Along another corridor, the prince paused, listening. Some tiny sound had stopped him, the scurrying of a mouse perhaps. Now the quiet lay heavy, and there came the muffled sounds of the city of Zankos outside the palace grounds, the lonely clang of ships' bells. The city never slept, or so the Grand Envoy said.

Another smaller staircase led Thayne to the highest level, an open-sided cupola. The view dazzled him. Zankos seemed close enough to touch. Behind lighted windows, he saw women in bright garb, and the streets below were crowded with celebrants. The Inland Sea lay dark and empty to the south. Somewhere horses nickered, sleepy night sounds. Sojii would be among them, and suddenly Thayne longed more than ever to be home at Castlekeep with his old playmates and Davi. There his mother was also a queen, but happy.

The prince and heir of Wynnamyr and Xenara leaned against the iron railing and drew a deep breath of moist salt air rich with the scent of night-blooming jasmine. This would be his kingdom one day, or so the Grand Envoy told him. Behind him came the quick patter of slippered feet upon the tiles. Thayne never had a chance to turn and face his attacker.

# Other TSR® Books

# Book of Stones

### L. Dean James

# BOOK OF STONES

First Printing: August 1993
Printed in the United States of America.
Library of Congress Catalog Card Number: 92-61096

9 8 7 6 5 4 3 2 1

ISBN: 1-56076-639-5

TSR, Inc.
P.O. Box 756
Lake Geneva, WI 53147
U.S.A.

TSR Ltd.
120 Church End, Cherry Hinton
Cambridge CB1 3LB
United Kingdom

For my daughters,
Shanan and Jessica

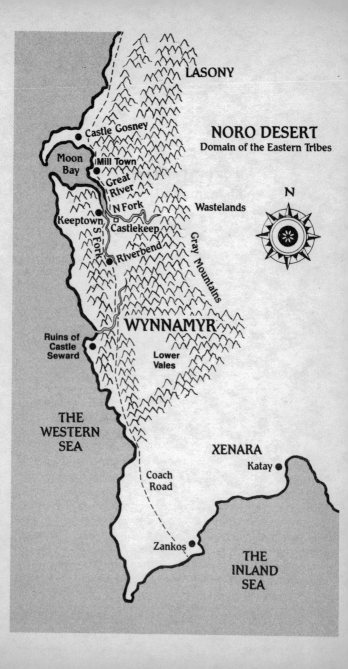

# Prologue

Eowin D'Ar, Grand Envoy of Xenara, huddled close to the campfire, his gnarled hands with their swollen-knuckled fingers buried deep in the wide sleeves of his robe. The chill night air troubled his rheumatism and caused his joints to ache, while the willow bark tea in the cup at his feet had done little to ease the pain. Nowadays the cold settled deep in his bones, and the hottest fire couldn't seem to warm him. Old age had its drawbacks, taking a toll on both mind and body.

"Sir? More tea?"

D'Ar glanced up into the earnest face of a young Xenaran soldier. "No, thank you. I've had enough."

"If there's anything else . . ."

"No, no. I'm fine." Eowin waved the man off and watched him return to his fellows at one of several other campfires beyond the pair of wagons.

Cidry, his faithful manservant of forty years, had died last summer, and Eowin, cranky with age and saddened by the loss, had found no one worthy to take his place. This small troop of soldiers attended him as best they could, in awe of the august personage of the Grand Envoy. Mostly they annoyed him. He'd never cared for the company of military men. They rarely thought deep thoughts or appreciated much beyond their horses and their weapons and a good game of dice.

"Ah, Cidry," Eowin muttered, eyes fixed on the flames. "I miss our philosophical arguments. . . . They at least warmed me, if nothing else."

An icy, dry wind ruffled the downy white hair that covered his head. Smoke stung his eyes and throat, and he tilted his head to gaze upward. A sliver of moon hung high overhead, snagged in a thick web of stars. Such bright splendor on a spring night. During his long lifetime of service to the Xenaran court, the Grand Envoy had traveled to many lands and seen many wondrous sights, but none rivaled this desert sky as it swept to the far eastern horizon.

The Gray Mountains lay close behind him, a barrier visible only as silhouettes jutting against the stars. Their high peaks snagged the moisture-laden clouds off the Western Sea and stole all the sweet rain for Wynnamyr's forests and valleys, leaving nothing for this thirsty land.

Ah, what a beautiful and wild country was Wynnamyr, with its ring of guardian mountains and rugged coastline. Xenara had long coveted the tiny kingdom's natural resources, and if not for the impossible terrain, would have absorbed Wynnamyr into its huge empire centuries ago. Year after bloody year of confrontation had always ended in a draw, followed by times of uneasy peace . . . until now. Now that peace was utter and complete. Eowin returned his gaze to the fire, a frown on his thin lips.

Seven years past, one more war had been fought between the two countries, and this time, Wynnamyr had won, though both nations had been horribly broken. In the midst of a desperate battle for the sea pass that bordered the two contending lands, Gaylon Reysson, sorcerer-king of Wynnamyr, had done the unforgivable. He had taken up the cursed magical sword, Kingslayer, and had slaughtered over half a million souls—not only Xenara's huge army, but the men, women, and children of Zankos, Xenara's capital city.

The memory of such devastation made the Grand Envoy's stomach clench. After his horrible victory, Gaylon Reysson had returned home with his few remaining troops, and little had been heard from, or of, him since. The people of Xenara had waited in constant fear for Wynnamyran vengeance to fall again. But it never had. Some finally dared believe the evil sword of Orym destroyed.

Whatever the truth, the fact still remained that the Red King was a murderer, cold and cruel, and Eowin must travel now to that man's court in hope of saving his own kingdom. The thought of begging favors shamed him, but in the destruction of Zankos and the palace there, the royal house of Gerric had been lost, King Roffo's direct bloodline nearly obliterated. All but one daughter—Jessmyn, who was also wife to Gaylon and Queen of Wynnamyr.

There were bastard sons aplenty, however, to contend for the Xenaran throne. The southern kingdom had survived the war only because of its vast size and location around the Inland Sea. A nation of wealthy merchants and traders, most of its vast sailing fleet had survived, and so trade continued. Only now the remaining merchant families had chosen sides and squabbled viciously among themselves and with the aristocracy for control of the throne and the parliament. So far, every claimant of the crown had been assassinated.

But the situation at home grew even worse with each passing day, so Eowin, nearly eighty years old and long retired, must perform this one last duty to his lost king. Somehow the Grand Envoy must convince Jessmyn D'Gerric to return to the land of her birth and take her place upon the throne of Xenara. Only she could bring the vying factions together—but would Gaylon Reysson let his wife go? There were certain paragraphs among their marriage contract that provided the envoy with some small leverage, should children have finally come from the royal union.

Eowin had met the young daughter of Roffo once long ago while negotiating treaties with the Wynnamyran usurper, Lucien D'Sulang. Then a princess betrothed to King Lucien, Jessmyn had appeared sickly and dull-witted—hardly a promising leader of a country. There hadn't been a ruling queen in Xenara for over four centuries, and that last reign had been disastrous. No matter. If Jessmyn or her offspring proved to be mentally or emotionally deficient, Eowin would surround them with sage counselors. The house of Gerric, on which the very foundation of Xenara was built, must not end.

Eowin glanced across the flames, drawn by the sounds of sweet feminine laughter that drifted softly from the wagon closest to the Grand Envoy's fire. Along one shadowed partition, a tall shape leaned against the planking, and the heavy silk cover above the boards had been pulled up just enough to emit a small amount of lamplight.

"Here you!" the envoy called angrily. "Get away from there!"

The silk dropped, and he heard steps move quickly away into the dark toward where the horses were picketed. Blasted soldiers couldn't be trusted, but then, the temptation was great. Along with gifts of fine cloth, spices, and exotic foodstuffs for the court of Wynnamyr, the envoy had brought three young noblewomen from the Xenaran city of Katay. Eowin had hopes that the grace and courtly manners of these ladies-in-waiting would remind Queen Jessmyn of her Xenaran heritage and of her duties to her deceased father, King Roffo.

The laughter came again, and then the wagon's door flap opened. Sandaal D'Lelan—at nineteen the youngest of the three ladies—stepped over the tailgate and climbed carefully to the ground. Her heavy cloak snagged on a corner, and she pulled it loose. Eowin watched with mild curiosity as the young woman silently found a place beside the fire. In one slender hand, she carried a small round-bodied mandolin of gilded ebony.

"A bit late for music, milady," the envoy said. "And a bit cold."

"I grew tired of empty-headed chatter," Sandaal answered curtly and ran long fingers over the mandolin's glossy black wood.

Undone, her raven hair fell well below her waist, and her dark eyes glittered with firelight and mystery. Women in general were a mystery to the Grand Envoy, but Sandaal D'Lelan he could not fathom at all. She was strikingly beautiful, tall but small-boned, almost delicate, and yet she emanated an incredible strength and intelligence for one so young. In later life and married to some wealthy nobleman, Sandaal would be a lady of formidable presence. At the moment, however, she was merely another impoverished aristocrat who had lost her entire family and inheritance in the destruction of Zankos.

Eowin had considered her unsuitable, at first, as a lady-in-waiting—too outspoken and even somewhat hostile—but then again, somehow appealing. Later, after so many interviews with the bland gentlewomen of Katay, the envoy had chosen her gladly. If nothing else, she made the long journey more interesting.

Sandaal began to play, her gaze focused inward. The instrument's strings were of steel wire, not catgut, and each time she plucked it, a note rang out hard and clear before fading into the night. Floating behind the doleful melody, her soft voice was no less fine.

> *"On the good king's orders,*
> *I left my love*
> *And sailed to distant shores.*
> *On the good king's orders,*
> *I left my home*
> *To die in distant wars."*

The Grand Envoy surveyed the stars once more as the sad ballad unfolded. Sandaal's choice of music always brought an ache to his heart. While Katina and Rose D'Jal, her companions, would sing of maidenly pursuits, of their dreams and hopes for true love and marriage, Lady D'Lelan's songs were invariably of despair and loss.

Even the noisy game of knucklebones at the nearest campfire had quieted. All the soldiers were listening to the refrain written in ages past by one of their own.

> *"I will away to other lands.*
> *I will away, my wife.*
> *I will away and say farewell*
> *To all I loved in life."*

The last note trailed off, and in the long silence that followed, only the flames crackled and snapped.

Finally a male voice called, "Play us a bawdy tune, pretty one!"

It was outrageous for a soldier to make such a demand of a lady. Eowin caught Sandaal's eye and gave a slight shake of his head. One side of her mouth quirked, and then she lifted her chin, a clear indication of impish intent, and strummed a major chord.

By the second rollicking verse, the guards were roaring. The elderly man tucked himself deeper into his cloak and cringed. There was nothing overt in the lyrics of the song, but they were filled with so many double and triple entendres of a most unsubtle kind that even the Grand Envoy, a longtime frequenter of taverns, felt his cheeks redden. From the door flap of the wagon, two round girlish faces peered, eyes wide with shock and some confusion.

The song ended to the soldiers' appreciative hoots, but when one asked for another ditty, Eowin growled, "No more." He leaned toward Sandaal. "I had hoped to bring Her Majesty a lady of high birth . . . not a tavern wench."

"Did you?" The young woman stood and shook out her long skirts, black hair cascading over her shoulders. "Have no fears, Milord Envoy. I won't disappoint you."

# One

The oriel at the northwest corner of Castle Gosney was cramped and poorly lit, its windows having been designed for use by archers, not accountants. Davyn Darynson, the young duke of Gosney, squinted at the inventory papers on his desk and tried to ignore the small child who galloped in circles around him. It was an impossible task. The flickering candle finally went out in the boy's backdraft.

"Milord, please!" the duke said irritably.

Thayne halted, breathless. "This is boring. I want to go riding. Now."

While the order was decidedly royal, the six-year-old, in frayed clothing and worn boots, hardly looked a prince of the realm or heir to the throne of Wynnamyr. But then Davi, in no better attire, looked very little like a duke.

"I promised the king I'd do these accounts."

"You should have brought a clerk," the boy stated.

Davi only grunted. "I can't afford one."

Or much of anything else. These were poor times for lord and commoner alike in a country that had never been wealthy to begin with. For seven long years, Wynnamyr had suffered the aftermaths of war, the hunger and deprivation. This year might finally prove the turning point—if the weather stayed kind. Many of the children who had seen their fathers march to battle and never return had finally reached adulthood. There were far more crops in the fields this spring and strong young men to tend them. Sadly, though, nothing could replace the lost skills and knowledge that farmers and artisans might have passed down from father to son had they survived the war.

"It's going to rain again," said Thayne, and the duke glanced up, his dismal chain of thought broken.

The boy leaned over the thick, slanted sill of a window aperture. Glass had never been a consideration for gloomy Castle Gosney, though once there'd been oiled paper placed to block the wind. Tiny brittle pieces still clung to the wooden frames.

"Come away from there, milord," Davi cautioned. The window openings were narrow, but not so narrow that a young prince mightn't slip through and fall to his death.

In a more reasonable mood than usual, Thayne dropped back to the splintered floor with a thud. A bit of stocking peeked from a split seam in the toe of his left boot, and he bent to poke the material back in place. Then, with bright blue eyes flashing, he considered what other mischief might be found in the small barren chamber. Not for the first time, Davi regretted allowing the child to journey north from Castle-keep with him to the Gosney estates, but saying no to the boy was almost as impossible as ignoring him.

Energetic, impetuous, and far too clever, the prince of Wynnamyr was already a head taller than any of the other boys his age. He'd taken his looks from his father's father—the copper red hair and deep blue eyes, the large-boned, lanky form that promised great height one day. From his mother, Queen Jessmyn, Thayne had inherited more refined features—a full-lipped cherub's face, certainly handsome and almost beautiful in a child. Jessmyn's wit and thoughtful intelligence were also his, along with a fairly even disposition, despite his rambunctiousness.

Truth be told, Davi was grateful for the child's company, though they were often at odds. The young duke, barely beyond childhood himself, had a better rapport with Thayne than with anyone else at court, including the boy's parents. Tradition had a Gosney always at the Red King's right hand, to serve and defend. Over the millennia, there had been an almost mystical bond formed between the two families, and for Davi, the ties had formed as strongly with this small son as with the father.

"There's someone coming." The prince stood on tiptoe to peer through another window.

"Who?" asked Davi without much interest.

The boy took a sudden noisy breath of air. "Visitors!" he whooped joyfully. "We've got visitors!"

Before the duke could react, Thayne had galloped across the floor and dodged out into the stairwell.

"Be careful!" Davi shouted after him. The narrow stone steps were uneven and steep.

Visitors . . . In the two quiet weeks since their arrival, there'd been few callers, only a few bold tenants with questions of policy for the new young landlord. The duke left his desk to gaze out the same window at a cool overcast day.

Visitors indeed. A strange procession rode out of the north through the upper valley, skirting the newly planted fields as they came. Ten . . . no, a dozen men, in white caps and dark uniforms, all mounted on white horses, pushed at the gallop.

A sudden apprehension touched Davi. Those weren't white caps on the riders' heads, but hair the color of snow. These must be men of Lasony, Wynnamyr's northern neighbor. Not a word, kind or unkind, had been exchanged between the two countries since the Xenaran war, when Zorek, King of Lasony, had refused sanctuary to Queen Jessmyn and the unborn child she carried.

"Fitzwal!" the duke shouted down into the little courtyard below. "Fitzwal!"

A moment later, the sergeant appeared, his long, narrow face upturned, eyes searching the tower wall.

"Milord?"

"Gather the guard! Strangers approach the castle."

Fitzwal looked slightly confused. Strangers in this quiet land were no cause for alarm, but he moved to collect the three men-at-arms. Their duty, above all, was to protect the prince. Davi hurried from the chamber, his own worn boots clattering on the steps.

His small guard, including Thayne, were all milling about in the courtyard by the time the duke arrived.

"Go to your chambers, milord," he told the boy, then added, "Please," at the sudden obstinate flare in the youngster's eyes.

"I don't want to."

"Highness, your father, the king, has given me the responsibility of your safekeeping. As soon as I'm certain of our company's good intent, you may return."

Thayne seemed about to object, then sighed heavily. "All right. But I better not miss anything interesting, or I shall be very angry."

Davi saw Fitzwal turn away to hide his smile. The old sergeant was Thayne's weapons master and especially fond of this eldest son of the Red King. Davi did not smile. He could hear the thunderous approach of many horses in the distance, and it troubled him.

One of the men-at-arms hustled the prince from the courtyard, then returned to stand in the short line of Castle Gosney's defenders. The sound of hooves grew louder, closer, and the duke went to the heavy wooden gate set in the courtyard wall. He could see them now, the white-haired men of Lasony on their small white mounts weaving past a nearby copse of tan oak. A gentle mist began to fall just as they arrived in the outer yard.

Every man among them wore a sword, but none were drawn. Only the two banner carriers held poles as well as their reins. Davi found himself staring with great interest at the leader of the band, dressed in a huge cape of soft white animal pelts. He was a slender elderly man—no, ancient—with a long white beard that reached to his belt. His hair was also quite long, and glinting across his forehead was a slender golden band. This must be Zorek himself, king of Lasony.

"Majesty," Davi said and opened the gate wide before bowing.

"And you are the newest duke of Gosney—Davyn, son of Daryn," the man answered in a brittle, aged voice, gesturing to a couple of his riders.

Two men behind him dismounted hurriedly and came to

assist the elderly king from his steed. There were silver bands across their foreheads—princes, perhaps. Davi cursed his inattentiveness to his lessons in Lasony royalty.

"May we offer you refreshments, Lord?" he asked. "And lodging, though I'm afraid the castle has long been empty, and we have few servants."

"We'll gladly accept whatever courtesy you have to offer, young man," the king said. "It's been a long journey, and I'm not the rider I once was." He rubbed the seat of his breeches and laughed.

Davi smiled politely. "My men-at-arms will see to your riders and horses. If you'll follow me, I'll find quarters for you and your sons."

Lasony and Wynnamyr had been allies for centuries and even shared a common, though differently accented, tongue, yet Davi's apprehension persisted. It was not a fear for the little prince—these men had shown nothing but goodwill—but a deep unease that refused to leave the duke. He led his royal charges over the moss-covered stones of the bailey, slick with the mist that had begun to turn to outright rain.

The castle within was dim and dusty and very cold, even in the great hall, where a fire raged on the massive hearth. The hall was embarrassingly huge and empty, but for two sections of a trestle table and a few rickety chairs and benches. Davi took Zorek and his sons to the long benches before the fire to shed their wet outer garments and warm themselves. The duke himself took their cloaks and hung them on racks beside the huge hearth to dry. Then, begging their pardons, he went to order mulled wine from the kitchens and warn the cook of guests for supper.

Even compared to rustic Castlekeep to the south, Castle Gosney was a large, sprawling, ugly structure. Once, when the tribes of ancient Wynnamyr had been at constant war among themselves, it had been a crude fortress. Then later it had been enlarged to hold the cruel sorcerous Dark Kings, who ruled the land until their own inbred madness led to their defeat.

The third Red King had given the castle and all the lands

surrounding it to the Gosneys over eight hundred years ago in exchange for their long and loyal service to Wynnamyr. Unfortunately, no amount of renovation over the centuries had ever seemed to lighten the castle's grim atmosphere. Many of the local peasants believed the myriad stone chambers to be still touched with the Dark Kings' evil. Ghostly sightings had been reported now and again, though usually from the most unreliable sources. Davi, having inherited the Dark Kings' blood through his paternal grandmother, had felt the faintest magical essence, but nothing more. What evil had been perpetrated here had faded with time, or been overcome by many years of residence by the congenial and earthy Gosneys.

Davi returned to the hall just before the wine arrived, brought by Tepson, their testy cook. Behind the man, Thayne followed almost timidly. The wine served, Tepson was sent back to his kitchens, though, much to his displeasure, his two young aides were sent to help Fitzwal prepare rooms for their guests. Finally Davi brought Thayne forward, a hand on the boy's shoulder.

"Milord Thayne, prince and heir to the throne of Wynnamyr," the duke said formally. "Allow me to introduce to you Zorek, king of Lasony, and his sons, Prince . . ."

"Calwin," said the younger son, smiling, and stood to offer the boy his hand. "And this is my brother and heir to the Lasony throne, Banak."

Banak also stood to shake Thayne's hand graciously. A closer look showed him to be a man of middle age, but youthful in his movements, with a pleasant unbearded face. Prince Thayne remembered his manners enough to bow to Zorek.

"Well, well," the old king said, stroking his beard so that rainwater dripped onto his forest green tunic. "There'll be another true Red King on the Wynnamyran throne one day."

Self-consciously Thayne ran fingers through his coppery hair. "My father's beard is red."

"So I've heard. Now, your grandfather, Reys, had hair as bright as yours. We were friends for a good many years, but unfortunately I've had no chance to meet your father. At my age, a ride to Castlekeep now would be beyond me." Zorek glanced at Davi. "In fact, I've waited a good many years for a Gosney to return home."

"Just how old are you?" Thayne asked, curious.

The duke frowned, but Zorek said proudly, "I may, if the gods so decree, celebrate my one hundred and third birthday this very spring."

The prince of Wynnamyr's jaw fell open. "And you rode all this way?"

"Nearly thirty leagues. A good deal farther than I have in a long, long time."

Thayne took a step nearer. "Is it true? Do you live in a castle made of ice?"

"Too true," Banak laughed. "But only in winter."

"How do you stay warm?"

"Oh, we have fireplaces just like you, so we do stay warm—wet, but warm."

The young prince looked to Davi, uncertain whether this was perhaps a joke, but Calwin took pity.

"The hearths are of stone, of course. And you would be quite surprised how well thick blocks of ice insulate a chamber. It's as comfortable as any drafty old stone castle. You'll have to visit us some winter and see for yourself."

"But it must melt in the summer. And you build a new one every year?"

Zorek answered this time. "No, child. The ice palace is well north, where the snow stays year round. It needs only minor repairs each winter."

Fitzwal appeared through the entrance nearest the kitchens and bowed. "Milords, the rooms have been readied and your baggage placed there. Our cook says there will be time to rest before dinner if it pleases you."

"Indeed!" said Zorek and slapped a damp, steaming knee. "A short nap will be much appreciated." Then he caught Davi's eye. "I would see you alone in my chamber first, Milord Duke."

Davi's unease grew suddenly stronger, but he bowed. "Fitzwal, please attend Prince Thayne while I'm gone."

"But I want to come, too," Thayne said, indignant.

The king of Lasony leaned close to him. "We'll enjoy each other's company at supper, young lord, but . . ." He looked again at the duke of Gosney. "I made a promise long ago to Edonna, your duke's grandmother, which I must fulfil in private. It is a matter of honor, Your Highness."

A quick, knowing glance flashed between the royal brothers of Lasony, and Thayne lifted his chin, regal but appeased.

"Matters of honor are most important," the boy agreed. "Come, Fitzwal. I wish to see the Lasony ponies."

The sergeant bowed indulgently. "Of course, milord." He bowed to Davi next. "Lord, King Zorek's quarters are beside yours in the north wing, and the princes' rooms are just across the hall from their father's."

The duke nodded, already aware of that. The north wing was the only one in the castle that hadn't fallen into complete ruin. His royal birth forgotten for the moment, Thayne began to gallop down the long chamber, whinnying and chuffing in excellent imitation of a horse, while Fitzwal hurried after him.

"A fine lad," Calwin said. "Reminds me of my oldest boy, Janic, when he was that age. Near drove me insane with his little misadventures." He grinned. "And it only gets worse, Duke. Believe me."

Davi grimaced as he led them away through the north entrance. "I've no doubt of that. His younger brother, Robyn, is as different as night from day. Far more sweet-natured, though he has his moments of temper."

"Perhaps it's as well he's second-born. Sweet-natured men," observed Prince Banak, "do not always make the best kings."

The duke could find nothing to say to that. He showed King Zorek to the apartment just beyond the one he shared with Prince Thayne. The chambers were hardly fit for a king, but his majesty seemed well pleased. The Lasony princes' rooms, across the corridor, were much the same as their father's, only slightly smaller. They, too, politely complimented the duke on their accommodations. Their own personal servants arrived to help them settle in, and Davi returned immediately to Zorek's chambers, a strange flutter in his stomach.

"Come in, come in," the old king called at his knock.

He'd shed his damp clothing already and had begun to don dry breeches and a shirt from one of his three trunks. His legs as he drew on the trousers were little more than bone and sinew. A fresh fire burned cheerfully in the sitting chamber's hearth, but the room was still cold. The king indicated one of the straight wooden chairs before the fire, and Davi took a seat.

"You have no manservant like your sons?" the duke asked, confused.

"Yes, of course I do, but he'll attend me later—after we've talked." The king took a chair for himself and sighed heavily, the toes of his buskins pointed at the flames. "Would you serve us more wine? I'm afraid it'll be a while yet before I can move again."

The cups and pitcher were on the hearthstones, close to the heat. Davi poured them each a cupful, the scent of cloves and cinnamon spicing the cool air. His ancient, craggy face weary, Zorek took a long pull of his drink, then turned ice-blue eyes on the duke.

"Some thirty years ago," the old man said, "your grandmother, Edonna, ventured north alone to Galwey, my summer keep in Lasony. It was a difficult journey for her, since she was quite ill at the time. A wasting sickness. There was nothing the physicians of Wynnamyr could do for her. Sadly, neither could ours in Lasony."

Zorek stared into his cup. "Her husband, Emil, the duke of Gosney, and his eldest sons by a previous marriage were with King Reys in the south . . . at war with Xenara. Only your father, Daryn, remained with the Wynnamyran court, too young yet to take up arms. But this much of your family history you may already know. Some things you won't know, since there's no one left to speak of them." The king looked up, his gaze distant, smiling faintly. "Ah, Edonna . . . Your grandmother was one of the most beautiful women I have ever known—tiny and delicate, with full blue-black hair that fell to her ankles. But she hadn't traveled to Lasony in hope of healing. She'd come to exact a promise from me. While I swore to do as she asked, fate was to take a hand, and it is to the grandson, not the son, that I must fulfill my vow."

The tiny hairs on Davi's arms prickled, and he shivered from more than the cold. Zorek held out his cup for more mulled wine, waiting perhaps for the young duke to say something, perhaps ask a question. Davi only filled the king's cup, silent.

"Look there," Zorek said finally, "in the trunk beside the armoire. There's a small metal box, locked . . . quite heavy. Bring it out. It is yours."

The young man went slowly to the trunk and even more slowly lifted the lid. Something lay at the very bottom, covered by neatly folded royal clothing. The dull gray sheen of the metal box told him it was made of lead, the soft material scratched and dented over time. Davi leaned to slip fingers under the edges, since there were no handles, then strained against the weight.

The container was rectangular, a small chest a hand's length on the narrow end and not much longer on the sides, but deep. Davi lugged it to the hearth and set it at Zorek's feet.

"What's in this?" the duke asked, partly curious, partly afraid.

The old king shook his head. "The lady never said, nor did I ask. The secret died with her." He pulled a small iron key from a pouch at his waist. "This will open it."

"Now?"

"No." Again Zorek shook his head, white beard swaying. "Edonna was quite clear about that. No one should see the contents except . . . Daryn . . . when he had reached his majority and had mastered his Sorcerer's Stone." The king stared into the flames now. "She gave him the Stone later, on her deathbed. He was but a boy, no more than twelve, and he took her death hard. Daryn was sensitive—a scholar and a musician, unlike his half brothers, who were fighting men— and his father treated him harshly."

Zorek took another swallow of wine. "Daryn took the Stone from his mother and ran away. She'd asked him to become a sorcerer, which must have terrified him. You see, magic then was even rarer than it is now. People were still very afraid of sorcery, and to become a sorcerer, Daryn would have to find a master to teach him."

"Sezran," Davi said with distaste.

"Just so. But the rest of the story you must know better than I. Daryn never truly mastered his Stone, but he helped to train Gaylon Reysson, King of Wynnamyr, to be the sorcerer he could never be. I was to bring this box to Daryn, but you are the last living Gosney, so the box is yours."

The young duke's stomach twisted. "I'm no sorcerer. I have no Stone. What can I possibly do with this?"

"My advice," Zorek said, "is to leave it locked. There is obviously something of great power inside—something Daryn, the sorcerer, might have been able to deal with. But not you. Find some deep, dark place to hide the thing and never think of it again." The king drew a breath. "My duty's done as best I could. The promise is fulfilled, and I can lie at rest finally. Banak has waited long enough for his crown."

"Milord!" Davi said in alarm. "Are you ill?"

Zorek chuckled. "No. Only old. Don't worry. I'll find my way home first. Do you think I fear death? Not at all. I have lived this long only to make good on my vow to your grandmother. Now take your treasure and let me nap before supper."

Davi rose, lifting the box with effort, and started toward the chamber door.

"You're a bright lad, Davyn," the king said behind him. "You've your grandmother's cheekbones and jawline, her full lips—and her fine keen mind. You'll do well, young Duke of Gosney, sorcerer or no. Never fear."

Davi didn't answer, his attention focused on the difficulty of opening the door latch with his hands full. But he did hear, and he knew that all he felt was fear—an unreasonable fear mixed with unreasonable hope.

His chamber door across the hall was unlocked, and Davi carried the heavy lead box to the bed. Despite a good cleaning, these rooms looked no more inviting than the rest of the castle—tattered drapes and tapestries, rickety furniture. And no money with which to change all that.

The narrow windows faced east, and morning light, even dimmed by the heavy clouds, brightened the bedchamber. The air tasted of sweet spring rain. Davi stared long at the container there on the blankets before him. With a dim sorrow, he wished he'd known his grandmother—and truly known his father, but these were useless wonderings. Perhaps the contents of the box would give him some vision of the woman who had sent it across time and distance.

The king of Lasony's advice, though, echoed in his ears. This chest had been meant for Daryn, a sorcerer. Best to slip away into the woods and bury the thing as deep in the earth as possible. But, no, not yet. What harm could there be in looking inside first, so long as he touched nothing? Easy enough to ignore his earlier unease here alone in his room.

With his dirk, Davi carefully broke the lead seal that covered the lock, then inserted the key, turned it, and just as carefully lifted the lid. A tightly fitted and shallow inner shelf of lead lay just beneath the first, and there the young duke found a folded paper, yellowed and brittle with age. The page cracked as he opened it.

*My Darling Son Daryn*, the letter began in an ornate feminine script. *I will miss you so—your poetry, your music, and your laughter. I pray that wherever you may be you have found some peace and happiness. I know I have laid a great burden on you, but it was necessary that I give you your great-grandfather's Sorcerer's Stone in hope that you may gain its power. I have sensed the gentle magic in you since your birth. Now is the time to master that magic—no easy task, but one I know you will fulfill for my sake."*

Davi's fingers tightened on the paper, and the edge began to crumble. He held it lightly and read on.

*Yet on your return to Castle Gosney, I have set another task, even greater, for you. A most dangerous one. Within this box, you will find the Dark King, Orym's, Sorcerer's Stone, handed down within your mother's family for these hundreds of years, always female to female and in secret, for fear of what might happen should the Stone fall into a male descendant's hands— one with the talent to master and use it.*

Now Davi's heart had begun to pound, a thundering in his ears as he scanned the delicate handwriting.

*Orym's evil lies dormant within, its influences trapped by the lead of this box that our dear friend and ally, Zorek, has delivered to you. With dying eyes, I see so much more clearly now, my darling. I have no daughters to pass Orym's Stone to for keeping. It is time the Dark King's powers end. Only another sorcerer may destroy a Sorcerer's Stone, and that is what I ask of you, my darling. Orym's pendant must never fall into another's hands, nor must his Book of Stones.*

*Yes. Even that survived. In the cellars of Castle Gosney, you must search the small storage chamber farthest from the entrance. Count ten flagstones out from the center of the west wall, and beneath this you will find another, larger, lead box. Within it lies the Dark King's Book—the original Book from which all others are copies. This too must be destroyed, for it is as corrupted as the pendant.*

The duke of Gosney dropped the page to the blankets and balled his hands into fists. Sorcery! The blood of the Dark Kings ran in his veins, just as it had his father's. At fifteen, when Davi had first arrived at Castlekeep, first tasted and felt the strong magic King Gaylon possessed, the boy had wanted magic of his own. The power was in him, of that he was certain, but without a Sorcerer's Stone, he could never hope to use that power, and Stones were rare.

For months, the boy duke had used all his spare time to wander the banks of the Great River near Castlekeep in hope of finding a Stone as Gaylon Reysson had. Davi had hoped for that blue glimmer of light out of the corner of his eye that meant that one small gray pebble among all the rest was truly special. After so many fruitless searches, he had finally given up, his hopes for magic dwindling.

Now those hopes resurged a thousandfold, despite his grandmother's dire words of warning. The young man focused on the letter once more.

*Know, dear son, that I do not leave you willingly and that my love for you will not die with this body. Be kind to your father, Daryn, for my sake. To you, Emil's love seems harsh and cruel, but that is only because it is so strong.*

*Destroy Orym's Stone and Book. Do not be tempted to preserve them. If you have ever loved me, you will do this thing. It is my dying wish.*

The final paragraphs and her signature were shaky, as though her strength had waned at the last, and Davi found tears in his eyes—for his father's loss, for his own. Then the excitement and fear reasserted themselves suddenly, followed by guilt. Edonna's dying wish should be fulfilled, the Stone and Book taken to Gaylon Reysson to destroy. The king had learned the dangers of Orym's influences firsthand through the ensorcelled sword, Kingslayer. Even Davi, Stoneless, had once been sucked into the weapon's ruthless power while they battled the Xenaran forces at the Sea Pass.

He laid the letter gently on the blankets, his eyes trapped by the chest. What willpower he might have had to resist temptation had disappeared with the memory of his hand around Kingslayer's hilt, the memory of the wild energy that had surged through his young body. The sword was gone, destroyed, but before him lay the answer to all his dreams. Dangerous thoughts, dangerous dreams. Slowly the duke pulled the shelf from the chest.

Despite the dull, cloudy light from the windows, the thick gold chain beneath blazed into rich, brilliant life. Breathless, Davi reached in to wrap his fingers in the precious metal links and lift it out. Now Orym's Sorcerer's Stone dangled before his eyes, a gray egg-shaped pebble nearly twice the size of the one in King Gaylon's ring. The gold setting had been molded into the claws of some bird of prey that clutched the Stone in a tight grip.

Davi felt nothing from the pendant. Somehow after Edonna's words of warning, he'd thought Orym's evil, bound and concentrated over hundreds of years, would radiate strongly enough for even the young duke's faint magical senses to pick up. There was nothing evil here, though, only the strong urge to take the Stone in hand and to become its master—a very foolish desire.

Orym was a distant relative, and sometimes, rarely, a Stone

might accept another master of the same bloodline. But to touch another's Stone with bare flesh could bring great harm, even death. Suddenly cautious, wisely afraid, Davi started to replace the pendant in the box. Momentum made the Stone swing away, then swing back, and the duke, eyes on the lead chest, saw a spark of brilliant blue at the periphery of his vision.

Great need and a strong imagination could sometimes be cruel. Davi stared at the gently swinging pendant and saw nothing but the rough gray pebble bound in gold—until he looked away again. Another deep blue glitter flashed at the corner of his eye, and the young man froze. With the flash had come a tiny hint of power.

All choice was lost at that moment, and now his body trembled in anticipation. Whatever the price, even death, Davi had to know if the Stone would accept him. The pendant swung back toward him on its chain, and he closed his left hand around the pebble. Azure light flared between his fingers. Icy heat stung his palm, then quickly turned to burning fiery pain that raced up his arm. He bit back a wail of agony, but held on all the tighter, willing the Stone to obey him. Even in his anguish, Davi thought he heard an echo of distant laughter.

The room began to spin around him, faster and faster, and he felt the Stone leeching the life out of him. Darkness came, swallowing him whole.

*My child*, someone whispered in his mind. *Son of my blood. Release the Stone, or you will surely die.*

"I want . . . its power," Davi moaned through gritted teeth, even against the agony.

*In time, young one*, the voice murmured. *In time.* Then a great emptiness washed through him, blotting out all sensations.

The duke woke sprawled across the bed, left arm flung wide, hand open and throbbing in time to his heart. The Sorcerer's Stone lay on the blankets close by. In the center of his palm was a small blackened hole, the flesh charred away as if he'd clutched a hot coal from the fire. The tips of his fingers were blistered. His entire body ached, and yet through the pain came a sense of wonder and hope.

*In time*, the voice had promised. *In time*.

Magic. The sharp flavor of it permeated the air of the room. Davi sat up on the mattress, exhaustion in his movements. Dinner would be soon, but Orym's Stone must be put safely away—for now. He snagged the chain and replaced the pendant in the box, along with the inner shelf and letter, then relocked the lid. The little chest fit perfectly under the bed.

On the washstand near the door were several jars of unguents and oils. The duke chose a green creamy mixture of comfrey, aloe, and beeswax to fill the hole in his hand. Easy enough to tell the others he'd burned himself stoking the fire. The wound was bound with a thin strip of linen, which Davi tore and knotted using his teeth and one good hand.

His thoughts were scattered as he changed clothes for supper, careful of the hand, which continued to throb. Thayne soon arrived alone at his door, and the duke answered the tentative knock.

"Fitzwal's already asked the others to come to table. I said I'd get you and our royal guests." The prince had changed, too, into his best attire—a black velvet doublet he'd nearly outgrown, and dark green breeches. "Are you ready, Milord Duke?"

"Yes, Your Majesty," Davi answered and stepped into the corridor, his injured hand held behind him. "I hope Tepson doesn't try out any new recipes on us."

Tepson was not a happy cook. A local cobbler by trade, he had come on hard times and had taken this job on a temporary basis. It had not been a bargain on either side.

The prince smiled broadly. "Fitzwal told him that whatever we couldn't eat, the cook would. Every bite."

That made Davi smile, too, despite the throb of his hand. Behind him in his room, Orym's Sorcerer's Stone waited, and below in the cellars lay the orginal *Book of Stones*. The thought of food didn't appeal to him at all. He wanted dinner over and done, wanted late night to arrive. Then he could spend time with Orym's Stone while the others slept, unknowing, in their beds.

# Two

Warm afternoon sunlight poured through the elms into the small sheltered courtyard behind Castlekeep. On the grassy grounds beyond, children played. Lilith had finished nursing on one side, and Jessmyn turned her little blanket-wrapped body to offer the other. The baby nuzzled a moment, then found the nipple and began to suckle, her dark blue eyes fixed on her mother's face. The queen of Wynnamyr smiled down on the tiny princess, the joy of the moment so strong she felt she might burst.

The ladies of the court had been slightly scandalized that the queen would nurse her own children. With the birth of each baby, a wet nurse had been brought to the keep, and each time Jess had sent her packing. She had waited long for the pleasures of motherhood and intended to enjoy them fully. Even Gaylon, sorcerer-king and warrior, would gently cuddle them close in bed at night, watching the baby nurse with wonder on his red-bearded face.

Prince Robyn, nearly four years old now, began to cry noisily somewhere beyond the courtyard wall. They were angry, frustrated tears that failed to cause any motherly concern. Jessmyn recognized Bennet's equally angry squalls with Robyn's. No doubt they'd discovered the same toy at the same time. Bennet's mother, Lady Keth of Oakhaven, ended the altercation in her gentle, reasonable voice.

There were only two aristocratic families, with five children between them, visiting the keep at this time. Financially, the king could afford to invite no more than that, but Jessmyn was grateful of the company, however small, of playmates for Robyn while his brother Thayne spent a month away at Castle Gosney.

Lilith had fallen asleep with the nipple still in her mouth. Milk dribbled from her pink lips. Jess shifted her gently, then tucked the loose blouse into her skirt with a free hand. Humming, she placed the baby in her bassinet and covered her warmly. Even with the sun shining so brightly, the spring air held a chill.

"Mummy!"

Jessmyn turned quickly at Robyn's howl. He rushed toward her across the flagstones. The queen hurried to meet him, lest he wake Lilith.

"Isn't Dubin mine?" the little redheaded child demanded, his dirty hands snagged in her long skirts. "Isn't he?" There were tear tracks running down his equally dirty cheeks.

Dubin was a well-worn stick horse with a stuffed stocking for a head, yarn mane, and dangling button eyes. Technically he belonged to Thayne.

"Bennet's ridin' him," the boy continued, aggrieved.

"Who found Dubin first?" Jess asked.

"Bennet . . . but I'm the prince! He has to do what I say."

The queen kept her expression serious. "You are a prince with princely duties. Princes are generous and kind and honorable. Princes treat their subjects honestly . . . and always share their toys."

"They do?"

"Always." Jessmyn nodded.

This didn't make Robyn happy. "I don't want to be a prince, then."

"But you were born one, all the same. That's something that can't be undone. Go back and play with the others. Be nice to Bennet. He'll be a baron one day and serve the Red King well. And you'll have Dubin to ride many times later on." Jess smiled. "Besides, you'll be riding a real horse soon."

"All by myself?" Robyn's face lit.

"Of course. You're getting to be such a big boy."

"I am!" he shouted, already at a dead run back toward the lawns, no doubt to brag to Bennet, who was slightly younger.

The queen checked Lilith, then returned to her stone bench and took up her book, a small volume of anonymous fourth century Wynnamyran poetry. Not the usual dark and dour fare of that age, but light and lyrical, written in the delicate script of a woman whose eye had been keen for beauty in the rough world around her.

"May I join you?" Lady Keth asked gently and, without awaiting an answer, plunked her hefty self down on the bench beside Jessmyn. She was a round, pretty young woman with dark hair and a pleasant disposition. Her eyes came to rest on Lilith in the bassinet. "Two are making me crazy," the lady said with a sigh. "How you'll manage with three to chase after . . . But then a queen should be able to find others to do the chasing."

"Just think of the wonderful exercise, Kethi."

The woman only groaned. "Talena's the worst, racing about with the others. She should have been born a boy with all that energy."

Yes, thought Jessmyn and remembered her own childhood when she'd much rather have learned to use a sword than a crocheting hook.

"I'm told they'll arrive today," Kethi said, changing subjects, as always without warning.

"Who?"

"The Xenaran Grand Envoy, of course, and his party."

"Oh."

"Aren't you the least little bit excited, milady? Can you imagine?" Lady Keth's dark eyes glittered. "Wagons made into houses with wheels? Only in Xenara would they think of such a thing."

"They're more a tent with wheels, I hear." The queen gazed down on Lilith, asleep, the tiny fingers of one hand pressed against a cheek.

"But big tents. Won't it be wonderful? A visit from the Grand Envoy of your homeland?"

Jessmyn bent to lay the book alongside the sleeping baby, then gathered the bassinet in her arms. "Wynnamyr is my home, Lady Keth. I've never known any other." She headed across the flagstones to call Robyn in for his afternoon nap.

*     *     *     *     *

They had left their arid homelands a fortnight past, and still Sandaal D'Lelan marveled at the green world around her. She sat beside the driver on the hard wooden bench while the huge wagon wheels jolted and thumped in the potholes of the coach road. The horsemen rode ahead—two dozen men-at-arms leading the envoy's wagon, with the women's wagon behind. A pair of guards followed the train.

The saffron silk wagon covers fluttered in the chill breezes that flowed along this series of narrow valley floors. Forested mountains hemmed them in. They traveled beside a flowing river, while trees rose on either side, the most astonishing of which were huge evergreens with reddish boles as straight as pillars and far thicker than a man was tall. Even with her neck craned back as far as it could go, Sandaal couldn't find the tops of them.

Wildlife thrived in the dim branch-filtered light here. White-tailed deer and elk, squirrels, raccoons, and ferrets ignored the humans' presence while they traveled, only to disappear when camp was made and the soldiers went out to hunt for dinner. There were species of birds far too numerous to count, and even a mountain lion had paused along the road once, unafraid. Sandaal drew the sweet moist air into her lungs and regretted their imminent arrival at Castlekeep. At each campsite, she had spent much of her time alone in the woods, gathering sweet-smelling lilies and wood irises—much to the envoy's displeasure, but there was nothing in this beautiful untamed land she feared.

Katina D'Jal pushed her fair head through the door flap behind the driver. "Meo, do you look for holes to drive into? How can we get dressed when we can't even stay upright?"

The driver grunted noncommittally, exactly as he had

throughout the entire journey, and Sandaal glanced back. Katina's rouge and kohl and lip paint had obviously been applied with an unsteady hand. The young D'Lelan lady looked away to hide her amusement. She had no use for face makeup or fancy gowns with their impossible, unbearable undergarments. Neither should Katina or Rose, since they were both naturally beautiful girls.

The wagon hit another deep hole with a thud, first one wheel, then the other. Within the tent, Rose cursed in a very unladylike manner. Sandaal ignored the complaints and discomfort, her attention already caught on their journey's end. They had come to a fork in the coach road that led to a huge heavy bridge, and beyond that bridge lay a quaint little town with houses and businesses of stone or brick or wood. She smelled roasting meat, pastries, bread, with a faint scent of offal behind them.

The quiet struck her most. People, carts, and horses moved up and down the main street, but without the shouts, the color, the teeming bustle of Katay. Beneath Sandaal, the wagon rumbled across the bridge planks, creating a muffled thunder that echoed back from the riverbed below.

"What a miserable little place," Rose said next to her ear. "I hope we don't have to stay long." She disappeared back behind the flap before Sandaal could answer.

All movement in Keeptown seemed to come to a dead halt as their train passed down the cobbled street. Curious eyes followed them, and Sandaal searched the faces, old and young. They were open faces, full of passion. How odd. These people hid nothing of themselves, but then perhaps they had nothing to hide.

In turn, the young southern woman offered the roadside watchers none of herself, except a haughty, distant, cold beauty. Xenarans were born to secrets—to calculations and bids for power. A few of the onlookers smiled, and a small girl, her eyes on Sandaal, waved shyly. Sandaal only looked away.

The town ended abruptly, and now the road grew steeper, the horses straining at the harness. They entered another small wood briefly, then found level ground again that opened up on a view of an ancient rambling castle. Sandaal studied the moss-and-lichen-covered stones and finally allowed herself a tiny frisson of anticipation.

The soldiers halted before the stable gate, which was opened wide by a servant. The men dismounted and led their horses into the saddling area, but the wagons were far too large to enter. Meo drew his team up just behind the Grand Envoy's wagon while they awaited directions from the stable master.

In the midst of the confusion, a lone man on horseback rode back to the second wagon. His young animal, a dark dapple gray, fidgeted under him, though his gloved hands were light on the reins. The Wynnamyran wore rust-colored riding leathers that matched his close-shorn red beard. His short, sandy blond hair was disheveled, and a warm winsome smile formed on his handsome face when he spotted Sandaal.

"Good afternoon, ladies."

Behind Sandaal, where they had parted the curtains, Rose and Katina giggled.

Katina, the eldest, said boldly, "Good day to you, sir."

"Welcome to Castlekeep," the man offered with a polite dip of his head. Then, distracted, he turned his horse and trotted away toward the envoy's wagon.

"Is he a lord, do you suppose?" Rose asked.

"Of course," snapped Katina. "The important question is, is he married?"

Sandaal rolled her eyes. Meo grunted and snapped the reins to send his team of horses forward. They halted directly before the castle's bailey, and servants rushed to help them down from the wagon and unload their belongings. Sandaal refused their help on all counts, carrying her single cloth bag and mandolin herself. The others struggled with the D'Jal sisters' enormous trunks.

The red-bearded man had given his horse over to a stable-boy and was in earnest conversation with the Grand Envoy now. His gloves were gone, and a heavy gold ring encircled the man's right forefinger. With a sick jolt, Sandaal realized

who this lord must be—Gaylon Reysson, the sorcerer-king of
Wynnamyr himself. The sickness turned to loathing when the
two men, young and old, turned and came toward the women.

"Your Highness," the Envoy said in his gravelly ancient
voice, "may I present Ladies Katina and Rose D'Jal and Lady
Sandaal D'Lelan."

The sisters curtsied deeply in their full-skirted pastel gowns
of blue and green, and each received a gracious kiss on the
hand from the king. But Sandaal's hand he held longest, his
hazel eyes searching the young southern woman's face.

"D'Lelan . . . ?" the king said softly.

"Yes, Your Majesty," Sandaal answered, demure, though the
close proximity, the touch of his skin against hers, made her
ill.

"You are related, perhaps, to Arlin D'Lelan?"

Eyes downcast, the young woman carefully hid the rage
that name brought. "He was my brother."

"He was my closest friend," Gaylon Reysson muttered, "and
a braver, better man I've never known. My condolences so
many years late, Lady D'Lelan, are poor recompense for a
brother's life. If there is anything I can do for you, you have
only to ask."

"Thank you, milord." Sandaal curtsied in her plain gray
gown and watched as king and envoy moved away toward
the stable yard.

There was only one thing Gaylon Reysson could do for her
—die—and that she would arrange somehow, no matter the
cost. Nothing else could ease the anger and pain of the last
seven years. In a single stroke of his magical sword, Kingslayer,
the king of Wynnamyr had destroyed Zankos, the capital city
of Xenara. Sandaal had lost everything—mother, brothers, sisters, aunts and uncles . . . and the D'Lelan family fortune.

Only the fact that she'd been visiting friends in Katay had
saved the young southern woman. Life, though, would never
be easy. At the age of twelve, she'd been left a penniless
orphan passed from family to family in Katay, unwanted by
anyone while the country recovered from a devastating war.
She had steeled herself even at that young age, refusing to

grieve until justice was finally served. And it would be served. That she had sworn long ago.

"Sandaal, quit daydreaming," Rose called from the courtyard. A female servant had arrived to show them to their quarters. They followed the servant across the bailey and inside.

"Isn't this place just awful?" Katina confided in a whisper as they passed along the corridors of the keep.

Sandaal nodded. The air held a dank mildew odor, and the candles along the halls did little to dispel the gloom. The servant led them up a staircase. Here there were high slotted windows to give light and even a little warmth. Dust motes danced in the sunbeams.

"Your things will be brought up directly," the middle-aged servant woman said and curtsied before opening the door on a spacious sitting room. A fire already burned on the hearth. "Her Highness thought you would rather share a large apartment than have separate chambers."

Lady D'Lelan was not at all pleased. The two months crowded in a single wagon with the sisters were enough to last a lifetime, but instead of complaint, she said, "Tell the queen thank you. This will do nicely."

"Yes, milady." The servant smiled and turned away back down the passage as Sandaal heard other voices approaching.

"Thank all the gods," Katina sighed.

Already the first of their trunks had arrived. Excited and laughing, the sisters entered their apartment and the confusion of unpacking. There were two bedchambers, and Sandaal stepped into the smaller one alone, closing the door. This bedroom had a cubbyhole library. There were also large windows set at angles in the outer wall, which created a little alcove for a window seat. In the gardens below, roses already bloomed, red, yellow, pink.

Castlekeep might be rustic, but it seemed a pleasant enough place to live. Cloud shadows drifted over the lush green lawns, and Sandaal fought the charm of this quiet land. She must never lose sight of her purpose.

*   *   *   *   *

With the first posted letter from the Grand Envoy, nearly four months ago, Gaylon Reysson had been touched by an uneasiness. He realized that his country's political relationships with Xenara would someday have to resume. Still, it had taken seven long years to ease the burden of guilt that disastrous war with their southern neighbor had caused him.

Eowin D'Ar was a crafty old fox, too, his letters worded in fancy high language with twists and turns that seemed to lead in no particular direction. But there were promises of a lasting peace between the two nations, an offer of mutual reparation and succor—for Jessmyn's sake, the daughter of King Roffo, who had died at Gaylon's hands in the final battle.

Alone with his thoughts before the hearth in their apartment, fleeting, unwanted images passed through his mind . . . of the destruction he'd wrought, the friends he'd lost . . . until the queen's hands came to rest on his shoulders. She bent to kiss his hair.

"You've been awfully quiet," his wife noted. "What troubles you, my lord?"

Gaylon managed a smile for her. "The Grand Envoy and his smooth tongue." Then he changed subjects abruptly. "How she must hate me. . . ."

Unseen behind him, the queen paused to contemplate the track his thoughts now followed. "You mean Lady Sandaal? I very much doubt she'd come to serve our court if that were true." Jessmyn leaned to kiss his cheek. "You did what you had to do. She can't blame you any more than one can blame a storm for rain and thunder. Let the guilt lie where it belongs—with Kingslayer and Sezran, who forged the sword. And with my father, who began the war."

Gaylon tried to do as she suggested, but the memories were hard to lose. She knew him better than he knew himself, though, and only in the reflection of her eyes could he see his own worthiness and accept the past. Over the years, Jessmyn's love, her gentle, persuasive voice and irrefutable logic, had brought him comfort. The tremendous magical forces within him had calmed.

"Are you ready?" Gaylon asked.

"I suppose." His wife sighed. "We haven't had a formal dinner in so long . . . and none of my gowns fit yet, so soon after the birth."

The king turned to look into her lovely unlined, unpainted face and cool jade eyes. A narrow gold coronet encircled her reddish honey-gold hair, all caught up in high curls. She'd chosen a pale green satin dress with a high bodice to hide her still-thickened waist, but her milk-swollen breasts strained at the material.

"You look beautiful," Gaylon told her and stood. "In rags you would look beautiful, my lady."

The young woman grimaced. "By Xenaran standards, I am in rags." She hooked an arm in his and let him lead her to the door. "What's this about the Grand Envoy's 'smooth tongue'?"

"Nothing really," the king muttered. "Only he hasn't come just for trade and peace agreements. There's an empty throne in Xenara. We both know he's come for a queen to sit in it."

They walked the hallway now, and Jessmyn never faltered. "Then he's come for nothing. I'm content with the throne I share."

Gaylon let the relief wash over him. The thought of her leaving him to go south was untenable. The lure of great wealth and power over such a huge nation might tempt anyone but Jessmyn. No, he could depend on her love always.

As they entered the great hall, all conversation and movement ceased. There were only a dozen at table tonight, but the trestles had been set up and places laid out with the court's best silver. King and queen acknowledged the bows from all present. The Grand Envoy with his ladies-in-waiting approached first.

"Your Majesties," the elderly man in long rich robes said and bowed stiffly before Jessmyn. "I am Eowin D'Ar, milady, and as Grand Envoy of Xenara, I have the rare privilege of introducing these young women sent to wait upon your person."

"My person," the queen mused, eying the ladies. "How shall they wait on me? My needs are rather simple."

"They will be companions, milady. You shall have music,

poetry, humor, and friendship. These are such things that royalty deserves."

The D'Jal sisters were presented first, with deep, graceful curtsies in their colorful, full gowns. Gaylon could not keep his eyes from Sandaal D'Lelan, though. She wore blue tonight, a rather severe gown without frills, but lovely nonetheless. Jessmyn seemed most taken with her.

"How kind a soul, my dear," the queen murmured to the young woman, "to serve the court your brother died to protect."

Sandaal's serene features never altered, but behind her dark eyes, Gaylon saw a momentary sorrow, and it cut him deep. His dearest friend, Arlin D'Lelan, had died at the king's own hand.

"I loved my brother very much," Lady D'Lelan answered quietly. "So I should also love the ones he loved."

"Shall we eat?" Gaylon shook off the guilt and signaled to the servants to bring the food.

Tonight they had music, a small group of players on lute, drums, and recorder. Unfortunately, the king thought as he took his seat at the head of the table, the musicians were young and not very good. Steaming dishes arrived, and however poor the music, the food turned out to be wonderful. The Grand Envoy had brought the court of Wynnamyr many gifts, not the least of which were kitchen supplies of exotic spices, rice, flours, sweets.

Wynnamyr was no longer starving, but its mainstay diet was of potatoes and meat. Many Xenaran dishes were served hot with ginger or peppers. Gaylon felt Sandaal's cool eyes on him now and again throughout the meal, and for the first time in several years, the king drank heavy amounts of wine with his supper. Jessmyn, seated beside him, refused to take notice.

The Grand Envoy enjoyed his wine as well.

"This," he said, happily refilling his cup, "works far better than willow bark tea on my poor aching joints. Sadly, though, there's no real cure for old age. . . ." The envoy leaned close to Gaylon and chuckled. "Except death, of course."

The king took a long drink from his own cup. "You haven't come all this way to deliver foodstuffs and enjoy our wines."

"True, Sire. This is not a social visit, but politics must wait until morning. 'Tis best, I think, to enjoy our meal. It's a good foundation on which to build better relations between our two countries."

"I can tell you now," Gaylon said, his voice a little muzzy with drink, "the answer is no."

Eowin's craggy face smiled. "Really? Nevertheless, I won't ask the question until tomorrow. Come, try the curried lamb." He dished a serving onto the king's plate himself. "But careful. It's hot."

\* \* \* \* \*

Well into the night, when all but a few guards slept, Davi took a candle lantern and traveled the stone steps that led deep under the castle's foundation. Prince Banak had inquired about the duke's wounded hand at dinner and accepted the duke's lie, but Zorek, silent, had looked troubled. The burn had continued to throb, a constant reminder of Orym's pendant hidden in his chambers. Davi had little appetite and even less attention for Thayne, who had begun to behave rudely by the time the meal ended.

The rest of the day the duke hardly remembered. Its passing seemed to take forever, but at last night fell. Now he held the lantern high at the base of the final stair, trying to get his bearings in this windowless underground. West wall . . . The light trembled in his good hand, and shadows fled before him. Oddly, this cellar, though considerably dusty, was in far better repair than the rest of the castle. Discarded furniture and boxes of scrolls and clothing were neatly stacked all around, and dust lay everywhere. Davi left footprints as he crossed to the most likely wall.

Wooden cartons covered the tenth flagstone. The duke set down his lantern to move them aside, then, with his dirk, cleaned the dirt carefully from the edges of the stone. With the knife wedged into one corner, he levered the flagstone loose from its bed and slid it aside. Beneath, someone had dug a shallow but wide hole that ran under the eleventh stone as well. In that hole lay another lead box.

Davi struggled to pull it from its bed. This one had no lock and was heavier than the chest in his room. He replaced the flagstones, then, the lead container awkward in his arms, the duke felt his way back up the stairs and down the long hallway to his rooms. This chest was laid upon the bed just as the first had been. Trembling all over now, Davi pulled the lid open.

A massive tome, the *Book of Stones*, lay within. The leather binding, cracked with age, was edged in gold and carved with unknown symbols. Almost against his will, the young lord reached out a fingertip and lightly touched the cover. No searing, fiery pain came this time, only a faint magical tingle that enticed him to open the Book. The first page was blank, the paper incredibly snow-white despite the ages that had passed since the Book's creation.

The second page Davi found filled with line after line of tiny runes without punctuation or indentations. Every page was the same, so completely covered with writing that little of the paper showed through. And all of it was incomprehensible to the duke. Gaylon Reysson had a copy of this fat volume in his library at Castlekeep, but no one dared disturb it. Even Davi, so desirous of magic, had never touched the Book nor looked within.

Now he had one of his very own, but what good would it do him? Stone and Book were closely tied. Here lay all the knowledge a young sorcerer would need to master his Sorcerer's Stone, and yet Davi could make no sense of it. He abandoned the Book for the moment and pulled the chest with Orym's Stone from under the bed. This time, he removed the stone carefully by its golden chain, then took the end of the clasp in his fingertips.

But as he brought the Stone near the Book, a faint blue glow began deep inside the pendant. The closer it came, the brighter the glow, until a clear blue light shone on the page. In that light, the runic lines blurred, reassembling into words Davi understood.

*To the mind that seeks true power, let these words be well remembered.*

He scanned the lines and found them, though translated, too esoteric for his limited understanding of magic. This was some sort of scrying spell and of no use to him. Arbitrarily Davi opened the Book near the middle and leaned closer.

*If a Stone be mastered already, that Stone will deny all others, bringing great harm or death to any who would touch it with bare flesh. If the master of the Stone dies, rarely may it accept someone of similar blood. This must be done slowly and with great care. Wrap and tie the Stone in silk and keep it about the person of him who would be its new master. Only then, and in time, will the Stone possibly come to obey another's commands.*

There in his candle-lit, stone-walled chambers, Davi drew a deep, shuddering breath. How had he found the one passage he so desperately wanted and needed among the hundreds, perhaps thousands, of pages in the *Book of Stones*? However it had happened, the young duke intended to use the Book's advice.

He found a silk handkerchief in a dresser drawer and carefully wrapped Orym's Stone, then tied it tight with a bit of thread. With equal care, he pulled the gold chain around his neck and slipped the pendant under his shirt. No one must see it. No one must know . . . not until the power was truly his.

# Three

A formal audience had been planned for the next after-noon, but morning brought three young ladies-in-waiting to Jessmyn's chamber door for the first time. The sisters' gar-ments were plainer today, but still rich and colorful by Wyn-namyran standards. Sandaal wore gray again and carried a mandolin of polished ebony wood as black as her long, straight hair. Katina and Rose had dark blonde locks, which had been forced into bizarre curls somehow knotted atop their heads.

A servant admitted the women, who curtsied politely before the queen. Jessmyn, smiling, nodded at them.

"Good morning, miladies." She stayed in her rocking chair before the fireplace, with Lilith snug in her arms. The baby had just finished nursing and now drifted to sleep.

"Good morning, Your Highness," the others murmured in return, eyes downcast.

For the first time, Jessmyn felt a touch of embarrassment over the shabby furnishings in her apartment. The tapestries were fading, the braid rugs threadbare, the stone walls gray and gloomy and mildewed. These ladies came from wealthy families. What must they think?

The queen continued to rock gently in the maplewood chair, her attention on the young women. "I've never had ladies-in-waiting before." Her gaze came to rest on Rose's fine-boned aristocratic face. "I'm not quite sure what I'm supposed to do with you."

"Let us do for you, milady," the younger sister said eagerly, her Xenaran accent exotic to the queen's ear. "I've brought a volume of Napier's poetry to read aloud, and Katina's brought games—"

"Napier?"

"A new poet in Benjir—a great warrior with the gentle soul of a peasant. He's one of the very few who survived the Wyn-namyran War."

Katina gave her sister a tiny jab with an elbow. "He's very popular in the south. All his poetry's been translated into Xenaran. We've brought you new books of all kinds, Your Highness. New music, as well."

Only Sandaal seemed reluctant to join in the conversation. Her mandolin set carefully on a low settee, she had gone instead to the hearth to fetch the kettle and refill the queen's teacup.

"How long do all of you intend to wait on me?" Jessmyn asked, amused.

"As long as it pleases you, milady," Katina answered and stepped forward. "May I?" She gently gathered the baby from the queen's arms and carried her to the crib, then covered her with quilts. "What would you like today, Your Majesty? Shall we take the morning air in the gardens? Or knit, or sew? I have rastik and feirie boards."

Jessmyn shook her head. "I'd rather get acquainted first. Sit. Tell me of yourselves and your families—how you've come to be here."

"Certainly," Katina said and motioned to the others to find seats.

The elder D'Jal sister obviously felt in charge here, and the others did as she bade, though it was equally obvious to Jessmyn that Sandaal did so only because it pleased her. The morning passed quickly and very enjoyably while Rose and Kat talked of themselves—subjects much to their liking. A servant brought tea and cakes at one point. The tray was filled with tiny sweet pastries made by the Grand Envoy's personal cook.

Sandaal D'Lelan avoided attention by taking the mandolin

to a window seat and playing quiet, achingly beautiful melodies in the background. Jessmyn found each of the ladies fascinating in very different ways. Katina was twenty, firstborn in Lord Rema D'Jal's house and very much used to having things her way. Jessmyn's royalty did not intimidate her, and Kat used the subtlest manipulation to gain whatever she wanted from her younger sister. Rose, on the other hand, at nineteen, was a babbler and a gossip, though not simple by any means—only young and happy and rather innocent. Sandaal remained a mystery that the queen could decipher at her leisure, but the beauty of her mandolin playing already showed some of the young woman's soul, and there was a sadness, a darkness within.

Prince Robyn arrived with the noon meal, face and hands grubby. He let Rose use a wet cloth to clean them without his usual complaints. At only four, he could be quite charming, even flirtatious, when there were pretty women around. The little boy entertained them while they ate with rambling stories of his adventures in the keep's gardens. Lilith woke hungry and wet, and Rose, on Kat's orders, went to change her diaper before bringing the infant to her mother.

"More apple cider," Robyn said, slightly jealous of the attention the baby was getting. He held out his cup.

"Please," Jessmyn insisted as Rose reached to pour him more.

"Pu-lease," the boy said, grinning. His freckled nose and cheeks were slightly sunburned.

He finished his drink, then abruptly climbed into Katina's lap.

"Robyn—"

"It's all right, milady. I don't mind." The older D'Jal sister wrapped her arms about the child and hugged him till he giggled happily.

The food trays were set aside, and stories of Katay and the Inland Sea begun. Katina had a flare for description, and Jessmyn found herself imagining, with just a touch of longing, the crowded, colorful streets, the smells of food, the shouts of vendors.

Midway through her tale, though, someone scratched at the door and broke the spell.

The queen called, "Come."

Their elderly stoop-shouldered chamberlain, Temric, entered, bowing. "The audience is about to start, milady. His eminence, the Grand Envoy, and His Highness, the king, await your arrival."

Reluctantly Jessmyn stood. Her present company was so much more pleasing. A tedious afternoon of treaties and agreements did not appeal to her in the least. But there were other reasons for her to attend this particular audience, reasons she refused to think about. Kat once more took the baby.

"I'll bring her to you later, when she grows hungry again," the older sister promised. "Don't worry. I've raised eight little brothers and sisters. We'll all take good care of her. Isn't that right, Lilith?"

The infant cooed and spit up some curdled milk for reply. Jess wasn't worried—the baby's regular nurse would be sent to help. Even so, she trusted these young women already and found that she liked them very much. Sandaal, with the shiest of smiles, offered to escort the queen to the audience chamber, but Jessmyn declined. While she enjoyed their company, she hoped the ladies didn't become an entourage, traipsing on her heels at every moment.

Instead, the old chamberlain went with her along the dim corridors of the lower level to the audience chamber. Within, light poured through high, narrow windows in the far wall.

"Your Majesty," the Grand Envoy said, bowing to her, his voice gravelly with age.

The king, seated on his throne, stood and descended the stairs from the dais to the floor. Her hand in his, she was led back up the stone steps and seated on the cushioned velvet. It felt strange. Never once in all these years had she sat upon the throne. Everyone knew that under the original marriage contract, Jessmyn was to be joint ruler of Wynnamyr, yet she had always left royal duties to her husband, offering advice only when it was asked for.

"My lady," Gaylon whispered and kissed her hand before

releasing her fingers.

"Was the council not invited?" the queen asked. Other than the three of them, the large chamber was empty.

"Lord D'Ar suggested we speak in private first," her husband said, and Jess noticed a tension in his words.

The queen eyed the Grand Envoy. "Then speak, milord."

Eowin bowed again, though that simple act obviously pained him. "May I ask first how you find your ladies-in-waiting, Highness?"

"They found me, first thing this morning." Jessmyn smiled. "But I find them very pleasing, Milord Envoy. I'm grateful of their company, however long a time that might be. But what, sir, prompted you to bring them?"

"Milady, they are simply a reminder of your southern heritage. You must know why I have come. . . ."

The queen's lips tightened. "I know, and I tell you honestly that nothing you offer will entice me from my husband and this kingdom. Surely you have others to rule in Xenara."

The Grand Envoy pursed his lips. "Your father left behind numerous bastard sons and daughters, but none are suited to the throne. You alone survive the house of Gerric, Your Majesty. You alone can bring the aristocracy under control again and balance the power they share with the merchant families." He paused to straighten his robes with a gnarled hand. "These last years, Xenara has lived under the constant threat of civil war. While my health fails with age, I've done everything I can to preserve the throne. Now I implore you to take your rightful place upon it."

"Do you think we care about your troubles?" Gaylon demanded, voice tight. "Whatever hardships you've faced, we've faced far worse—and survived. Wynnamyr didn't start the war. Xenara did."

Eowin D'Ar gazed at the flagstones. "This is true, milord. But you ended it."

Jessmyn saw pain wash over the king's pale features and felt his agony as if it were her own. All those deaths he had carried on his shoulders for so long, and now, finally, when he had just begun to live again, the memories were brought back to haunt him.

"Milord Grand Envoy," the queen said coldly, "do you realize what you are asking? This is the only home I have ever known. I was taken from my mother at birth and given to my husband's father, betrothed to Gaylon in hope of bringing peace to our two countries—a peace my father chose to break. I have no obligations to Xenara, no matter my blood ties."

"I beg your pardon, but you do, Your Highness. Have you reviewed the marriage contract recently?"

Gaylon put a hand on his wife's shoulder. "Our copy was destroyed before I took my crown back from Lucien D'Sulang."

"Then read it now, please," the envoy said and drew a scroll from one wide sleeve of his robes.

Bowing, he carried the paper up the steps of the dais and held it out to the king. Gaylon stared at it for a long moment before finally accepting the scroll. Jessmyn plucked the roll from his fingers and slipped the ribbon off.

This copy was in the Xenaran tongue, ornate and pretentious. It delineated the exchange of a tiny princess for mineral and water rights and a chance to gain influence and power over the Wynnamyran crown with her marriage to the prince and heir. Except for the double seals of kings in red wax at the very bottom, this might have been a receipt for the sale of a prize horse. Irritated, Jessmyn scanned the tiny, precise script.

"The twelfth paragraph down, milady," Eowin offered.

Her eyes found the lines, and they chilled her heart: *Should the house of Gerric fail for any reason, the line of Xenaran succession shall fall to Jessmyn D'Gerric and her heirs. Therefore, should Jessmyn D'Gerric be unable or unwilling to mount the throne of Xenara, so shall her firstborn son or daughter rule instead. Should this offspring be in his or her minority, a regent shall be chosen by the houses of Miren, Koshen, and Falsted to guide the child until of age.*

"Jess?"

Gaylon's voice seemed to come from some great distance.

"The house of Koshen was lost in Zankos with your father's,

milady." The Grand Envoy stood near the throne. "But the D'Mirens and D'Falsteds remain strong in Katay. There's been no communication between our two countries, so I wasn't certain that you had borne any children, but I forewarned the houses in question."

"What?" the king demanded. "Forewarned about what?"

Eowin D'Ar had to know exactly whom he dealt with—a mercurial and deadly sorcerer-king—yet he answered willingly enough. "The choosing of a regent for your son, Thayne, who will inherit the Xenaran crown if your wife declines. This was contractually agreed upon by both your fathers, and you are bound by it."

Eyes wide with dismay, Gaylon looked at Jessmyn. "Is this true?"

She nodded, unable to find words of comfort for him or herself. The gray Stone in the ring on the king's right hand flared a sudden brilliant blue for just an instant, and the paper in Jessmyn's fingers vaporized. Unhurt, she still gasped in shock.

"So much for contracts," Gaylon said and offered the Grand Envoy a twisted smile.

"There's another copy at the royal library in Katay," the old man muttered. "It, too, is but a piece of paper. Only the words and their intent are binding. Your honor, Sire, must guide you in this. Remember, though—your father willingly signed the contract, trusting his heir to honor it." He bowed awkwardly. "My bones ache, and I tire easily, Your Majesties. If you would forgive me . . ."

"Of course, Lord D'Ar," Jessmyn agreed. "Please take your leave. I'm sorry if our reception to this news has been less than hospitable, but I'm sure you understand why. I promise, we'll think on all you've said and shown us."

"I can ask no more." The Grand Envoy tottered down the steps to the floor and made his way to the chamber exit, where a pair of his soldier-servants met him in the hall.

The doors closed once more, and in the silence that followed, the queen watched her husband fight for control of his emotions. Not very many years ago, she would have feared for the old envoy's life, but Gaylon had matured as a man and a sorcerer. Now he turned to her.

"How can we be held to contracts written when we were mere children?"

Jessmyn stared at her empty hands. "Because royalty has always been at the mercy of its ancestors and its subjects. Our choices are often made for us even before we're conceived. And so it was for Thayne."

"I won't let them have him," the king snarled and began to pace. "I won't have him raised in a court that thrives on intrigue. I won't be forced into another war one day with my own son."

"No," the queen agreed. "But there's only one way to insure that doesn't happen." She waited until Gaylon paused beside her. "I must take the throne myself."

The king paled again, then flushed with outrage. "Jessmyn, no!"

"It can be done, my lord," she murmured gently. "With Lord Eowin's help, I can set up a council to rule, in time. When Xenara has stabilized politically, I'll come home to Wynnamyr—where I belong. If the two countries become as one—as our fathers hoped—then I can rule Xenara from here. We can rule Xenara."

"By all the gods, Jess," Gaylon moaned. "You don't know what you're saying. You'll never return to the poverty and solitude of this place once you've tasted the wealth of Xenara. There would always be something to keep you from leaving. And the danger . . . These people backstab and poison one another simply for the sake of enjoyment." He went to his knees at her feet, his face filled with hurt. "I couldn't live without you, my lady. You and the children are all that keep me sane."

Jessmyn leaned forward to catch her husband's head in her two hands. "Then you must come with me." She kissed him lingeringly on the lips. "Because neither can I live without you."

\*   \*   \*   \*   \*

The dense cloud cover had blown in from the ocean again, but no rain fell this morning. A blustery wind snapped the green banners the two white-haired soldiers held and dragged at Thayne's cloak. He watched Zorek and his sons exchange solemn farewells with Davi, then the king of Lasony clapped his hands.

From somewhere at the rear of the line of horsemen, someone rode forward leading a small white mare with thick mane and tail and shaggy fetlocks. Zorek turned to the prince.

"This is my parting gift to you, milord," he said. "She's young and as yet unnamed, but she's swift as the wind and very good-natured and will make you a fine mount. Will you accept her?"

Flustered, Thayne took the reins. "She's beautiful, but I have nothing to give you in return. . . ."

"The pleasure of the gift is all I want, Your Highness."

"No, wait!" The prince caught the edge of his cloak and reached into a deep pocket in the lining. The long wooden whistle was old and battered, but one of his favorite toys. He held the thing out to Zorek. "It gets full of spit if you blow on it for too long, but you can make some pretty sounds."

"Thank you," the king said graciously. "I shall cherish it always."

His sons came forward to help the ancient monarch into his saddle, then mounted their own animals. Zorek led his troop away at a jog, headed north once more through the fields. The little mare, confused, tried to follow them, but Thayne's tight grip on the reins stopped her.

"What will you call her?" the duke asked, smiling.

"I don't know." Thayne looked up into Davi's face. Despite the smile, the man had puffy shadows under his eyes, and his face looked haggard. "It'll have to be a special name."

The mare stretched her neck out and neighed after the other horses, her whole body shuddering with the effort.

"She wants to go home," Thayne said sadly.

"But she'll learn to love it here in Wynnamyr in time." The duke motioned to Fitzwal to take the horse. "Put her in the stall next to Crystal. I want them to make friends."

"Aye," the sergeant-at-arms agreed and led the animal away. Her hooves beat a muffled rhythm on the stones.

"She'll need to be shod," Davi called.

Thayne continued to gaze after the retreating men of Lasony as they dwindled in the distance. He would have to go there someday—to that cold, snowy land. There were many marvelous places in his world to explore. The prince was only just beginning to grow confident in his reading skills, and enjoyed his lessons in geography and history the most. To be truthful, he longed to return to Castlekeep and his tutors. Castle Gosney had turned out to be a dull, dull place, and Davi, preoccupied with his estate accounts, paid little attention to his prince.

"Your Highness?"

The wind whipped the boy's cloak up again and sent a chill through him. "I'm coming," he answered distractedly and followed the duke back inside.

Another boring gray day proceeded to pass slowly. Thayne tried to read from the books he'd brought along, but his own naturally high energy kept him from sitting still for very long at a time. After dinner in the kitchens, with only the grouchy cook for company, the boy took a handful of carrots to the dilapidated stables.

Davi's gray mare, Crystal, came to him immediately and blew gusts of hot air through widened nostrils as she searched him for the treats. The new mare, though, would have nothing to do with him. It continued to pace in the small box stall.

"Come, lady, come," Thayne sang to her without much hope. Having been raised around horses, he understood her distress at being left behind by her companions.

This was the very first mount the prince could call his own, and that thought pleased him. Though not a pony, the mare was small enough to allow him more confidence. He might even be able to saddle her himself if he stood on a stool, and any little bit of independence to a six-year-old was welcome. But she needed a name, something regal and worthy of her fine-boned, purebred beauty. Sojii, in the Benjiran tongue, meant "wind," which King Zorek had claimed her to be as fast as.

"Sojii," the boy called gently, tasting the word.

The mare paused and swung her head to look at him, then went back to pacing. Sojii it would be. Yes, the name definitely pleased him. One of the men-at-arms, a youth called Toad, had begun pitching hay into the stalls with a three-tined fork—last year's sweet timothy, dusty and dry now.

"Highness," the young soldier said amiably and tossed a forkload over Sojii's half door.

Thayne eyed the hinges and hasp on the old wood. "Do you think this door'll hold her, Toad?"

"Aye, milord. Strong enough, I 'spect."

"I don't want her to run away."

"Naw, she'll settle down. Won't ya, lass?"

Toad made kissing noises to the mare, and she turned and came right to him. For an instant, Thayne felt betrayed.

"It's how they call 'em in Lasony," the soldier explained. "Give her the carrots, and she'll take to you right quick."

"Sojii," Thayne said, holding out a piece of carrot on the flat of his hand as his father had shown him.

She picked it up delicately with soft, warm lips, and he gazed into one liquid brown eye, already deeply in love with his very first horse. Behind them came a clattering of shod hooves on the flags of the bailey. Castle Gosney, as a fortress, had its stables in the protected inner courtyard.

"Halloooo the castle!" someone shouted, and the words bounced off the stone walls.

"Wait," Toad commanded and hurried away.

With a quick glance at Sojii, Thayne hurried after the soldier. More visitors, all in just a few days. Perhaps the journey north had been worth it after all. Fitzwal arrived in the outer courtyard at the same moment as Toad and Thayne. There was only a single rider in the bailey, though—a young herald wearing the tabard of the royal house. He rode a sweaty horse that danced nervously on the stones and fought him for the reins.

The herald waved a sealed envelope. "I've brought urgent news for the duke of Gosney from His Majesty, the king."

# Four

By dawn a thick white fog had rolled inland off the Western Sea, drifting across Moon Bay near the mouth of the Great River. In the chill wet air, the Gosney retainers made ready for the journey south to Castlekeep. Fitzwal had saddled the new Lasony mare and ridden her first, declaring her sound and well mannered enough for a young prince to handle, which pleased Thayne.

Davi paid the sour-faced cobbler-cook and his helpers a little extra to make up for their early departure, then went out into the misty morning, his cloak pulled tightly about him. Exhaustion tugged at him as it had constantly these last few days, but Orym's Stone lay snug against his chest. All his nights had been spent reading the Dark King's grimoire, trying to absorb page upon page of incredible spells, not that he'd had the courage yet to put its lessons to work or even take the Sorcerer's Stone in hand again.

"Careful with that trunk," the duke said irritably to Gabe, the man who struggled to lash it on one of the pack animals. The *Book of Stones* in its lead box lay buried in the clothing of this particular chest. It was madness to carry Orym's Stone and Book back to the keep. Should the king detect their presence, he'd certainly destroy them, but what other options did Davi have? He couldn't bear to leave them behind.

Torches in sconces along the inner courtyard walls cast feeble light through the fog. The flagstones were wet and slick underfoot. Someone brought him his saddled mare, then gave him a leg up. Crystal did a sideways jig, bobbing her head, eager to go, but the duke held her in check. His sword was handed up to him.

"Milord Thayne," he called, and the boy appeared immediately, already mounted, his white horse melding ghostlike with the mist.

"Why has my father called us back so soon?" the prince asked, stifling a yawn with a mittened hand.

Davi heard a touch of worry in his voice. There had been nothing in the king's message except the order to return to Castlekeep immediately. "No doubt it's something to do with the Xenaran Grand Envoy's visit. If there's been illness or accident, your father would have said, so don't fret." He glanced down at the little mare. "How is she in the bit?"

"Fine." Now there was a hint of pride. "I've named her Sojii. . . ."

"Sojii," the duke repeated and envisioned the wind in the mare's silver mane. "A good name." He turned in the saddle to peer through the mist. "Hello back there. Are we ready, Fitzwal?"

"Aye," came the answer. "If Toad'll ever get a foot in his stirrup."

In moments, the group had filed out through the bailey and onto the rutted, little-used wagon trail that would lead them to the coach road at Mill Town. Crystal broke into an excited jog, and Davi felt the silk-wrapped Stone in its golden clasp bounce lightly against his breastbone. There was never a moment he wasn't aware of it, never a time he didn't long for its power. Already, subtle changes had begun in his perceptions.

The world around him had grown clearer, more distinct, over the last few days—colors brighter, sounds more lucid. Even through the silk that protected him, the duke instinctively recognized the first signs of bonding. The thought brought elation and stark fear. Perhaps the Stone desired him as much as he desired it.

"Davi?"

The duke glanced at the small fog-shrouded figure who rode beside him. "Yes, my prince?"

"Are you all right?"

"Of course. Why?"

"You haven't talked to me much lately. And since King Zorek's visit, you seem . . . sort of tired and grumpy all the time. I thought maybe you could be coming down with a cold."

"Could be." Davi forced a laugh. Young royalty tended to be precocious, and this perceptive little prince was no exception, sometimes behaving more like an adult than the adults around him.

"Well, when we arrive at the keep," Thayne said imperiously, "you're to see Girkin immediately."

"Certainly, Your Majesty," the duke lied. The elderly keep physician with his nasty concoctions and ridiculous remedies was the last person he cared to see on their return.

"And bundle up. It's cold."

"Yes, Your Majesty."

Behind them, Fitzwal chuckled. Davi abruptly nudged Crystal into a trot through the milky fog, and the others were forced to follow. The king had said to come with all haste, and if they hurried, they would reach Mill Town in time for a quick dinner while the horses rested. Impatience and irritation were common emotions to the duke recently. The simple reality around him seemed extraneous, devised to keep him from the one thing he truly wanted and needed to do.

Davi pushed them hard until his knees began to ache from posting the trot, and Cil, one of the men-at-arms, began to grumble. They would much rather gallop, but that would tire the horses far more quickly. Thayne kept pace without a word of complaint, though part of the time he was forced to sit the mare's bouncing gait.

By midmorning the fog had nearly burned off, and Thayne pointed out the chimney tops of Mill Town beyond the trees. It was a sprawling, teeming lumber town, Wynnamyr's only seaport, and far larger than Keeptown near Castlekeep. The fine hardwood lumber from the many mills was exported to

the arid southern countries all along the western coast, mostly
for use in ship building. The beautiful softwoods, redwood,
yew, and cedar provided lumber for homes and establishments.

A strong scent of sawdust and rotting fish mixed with moist
salt air met them on the outskirts of town. There were several
more ships in the harbor than on their first visit—all of them
Xenaran, for some reason—and the cobbled streets were filled
with busy people. The crowds made Davi nervous. Fitzwal
took the lead now. "Make way!" he shouted at the throngs.
"Make way for a prince of the Red Kings!"

The foreigners only gawked at the redheaded child on the
cream white horse, while some of the townspeople managed
awkward bows in cramped quarters. The first few places the
royal entourage stopped, they found the inns and taverns
jammed to capacity. Finally, despite the noontide crowd, a
harried innkeep at the Sailor's Roost found them room at a
table and brought them a decent meal—all but poor Toad,
who had to watch the horses and their belongings against
theft.

Davi had little appetite for his fish chowder. The noise and
stench of the packed common room set his teeth on edge.
Though he remembered finding Mill Town exotic and exciting
before, it made him anxious now.

"You should eat, milord," Thayne said from beside him.
"We've a long ride ahead of us."

The duke found a smile for him. "I should say the same to
you, my prince."

"I don't like fish. It's too . . . fishy tasting." The child
screwed up his face. "I wish they'd had venison." He took a
sip of his watered-down wine. "I can't wait to get home. I
really miss my mum and . . ." His voice trailed off, and his
cheeks reddened.

Fitzwal leaned across the table toward him. "Even the
bravest soldier gets homesick, Your Highness. There's no
shame in that."

Beside him, Thayne turned, and his eyes met the duke's for
just an instant. A tiny shock rippled through Davi, and he

felt—no, experienced—the boy's longing for his family as if it were his own. The Stone warmed perceptibly against his chest, feeding the empathy the duke of Gosney shared with this son of his Red King. Magic, subtle yet strong.

"Milord Davyn," said Fitzwal quietly and nodded his chin at the table behind the duke where low, angry voices began to rise.

"I think our meal is done," Davi said just as quietly, holding his purse out to the sergeant. "Pay our debt and meet us outside. Don't forget Toad's dinner." He gazed at the other two men-at-arms, Gabe and Cil. "Should trouble start, keep clear of it. The prince is your only concern." Already he had Thayne's arm in hand, helping him out from the bench, but his attention remained on the argument.

They were two heavyset Xenaran sailors, and well into their cups for so early in the day. Davi pulled the prince free of the table just as the two began to grapple drunkenly. All would have been well if not for a third man, a fellow sailor, who rushed to try to part the wrestlers. His good intentions earned him a knife blade in the belly.

The wounded man staggered back, blundering into Davi and the prince. Thayne was jerked from the duke's grip, and in fright, the boy dodged away—into the sailor with the bloody dagger. Davi, still somehow connected empathetically, felt a searing pain in his own body as the blade pierced Thayne's flesh, then something snapped inside the duke—a cold, clear rage that awakened the Sorcerer's Stone even in its silk wrapping. The knife suddenly took life of its own, was somehow ripped from the sailor's fist and sent flying into the wall behind them, where the point lodged deep in the wood.

At the very same instant, the duke of Gosney had drawn his sword and struck off the hand that had held the dagger in one swift, unconscious move. Only Fitzwal's grip on his arm kept him from running the screaming man through.

"The prince!" his sergeant cried urgently.

Every Xenaran sailor in the tavern, friend or foe of the wounded men, had drawn his weapon. Others scrambled for the exit in hope of avoiding trouble. The innkeep had wisely disappeared altogether. Davi scooped the whimpering prince into his arms and let his three men-at-arms make a path to the door.

"This is the son of Gaylon Reysson," Fitzwal snarled at a sailor who made a threatening move toward them. "If ye've any sense, ye'll keep yer distance, man."

That made them all pause, at least. Davi clutched the prince to his chest, feeling the throb of the wound in the boy's side and hot blood on his one hand. If they had even looked the part of royalty, this might not have happened. What madness had brought them here in the first place? Toad met them, wide-eyed, where the horses were tethered in a shady thicket of myrtle behind the inn.

"There must be a surgeon in town," Fitzwal offered, as pale and sick with worry as Davi was.

Thayne struggled free of the duke's grasp and pulled his blood-sticky shirt loose for them to see the wound. The knife had pierced the right side so close to the edge of his waist that it had gone completely through. Bloody it was, but not bad.

"Am I going to die?" the boy asked, afraid but without tears.

"No," Toad laughed. "But you'll have a grand scar."

"Really?" Now the prince and heir was pleased.

Fitzwal straightened. "Break out the bandages, Toad, and the golden seal." He shook his head. "Well, I don't want to be the one that tells the king we nearly lost his firstborn in a tavern brawl."

"This is gonna sting, milord," Toad said as he brought the medical supplies.

Sting was too mild a word. Thayne, brave and stoic so far, squalled when the golden seal powder was dusted into the open cut, and the duke suffered with him. By the time the pain passed, the boy's face was streaked with tears. Davi wrapped the linen bandage around Thayne's waist and tucked the edges in while Fitzwal brought a clean shirt.

They rode away from the inn, ignoring the havoc that raged unabated.

"Well, we saved the price of a meal," the sergeant grunted

and tossed the duke's purse back to him.

Toad looked morose. "And forgot my dinner."

"I saved some biscuits," Cil told him and passed them over.

Now Thayne rode before the duke on Crystal's saddle, held firmly in his guardian's arms, Sojii led behind by Toad. Davi didn't push them at a trot, since even the plodding pace of the mare hurt the prince's side. The boy didn't complain. He only bit his lip and kept quiet. They wouldn't be able to make haste as the king had asked, but that couldn't be helped.

"What happened to the dagger?"

Thayne's question shook him. "I don't know," Davi answered carefully.

"But you saw it, didn't you? You saw it jump out of the sailor's hand."

"He must have thrown it."

"No," the boy insisted. "The blade jumped out of his fingers and flew at the wall by itself. I saw it . . . just as you . . . How can he be a sailor without his right hand?" Here was compassion and concern for the man who had so callously injured him.

"He'll manage." The duke looked away. "I'm sorry, Your Majesty. I'm sorry you saw that, and I'm sorry you were hurt. The king trusted me with your safekeeping, and I failed him. I failed you."

"No," Thayne muttered, one small hand pressed to his aching side. "It wasn't your fault. But I did see it. I did see the dagger fly." When Davi kept silent, he asked, "Did we just have an adventure?"

"I believe you could call it that."

"Oh." The prince tilted his head back to gaze up into Davi's face, and his mouth twisted ruefully. "It wasn't nearly as much fun as I thought."

\* \* \* \* \*

Laborers, both slave and freemen, worked diligently on the palace and the grounds. Of all Zankos, this one structure had remained standing after the war, its marble sooted and black where Kingslayer's fire had washed over it. The interior—walls of wood and plaster—had not survived, nor the lovely gardens with their ancient bent olive trees and flowering citrus.

Perched on the high stone wall that surrounded the royal grounds, young Raf D'Gular watched a team of horses drag another full grown olive to the great pit dug in the dry ocher soil. New trees had been brought from Katay in the east, and already the grounds began to take gracious shape. Over five hundred men had been set to repair the palace, and even in all the confusion, the work continued.

"How's the view?" someone called from below.

Nials Haldrick peered up at Raf, one hand shading his eyes from the sun. He was a tall, slender man in embroidered white robes and sandals, with a head of thick dark curls and a pleasant serene face. He would be the new palace physician when the Grand Envoy's royal family arrived to take up residency.

Raf shrugged. "Decent enough." He swung himself over the edge of the wall, then dropped to the ground, absorbing the shock with flexed knees. It was considerably dustier down here.

"Careful, or you'll end up my patient," Haldrick said amiably. "Let me see your hand." He took the young man's left hand before he could protest.

Raf endured the gentle probing touch of the physician's fingers. He was foreign trained and used esoteric medicine as well as Xenara's modern skills and instruments.

"Hmmm," Nials muttered. "Too much wine, my boy. You must concentrate on eating green foods and fish as well, and leave red meats alone." He released the hand. "Let's find someplace where the air is a little fresher."

Young D'Gular, his left hand tingling strangely, followed the physician across the grounds, around and through the work crews. "This is all very nice," he said, observing the new flower beds. "But you could be going to all this trouble for my royal bastard brother's sake."

"Perhaps," Nials answered. "How is your father?"

That question brought a bitter laugh from Raf. "As always. He'll have Kyl on the throne at any cost. Eowin D'Ar is a fool to bring Roffo's daughter back to Xenara. If she's any wits at all, she'll refuse him."

"I'm afraid she can't." The physician led him into the courtyard, where wide red tiles were being laid. "And what of you, Raf? What part in all this is yours?"

"You'll have to be more clever than that to wheedle Harren's secrets out of me."

Now Nials laughed. "I'm afraid I'm not much suited to intrigue. But it isn't secrets I'm after. I see you always on the outside, watching, listening. One simply wonders where exactly you stand."

"Here at the moment," Raf said lightly. "I'm of the house of Gular, born and bred, Master Haldrick."

"And so your loyalties lie there."

Raf looked away. "I'm a younger son with little to inherit. My father cares for nothing but his royal bastard half-wit, so you might say my loyalties lie with me."

"Then perhaps you might find succor at the side of the true queen of Xenara," the physician said. "Your knowledge of the opposing houses would be welcome."

They had come into a wide bright chamber that had once been the morning room. New walls with fresh coats of plaster enclosed it. Raf wrinkled his nose at the scent.

"No," he said, listening to his words echo in the emptiness. "As you say, I prefer to watch the games." He turned away, headed back the way they'd come.

Haldrick didn't follow, but he called, "Don't be too surprised if you're forced to play."

*  *  *  *  *

The roses bloomed early this year, or so the queen had told them. In Xenara, the roses bloomed almost year round, but never so spectacularly as this. Sandaal wandered with basket and scissors through the bushes, bemused by the riotous colors and fragrances, unable to decide which flowers to cut.

Katina, in a gown with hues to rival the flowers, had already nearly filled her own basket.

Climbing roses, a rich deep red, sprawled over the keep wall and tangled themselves in the balconies above, while tiny perfect white tea roses were set in neat rows on the borders of the garden. In between lay every possible color under the warm spring sun—purples, pinks, yellows, and reds.

Sandaal chose a perfect yellow bloom finally, just opening, the petals streaked with pink, then moved deeper into the garden where a bush with soft lavender blossoms had caught her eye. As soon as she had reached the bush, the young woman heard the crunch of gravel. A man led a dapple-gray horse out the rear doors of the stables and into the wide yard behind the garden.

He was poorly clad in travel-stained breeks and a dark knit shirt with a worn leather jerkin over it. His knee-high boots were in desperate need of new soles. His hair, cut at the shoulder and tied back, was as black as Sandaal's, only wavy. Both he and the animal seemed weary.

"They've finally arrived," Katina said from beside her.

"Who?"

"Really, Sandaal," the young D'Jal woman muttered with barely concealed contempt, "if you'd ever listen instead of daydreaming . . . That's got to be the duke of Gosney. It's all the old man's been talking about for days." She and Rose always referred to the Grand Envoy as "the old man," an odd mixture of disrespect and affection. "He's been waiting for Prince Thayne and the duke to return from the Gosney estates up north. Now maybe we can go home. I'm sick to death of Wynnamyr."

"He doesn't look much like a duke." Sandaal watched the young man tie the horse to a pole on the far side of the yard, then disappear into a shed. Despite his outward appearance, though, she'd noticed the fine aquiline nose and high cheekbones of a nobleman.

"He's poor . . ." Kat said meaningfully. "And not worth your bother."

Sandaal felt a tiny flush touch her cheeks, then felt anger at herself for letting Katina's words bother her. The men of this small rugged country, lord and commoner alike, were generally crude and unlettered and of absolutely no interest to her. Still, that momentary glimpse of the duke of Gosney had disturbed her for some reason.

"Come on." Katina broke her companion's chain of thought. "You're taking too long. My basket's already full." She began snipping roses from the nearest bushes and handing them to Sandaal. "We don't have all morning."

Both baskets filled, the D'Jal sister led her back into the keep, back into the dimly lit, damp corridors of gray stone. Sandaal regretted leaving the gardens, but Her Majesty had come down with a cold, and the fat little keep physician had ordered her to stay inside. Ridiculous—the spring air and sunshine would be far more healthful.

Lilith had been removed to the nursery and was tended by a wet nurse for the while. A small cold in an adult could turn deadly for a baby princess. Katina opened the door to the queen's apartments without knocking. The young noblewoman was aggressive and tended to take liberties, but Jessmyn didn't seem to mind. Vases filled with water waited on a table, while the queen lay abed in her bedchamber. Rose's soft voice came to them, reading from one of the numerous books the Grand Envoy had brought.

"Did your mother never teach you how to arrange flowers?" Kat snapped irritably and snatched away the pink bloom that Sandaal tried to add to a bouquet of red. Then the anger melted. "I'm sorry. I didn't think. . . ."

"No matter." Sandaal wandered into the bedchamber with the yellow rose in hand. "Your Majesty." She curtsied at the foot of the bed, then brought the flower to the queen.

Jessmyn smiled under a reddened nose, and Rose's voice faded.

"This is so beautiful, but I'm afraid I can't smell it." Her Highness's voice was rough, and she clutched a well-used handkerchief. "How were the gardens?"

"Wonderful," Sandaal said quietly. "Would you like some music, milady? Or should we leave you to sleep?"

"But I'm only halfway through this chapter," Rose complained from her chair.

"We'll finish it another time." The queen gestured to Sandaal's mandolin where it rested on a corner table. "I would rather have music for a while. If you would, Rose, I'd like some more hot tea."

The younger sister marked her book and set it aside willingly enough, but frowned at Sandaal as she passed by to the doorway.

"Come sit on the bed and sing to me, child." Jessmyn patted the blankets beside her.

Sandaal brought the instrument. "What would you have me sing, milady?"

"Anything. I'm bored to death." But when the young woman put her fingers on the strings, the queen laid a hand on her arm. "Do you have a sweetheart, Sandaal? Are you betrothed to anyone?"

The questions were far too personal, even from the queen. Sandaal let the anger go.

"No, milady. I have no dowry to offer."

"You have your beauty and your voice . . . and a fine bright mind."

The Southern woman smiled ruthfully. "In Xenara, a lord must see the gold before the girl."

"And they think of *us* as barbarians," the queen said, indignant. She blew her nose into the hanky. "Well, there's time yet. We'll find someone suitable." Then, at Sandaal's stark look, "And acceptable to you, of course. Sing for me, please, my dear."

\* \* \* \* \*

The king had left the keep—gone deer hunting in the coastal mountains for the day. So the stable master told Davi when he and the prince first arrived. The duke felt nothing but relief over that. Thayne was taken immediately to Girkin, and Crystal, who had thrown a shoe, was taken to the smithy. Afterward, Davi went with his belongings to his own apartments in the southeast wing. There he hid the *Book of Stones* beneath the bed for lack of a better idea, then bathed and dressed quickly and headed for the queen's chambers.

A lovely blonde-haired young woman in a fine blue gown let him in. Another, dressed in pink, sat in a chair by the hearth. They were sisters and close enough in looks to be confusing at first. Someone in the bedchamber played a mandolin—someone with agile fingertips that plucked an intricate melody. The lady in blue went to announce him to the queen, and the music stopped abruptly.

"Davyn," Jessmyn said warmly and reached out both hands to him as he entered.

He bowed to kiss the slender fingers, acutely aware of the beautiful solemn girl that sat on the far side of the bed, the mandolin held in her lap. Unfortunately there were other things that must be dealt with first.

"Highness, Thayne is in the apothecary with the physician," Davi blurted. "He'll be fine, but we met with some ill fortune along the road."

"I know," the queen said gently. "Both Girkin and Thayne have already been here. Girkin says the prince is healing nicely, while Thayne has decided he would like to have another such adventure as soon as possible."

"Gods, no!"

Jessmyn chuckled. "I agree. Here, milord, let me introduce my ladies-in-waiting, thoughtfully provided by His Graciousness, the Xenaran Grand Envoy. Katina and Rose D'Jal you have already met." The women curtsied in turn. "And this is Sandaal . . . D'Lelan."

Davi somehow missed the emphasis on the family name. The dark-eyed, black-haired woman on the bed nodded, but had no smile for him like the others.

"Your playing is exquisite, Lady Sandaal," Davi said.

"Her voice even more so," said the queen. "Our young duke of Gosney has great skill on the lute and a fine voice as well. I might like to hear you play together sometime soon, if it pleases you both."

Oh, yes, thought Davi, his eyes fixed on the young southern woman. Her dark beauty entranced him, held him charmed almost as strongly as Orym's Stone. The two sisters were forgotten completely. Sandaal . . . D'Lelan. From the house of Lelan. That realization brought a tiny jolt.

"Are you . . . are you, by any chance, related to Arlin D'Lelan?"

"He was my brother," came the soft answer. She refused to meet his eyes.

"I'm so sorry. . . ." The words were painful.

"It's not necessary. I long ago gave up the grief."

Davi heard a false note in that last statement, but had no time to wonder. Jessmyn motioned him to a chair.

"I sent the king on his hunt today because it may be the last for a while."

"Milady?"

"Marten Pelson has been sent for and will arrive soon. The council agrees the fourteenth earl of the Lower Vales is best suited to rule Wynnamyr in our absence. And you, Milord Duke, must decide whether to remain here and help him or leave with us."

"Leave?"

"Eowin D'Ar, the Grand Envoy, has persuaded me to ascend to the throne of Xenara." Stunned, Davi stared at her. The queen glanced at the women. "Leave us, please, for the while. I'll send for you later."

The duke, with momentary regret, watched Sandaal leave, then Jessmyn's news flooded back in a wave of confusion.

"You are leaving Wynnamyr? And the king goes with you?" He couldn't keep the incredulous tone from his voice.

"For a time. It's Gaylon's decision, but I'm glad. The Grand Envoy has left me no choice, Davi. If I refuse, then Thayne must go in my stead. One day he may rule both countries, and Wynnamyr can only benefit from that, but raised alone in Xenara . . ." The queen looked up into her duke's face. "Will you stay and aid Marten? I'm sure he'll need all the help he can get."

Davi shook his head. This wasn't even a consideration, and Jessmyn knew it. "Where the Red King goes, a Gosney follows. The children will also come? And Thayne?"

"Yes," the queen said. She smiled. "His adventures are really only just beginning, I'm afraid."

The duke couldn't answer her smile. "Xenara is a snake's den. Your lives will all be in danger . . . and how will Gaylon Reysson be received, the sorcerer-king who took so many thousands of Xenaran lives with his own hands?"

"His protection I leave to you. All our protection may be on your young shoulders, Davyn Darynson." Jessmyn glanced down at the blankets. "D'Ar has made many promises, and I feel he'll do his best, but he's a very old man and not in the best of health."

"I won't forsake you, milady." Unthinking, the duke touched his chest where Orym's Stone lay hidden. Now, more than ever, he must gain its sorcerous powers. Xenara's many religious sects had dangerous magicks of their own.

"You must be tired from your journey, Lord Gosney," the queen murmured, but Davi could see her own exhaustion from the illness. "Go and rest. When the king returns, you'll have much to discuss."

"Your Majesty." The duke bowed and turned toward the door.

"One thing more," Jessmyn said from behind him, and he turned back. "How do you find the Lady Sandaal?"

"I beg your pardon, milady?"

"Lady Sandaal . . . does she not please you?"

A small uncomfortable knot formed in Davi's throat. "She is . . . very lovely."

The queen studied his face carefully and seemed to find what she sought. "Good. Then you won't object to keeping her company from time to time . . . in order to practice music together, of course."

"Of course."

"Can you do this without hurting Cally's feelings too badly?"

Sweet Cally. He'd forgotten all about the pretty kitchen wench who shared his bed occasionally—in secret, he'd thought until now. Jessmyn had always been the perceptive one, though. A touch of frustration came. His life had suddenly grown so complicated, it would take a sorcerer to sort things out.

"I'll try my best, milady," Davi promised.

The queen waved him away. "If you accompany us south, you'll have to tell her farewell in any case. Go on, then. Rest well."

"And you, my queen."

The duke backed out the door, thoughts torn between the magic of his Stone and the earthy magic of the dark-eyed Sandaal D'Lelan.

# Five

In spring the does dropped their spotted fawns, so this day Gaylon hunted only the bucks, with their mossy new-grown horns. The still-damp ground from last fall's molding leaves made for silent stalking. They had left the horses tethered well down the mountainside.

Lord Ferges, Eighth Baron of Oakhaven, now signaled the king silently from a thicket of whitethorn.

"Day bed," he murmured when his monarch arrived, and he pointed at the little sheltered nest within the bushes. "The droppings are very fresh. He's somewhere about. Look for tracks."

They had already seen the peeled bark on the young firs in the area where a buck had rubbed his antlers. Gaylon studied the damp soil. The narrow double slots made by cloven hoofs were easy enough to spot, but which were newest? One thin path among the weeds seemed the most used, and the king followed it carefully up to the edge of a small glen. There, near the uppermost rim, a buck grazed, tearing hurried bites of grass, dark liquid eyes watchful, long ears flickering.

Both men froze, their leather clothing of greens and browns a perfect camouflage against the trees. The breeze blew toward them off the mountain, keeping their scent from the prey. Gaylon stared in awe at the size of the creature, the great rack of horns—twelve points at least.

"He's yours, milord," Ferges whispered barely.

"Then back me, should I only wound it."

The king drew an arrow noiselessly from the quiver at his shoulder and nocked it in the longbow's taut string. Beside him, the baron followed suit. Gaylon drew, feeling the powerful resistance of the wooden bow. Thirty paces above them, the deer seemed to sense danger.

Its head jerked up in alarm just as the king let fly. The animal backed suddenly, and the arrow cut it across the base of the neck, just above the muscled chest, driving on into a tree on the far side. Ferges's shaft missed altogether and skittered away along the ground as the buck bounded away into the forest.

Gaylon cursed lividly and started after it.

"We'll never catch it now," the baron cried after him.

"It's injured. We can't leave it suffer."

"You only nicked the animal. He'll survive, all the wiser now."

The king ignored him, already headed up through the tiny glen, certain that Ferges would follow. Where the deer had stood were bright splashes of blood that led away to the south—far too much blood for the wound to be considered a nick.

They didn't have to go far, though. A hundred paces among the trees, the buck had fallen dead. The king's arrow had slit its throat, and the creature had run, pumping the blood all the harder from the slash.

"Dress it out, Milord Baron, if you please," Gaylon said. "I'll fetch the horses."

"Aye," the man answered, not happily, and drew his hunting knife.

The king headed back down the mountain, a faint smile on his lips. Field dressing a kill was never a pleasant task, and only made the worse by the fleas and ticks that deserted the carcass as it cooled. Now, though, Gaylon had time to think as he walked alone in the silent wood, and his thoughts were dark.

Davi and Thayne had not yet returned to the keep. Marten Pelson, whose estates were many more leagues to the south, would not arrive for at least another fortnight. Then . . . then the journey to Xenara must begin soon after. Gaylon fought a rising dread. Once again his happiness had been momentary, though that moment had managed to last several years this time. His fears were manifold now that he had so much more to lose.

Eowin D'Ar said they would go directly to Zankos, that the palace there, being of marble and stone, had survived the holocaust and been refurbished, its gardens redone. All around the devastated city, new establishments and homes had been built—the harbor there was still the finest along the shores of the Inland Sea, and so the people of Xenara returned to it, despite the ashes of thousands upon thousands of citizens scattered in the rubble.

How could Gaylon Reysson, man and sorcerer, stand among those same ruins? By his own hand, all those men, women, and children had died. Dim memories whispered to the king of the mindless joy that destruction had brought him—memories that he tried so hard to hide from himself.

Only Jessmyn's fierce love and determination had made it possible for him to survive, to rule Wynnamyr, to remain sane in the face of all he'd done. But the queen was a daughter of the house of Gerric. In her veins ran Xenara's hot blood. She might find even greater purpose in her father's land, surrounded by wealth, given the power to rule a mighty nation. The thought that Jessmyn might never return with him to Wynnamyr made Gaylon's stomach twist in painful knots.

A certain knowledge came to him suddenly, something akin to his constant awareness of Jessmyn's love and nearness. The duke of Gosney had arrived at Castlekeep. Gaylon knew that for certain, felt Davi's strong presence, more so than ever before.

Tali's gentle whicker jarred him from his waking dream. Their mounts and the one pack animal were tied close to slender evergreen boles near the coach road. He rubbed the blood bay gelding's soft velvet nose with a gloved hand, feeling its hot breath even through the kidskin, then removed the halter and mounted, eager to be home now. The other two horses were led up the mountain to Ferges, who, sleeves rolled back, stood over the carcass, bloodied to the elbows. He looked up, scratching furiously at his upper arm. Already the flies had found the entrails.

"Are we ready, milord?" Gaylon asked ever so sweetly, amused.

The baron only grunted in reply.

\* \* \* \* \*

Eowin D'Ar used the queen's illness as an excuse to rest in his own chambers. His own ills came with age, and there was little to be done for them. The solicitous Girkin tried, though. Even now he carried a hot mug from the hearth to the Grand Envoy.

"Now, this has a small amount of jimsonweed in the tea," the little fat man advised. "There are side effects, and it's to be used most sparingly, milord, but I find it eases the worst of the joint pain for the longest period of time."

Eowin accepted the mug gratefully enough until he tasted the brew. "Dear gods, this is horrible! Can't it be sweetened?"

"Honey only makes it worse, believe me. Force it down, milord. Do try."

The physician's round earnest face was not much younger than the Grand Envoy's, and the fringe of hair that circled his balded pate had gone as white as the Xenaran's. Girkin's pale blue eyes, however, still held a spark of youth, a bright curiosity in the world around him. Eowin envied him that. Dutifully he sipped the nasty concoction and soon felt the heat in his stomach sink deep into his bones. His head, on the other hand, began to feel light—relief from the pain was that strong.

Girkin smiled broadly. "A marvelous infusion, is it not?"

"Truly . . ." the envoy sighed. He swung his legs from the bed and sat up, then caught his head in his hands. "Oh, dear."

"The dizziness will pass, milord. But do not attempt to overdo it. Your bones, I'm sorry to say, are still ancient, however much better you feel."

"I shall keep that in mind. Would you find me my cloak?"

"Perhaps milord should rest awhile longer. . . ." The physician looked concerned.

"Thank you, but this bed has grown far too familiar. I have much yet to discuss with Her Highness."

Now Girkin looked worried. "Lord Eowin, the queen's cold has not abated. These sicknesses are as dangerous to the very old as to the very young. I advise you to wait."

"I must take the risk, my good physician." D'Ar patted the fat man's rounded shoulder. "But I promise not to approach the lady too closely." He headed for the door. "If you would, please write down the recipe for this particular remedy. I would show it to my healers in Zankos."

"Certainly." Girkin bowed, pleased. "Just remember it must be used sparingly. May I accompany you to the queen's chambers? It's time I looked in on her."

Eowin paused to consider. "Only if you promise not to stay long. I would talk to Her Highness in private."

The physician agreed, and they walked together toward the royal wing of the keep. The deep ache in the Grand Envoy's joints had almost completely subsided for the first time in many years. Such a release from pain made him feel euphoric. In the south, he had access to exotic potions imported from faraway lands, but they kept him in a drugged sleep, which was hardly useful to a busy man.

Used to huge bustling cities and courts, Eowin had still not gotten used to the quiet, empty corridors of Castlekeep. The silence tended to unnerve him sometimes.

"I've heard the duke of Gosney has returned with the prince," he said, his voice hushed for no other reason than the stillness of this place.

"'Tis true," Girkin answered.

"I was also told they met trouble along the way . . . that the boy was injured."

The physician wagged his head. "In Mill Town, our only seaport. I'm sure you're aware of the dangers of such places. Why on earth the duke would take such a risk—"

"Prince Thayne," Eowin interrupted, aware of Girkin's tendency to prattle. "I'm told he's fine, despite a knife wound."

"Quite well. An extremely fortunate youngster. The knife blade only pierced the fleshy area of his side . . . his baby fat, if you will. Painful, but the wound bled well and Gosney had the best herbal powder available—one I provided to guard against just such an occurrence before they left Castlekeep." The pudgy physician also tended to congratulate himself fairly often.

"Then he's in no danger of infection?"

"None whatsoever. The Red Kings are a hardy breed. The lad's healing quickly."

Satisfied, the Grand Envoy halted before the queen's apartments and let Girkin knock. A servant let them into the sitting room, then took her leave. Her Majesty was alone in the bedchamber, her ladies-in-waiting nowhere to be seen. For Girkin, she had a smile, but only a cool stare for the envoy.

"Milady," the two men said almost as one, and bowed.

"How are you feeling, Your Highness?" the physician asked.

"What color is my nose?" the queen returned irritably.

"Quite red, milady."

"That is how I feel, then." The woman blew her ruddy nose into one of a stack of handkerchiefs on the bedside table. The used ones were heaped on the floor, and her long, honey-colored hair lay in untidy waves about her shoulders. "I'm sick of being sick. I miss Lily. I hate this!"

Girkin ignored the outburst. "How does milady's chest feel? Any tightness?"

"No."

"Then be grateful, Highness. If the cold remains only in the head, you'll be well much faster."

"Wonderful," Jessmyn said and blew her nose once more.

"Ahem." The envoy caught Girkin's attention, then nodded toward the exit.

"Madam, if I may take my leave. . . ." The physician stepped back from the bed. "The Grand Envoy desires a word with you."

"Does he?" she growled. "Go, then. Find me a wonder cure, old man."

Alone finally, the two stared at one another, queen and

envoy. Eowin believed them to no longer be enemies, but not yet friends.

"You haven't come to inquire after my health," Jessmyn stated. "My eldest son's condition would be more important to you."

"Not so, milady. I would rather have a queen mother on the throne of Xenara than a boy. A regency presents a number of problems all on its own. And at my age, I will never live to see Thayne's majority." D'Ar studied his hands with their gnarled, thick-jointed fingers. "Have you come to a decision, Your Majesty? If so, I've not been made privy to it."

"Oh, I think you have. Your ploy has worked, Milord Grand Envoy. I am bewitched by your ladies-in-waiting and their stories of Katay and Zankos. The books and gifts you brought have only whetted my appetite for more. I must see my father's land for myself."

Eowin did not let her see the relief and joy her words created. Instead, he merely watched her with interest. "It is your land now, milady."

"Well, the king is unhappy with my decision," Jessmyn continued, "but then how else could he feel? He's made a decision of his own. Wynnamyr is to be left in the hands of a trusted lord and friend, while Gaylon accompanies us south. So you see, you'll have an entire royal family at your disposal."

This revelation put a damper on his earlier joy, but again the envoy kept his emotions to himself. "So long as His Highness understands that it will not be he who rules in Xenara."

Jessmyn sniffled noisily. "Believe me, sir, he wants nothing to do with Xenaran politics. His intentions are only to protect me and the children."

"Then his help is welcome, milady. But you and I have much to discuss. Our politics are volatile and constantly changing. The power balance between the aristocracy and the merchant families is always delicate. Alliances and feuds are formed and fought and forgotten in a single day. To harness such power will not be easy. Your father left you a nation in turmoil."

The young woman gazed directly into Eowin's eyes. "Do you feel I am capable of such a task?"

"It's too soon for me to make that judgment, milady," the envoy answered honestly. "But you are my greatest hope."

\* \* \* \* \*

Davi knew instinctively when the king and his hunting companion neared the castle, so he waited at the stables for them. With great care, the young duke ignored the Stone on his breast, denying its existence. Nothing of the pendant must be detected by Gaylon's strong sorcerer's powers. The knowledge that Davi must explain Thayne's injury to his lord helped keep his mind from the magic.

Before long, he heard the quick clop of hooves on the road—horses at the trot.

"Go on wi' ya," Luka, the horse master, called from the smitty's shed to two of his stableboys. They, in turn, propped their rakes against a wall and ran to greet the riders.

The king came into view first, bow and quiver over a shoulder. The baron of Oakhaven followed, leading the packhorse with a stag lashed across its saddle.

"Good hunting!" Davi shouted, and Gaylon pushed his tired mount into a short gallop to the yard.

There he kicked free of the stirrups and dropped to the ground, then grabbed the young duke in a hard embrace before holding him at arms' length.

"By the gods, boy. It's good to see you!"

"And you, Sire."

"You've heard the news?" The king tossed his reins to one of the helpers, then unslung his bow.

"The queen told me, milord. It all seems so sudden."

"Have you chosen, then?" Gaylon was suddenly interested in the buck being laboriously unloaded from the packhorse. "I wanted the council to give you the governorship, but they feel a nineteen-year-old duke too young. You could still help the earl. . . ."

"Marten's better suited to the job than I, Sire." Davi searched the king's face, his red beard barely touched with silver below the lips. "Where you go, lord, I go."

"I'm glad." Obviously relieved, Gaylon caught the duke in one more quick embrace. "I need to clean up and see how my lady is feeling . . . see Thayne. Did he behave himself?"

"Milord," Davi said, the guilt crashing down on him again.

The king paused, troubled. "Thayne?"

"The prince is fine, Sire . . . no thanks to me. We stopped to dine in Mill Town five days ago and were caught in a tavern brawl. Thayne was wounded."

"Not badly?"

"No, but he could have been."

"But he wasn't. Don't look so glum." The king grinned and clapped Davi on the shoulder. "Let him tell me the details first. I'm sure he's proud of the whole business." He started toward the bailey, dragging Davi along. The baron, forgotten, followed respectfully. Gaylon suddenly stopped. "Have you met the queen's ladies-in-waiting?"

"Yes, Sire."

"The dark beauty, Sandaal, is Arlin's younger sister."

"I know."

"She obviously comes of good stock. She's bright, talented, and might produce some fine Gosney children."

"I've barely met her." Davi's cheeks reddened. "At least the queen was more . . . delicate in her approach."

"Was she?" Gaylon only grinned all the more. "Well, we've a long journey south to face. I'm sure you'll get to know the Lady D'Lelan much better. Some good may come of this whole mess after all."

There was pain still behind that grin. Davi sensed it. Their lives, now finally growing settled and comfortable, were about to be turned inside out again. Even under Marten Pelson's sure, steady hand, Wynnamyr would suffer the loss of its royal family. The young duke experienced a surge of loathing. He remembered the waves upon waves of Xenaran soldiers they had fought in the close confines of the Sea Pass, remembered the deaths of his companions.

"Are you listening?"

Davi blinked. "I'm sorry, Sire."

"I only said I'd leave you here," repeated the king. "I'm going for my bath now. I'll meet you at supper in the great hall. Bring your lute, please." He nodded at his hunting companion. "Baron."

Both duke and baron bowed as Gaylon disappeared into the dim entrance of the keep. Immediately Oakhaven groaned and stretched his muscles, then scratched furiously at his chest. The man was far more dirty and disheveled than his monarch had been.

"Think I'll bathe as well," he said dolefully. "I doubt my lady wife will appreciate fleas in the bed tonight."

Davi nodded, smiling. "At supper, then."

In the quiet that followed the baron's departure, Davi noticed a vague throb against his breastbone. The Stone had wakened, and his fingers sought out the rounded lump under his jerkin. While in the king's presence, he had somehow forgotten the pendant, his connection with it severed completely. He had no control over Orym's Stone, and yet when his need was greatest, it had responded in the tavern at Mill Town.

This knowledge only frustrated him all the more. Davi wanted the Stone to respond to his direct commands. Only Gaylon Reysson could train him in the magical arts, and to him the duke dare not go. At least the king had detected nothing of Orym. For that much Davi was grateful.

\* \* \* \* \*

His shirt hiked up, Thayne sucked in his stomach and pulled the bandage carefully away from the wound. "See?"

Bennet, being the youngest boy, seemed properly impressed by the thick scab. Brother Robyn showed little interest. Bennet's older sister made a noise of disgust and ran away across the sward with her doll.

"Girls!" snorted the young heir to Oakhaven. "I want a knife or sword wound, too. Did it hurt much?"

"Lots," Thayne said casually. "But I only cried a little. Fitzwal says I'm very brave."

"Princes have to be." There was just a touch of jealousy in Bennet's voice.

Thayne caught Robyn's hand in his and leaned down. "Want to see my new horse? Her name is Sojii."

"Can I ride her?" the littler prince asked.

"Later maybe. She's tired now after so long a journey."

All three boys headed toward the stables, Robyn mounted still on Thayne's old stick horse. As they crossed the lawns, Thayne realized he was tired, too, but the chance of showing off his new pony proved irresistible. Luka worked a young colt on a long rope in the exercise yard. He brought the animal to a halt so the children could pass through to the long, low barn.

Someone already stood at the double doors to Sojii's stall, gazing in at her. Thayne remembered the black-haired woman as one of the ladies who served his mother now. She noticed their approach and curtsied respectfully, but somehow her dark eyes were cold. Robyn, though, noticed nothing but her great beauty and began to flirt immediately.

"Hullo, Sandaal," he said shyly, his *s* sounds still slightly *th*'s. The wooden horse was abruptly discarded, and the boy ran to clutch the young woman's plain skirts. "Can I have a hug?"

"May I," she corrected him, but bent down to gather the toddler in her arms. Her eyes softened briefly. Robyn reached out to stroke her impossibly long hair, then Sandaal straightened, the prince's small fingers held in one hand. She gazed into the stall once more. "I've never seen such a beautiful mare. I was going to ask Luka where she comes from as soon as he's finished his work, but perhaps you boys might know."

"She's mine," Thayne said, filled with pride and a new appreciation of Sandaal D'Lelan. "The king of Lasony gave her to me."

"A Lasony pony, then. I've heard tales of them, but never seen one. They're said to be wiser than most breeds . . . quicker and with more stamina. Is that true, milord?"

Thayne watched Sojii, her head in the manager, munching

hay. "I haven't had her long, milady. The duke wouldn't let me run her, but she's very sweet-natured and quick to learn."

"Thayne's going to let me ride her," Robyn stated. "Maybe he'll let you, too."

"No," said Sandaal, and the prince heard a touch of longing in her tone. "Too many different riders will only confuse the mare. Prince Thayne is her master now, and she should feel only his hand on the rein."

Thayne looked up at her. "How do you know so much about horses?"

"My family raised them. I had a Majeran mare when I was a child. I loved her so. . . ." The woman's voice trailed off, her eyes on some distant memory. "She was lost in Zankos, along with my family."

Robyn and Bennet looked confused by her words, but Thayne felt a sudden keen guilt. He was old enough to know that his own father had destroyed this lady's home. The reality of that time in history had never been made so clear to him, though.

"I'm . . . I'm sorry," the boy said.

Her eyes hardened again. "No need to be. It was my fate to survive." Sandaal swept Robyn up once more in her arms. "Anyway, the queen has sent me to bring you to supper."

Thayne balked at that. "I want to eat with the others in the great hall."

"Another year or two, Milord Prince," the young woman said, measuring him with her gaze. "The adults dine late in the evening, when little ones should be abed."

Robyn plugged a less-than-clean thumb in his mouth and twirled Sandaal's hair with the other hand. Thayne seethed. Little ones indeed. After all, he had a knife wound and a wonderful scab and a Lasony mare, swift as the wind. But then again, he was hungry. That small fact made him follow the others back to the keep.

# Six

The duke of Gosney was tired from his journey; Jessmyn could see that. With their supper nearly done in the great hall, he would be thinking of his bed. The queen had other, just as pleasant, plans for him, however. She leaned to whisper in Lady Keth's ear, who in turn passed the message down the table to Lady Sandaal. The girl glanced at the queen with a tiny smile and nodded barely.

"Milords and ladies," Jessmyn said loudly over the murmur of conversation, "I have a treat for you tonight: music from Xenara. The Lady Sandaal D'Lelan has kindly consented to play for us."

Sandaal had already gathered her skirts and left the table for a single chair set near the hearth. A servant brought the ebony mandolin to her. Seated beside the king, Davi watched her, his face still, but his bright green eyes intent.

This seemed such a perfect match. The queen had considered many a young Wynnamyran lady of high blood for her duke, but none had truly satisfied her. Davi had been somewhat young yet for marriage then, but now, at nineteen, he might start a family. From such a pairing, the children should be beautiful, highly intelligent, and healthy.

Lady D'Lelan began to play, then to sing in her native tongue—a song of sailing to distant ports in exotic lands. The beat was strong, and she slapped the small hollow body of the instrument between strummed chords. Jessmyn found her toe tapping in time under the table. Near the king, the Grand Envoy smiled with approval and pride. Gentle applause followed the end of the song.

The next tune was sung in Wynnamyran without a trace of accent, a familiar folk song that brought the diners into the chorus. Servants began delivering dessert, but no one seemed interested in the food now. Jessmyn saw the king nudge Davi with an elbow as the second tune ended. The young man's face reddened slightly, and he shook his head, but Gaylon grew insistent.

Finally the duke stood, embarrassed.

"Lady D'Lelan," Gaylon called, "it would please me greatly to hear my duke sing with you, if you would be so kind."

The woman bowed from her seat. Another chair was brought, along with Davi's lute, an instrument nearly thrice the size of the mandolin, though hardly as beautiful. Obviously old, the lute had seen hard usage, its lacquer worn and scratched. It had been Davi's father's once. The duke took his seat beside the lady. Both were plainly dressed, yet somehow elegant together.

"Do you know 'Desirey ut Veve'?" Sandaal asked.

Davi nodded mutely, his eyes on the strings of his instrument, his cheeks still slightly red. This was a love song in Xenaran, written especially as a duet.

The lady began, expecting Davi to join her, and he did moments later, obviously a little flustered. She took them through the first stanza with the music only, so they might get the feel of one another's style. By then the duke was snared completely in the tune, swept up in the crystal notes of lute and mandolin. The audience was lost to him.

He sang first, in Xenaran with a gentle but clear voice.

> "*Where have you been, my lady love?*
> *Where lay your head tonight?*
> *If you have found another love,*
> *My heart shall die this night.*"

She answered sweetly, the melody altering,

> "How can you doubt me, my dearest lord,
> When I have always been yours?
> Only with fear can you destroy my love,
> Only with trust can you keep it."

Now their voices joined for a time in exquisite harmony and
intricate cadence.

> "I feel your kiss upon my throat.
> My lips are for only you.
> Your touch is all that I desire.
> Death can never part we two."

The Wynnamyran translation would seem awkward to the
ear. There were no words to truly express the heat and passion of this Xenaran song. Some at the table would never
understand the meaning. Jessmyn did. Her husband met her
gaze across the table, and the heat of the song passed between
them. Then the queen's eyes were drawn to the singers. They
had begun separate verses again, and their gazes, too, had
met. Caught up in the song, they played the parts of the
lovers with complete abandon now.

Their voices blended perfectly as their fingertips danced
along the strings. Somehow an unearthly echo had begun
from the instruments, one or the other or both. Jessmyn
couldn't quite tell, but it was the same magical resonance that
Gaylon produced unconsciously with his Stone while playing
his own lute. Listening, the king's brow furrowed slightly.

But the magic could only be the combination of the two
young people, so talented, so well matched. The song ended,
and a long silence followed. The duke and Sandaal still touched
knees, their eyes trapped by one another's, and Jessmyn sighed
happily, certain of a romantic victory. Around her, the diners
began to applaud, calling for another song. Then Sandaal murmured something unheard. Davi jerked suddenly, as if waking.
He stood and strode quickly from the hall, lute in hand.

"What in . . ." growled the king and started to rise.

The queen shook her head. "Let him go, my lord. Please."

* * * * *

Davi pushed past the servants in the corridor. The air cooled his sweated forehead as he walked toward the southeast wing and his chambers—away from the lights of the great hall, away from the heat of Sandaal D'Lelan. Oh, gods! Her voice still rang in his ear with its promises of love, and the pendant on his breast seemed a hot coal, burning its way to his heart.

" 'Twas only a song, milord," the girl had told him, her eyes gone cold after the last fading note.

That had brought him to his senses, brought a curious ache to his chest, but worse, he'd realized that Orym's Stone had awakened of its own accord again. There! There in the same room with Gaylon Reysson.

Davi found his rooms and locked the door behind him, then dragged his jerkin off and untied his shirt. Even through the silk that bound it, the Stone glowed blue. The chain held away from him, he fumbled the string from the silk and let both fall to the floor. The half-healed scab in the palm of his left hand throbbed in time to the Stone's pulse. A warning perhaps, but the duke must try once more. He dropped the chain, his teeth gritted tight.

The pendant swung back against the bare skin of his chest. Instead of fiery pain this time, he felt an icy heat charged with energy and then a surge of triumph, of ecstasy. The world brightened, images sharpened, but not just as his eyes could see. No, this clarity came also from within. The duke reached up to touch the Stone with tentative fingers. It brightened in response.

*Good*, someone whispered in his mind.

The disembodied voice made him gasp and jerk his hand away.

*Do not fear me, child*, the voice murmured.

"Who . . . what are you?" Davi demanded, afraid.

The answer came, *See, then*.

In the mirror before the wardrobe, candlelight distorted, rippling, wavering, a creature formed, human seeming. The duke beheld an old man, stocky and dark-bearded, his hair dark, a wild mane about his round face. The eyes were the color of smoke, pale gray and red-rimmed. For the briefest of moments, Davi saw his father there, then realization struck.

Desperate, he caught the chain in his hand and jerked it hard, but the links refused to give.

*Wait!* the Dark King cried. *Please, child, wait.* His voice held infinite calm. *The changes within the matrix of the Stone have begun. To deny it now would be to deny yourself.*

"Better that than to have your evil hold over me," Davi said, his tone quavering with suppressed horror.

*Be calm,* the old man insisted. *What you see before you is only an image. My powers are weak.*

"You have this much power." The duke indicated the reflection.

*Only because my memory lies still within the Stone. As it grows more attuned to you, that memory will fade and finally die, and I shall be gone forever."*

Davi had read of Orym's madness in many a history book, had heard from Gaylon of his brushes with the Dark King's sly power. Gaylon, an incredible sorcerer in his own right, had overcome Orym's bids to regain life and control over the sword, Kingslayer. The duke of Gosney had little knowledge of the Stone's magic, with no way to protect himself. Orym seemed to hear that thought.

*Knowledge is all I have to offer, young one.*

Davi studied the reflection carefully. "In exchange for what?"

*In exchange for a chance to do one kind act before my essence leaves this world forever,* Orym said simply.

"You?" The word was incredulous.

*Do you think I don't feel the weight of the evil I've perpetrated? I've had a thousand years to consider my cruelty and insanity. By regaining Kingslayer's power through Gaylon Reysson, I sought to continue that reign of terror, but no more.*

An ineffable sorrow filled Davi, and the Stone pulsed slowly with his heart. Somehow he felt this old, old man's pain.

*Young lord,* the image implored, *give me this one last*

*chance to ease my soul. Let me train you from the* Book of Stones; *let me show you how strongly the blood of the Dark Kings courses through your veins. The Sorcerer's Stone you now wear is one of a kind. With it you will be more powerful than even Gaylon Reysson. I promise you.*

The possibilities whirled through Davi's mind. All that he had ever hoped and dreamed for was being offered by this shade of a long dead and dangerous king.

"How can I trust you?" he asked finally, desire and doubt tugging at him.

*Only by giving me the chance to prove myself. In training you, I offer you the means of my own destruction. Once you have gained some control over the Stone, you will be able to banish me from it forever as soon as you please."*

"Then this will be the first thing you teach me," said the duke, adamant.

The image in the mirror smiled faintly. *So be it. . . . Bring out the* Book of Stones, *and let us begin.*

\* \* \* \* \*

The ladies-in-waiting returned to their chambers much later in the evening. Despite the duke of Gosney's less than courteous departure, the entertainment had continued. Rose and Katina had joined Sandaal on their own, more ladylike, hammer dulcimers. The Lady D'Lelan had kept her emotions and her temper in check until now, when they were once more in their rooms. Even so, it must be a hidden, silent rage. She must not let the D'Jal sisters see or know her true feelings in any of this.

Why had she chosen such a song to share with the duke, a man she hardly knew? Why had she then broken the spell so cruelly? Fool, she snarled inwardly, idiot! By his close friendship with the king, the duke of Gosney, unwittingly or not, might help her attain her goal. His enmity was the last thing she needed.

Katina D'Jal had donned her nightgown already and sat at the shabby dressing table to remove her makeup. She glanced at Sandaal's distorted reflection in the mirror.

"I wouldn't worry overmuch, San. He's darling to look at and titled, but poor as a peasant. I know Her Majesty is set on matching you, but avoid it at all cost. As queen of Xenara, Lady Jessmyn can provide you with a dowry that will get you any man you please for a husband. The gossip is that the duke's involved with one of the kitchen girls . . . Cally, I think. Not that it matters. I'm told Wynnamyrans make terrible lovers."

Rose pursed her lips. "She's already made up her mind. It's obvious she wants Davyn Darynson, poor or not."

"Don't be ridiculous!" Sandaal snapped in anger. "I'll have no husband. Do you think I want to become as the two of you will—servants and slaves to Xenaran husbands with too many wives and not enough brains?"

"So long as they also have too much money and prestige, we won't mind." Kat began to laugh happily. "Finally a chink in that perfect armor of yours, Sandaal."

"How did it feel?" Rose sighed, eyes dreamy. "So close to him in the heat of the song?"

Sandaal found her own nightgown. "I prefer to forget the whole subject, if you don't mind."

"But he's so . . . handsome," Rose continued, oblivious. "With those thick long lashes and those green, green eyes." She turned to Katina. "Did you notice his hands? Did you see how he played?"

"Dear gods, Rose," Kat growled. "You're half in love with him yourself."

The younger sister wandered to a window, and Sandaal heard her murmur, "More than half . . . I'm afraid."

\* \* \* \* \*

Orym advised he sleep, and so Davi did, late in the night. The thought seemed impossible at first, his mind so filled with elation and energy from this beginning lesson in the *Book of Stones*. But the Stone itself soothed him into deep slumber soon enough.

"Davi?"

The feminine voice, a whisper near his ear, woke him partially, then fingers caressed his hair. Beneath him, the bed moved, the covers shifting.

"Cally?" he mumbled.

"Aye. Your door was locked, so I used the chamberlain's key." Her body pressed close to his.

"Cally . . ."

"Shhhhh." Lips found his, soft, questing.

A melody came unbidden to Davi's mind—an erotic Southern song, full of passion. The Stone stirred at his breast under his nightshirt, and desire filled him—a sudden hot lust unlike anything he'd ever experienced. After a slight hesitation, Cally responded to his strange breathless kiss. It was then he lost whatever control he might have had.

Always a gentle, considerate lover before, Davi laid hands roughly on the woman, ripping her gown to uncover her soft, small-breasted body. In his mind, it was Sandaal D'Lelan there among his blankets, dark-haired and fiery.

"Milord, please," Cally moaned, afraid and aroused in the dark.

He used her for his own pleasure then, completely, covering her mouth when she cried out. The Stone led him, heightening every sensation to the point of pain, but even the pain brought him exquisite joy. And all the while, some part of him watched his own actions with confusion and horror.

The duke fell aside finally, sated, sweating. Cally's fading whimpers seemed to wake him from some bizarre dream. Oh, dear gods, what had he done?

"Cally," he said, his voice husky. "Have I hurt you? I'm so sorry. . . ."

"It's all right, milord," Cally said quietly, almost dreamily. "You frightened me, 'tis all. I ain't hurt." He felt her gathering her torn clothing. "In fact, 'twas nice, all in all." She paused. "You've changed, milord, since your return—so strong and forceful now. But if ye'll be more careful with my gowns . . . I don't really mind."

"I'll buy you a new one," the duke promised. "Come here, please."

The girl came willingly, her rent garment discarded, and Davi gathered her naked in his arms. They slept until dawn, nestled there together under the quilts. With first light, though, Cally had to leave, since it was her duty to start the ovens in the kitchen.

"Shall I come help?" Davi asked sleepily.

"Goodness, no!" Cally said. "A duke doesn't stoke fires." Then she leaned to kiss him and added impishly, "At least not in the kitchen. Shall I return tonight, milord?"

He stared at her, remembering, and the Stone sent another surge of desire through him. "No . . . best to wait awhile."

"Certainly, milord." Cally glanced down at her ripped nightgown, hurt in her eyes. "I have to go." She hurried to the door and out into the passage.

The moment she had gone, Davi went to turn the lock. He gazed around the chill gray room, then stood before the mirror, a deep anger seething inside.

"Orym," the duke commanded and felt his Stone answer with warmth.

*Eager so soon for another lesson?* the image asked hollowly, rippling into existence in the dim light.

"Bastard! Answer me now and answer me truthfully, or I'll banish you from the Stone this very moment."

The Dark King gazed out at him. *Ask the question, then, child.*

"Are you using me? Was that you tonight who made love to Cally?"

*Not I.* Orym's face held amusement. *Already you are a sorcerer, albeit an apprentice, and sorcerers are most often a lusty breed. The Stone tends to free your true nature.*

Davi felt a touch of revulsion. "If that's so, I'm not certain I like my true nature, then."

*Control over the Stone is only half the task, young one. Control over yourself is the other half. That is a lesson I never learned, and so the world suffered horribly at my hand.* The Dark King looked into the distance now. *You have great talent, Davyn Darynson, but every step toward your goal will be a struggle. I will train you in the rituals, but only you can decide in which direction you will finally go—for good or ill.* His gaze returned to Davi. *Perhaps you should banish me and give the Stone to Gaylon Reysson to destroy.*

"No!" Davi said sharply and saw Orym smile.

*Just remember, child, whose blood runs in your veins.* The image winked out, and the duke of Gosney found his way back to the bed, exhausted and troubled.

His sleep was short, though. The day had brightened only marginally when Davi heard shouts along the passageway. He turned over and buried his head in the pillows, but the cries were too insistent. Something had happened, something to rouse the entire keep. Finally the duke pulled on breeches and buskins under his nightshirt and went out into the hall.

"What's going on?" he demanded of a servant rushing past.

"I ain't sure, milord," the fellow answered. "An accident, I think. Someone's taken a fall."

"From where?"

"The second floor balcony in the northwest wing."

Davi's heart began to thud erratically in his chest as he followed the servant to the back courtyard. The children—Thayne and Robyn—slept in the nursery at the end of the northwest wing. A sleepy nanny might have let the youngsters slip past her. No, Thayne was not the victim. The duke would have felt the danger, felt the boy's pain. On his breast, the Stone warmed imperceptibly with his distress.

A small crowd of household staff stood in a circle on the steps beneath a high balcony. Across the way, Girkin approached as quickly as his ancient stiff legs would allow. Davi didn't wait, only pushed his way roughly through the onlookers. Dark blood spilled over one step and down another, and for a long moment, he stared without comprehension at the crumpled form lying sprawled over the Stones.

"Cally," he whispered finally and crouched beside her.

Life had already fled her body, her lovely blue eyes staring into infinity. The torn nightgown lay open, and he gently covered her nakedness, then closed her eyes. How could this have happened? She would have gone immediately to her room to dress for work, yet for some reason had gone upstairs instead and to the opposite wing. Girkin squatted laboriously beside him, muttering.

"Poor child . . . poor dear child."

Davi found a bloody hand and brought the fingers to his lips. He'd promised her a gown. And he'd treated her so roughly, abused her love last night. The pain of that thought brought tears to his eyes.

"Milord is distraught," the physician said kindly, knowingly. Then their quiet affair must hardly have been a secret within the keep. "Leave her to me. I'll take good care of her." He signaled two of the male servants, who caught Davi's elbows and pulled him upright.

"No," he muttered. "Let me stay with her."

"Best not, milord." It was Fitzwal at his side now, guiding him away.

"How?" the duke asked, bewildered.

"An accident, milord." The sergeant shook his head sadly. "It's cold out here, and you need more than a nightshirt or you'll catch your death."

Davi glanced back. Now he could see the balcony above where bright red roses climbed through the balustrades. Someone stood there gazing down, long black hair drifting in the early morning breeze. Sandaal D'Lelan.

\* \* \* \* \*

Cally's funeral was held two days later, late in the afternoon, in the town cemetery, with her large family in attendance. They were greatly honored by the presence of the king and queen and the duke of Gosney, along with over a hundred others. Cally had been much loved by the people of the keep.

Jessmyn watched Davi stand over the grave, dry-eyed and numb. He had changed since his trip north, though she couldn't put a finger on just quite how. Even Gaylon had commented on it in passing. The young duke seemed to have less time to spend with his lord or his prince, and now spent far more time in his chambers.

If this were grieving for Cally, then it would pass eventually, and the queen had not given up hope of pairing Gosney with Lady D'Lelan. What truly mattered, though, was the fact that soon they would all be on their way to Xenara with the Grand Envoy.

Marten Pelson had arrived finally the day before. Nearly every moment of the day and night had been spent in the council chambers since then. There the king and council members labored over the documents that would give the earl of the Lower Vales the power to rule Wynnamyr in Gaylon's absence.

Girkin still felt Jessmyn's health too poor for travel so soon after Lilith's birth, but if it were up to the fat little physician, the queen would spend the rest of her life abed.

"My lady," Gaylon murmured to her. The funeral had ended, and the crowd dispersed. Only Davi remained beside the grave marker, a white rose clutched in his fingers.

"I'll be along in a moment," Jessmyn told her husband and watched him walk back to the small carriage on the road.

Davi remained motionless, one hand on the carved stone, head bowed.

"The hurt will pass in time," the queen said softly.

When he looked up, she was amazed to see a suppressed anger in his face. "No," the duke contradicted. "It won't. I still feel pain over Rinn and Karyl and Arlin. Why must the good ones die?"

"I don't know. . . . Milord, Cally was young and pretty . . . and a kitchen wench. To grieve overmuch would be unseemly for a duke."

Bitter, Davi threw the rose down among the other flowers. "Yes, of course. You want me to pay court to Sandael D'Lelan."

"Davi," Jess said carefully, "it's only my hope, not a command."

"I shall obey your hopes then, madam." The young man bowed and strode away—not toward where Fitzwal held his horse, but toward the town and, no doubt, a tankard of ale.

\* \* \* \* \*

Soon enough Gaylon realized that transporting his royal family and entourage to Xenara would be no easier than it had been to move the entire Wynnamyran army. Marten Pelson, his dark hair lightly streaked with gray now, proved, as always, to be invaluable in directing the confusion.

While the two friends had been in contact over the past years, the king had not seen his earl since the war. The Lower Vales in a way were a kingdom all their own and provided more than half the foodstuffs and wine for all of Wynnamyr. Plus, the greatest damage had been in those fertile valleys where the worst of the battles were fought. Marten had been kept as busy as the king in rebuilding the country, and even now there was little time to enjoy renewing their friendship.

The third morning in the council chambers, they, along with the Grand Envoy of Xenara, went over the lists of goods that must travel south with the royal train. Thayne and Robyn had joined them at some point, coming unnoticed through the drapes from the throne room. Now the littler prince shoved a tattered stick horse onto the table and scattered their pages.

"We mustn't forget Dubin," he commanded. "Dubin has to go with us. He's very strong, Da. I can ride him all the way to Zankos."

The elderly envoy glanced up, annoyed.

Marten managed a tired grin. "I'd give him a bath first." He gathered papers from around the filthy stocking head with its straggly yarn mane, the princes already forgotten. "This will not be a comfortable trip for the queen and the children, Sire."

"Please," said Eowin D'Ar. "Take my wagon for their use. Now emptied of gifts, it has far more room than I require."

"That's very kind, sir. Thank you. We'll prepare one of ours for your use," Gaylon said. He looked at Marten. "How was the coach road when you came?"

"Looks passable . . . with some minor repairs along the way." The earl shrugged. "It wasn't built to handle wagons of such grand size, but the envoy managed to reach here from Claw Pass. That's far worse going than the Sea Pass, though the desert route's quicker from Katay."

"Perhaps we should go back that way. . . ."

"I advise against it," the envoy said. "That would add many days to the journey to Zankos."

Marten agreed. "Girkin would have a fit."

"And rightly so," the king admitted, discounting his own idea. Of them all, Jessmyn and Lilith would least enjoy this journey. "Robyn!" The youngster had climbed a chair and emptied an ink pot on the floor. Thayne only watched silently from the doorway.

"Where are the jailers?" the earl cried in mock outrage. "To the dungeons with this prince."

Happy, Robyn drew a small wooden sword from his belt. "You'll have to capture me first."

Before Gaylon could stop him, the boy had whacked Marten hard on a kneecap with his blade. The earl dodged the second blow, and the king caught his youngest son by the scruff of the neck.

"By the gods," Pelson grunted, nursing the injured leg. "He takes after his father."

The Grand Envoy, always so proper and grave, had given in to a fit of wheezing laughter.

"Where's Nanny Delya?" Gaylon demanded.

"Helping Mum pack," Thayne said quietly. "The duke asked Fitzwal to watch us, but he had horses to tend to, so we left."

"And why isn't Davi with you? He didn't bother to show his face for this meeting."

"He's too tired to play with us." The king heard a hint of betrayal and pain in that simple statement. Thayne and the duke of Gosney had always been close.

"He's been tired a lot of late. Perhaps Girkin should have a look at him."

"It could be Cally's death. . . ." Marten's eyes clouded slightly. The pretty, sweet-natured kitchen wench had been a favorite of his once, years ago.

"No. He's been this way since his return from Castle Gosney." The king looked at Thayne again. "Did anything unusual happen while you were there? Besides the trouble at the inn?"

The prince shook his red head. "Only King Zorek's visit. But he did give Davi a gift from his grandmother."

"How come no one's mentioned this before?" Gaylon muttered. "What was this gift?"

"A secret. The king of Lasony promised he would deliver it to Davi's father, but couldn't," Thayne answered. "Davi never mentioned it after, so I forgot."

Marten Pelson tapped the table. "Antique gifts aside, just send Girkin with one of his nasty ale yeast concoctions, and Davi will recover quick enough. We've other things at the moment to worry about besides a tired duke."

"Yes," Gaylon said uneasily. He had little Robyn trapped under one arm now. "First we need to decide what to do with two loose princes."

"We could always tie them up."

"We'll go back to Fitzwal," Thayne offered as a compromise. "Maybe he'll saddle Sojii for me, and I can take Robyn for a ride in the exercise yard."

"Really?" the younger prince whooped and began to struggle in his father's grip.

The king smiled. Thayne was rarely so generous with his little brother.

"Go, then. And stay out of trouble."

The two boys fled as fast as their short legs would take them, sad Dubin left behind on the table. Marten propped the stick horse carefully against a stone wall.

"Once upon a time," he said, "I never thought you'd live to have children."

"Neither did I. . . ." The king cocked his head. "And now you even have a son of your own. The fifteenth earl-to-be."

"Aye, and another babe on the way. It certainly changes one's perspective of the world."

Gaylon shuffled papers, suddenly nervous. "Will you bring your family north to Castlekeep?"

"That depends on how long you plan to stay in Xenara, Sire."

"No longer than we must," Gaylon answered with vehemence.

The Grand Envoy, on the far side of the table, frowned.

Marten didn't notice. "About the troops. I think two dozen,

to match the envoy's, would be best. You hardly need the protection west of the Gray Mountains, but . . . excuse me, Lord D'Ar . . . Xenara mustn't forget who won this last war."

"I absolutely disagree, Your Highness," the envoy said in alarm. "A show of force, no matter how small, will not further your cause with my people. Your queen, being of the house of their beloved Roffo, will be joyfully welcomed, I promise you. You, on the other hand, are too well remembered. Do not come to Zankos as the conquering hero. You'll taint your wife's reign and quite possibly bring disaster upon yourself."

"Milord." Marten Pelson took the king's arm. "If this is the case, then it's madness for you to go at all. Stay here and keep the children with you. It isn't safe for any of you in Xenara."

Gaylon shook his head. "No. Jessmyn would never leave the children behind, and I would never let them go without me."

"We love our children in Xenara, Milord Earl," D'Ar said archly, "even as you do here. And these particular children are as much ours as yours."

The sound of that chilled the king's heart, but it was true. Such was the lot of royalty—born and bred for the people they ruled.

"I'll need no troops, Marten. It seems I can best defend my family from the background. So I shall."

# Seven

The caravan left early on a spring morning in the midst of a gentle rain. The two huge Xenaran wagons led the four smaller Wynnamyran ones through Keeptown, followed by the king and Davi with his sergeant and two men-at-arms on horseback. The troop of Xenaran soldiers came behind. Citizens watched silently from windows and doorways. No one waved or smiled. They had little cause for happiness. Gaylon Reysson, these past years, had become an excellent monarch, and his wife, the queen, was no less loved. Marten Pelson, whatever his qualifications, was not the king the people of Wynnamyr had come to trust.

Seated on the low bench near his mother in the lead wagon, Thayne felt only excitement. The jolt of the wheels failed to bother him, or the loud *thump-thumpi* as they crossed the planks of the bridge to the coach road. Lilith, though, wakened in the queen's arms and began to cry. His mother let the baby nurse.

Robyn tugged at her clothing. "Me, too," he demanded, jealous of the infant.

"Stop it," Thayne said in disgust. "You're a prince, not a baby. Just sit still."

"I don't want to sit here."

Their mother laid a hand on Robyn's shoulder. "There's a box of toys under your bed. Go find one you like."

The boy stumbled to the front of the crowded, swaying

wagon to obey, and Thayne looked up at the queen.

"Why can't I ride Sojii, Mum? I'm old enough to stay with the men."

"You are," she said, smiling. "But your father says you're to work on your music in the morning, and after lunch your scholastic tutor will join us for lessons. Then later, if you've done well, the king has said you may ride with him for a while in the afternoon."

Lessons. The joy of the adventure already faded before it had hardly begun. Then the rear flap opened, and there was Davi, his hair and clothing wet. He climbed in before removing his cloak.

"Your Majesties," he said and bowed, already hunched under the low cloth ceiling.

"Your boots, milord," the queen replied.

"Oh, sorry." He plunked down on the floorboards and worried the muddy boots from his feet, then set them carefully aside.

"Davi!" Robyn cried from somewhere behind the storage trunks. He scrambled forward to throw himself into the duke's lap.

Thayne watched the young man smile through his initial startlement, but his eyes were dark-circled and weary. Perhaps he grieved over Cally, not that it mattered. The elder prince still felt angry and deserted by his friend.

"What are you doing here?" Thayne asked coolly.

"I'm your new music teacher, since we couldn't bring the entire court along." Davi glanced back through the slit in the rear door flap. "Though it certainly looks like we tried." He hugged Robyn. "And how are you, my little redheaded imp?"

"I'm fine," the youngster answered and tugged at his copper curls, then whispered confidentially, "But Lily's bald."

"Some babies are born like that," Thayne said, so much older and wiser. "They get hair later."

Robyn shrugged. "I hope so, 'cause she sure is ugly."

"Robyn!" their mother said sharply, hurt.

"Well, she is," the child cried in his own defense. "Isn't she, Thayne?"

The older prince kept his mouth shut. Lilith was indeed unlovely to his young eyes, but he also knew how differently she was perceived by her mother. The duke of Gosney pushed Robyn from his lap and got unsteadily to his stockinged feet. A wagon wheel dropped into a pothole, nearly upsetting him again.

"Milady," he said, expression serious, "I doubt very much that lute lessons are possible under these conditions. In fact I can't imagine a journey of any length under these conditions." The wagon jumped again, and Davi sat suddenly on the hard bench behind him. "Crystal is a most trustworthy mount. Once the rain ceases, perhaps you'd care to ride for a while. I'll lead her if you like."

Jessmyn frowned. "I haven't sat a horse since . . . since I was eight years old."

"Why, Mummy?" Thayne asked, just now realizing that while the gentlewomen of the court often rode on the hunts, his mother had never done so.

"It hardly matters." A faint sorrow passed behind the queen's eyes and was gone. She smiled. "Thank you, anyway, Milord Duke."

"Well, the offer remains open—always," Davi told her. "Come along, Thayne. Let's see how badly we can play the lute today."

* * * * *

Wagon travel was not only miserable but slow. Jessmyn found she lived for the evenings, when at dusk the caravan would halt and make camp. They had fallen into a routine of sorts. To hold back the cold night wind, a pavilion would be erected, then supper served. Afterward, there'd be music and singing, but only for a short while. Exhaustion led them to their beds early. And despite all her hopes, Davi and Sandaal continued to avoid one another's company.

The Xenaran soldiers slept out in the open, rainy weather or not, while His Royal Highness slept in a bedroll beneath his wife's wagon, there being no room on her cot for them both.

The duke, his men, and the rest of the male servants shared the ground beneath the remaining wagons.

Not too many days into the journey, the queen had finally, in desperation, taken Davi up on his offer to ride the gray mare, Crystal. The ground seemed a frighteningly long way off at first, but soon Jessmyn had fallen completely in love with the duke's gentle animal. Dim remembrances returned. There'd been a time in her childhood when horses and riding had meant a great deal to her.

The back of her skirt hems tucked into her waistband made trousers of a sort, but soon the queen had commandeered a pair of Davi's breeks, a little large, and found a spare pair of boots among the soldiers that fit well enough. At times, Katina would take the baby and Jess would ride ahead on Crystal, Gaylon beside her on his big gelding, Tali. Then she could put the mare into a slow gallop, reveling in the graceful motion, the feel of control and power that came through the reins to her hands.

Gaylon wasn't happy. The nearer to the Sea Pass and the Xenaran border they came, the deeper his gloom. Nights without him were the worst. Sometimes, if the children slept soundly and the camp lay still, Jessmyn would slip out of the wagon to join her husband in his blankets and try to ease his apprehensions. His arms around her helped to ease her own. This had been no easy choice for either of them.

\* \* \* \* \*

Davi was restless tonight, wandering in the blue light of the full moon, searching for a comfortable spot to sit and play his lute. There were emotions that needed release. Three days ago, the caravan had passed through the town of Riverbend, and he had seen his mother for the first time since the war. Haddi still ran the Fickle River Inn, but she—and it—had aged.

There was far more gray than black in her long hair now, and she had gained weight. Only her disposition hadn't changed. She had greeted him emotionlessly, and underneath, through the Stone's faint influence, he felt her cold, bitter anger—at life, at fate, at a world that had given her Daryn of Gosney so briefly, then stolen him away again. Davi felt only sorrow for her and was glad when the caravan moved on.

He settled finally against a grassy hillock along a small creek that bubbled in the moon shadows. The voices and lights from the camp were dimmed with distance. The duke touched the pendant through the layers of cloth at his breast, his eyes on the sky. There would be no lessons in sorcery on this journey. The *Book of Stones* had been packed carefully away. No one, absolutely no one, must discover its presence. Orym had wisely stayed silent, no longer even felt within the Stone. Davi hated the deception, but the Dark King's Stone belonged to him now, and he to it. In some yet unforeseen future, he'd be able to prove himself worthy of the sorcery. Then Gaylon would know and understand.

He gathered the lute into his arms and began to play . . . only to remember the tune was a favorite of Cally's. The music faded away into the night. It was a time for melancholy ballads with lyrics that might let his hurt go. Davi tried another melody, one Gaylon had taught him, then eventually added his voice, soft and low. Sometime later, another soft voice joined his in harmony from somewhere among the trees.

"Who's there?" he demanded quietly, his hand flat on the strings to deaden their sound.

"I'm sorry," Sandaal D'Lelan said, moving into the moon-light. "I didn't mean to disturb you."

Davi stared up at her slender silhouette. "Yes, you did." He started to rise.

"No, please," she bade him. "I'll leave. . . ." The young woman turned away, then turned back. "First let me apologize for that night we sang together. I was rude."

"And so was I. Forget it."

"I'd like another chance," Sandaal continued. "To play music with you."

This sudden change in behavior disturbed Davi, made him leery. "Is this your idea? Or the queen's?"

"Mine, though I doubt the queen would disapprove. Do

you?" She boldly settled beside him on the grass, and he noticed her mandolin in her hands. "No one dictates to me whom I shall love or marry. Not even a queen. But I realize I've been using that as my sole reason to dislike you. It's not a very good reason." Sandaal picked an idle tune on her instrument. "I think we should find out if we like or dislike each other on our own."

The duke of Gosney remained silent, uncertain. He had watched Sandaal in the presence of others, and she rarely had two words to put together except when singing.

"We needn't be friends or anything like that," she muttered now. "I just wanted you to know that you're the finest musician I've ever heard, and it would please me to play with you again."

"The king plays far better than I," Davi said, fighting the pleasure her compliment had brought.

"I've never heard him."

"He hasn't had much time of late."

Sandaal's tune grew stronger, louder. Somehow she'd felt his melancholy mood. Her voice joined the mandolin's, sweetly, in Xenaran. Not a love song, this one, but a ballad of a commoner woman's hard life from birth to death. Davi had never heard it before, but found the chords and joined the young woman on the chorus. The words touched him, reminding him of his mother, of Cally. His chest began to tighten and his eyes to water. Ashamed, he kept his face averted as the song came to an end.

After a long silence, Sandaal spoke. "I'm sorry, milord. I'm so sorry for Cally and the baby."

Stunned, Davi turned to her. "The baby?"

"I . . . we . . . all the women knew," Sandaal said, stumbling over her words. "Cally was three months pregnant. She was so proud to be carrying a duke's child."

Davi buried his face in his hands. Why hadn't she told him? Their stations in life would never have allowed them to marry, but he would have acknowledged the baby, taken care of them both as best he could. A child. Anguish swept through him, and his Stone, its magic so carefully forgotten, flared against his breastbone, icy hot. He dropped the lute and rose suddenly.

Sandaal caught his arm in a strong grip. "Don't run away from me again, Davi! Don't run away from the pain. Stay here and tell me everything—every little thing you remember about Cally. Tell me how special she was."

"I saw you that morning," he said harshly. "I saw you on the balcony where she fell. What were you doing there?"

"Our chambers were nearby," the young woman answered, confused. "I heard all the noise and went to investigate."

The duke sank back to the ground. "Why would you want to hear about my lover?"

"Because you need to speak the words, milord. You need to share the sorrow. Share it with me."

Blue moonlight touched her lovely eyes and lips, shadowed her cheeks. Whatever her reasons behind this offer of kindness, the duke felt compelled somehow to stay. He had spoken to no one of Cally since her death. Now the memories poured out. Eyes on the stars, Davi talked, and an odd calm came over him. Cally had been a friend as well as a lover. There had never been any romance between them, just a mutual warmth and companionship. Being older, she had watched the young boy-duke mature, slapped his hands when he came to steal cookies from the kitchen, cared for him when he returned from war, wounded and heartsick.

So, he knew now, he grieved the loss of the friend far more than the lover. But the baby—there was the true tragedy. Cally had always wanted children and thought herself barren. What sort of cruel fate would take her life just as her dreams were finally being fulfilled?

Sandaal kept silent throughout, though once or twice Davi thought he heard her take a ragged breath. His tears had long since gone, and the ache in his heart had dulled. At last there was nothing more to say.

Except, "Thank you, milady, for listening."

Sandaal touched his arm, then gathered up her mandolin. Moonlight glinted silver on her cheeks now. Wordlessly she left him alone in the night.

* * * * *

The days grew warmer the farther south they traveled. The Gray Mountains moved away to the east, leaving the caravan within the first and smallest of the Lower Vales. Here the spring grasses were a mixture of green and yellow, already heavy with ripening seed heads, and there were planted fields along the road. The road itself had widened and was in much better repair.

King and queen rode ahead, unaccompanied today. Gaylon had to hold Tali in tight with the reins. The big bay gelding danced, full of energy this afternoon, and had managed to infect Crystal. Jessmyn only laughed as the mare jigged sideways, fighting the bit. Her laughter made the king smile. To ride beside her, to see the pleasure on her face, helped him forget for a small while where they were headed. Nearly two thirds of the journey had been completed.

The road opened up before them, a long stretch without turns. Jessmyn suddenly loosened Crystal's reins.

"No, my lady. Wait!" the king called.

If she heard his call, she ignored him, the mare already at a full gallop. Gaylon gave Tali his head. The horse lunged forward, following swiftly. It had rained lightly last night, enough to keep the dust down. Despite his gelding's long legs, Crystal continued to lengthen her lead. The king put the spurs to Tali. Blasted woman! What was she thinking?

The long straightaway played out, and the road veered right. Tali came into it on the wrong lead and made a flying change to catch his balance, but there beyond the curve stood Crystal, alone. Even her saddle was gone.

"Jessmyn!" Gaylon shouted, fear rising.

Tali fought the sudden jerk on the bit and plunged to a jolting halt, but Gaylon had already thrown himself from the horse. The queen lay on the ground in the high grasses by the road, one hand tangled in a rein.

"Jess . . ."

The young woman moved feebly, then opened her eyes. "It broke," she muttered. A tiny bit of blood edged her lips.

"What?" Gaylon demanded, feeling arms and legs. "Where?"

"No." She fended off his hands. "The saddle. The saddle broke." Her voice grew stronger. "It wasn't Crystal's fault."

"And you still managed to hang on to the horse. Where does it hurt?"

Jess groaned. "Everywhere . . ."

The king slipped careful arms under her and stood.

"I can walk," she protested.

"Absolutely not."

Crystal followed them back down the roadway, but Tali had disappeared in the opposite direction, intent, no doubt, on enjoying some freedom. Gaylon cursed under his breath at his stupidity, her foolishness.

The caravan met them a while later, and immediately the alarm was raised. Davi arrived first, on horseback.

"Get Haslic," the king commanded. "Bring him to the queen's wagon."

Davi spun his mount and sent it at a run to the farthest wagon back, where Haslic, their tutor and apprentice physician, resided. Gaylon carried the queen to the stairs her driver had hastily dropped into place. Sandaal climbed the steps behind him.

"What's happened?"

"The queen's taken a fall."

Jessmyn reached out to catch the girl's hand. "I'm all right. My lord makes a fuss over nothing."

"We'll let Haslic decide that." The king laid her gently on her narrow cot.

"Da!" Thayne cried from outside.

Sandaal raised the wagon cover a bit. The elder prince sat his white mare. Katina stood nearby, the babe in her arms, while Rose held Robyn by one hand. Lady D'Lelan motioned them for quiet. More people were arriving—some soldiers, the servants, even the Grand Envoy. Davi used his horse to push his way through the small crowd, leading the young physician on foot.

Gaylon called to the duke. "Go find Tali. And bring back Crystal's saddle."

The young man nodded, eyes troubled, and headed out just as Haslic entered. The Grand Envoy came after. His eyes were no less troubled than Davi's, but there was considerable anger on his face as well. He turned on Sandaal in the crowded area.

"Get out, Lady D'Lelan. Please."

She bowed her head and left immediately. Haslic had knelt by the queen, and with long slender fingers explored her scalp first.

"I'm not hurt," Jessmyn insisted.

The physician's hands began to knead her stomach and made her wince at one point. He removed her boots and felt along her legs. A prod at the left hip made the queen grit her teeth.

"Well?" demanded Gaylon and the Grand Envoy at the same time.

"Milady is lucky, milords," the young man answered. "I can find no fractures, no injuries to the head. There is some tenderness in the abdomen, but no indication of internal injuries."

"And the blood on her lips?" the king asked.

"She's bitten her tongue is all. There are scrapes and cuts, but I believe the injury to the hip will be the most painful. A skin of cold water will help keep the swelling down and ease the bruising." The apprentice physician smiled at his patient. "Your Highness will be more careful next time."

"There'll be no next time," Eowin D'Ar snapped imperiously. "Milady is not to ride again."

Gaylon looked at him. "You overstep yourself, sir."

"And you risk your wife's life, Majesty. Everything depends on the queen's safety. Think of the children, if you won't think of the lady."

Despite himself, the king's Stone glittered in the ring on his hand.

"Stop it, both of you," Jessmyn said angrily. "I understand your concern, Lord D'Ar, but if you think to make me a prisoner in Xenara, you're mistaken. I'll ride when I please, I'll do as I please, and my children are my own concern. Life itself is dangerous and ultimately lost. I'll enjoy what I can of it."

Eowin bowed his white head, eyes downcast. "Milady, for-give my words. I've let my worries run away with me."

"It's all right." The queen turned slightly on the cot and hissed with pain. "Send Lady Sandaal to tend to me, please. Haslic, you may instruct her on what needs to be done."

Gaylon leaned over her. "Would you have me stay, love?"

"And watch me moan and groan? Thank you, no. Go tell the boys their mother will live. I'm certain gossip and specula-tion have them both upset."

Everyone was upset. Nearly the entire caravan clustered near the front of the first wagon. The king let Haslic explain the queen's condition to them, but being Girkin's apprentice led him to use technical terms and flowery language that only confused the group all the more.

"She's going to be fine," Gaylon growled in frustration. "Just bruised and sore for a few days." He reached out to pat the knee of Thayne, who sat beside him on Sojii. Rose had gath-ered up little Robyn and tried to stanch his tears. While the physician spoke with Lady D'Lelan, the king wandered to the head of the eight-horse team that pulled his wife's wagon. What little of the road ahead that could be viewed from here was empty.

He had just decided to find another saddled mount when Davi appeared, leading Tali behind.

"Her Majesty?" the duke asked at his approach.

"Nothing broken," Gaylon said curtly. "Where was Tali?"

"Not far. But I'm afraid he demolished a corner of some poor tenant farmer's barley field. What he didn't eat, he tram-pled." Davi dismounted and brought his lord back to Tali, who carried the queen's saddle. He pulled it free and lifted the off-side flap. "The girth straps, milord. The leather had rotted."

"But how? The rest looks fine."

"Perhaps someone forgot to oil them, and they got damp. I don't know. . . ."

"It's still inexcusable." Gaylon felt anger flush through him, felt his Stone answer. "Find me the servant who saddled the horse. There'll be punishment of some kind for this lapse in judgment."

The duke of Gosney looked him in the eyes. "I saddled the horse, Sire."

"You? Dear gods, Davi, how could you miss this?"

"I've no excuse, milord," the young man said unhappily.

"She might have been killed. . . ."

Now Davi's gaze faltered. "I know."

"Is that knowledge punishment enough?"

"You must decide, Sire," the duke answered, thoroughly miserable.

"I think it is. Come give the animals to one of the grooms. You and I will spend some time with the children. They're frightened. Then when the queen has sufficiently recovered, you may offer her an apology for your stupidity."

"Aye, milord."

The king turned away abruptly, certain his duke would follow.

*  *  *  *  *

Rose brought him a plate of supper at dusk. The duke had taken himself into the trees east of camp in search of solitude. Food, drink, or company did not appeal to him, but the D'Jal sister had somehow tracked him down. She had shown him these little kindnesses all during the journey, and Davi could think of no way to reject them without hurting her.

She sat now beside him, the plate held out.

"Thank you," he mumbled and set his supper on the ground.

"The ants will get it, milord."

"Probably."

Rose looked at him, her pretty face worried. "May I know what bothers you, Lord Gosney?"

The king had said nothing to the others about Davi's failure, and no one seemed eager to place blame in any direction. Let it be a mischance, an accident, and leave it at that, since His Majesty seemed satisfied. But the duke's own guilt made him open his mouth.

"The queen's fall was my fault."

"Not so, milord," Rose said fiercely. "Why would you check

the off-side straps? They were already buckled." When Davi glanced at her, she continued. "The king said it was rotted girth straps, and no one's blame."

"It was my horse and my duty to check everything," the young man growled.

"Then a duke is not allowed mistakes?"

"Not where his queen is concerned."

"Ah, then." Rose placed a wineskin at his feet and stood. "His lordship prefers to wallow in self-pity. I'll leave you to it."

He caught her hand—not so slender and fine-boned as Sandaal's, but soft. "Please. I appreciate your concern, but I need some time to sort this out myself. I promise I'll eat the food before the ants do. Thank you."

The younger D'Jal sister smiled, pleased. "You're welcome, sir." She turned and stepped lightly away in the dusk.

The hot day had cooled finally, and night came alive around him, birdsong and crickets and bullfrogs. Davi put his head back against the myrtle bole behind him, sighing.

"She loves you, you know," a soft voice said from among the trees.

It was Sandaal.

"You mean Rose?" The duke sighed again. "I was afraid that might be the case."

Lady D'Lelan appeared in the shadows. "Would you prefer I leave as well?"

"Of course not. Come sit. Are you hungry? I can't seem to find my appetite tonight."

"I've eaten, thank you." She settled beside him, chin on knees, drab skirts draped to the ground. "Do you know what would happen in Xenara to so careless a duke?"

"I'm afraid to ask."

"You'd lose your head. Or worse."

"There's worse? Then I'd better keep my head about me in Zankos."

"I think your royalty is a bit more forgiving than ours."

Sandaal had sat quite close, her shoulder touching Davi's. Her nearness caused his heart to beat faster. Over the past fortnight, they'd become what he could only consider good friends, though the lady avoided him still during daylight in camp. Now he thought he understood why. She no more wanted to hurt Rose's feelings than he. But the young duke wasn't certain how much longer he could hide his feelings for Sandaal. She enthralled him. So far, though, she seemed to want only his companionship, and instinct told him that must suffice.

Their mental sets were much the same. They'd read many of the same books and, late in the night while the others slept, discussed them passionately for hours. Music was only possible if they went far downwind from camp.

"How do you suppose she'll react to such power and wealth?" the young woman asked in the warm, comfortable silence.

"The queen?"

"You've lived poor all your lives in Wynnamyr, even your royalty. Her Majesty has never ruled directly. We could fit ten Wynnamyrs inside Xenara . . . at least. I can't imagine wielding the power that will be hers soon."

"She's much stronger than she appears."

Sandaal shifted against him. "Yes. I've noticed."

"What worries me," said Davi, "is the Grand Envoy. Jessmyn is just a piece in some game of his. I can't even prevent her falling from my horse. How will I protect her against the merchant families and the noblemen who oppose her ascension?"

"Zankos is a dangerous place—even now while it's being rebuilt. Within the palace grounds, though, royalty has its safe haven. No king or queen has been assassinated within the walls in over three hundred and fifty years."

"That's very comforting," the duke said dryly. "Such an arid lifeless land. I'll miss my trees, my green mountains."

Sandaal laughed. "No. You won't have time. Xenara's port cities never sleep. There's so much to do and see." She pressed a hand to Davi's chest, over his Stone. "There's a courtier's heart in there somewhere. You'll dance till dawn and sleep throughout the day."

"Only if you'll dance and sleep with me." Even as he said the words, the duke regretted them.

Lady D'Lelan stood and shook out her skirts, pushing her long black hair from her shoulders. Fool! he thought. Two horrible mistakes in one day. The young woman looked down on him, and in the darkness, he imagined the disdain on her face. She only laughed again.

"Perhaps. We'll have to see."

Then Davi was alone again, but with a touch of hope.

# Eight

Davi watched Sandaal move in and out of the moon shadows, her hair spilling blue-black over her shoulder. It was nearly dawn, a long night's travel done, and she was making the beds in the sand beneath the ladies' wagon. Rose and Katina had gone to settle the children with their mother, the queen, in their own wagon.

"Milady," the duke said softly from where he squatted near a huge spoked wheel.

Sandaal froze, hands full of blankets. "Davi?"

"Yes." He sidled closer, all his careful thoughts jumbled and confused now. "I need to talk with you."

"Not now," she muttered and went back to her bed-making.

"I miss our music . . . our talks. We could slip away for a little while. . . ."

"To where?" the young woman demanded. "This is the Xenara Plain. There isn't a tree-filled dell or glen anywhere to hide the sounds of our instruments or our voices. Besides, I'm tired. Go away, Davyn Darynson."

Her tone was brusque, and Davi's confusion only grew worse. "The closer we come to Zankos, the colder you are to me, Sandaal. I don't understand. We've shared so many things on this journey. I thought . . . I hoped you felt for me as I do for you."

Sandaal paused again, her expression hidden by the shadows. "You think too much, Davi. You assume too much. A song and a kind word are not vows of love."

Davi gnawed his lip. This was wrong, all wrong. That last
night spent in the vales, he had never felt so strong a tie with
any woman as he had with Lady D'Lelan. Their music had
been unearthly and beautiful, even without Orym's magic, and
their voices had blended in perfect harmony under the stars.
Only for the past fortnight, as the caravan traveled ponder-
ously across the Xenara Plain, Sandaal had refused any contact with him. At first Davi believed it might be for Rose's
sake, but in their brief moments alone, Sandaal remained
aloof, a stranger.

"Go away, Davi," she said again, and the words brought an
ache in the duke's chest.

"What's that?" Katina asked, returning with Rose.

Davi didn't stay any longer, only faded silently back from
the wagon. The first faint color of dawn touched the eastern
horizon, the beauty of it lost to him. Anger, fear, and frustration gave way to more confusion. It was time to find his own
bed and sleep. Later he might make sense of Sandaal's behavior, but not now.

\* \* \* \* \*

The long, slow passage across the Xenaran Plain was a bitter one for Gaylon. Travel was done after dark, since late
spring brought greater heat at the lower elevation. They must
travel by night and sleep as best they could during the day.
This last leg of the journey would be thankfully short, however.

At least traveling in darkness hid most of the memories
from the king, but the wheels of the wagons would crunch
loudly over debris time and again. Dry branches, Gaylon told
himself, while his mind saw the white bones of soldiers and
horses laid bare in the final grim moments of the war.

By night, the king was forced to bundle up against the icy
salt wind that blew in from the western coast. By day, he lay
in the shade of the queen's wagon, sweating, his sleep further
disturbed by nightmares. Over and over in his dreams, Gaylon

found himself standing on a promontory above the plain, Kingslayer in hand, its power surging through him, spewing from the blade's tip.

His uncontrolled rage sent a flood of molten starfire over the land below, consuming everything that lay in its path. Then something huge and winged swooped toward him out of the sky.

"Dada . . ."

The word was whispered in his ear, and the king opened his eyes. Robyn leaned over him, his small face flushed with the heat. The camp around them was still except for gusts of hot wind.

"What are you doing down here?" Gaylon asked the boy.

"You woke me up. Why are you crying?"

The king scrubbed the tears from his cheeks, felt grit there as well. "I had a bad dream, that's all. Go back to bed."

"Can your Stone make good dreams?" Robyn still leaned close, eyes wide.

"Yes."

"Then tell it to, Da."

"I will. Get to bed. Quietly."

The prince stood up, the wagon floor well over his head, then scrambled up the steps. Gaylon settled back on the blankets, weary. Once he would have found peace in Dreaming, exploring the universe through his Sorcerer's Stone, but no more. The will to Dream had left him with the death of his friends and the destruction of Kingslayer. In fact, he'd made little use of his Stone in these last few years. A king's business involved far more than magic. But that magic might be needed to protect them in Zankos.

Gaylon found his waterskin and drank sparingly. Water here was precious. They had barely enough for the horses. Another day, the Grand Envoy said, or rather another night's travel. The caravan would arrive in Zankos by tomorrow morning. Another day. Gods, he wanted to be home in his cold drafty keep. Anywhere but here.

The wind drove under the wagon, and the king squinted against the small cloud of salty dust. The sun westered, though still high enough in the sky to bake the parched earth and glint on the bleached bones scattered in every direction. These were mostly the skeletal remains of animals—great open rib cages of horses, porous from years in the sun. Apparently the Xenarans had laboriously gathered their soldiers' remains. This land held many gods, worshiped by a diverse folk. The dead had not been left untended.

Afraid of sleep, the king of Wynnamyr stared sightlessly at the planking of the wagon bottom. Finally the sun drifted to the horizon and the air cooled. There came bootsteps in the sand.

"Sire?" Davi bent to peer under the wagon. "Lord D'Ar says if you please, we might take our evening meal on the move and arrive a little earlier in Zankos."

Gaylon nodded. "Nothing would please me more." He crawled free and stood.

Around them, soldiers stirred, carrying heavy skins of water from the barrels to the horses. Davi moved to gather the king's bed. The wagon covers had been rolled halfway up, and Robyn hung on to the side, chin on the boards.

"Hello, Da."

The king ruffled his son's hair, then leaned in under the silk. "How fares my lady?"

"Well, kind sir," Jessmyn answered from the edge of her cot as she brushed the tangles from her hair.

The bruise on her cheek had turned an even darker purple in the last two days, and she moved rather slowly still—without complaint, though. Gaylon smiled at her, scratching slowly at his red beard.

"The Xenarans will think me a wife beater as well as a wholesale murderer. Perhaps you should wear a veil." To make light of the situation seemed the only thing to do.

Jessmyn pursed her lips. "My husband is neither. When war is forced upon a king, he does what he must to protect his own."

"Perhaps you can explain that to them as their queen."

* * * * *

Zankos had once rambled for a great distance along the Inland Sea and up the steep slopes to the plain, where it had rambled some more. It had been the great beating heart of Xenara, and perhaps it would be again someday. Now the city was a tenth its former size, but still far bigger than any town or borough in Wynnamyr.

The Grand Envoy's caravan came upon the remains of the old Zankos first, nothing more than sooty ground over which charred timbers were scattered. Where four- and five-story establishments had risen lay broken, blackened stone foundations—nothing more. The devastation spread away to the east and west as far as the eye could see, while the Inland Sea glittered to the south. Sandaal stared bleak-eyed, without the vaguest notion where her family mansion and grounds had been, though she remembered watching lighted ships move across the night waters from her bedroom window.

She remembered their large gardens, some of them growing on the steep slopes, and the stables filled with beautiful dark horses. And she remembered Arlin, the one brother who'd taken the time to show the littlest daughter how to ride. Of all her family besides her mother, his was the clearest face in her memories, though he'd left home when she was only seven. That had been the greatest tragedy of her young life at the time.

Of him, of her child's life, there was nothing left. The wagon rumbled on through the ruins, swaying, then headed down the slopes toward the living city with its ornate new structures. A blessed cool breeze blew in off the water, bringing the faint clang of bells from the docks and the shouts of laborers.

"Sandaal?" Katina sat beside her on a bench, her eyes on the same desolate landscape. "This is the first time you've been back . . . since . . . Are you all right?"

The young woman nodded, unable to trust her voice.

"Her Majesty will need to be dressed soon," Rose warned from the back, where she dug through a trunk. "I can't find my hairpins."

The new Zankos had been alerted of their arrival, and the

caravan paused before entering. Within the queen's crowded wagon, trunks and cartons were stacked out of the way to leave room for the ladies-in-waiting to work. Sandaal helped Jessmyn into the gown that Katina had sewn for her. It was plum silk, cut low in front in the ancient royal Xenaran style, with a long straight skirt, slit to one side. Silk slippers in the same color completed the ensemble.

The queen looked down in dismay. "Dear gods, this is far too revealing. At the worst possible moment, it'll all come undone."

"Milady, don't worry." The Lady D'Lelan carefully slipped a tiny plum shoe on Her Majesty's foot. "Katina is a wonderful seamstress. She knows exactly what she's doing."

"Your hair, Highness," Rose said. "Just a few more pins."

She stood on a stool, trapping red-gold curls. Kat brought a small jeweled coronet, the best Wynnamyr had to offer, while Sandaal stood back to admire the overall effect. Her countrymen appreciated beauty, and in Jessmyn D'Gerric, they would see their lost queen, Jarath. The people would welcome her, if not the factions that warred for power.

Someone rapped on the wood near the steps.

"May I see my lady?" the king called.

"Come," Jessmyn told him.

Sandaal turned her head away as he entered, finding something else to trap her interest. Sometimes she feared her anger would betray her. The Grand Envoy had convinced Gaylon Reysson to stay within the wagon. He would not be welcome here in Xenara, though D'Ar felt certain the king of Wynnamyr would be tolerated eventually, if not loved. Sandaal doubted that, not when every man, woman, and child in the land had lost some relation to him and his cursed sword and Stone.

The young woman swallowed back the bitterness and brought the queen a fan of pheasant plumes. Her Majesty, with her ladies-in-waiting, would be carried in an ornate open carriage along the wide cobbled boulevard that led to the palace. It was something the king had violently opposed. Now he stood nearby, silent, beaten into submission by the queen's logic and the envoy's shrewd tongue.

"You mustn't worry, Majesty," Katina told him kindly. "The guards will be close by, and we shall all be armed." She showed him the little dirk in a jeweled sheath strapped to her wrist and hidden under sleeves of billowy silk. "We were trained in their use."

"No doubt," Gaylon said with a hint of sarcasm. "I will see you at the palace, then."

"My lord." Jessmyn tried to turn to see him.

Rose squawked, "Don't move yet!"

The king's boots thumped down the steps, and Sandaal heard his voice. "Find Gosney for me. I want to see him at the last wagon. Immediately."

"Milady, please," Rose said, exasperated when Jessmyn tried to move again.

Horses approached, their hooves dancing over the cobbles, very unlike the plodding pace of the tired animals that pulled the wagons. Sandaal peered out from under the cover and saw the royal coach, draped in rich purple silks and satins. It was Fitzwal who came to help the queen down the steps and into the carriage, then assisted each lady-in-waiting to her seat near Jessmyn. The children with their nanny would follow in the caravan.

Jessmyn searched the small crowd, no doubt looking for her husband. He was not about, nor his faithful duke. The soldiers arrived, dressed out in helms and cuirasses, a lance shaft cradled in the edge of each right stirrup. Light glinted from the spear tips above their heads. A dozen men rode to the fore, a dozen behind. The Grand Envoy was helped into a litter chair that would be carried before the queen. At his signal, the procession finally moved.

The ashes left behind, they entered the city. On either side of the concourse tall buildings rose, surfaced in stucco of pale beige or pink—new, but already weathered by sun and salt breezes. Every wrought-iron balcony was crowded with citizens and visitors, every inch of walkway thronged with people in bright garb. On her satin cushions, Sandaal turned her gaze from street to walls and back again. Silence reigned, an eerie quiet broken only by the beat of hooves and the squeak of wheels.

Confused, the queen looked around, too, pale and wan in the morning sunlight. Then she smiled and raised a hand to a group in the nearest balcony. Sandaal had never seen her smile so—it lit Jessmyn's face and transformed her. It wasn't to the adults she waved, but to a small child, a beautiful girl in a tiny red dress, standing to the front, hands wrapped about the iron scrollwork. Shyly the girl reached an arm through the railing and waved back.

They'd been ready to decide one way or another on how to accept Jessmyn D'Gerric, this crowd. A small silk streamer suddenly fluttered down to the cobbles, then another and another, and the people of Zankos began to shout. The roar echoed back and forth across the small canyon of buildings until Sandaal's ears rang. Their driver fought for control over his team, and the soldiers fought unruly mounts. Colored ribbons, unraveling in the air, did nothing to calm them.

To the rear, Sandaal saw that the two soldiers closest to the carriage still held a tight rein on their animals, their attention on the crowds above and below. Something familiar touched her, something in the way one sat his horse. The Xenaran helm had leather flaps sewn with ring mail that covered the neck, but only a broad iron nosepiece to protect the face. This soldier's gaze swept upward again, and Lady D'Lelan saw a flash of bright green eyes. Davi. The fool.

Beside him rode the tall Wynnamyran king, Sandaal realized—a determined man and husband, who had shaven his rich red beard in order to play the role of a Xenaran soldier. If they were somehow found out, the queen's triumphant entry into Zankos could turn to disaster. Gaylon Reysson just might bring down the Xenaran ire he sought to protect his wife from. An idle thought, but interesting. Even a sorcerer would find it difficult to survive such a mob.

Sandaal turned her attention elsewhere. Jessmyn, hiding her confusion, accepted the roaring welcome of the people. This was her birthplace, and yet she rode the streets of a strange city in a strange land. The riotous colors and cries would inspire confusion in anyone. Small children had begun to approach the slow-paced carriage, eager to hand little cloth-wrapped gifts to the daughter of Roffo. They would be mostly food—dates and sesame cakes and other delicacies—none of which the queen could taste. The foodstuffs were handed out to the poor later at the palace gate, where hungry people gladly risked poisoning for something to eat.

The next crowd of children surged forward, some of them getting under the feet of the two odd soldiers who rode behind. Lady D'Lelan paid them no mind, her eyes on a young Katay nobleman she'd recognized, who stood on the walkway beside a lamppost. Raf D'Gular's speculative gaze was on Jessmyn, and while those around him shouted their welcome, he remained silent. A vague frown touched his handsome, swarthy face.

The House of Gular had their own contender for the throne—Raf's eldest half brother, Kyl, who was also Jessmyn's bastard half brother, many years her senior. Raf took note of Lady D'Lelan, and his thin lips curled into a feral smile. The men of Xenara had little facial hair, and most shaved even that, but Raf wore a narrow mustache and goat's beard at the point of his chin. Sandaal had always thought him rather charming, a renegade even within his renegade family. With a small dip of his head, the young man turned and slipped into the crowd.

The boulevard began its long winding curves down the slopes to the Inland Sea and the palace. Where the Mezon temple had stood a new temple had been built, but to which god Sandaal had no idea. The warrior god, Mezon, no longer had priests to honor him nor followers to support him. Gaylon Reysson, a sorcerer, but a man all the same, had destroyed the cruel god with the power of Kingslayer.

Beyond the glowing white marble temple, the palace rose above the high wall that surrounded it and the gardens, the kiosks, and patios. Of all Zankos, only the palace had survived the Wynnamyran king's revenge. Sandaal remembered it still, set against the golden sunlit waters. The structure was far more a fortress than Castlekeep, yet instead of uneven gray stones haphazardly mortared, here were huge blocks of marble and granite, fitted almost seamlessly.

Even in the midst of the roaring crowd, Jessmyn had seen the palace, too. Eyes trapped, she looked in wonder. Yes, Sandaal thought. Enjoy the beauty of your new home, Highness. Accept the adoration of your people, for they'll never let you return to Wynnamyr.

\*     \*     \*     \*     \*

The soldier who'd loaned Davi his uniform, however unwillingly, had also loaned him the smell of his sweat and his hard-mouthed, ill-tempered mount. The little beast had a jarring trot which it insisted on using even while standing in one spot. Hopelessly the duke juggled reins and lance and tried to keep track of thousands of shouting people to either side of the queen's carriage.

Strips of colored cloth continued to shower down from the balconies, spooking the animals. Several times, Davi and his king collided horses painfully in the center of the boulevard. Gaylon only growled at him in gutter Xenaran, which included some profanity as colorful as the streamers. The sun only made matters worse. While a stiff breeze cooled Davi's face, the iron helm and leather cuirass only drew the heat until sweat trickled from his jaw.

Sandaal, sitting across from the queen, drew his eye far more often than he should have allowed. Madness. All of this was madness—the throngs, the shouts, the towering buildings. Yet in the faces of the people who crowded around them, the duke saw a strange joy. The house of Gerric had returned to Xenara, and nothing else seemed to matter.

The concourse made its way in three long loops down the slope to the Inland Sea. How structures could be built on such a steep incline mystified Davi, but there they stood in long ragged rows, with alleys so narrow the balconies almost touched. Some of the buildings had small bridges between the uppermost stories, and while the streets were lined with muck, flowers bloomed in window boxes that filled every aperture. Some of the flat-topped roofs farther down the slope had lush gardens planted on them.

What a wondrous city. Sandaal was right—already the duke felt himself drawn by Zankos's teeming life and energy.

"Get your eyes open, by the gods!" the king snarled loudly as Davi's mount swung sideways toward a group of children.

"Aye, sir," the duke answered under his breath, contrite. He spurred the animal hard to force it back into the road.

But those open eyes first found Sandaal briefly, found her smiling back at him—a little amused twist of her lips. Embarrassed, Davi looked away to search the roofs for an attack he now felt certain wouldn't come. Oh, there was danger in this place, but not today. Today Xenara loved the woman who would be their queen.

Finally the procession arrived at the temple, and except for the citizens who had flooded the boulevard to follow them, the roaring crowds were left behind. Davi took a shaky breath and let the tension go, allowing himself a guilt-free moment to take in the tall pillars of the temple. It was cool here in the shadows. Marble statues of lithe gods stood at the head of wide stone steps, and incense wafted on the sea air. Would they require Jessmyn to worship their gods? And if they did, would she? No, the lady was anything but false in her dealings.

Wide gates of oak beams swung slowly open to admit them within the palace grounds. The palace itself rose at the far end of the enclosure, a gleaming many-domed structure that captivated the beholder. Far larger than Castlekeep, its lines and form were beautifully simple, yet somehow complex, leading the eye from tower to dome to terrace.

Eowin D'Ar disembarked from his litter when the last wagon had arrived and the gates closed. The old man's face held pleasure.

"Milady has won the hearts of her people," he said enthusiastically. "You have done all I had hoped for and more. Thank you, Your Majesty."

"Hearts are too easily broken, Lord Envoy," the queen replied from her cushions. "I must win their minds as well."

Ancient and stiff, D'Ar bowed to her. "It will be an honor to serve you, Highness." He reached out to help her down from the carriage, then led her to another litter. Jessmyn moved slowly to hide the pain from her hip. The envoy returned to his own litter as a group of palace guards arrived to lead their way. Davi watched them leave.

"You there. Corporal."

Sandaal's imperious voice rang out in the comparative quiet. The duke looked behind him in hope she called another. The others were gone.

"Milady?"

"Help us down, you stupid lout." The young woman lifted her chin, daring him to disobey.

Davi dismounted, glad to be quit of the soldier's mount for the moment but reluctant to be pulled into Sandaal's game. Lady D'Lelan put out a hand to him while the D'Jal sisters looked on in amazement. The duke helped her to the ground.

Sandaal sniffed. "You are in desperate need of a bath."

"Not me, milady. It must be the horse."

Davi handed Rose down, then Katina. Both wrinkled their noses in disgust.

"Impudence will get you whipped, Corporal. You're no longer in Wynnamyr."

A reminder, as if he needed it. At the sound of hooves, the duke turned. Gaylon, still in Xenaran uniform, had ridden back from the wagons. He pulled up beside them.

"Miladies, is this man bothering you?" the king asked.

"Only his stench," Sandaal said, and offering them a private grin of mischief, she left to join her companions.

"She knows who I am," Davi muttered glumly as the two men rode to the rear of the caravan.

"Now she knows us both. Which is why we were supposed to disappear the moment the queen was safely within the compound." There was irritation in Gaylon's voice.

"Will she tell the envoy?"

The king shook his head. "It hardly matters. Our soldiers certainly will. After leaving them bound and gagged in the provisions wagon all morning, I don't have the heart to slit their throats as well."

"That would be too Xenaran," Davi agreed. "Is the smell really that bad?"

"Not when you stand downwind." Gaylon laughed. "You aren't the only one, my duke. None of us have bathed in four days. But thanks to Wynnamyr, Zankos has an endless supply of fresh water." He nudged his mount into a short lope. "Let's release our soldier friends, give them back their foul clothes and ugly horses, then find ourselves a bath."

* * * * *

The palace guard was a healthy, handsome lot, Jessmyn decided, no doubt picked for their pleasing looks as well as their military skills. Everything in this place seemed designed near perfection. The men wore lightweight leather cuirasses, pleated kilts of leather over white linen, and cross-tied sandals. Their muscled legs were tan. Unused to seeing so much bare skin, the queen averted her eyes, embarrassed. The small band brought her litter through the lower gardens toward the palace. Behind them, the queen heard sweet laughter and wondered if her ladies-in-waiting found this place as awe-inspiring as she.

Young olive trees lined the paths, and potted dwarf citrus trees, heavy with fruit and flowers, were everywhere. Shady kiosks stood among tall, feathery date palms. No lawns here, just raw yellowish dirt, neatly raked, and stone-lined flower beds filled with a multitude of blooming plants that Jessmyn couldn't put a name to.

A huge central fountain sprayed a silver curtain of water into the warm air. The rich scents of this seaport, fish and spices and exotic perfumes, filled the queen's nostrils. Gardeners watched her approach from the terraced slope within the northern wall of the enclosure. Male and female servants, all in the same sleeveless white robes, met their new mistress at the closest palace entrance, bowing deeply.

Dear gods, there were at least a hundred of them, eyes respectfully downcast. Jessmyn felt the litter settle to the shiny red clay tiles of the patio, then Eowin D'Ar arrived to help her climb from the chair. He led her forward.

"Nials!" the old man called in his scratchy voice.

"Yes, lord." The man who pushed forward through the little crowd had impossibly curly black hair and wore embroidered robes. His pale blue eyes regarded the envoy, then the queen, and she saw kindness and concern in them. The myriad tiny wrinkles on his face proved him older than he first appeared.

"Milady Jessmyn, this is our physician, Nials Haldrick." Eowin waved the man closer. "You'll tend the queen first, then have Wees show her to her apartments."

Nials nodded. "And you, milord? Shall I look in on you?"

"Later. I've messages to send first." The elderly man bowed to Jessmyn. "If I may take my leave, Highness?"

"Of course . . . but . . . when will I see the children?" The queen felt panic at being deserted in unfamiliar surroundings.

"Soon, milady. I promise." The Grand Envoy turned toward the servants. "Go back to work. After Her Majesty is rested, you shall be introduced to her."

The crowd dispersed silently, and D'Ar took his own route across the wide patio and into the palace. The guard had already disappeared. Nials smiled at Jessmyn, then reached to take her hand, though not to lead her anywhere. Instead, he kneaded her right palm with gentle fingertips. She winced when he squeezed a spot just below her thumb.

"Your Majesty is in pain," the physician said. "Her right hip has been injured."

"The envoy told you. . . ."

"No, milady. Your hand told me."

The queen smiled in amusement. "Such a clever hand. I never realized . . ."

"Your Highness, healing is an ancient art, but so is diagnosis. Your body speaks in many ways." Nials's fingers continued to explore her hand. "There are pressure points on the hands and feet that connect to every major organ, every bone and joint. Here the heart, there the stomach." He released her at last. "Yours is a healthy body, milady—aside from this recent injury. If I may take you to my apothecary, I believe I can speed the healing and ease your pain."

This gentle man amazed her as much as her surroundings. He was so unlike the haughty keep physician, Girkin, and his self-conscious apprentice. Jessmyn found she truly liked Nials Haldrick, though it seemed unwise to place unreserved trust in any Xenaran yet. Awed, she let him lead her through a gleaming arch into the palace.

# Nine

A young female servant led Rose, Katina, and the Wynnamyran princes deeper into the palace. Thayne lagged behind, in awe and just a little uneasy in this maze of corridors and the great empty chambers they crossed. Underfoot, the floors were covered with fired reddish tiles, while the walls were smooth and whitewashed. Soft light flowed in through apertures in the high vaulted ceiling. Cool breezes drifted along the passages.

Thayne gazed around himself, unhappy. The dark, cold halls of Castlekeep seemed distant now.

"Where are my mother and father?" he asked finally and heard his voice come back to him in quiet echoes.

Rose had Robyn by the hand, and she paused. "Your parents are being shown to their own quarters."

"Where're we going?" Robyn demanded. He was tired, his eyes dark-circled, his mouth puckered into a pout.

"We're going to your chambers," Katina answered. "There you'll have some dinner and a nap."

"Don't want a nap. I want my mum," the little prince whined.

"You'll see her soon, I promise." Rose caught his hand in hers again. "But wait until you see the nursery. It's the most wonderful place in all the palace."

They continued on. Distant voices and music drifted to them on the breezes, and once a waft of cooking food, heavy with spices. Thayne's stomach grumbled. They passed through high arches into an inner courtyard filled with huge potted plants and low couches and tables. Small trees, heavy with ripening fruit, had been planted in barrels, and white water rushed over rocks in a fountain. The roof above was a series of ornate wrought-iron grilles, open to the bright Xenaran sky.

The servant brought them to the center of the courtyard to a table laden with platters of fresh fruits and cakes. Robyn didn't wait for an invitation. He jerked free of Rose's grip, scrambled up onto a settee positioned nearest the laden table, and began to stuff grapes into his mouth.

"Your Majesty, wait!" Katina cried and tried to gently empty the boy's mouth.

Rose gestured abruptly to the servantwoman, and, bowing, she came forward to sample a small amount from each plate. Moments later, the woman nodded, pale face filled with relief.

"Leave us," Kat told her, then turned to Thayne. "Milords may eat."

The elder prince stared at the fruit. "What's wrong with the food?"

"Nothing's wrong, Your Highness," murmured Rose, cutting a slice of sweet bread for Robyn. She poured grape juice into two cups. "In Zankos we must be more careful of your persons is all. Robyn, wash your hands in the bowl of water first, please."

The boy dutifully splashed around in the bowl, then used a soft white towel to dry his hands. Much of the grime remained on the material. Thayne cleaned his own hands more meticulously, thoughtful. The food tasted fine, even wonderful after weeks of stale traveler's fare, but the memory of the servant's colorless face bothered him. Poison. His father had discussed the subject before they'd left home, though it had never occurred to Thayne that someone else must risk her life in order to test the royal meals. It had also never occurred to him that someone completely unknown would want to harm him or his family. These were not pleasant considerations.

"Is this the nursery?" Robyn asked, his mouth full of bread.

"Part of it." Katina nodded.

"It's big," the boy said. "I like it."

Rose only smiled knowingly. "The Lord Envoy will choose a governess for you soon. Until then, I shall stay with you."

This pleased Robyn, but not entirely. "I want a pretty nanny, Rose. I want you."

"And who will wait on the queen?" The young D'Jal woman laughed. "Don't worry, Robyn. We'll ask Lord Eowin to hire a pretty one."

Thayne cringed. He wanted no governess at all. He wanted to be with the soldiers, making certain that Sojii was bedded down properly. Most of all, he wanted to know where Davi was, and his father. They ate in quiet for a time. The elder prince discovered the wonderful taste of dates stuffed with nutmeats and rolled in powered sugar. There were some things, then, that this land had to offer.

Robyn had fallen asleep, his tousled red head laid on the table. Katina scooped him up and carried him toward the far courtyard exit. Rose and Thayne followed, after rinsing their fingers in water. The next chamber was also light and airy and far larger than the courtyard. Huge thick carpets with intricate patterns covered the tiles, and slender mats had been laid out as beds. Silk cushions were scattered everywhere. Thayne barely noticed any of that, for on the opposite side of the great room stood a number of mysterious objects.

"Let's go look," Rose told him. Kat had already placed Robyn in one of the beds and remained to tuck a lightweight sheet around him.

Hardly aware of Rose beside him, the elder prince crossed the chamber. Someone had carved horses from wood, and pony-sized, they pranced in a circle—four of them—held from the round wooden flooring beneath them by thick metal poles. The platform was raised three steps from the ground. Thayne gazed up at Rose.

"There's a crank that winds a spring inside the mechanism," she told him. "When it's wound, the horses go round and up and down. It makes music, too. King Roffo's grandfather brought the carousel back from the Tuyali campaign. Many Xenaran princes have ridden it since then."

"I'm not a Xenaran prince," Thayne said, idly brushing a hand over the shiny white paint. The bridle and reins were real leather, while the saddle had been carved from wood and painted with gold trim. The tails and manes were of long horsehair, silvery like Sojii's. "What's this?" he asked and walked to another intricate structure of wood and metal that resembled nothing he'd ever seen before.

Rose shrugged. "No one's decided exactly what that is. We can't even remember how it came to be here, but if you pull the levers and knobs, you can make music of sorts. Pretty colors flash and spark as well."

"Hmmm . . ." Thayne muttered, but refused to touch the thing.

"These are goat carts." The young woman led him to four marvelous wagons built in the shape of sailing ships and rigged with tiny sails. Each had room for one small child inside. "These trunks are filled with other toys."

Large wooden chests lined one wall, a dozen of them. Despite himself, Thayne was intrigued. What marvels might they hold? He turned his back to show Rose his disdain. She only smiled again.

"Will you rest now, milord?"

"I'm not tired."

"Nevertheless," Katina said as she arrived beside them, "you'll lie down for the while. And later, before supper, you'll bathe."

The thought made Thayne wince, but he returned to the mats and stretched out on the one nearest Robyn. In moments he had fallen sound asleep.

\* \* \* \* \*

Davi stood in the midst of his belongings, uncertain. His trip had been short, his accommodations being rather small and near the palace's western entrance. He had no idea where the king had gone. They'd parted company at the stables while Davi made certain Crystal and Sojii were bedded down comfortably.

The size of Zankos Palace intimidated him—nearly triple that of Castlekeep. The grounds swarmed with servants and kilted guards, all of them busy yet respectful. Davi gazed out the single long window of his main chamber at rows of olive trees leading to the palace wall and the city buildings that climbed the steep slope beyond. What he needed desperately was to be clean and rested. What he wanted was some time alone with Sandaal, but as usual she'd ignored him.

Finally the duke found the energy to move. Through a small doorway to the left, he found a tub and a low platform with a hole in it. The sound of running water came from the darkness below. A basin in the corner had spigots, and when he twisted a knob, water splashed into the porcelain bowl, growing hot as it flowed. Amazing . . . In moments, he'd discarded his clothing and climbed into the tub. Adjusting the water temperature frustrated him at first, but not for long.

Gods, the luxury of it—a bath anytime he chose, without a half-dozen servants slopping water out of buckets. Davi slipped down into the warm water, content, his eyes on the pendant on his chest. The Stone remained cold and dark, and all that had gone on before seemed dreamlike, imagined. Would it answer him now? That thought brought a prickle of anticipation.

The water rippled around him, distorting the pendant. For the first time in what seemed to be forever, Davi reached for that memory of fire and ice. The Stone woke, blue light diffused and shimmery, and instantly another presence imposed itself.

*Child of my blood,* Orym whispered in his ear.

"Go away, old man," the duke growled. "I'll call you when I need you."

*So angry,* came the disembodied voice. Then the Dark King's wavering visage took form upon the water. *You have much still to learn and yet would send away your teacher.*

Davi gritted his teeth. "Let me bathe and rest first."

*Beware you don't rest too well, child.*

A long silence followed in which Davi pondered those ominous words.

"What do you mean?"

*Ah . . . that interests you. Listen well, Davyn Darynson.* The old king's face contorted with ripples. *This is a place fraught with dangers.*

"You tell me something I already know," Davi snapped. "This is Xenara, Zankos—"

*Listen! These chambers are set to kill the unwary.*

That made the duke pause. "They plan my death already?"

*Not yours, but he who had this chamber before you. A shame to die by accident.*

"A shame to die by any means. Where? Where is the danger?"

*That I cannot say.*

"Or won't."

*Be grateful the man's essence remains to tell the tale. The death was recent, his body found on the bed as if he died in his sleep.*

Davi cursed quietly. "So I sleep on the tiles. Wonderful."

*When you've rested, call me. We'll work in the* Book of Stones. *It's time you learned to Dream.*

Orym faded away, and the Stone's glow faded with him. The duke scowled at the water, unhappy with his thoughts. He'd come to protect the king and his royal family, but first must protect himself. Not a good beginning.

A shelf behind his head offered up sweet-scented soap and a rough cloth to scrub a fortnight's grime from his body. There was even a little mirror and a strange sharp knife obviously meant for shaving. His beard had grown heavy during the last leg of the journey. Clumsy and unfamiliar with the blade, he managed to nick himself.

The sight of bright scarlet blood on his chin brought a moment's panic. Fool! Orym had warned him, yet he'd taken an unknown knife and cut himself. If the blade had been poisoned . . . Yet nothing untoward happened, and Davi relaxed at last. A soft towel wrapped around him, he returned to the main chamber to dig fresh clothing from one of the three trunks.

There were thick rich rugs on the tiles, but the furnishings were sparse, and there was no fireplace—no need for one. Someone had placed a platter of fruit and biscuits on the low table. Davi ignored the food and kicked silky cushions out of his way in order to get to the bed. It looked inviting, though only a thick mat covered with lightweight sheets. Still, somehow this had been an instrument of murder. Or so Orym said. Perhaps the fellow had taken poison in his food, then lain down to die.

The cushions were lumpy, meant for seats, not for sleep. Davi sighed and found himself a length of carpet to stretch out on, then dragged the sheets from the bed. Even in the warmth, his damp hair had cooled him. But the material snagged on his sleeve as he pulled it across. While stickers and straw were often woven into woolen blankets, these were linen and extremely fine.

Davi unhooked his sleeve and slid his fingers along the sheet, then stopped. To be twice a fool might be tragic. Wary, he took the cloth to the window and searched it visually. The light glinted finally on something shiny—a slender needle, so fine and small as to be almost invisible. It had been hidden in the upper edge, where a man might run a hand into the point when he pulled the sheet over him.

Exhausted, the duke tossed the material into a corner and sat heavily on the bed, cross-legged, his hand clutching the Stone at his breast. It seemed impossible to live in a land where enemies, known and unknown, stood on every side, where another man's death might just as easily be your own. Sandaal D'Lelan had spent her entire life in this land. No wonder she found kindness and love suspect.

A knock at the door roused Davi from his thoughts. "Come," he called, uncertain whether to greet the caller as friend or enemy.

The man on the threshold was small and slender, with copious dark curls on his head. His large eyes, set deep in a swarthy face, seemed kind enough. Behind him stood servants with folded linens in their arms.

"Milord, I am Nials Haldrick, the palace physician. May we enter?"

"At your own risk," the duke said heavily.

Haldrick stepped inside, pale eyes filled with sympathy. "I asked that you be told to wait before entering your chambers—until I had tended the queen."

"A message I didn't receive. But as you see, I'm still alive."

"Ah . . ." The physician signaled the servants, and they entered, a half-dozen of them, to go over the room's furnishings and decorations with considerable care.

"There's a needle in that," Davi said quickly, when one man reached to gather up the discarded sheet. "And I don't think it was intended for sewing."

Nials Haldrick grimaced. "I apologize, milord. The palace guard have their own physicians, and I was informed of the death in this chamber only today." He gazed at the tiles. "It's one of my duties to make certain the palace is safe for the royal family. Unfortunately neither your apartments nor the king's were ready on your arrival. His Majesty will share the queen's chambers for the while, but you were given these less than adequate rooms. I'm grateful you recognized the danger."

"No matter," Davi said tonelessly.

"But it does. May I examine milord?"

"Why?"

"My duty . . ." The physician came forward to take Davi's chin in hand and tilt his head to the afternoon light. Next he examined the duke's teeth with gentle fingers.

"Are you sure you're not a horse doctor?" Davi demanded.

Nials laughed. "Quite sure. Your gums are pale, milord, your eyes discolored. As with the others, you suffer dehydration and exposure. I have elixirs to replenish your body, but rest is the most important thing." Around him, the servants had finished, leaving the bed made, the chambers neat and tidy and hopefully danger-free. "Supper will be at dusk in the main dining hall, if you feel up to it. Otherwise, order a meal brought here and sleep." The physician waved one young white-robed servant to him. "This is Rauly, an apprentice of mine. He'll attend you personally, taste your foods, and guard your rest."

Despite Haldrick's kindness, Davi felt contrary. Besides, a manservant underfoot would seriously interfere with any work in the *Book of Stones*.

"I don't want him."

Nials frowned. "You find him somehow disagreeable? Perhaps another . . ."

"No. I've my own men to serve me."

"Milord, here in the guards' quarters, the supplies cannot be as closely monitored. Rauly is trained in the detection of tainted or blemished foods, while your own servants are not. Please. The royal family holds you in high regard. For their sake, accept my apprentice."

"I said no, but thank you all the same. If you plan to protect me, then get my apartments ready as quickly as possible." Davi returned to the bed, feeling far more uneasy than he'd let on to the physician. "Thank you for your diligence, Lord Haldrick, but I'll rest now."

"The elixirs—"

"Leave them outside the door."

Unhappy, Nials bowed with the others and took himself from the room.

*　*　*　*　*

Raf D'Gular returned to his father's house on upper Potters Street in the late afternoon—more than a little drunk on wine and anger. A young female slave elevated his wrath by refusing to bring him more wine.

"The master's orders," Lisi said, fear in her eyes. Raf had mishandled her more than once, but her fear of his father was stronger.

"Where is the old bastard?"

"Upstairs, milord, readying himself for council. He says you're to get ready as well."

"And Kyl?"

"In the library, milord."

"What for? He can't read." Pleased with his own humor, Raf tottered up the staircase to his room, chuckling.

He hated his half brother, Kyl, for many good reasons, but mostly because he was a king's bastard son and everyone's hope for power. He hated Kyl almost as much as he hated his domineering father and his catty sisters. And his mother, who'd produced a contender to the Xenaran throne, then married Raf's father. Kyl, of all of them, was hardly to blame—just a huge dim-witted lout, bewildered by it all—but Raf still hated him on principle.

His clothes had been laid out, rich silk breeks and lawn shirt, with a light dress jacket, which would still be uncomfortable. The night was warm, and while the palace remained cool, the crowded council chamber would not be. Raf found an open bottle of wine stashed in his closet, an old one, a little vinegary, but it was something to drink while he dressed and thought.

She was pretty, this Jessmyn D'Gerric. No, beautiful. Her hair had glinted red-gold in the sunlight this morning. She'd left a throne in the north to die for one in the south. What stupidity. What a waste. And Sandaal had sat there near the Wynnamyran queen, dark and lovely in her own right. Raf had fancied the girl for a while, but she remained aloof, which only made her all the more desirable.

There were voices below in the entry hall. He straightened his clothes as best he could and followed the patterned carpet back to the stairs. From there the voices led him down to the library. The room was packed with the leaders of some of the richest houses in the land; Troya, Brennar, Layne, and Aikim, all aligned to the House of Gular in their bid to put Kyl on the throne. No one took notice of Raf when he entered—except his father, who frowned at his youngest son's disheveled appearance. Kyl sat in a corner, his full lips tucked in a pout.

"Harren," Stef D'Layne growled, his beefy face red in the lamplight, "you promised us she'd never arrive in Zankos."

"And when do I ever make such foolish promises?" Raf's father demanded. "I told you we'd do our best to stop the Wynnamyran queen, to give her good reason to stay at home. The attempt in Mill Town failed, but we've other resources."

Damin of Aikim shook his head. "Sailors aren't suited to

assassin's work. And to scatter a whole crew through the town to wait and hope for a chance at a prince borders on idiocy."

"Hindsight is a marvelous talent," Harren said with asperity. "Chances are something I'll gladly take. Perhaps you wish to rethink your membership here?"

D'Aikim shook his head once more, mouth clamped shut in anger.

Harren gazed at the others. "Jessmyn D'Gerric sits in the palace, and D'Ar has the upper hand at the moment. But I remind you, gentlemen, we still have someone close to the queen, someone who'll do our bidding, so the game isn't lost yet." Raf's father took a sip from a cup, smiling. "We'll keep our work subtle for the while. If that fails to convince the Wynnamyran royal family to return to Castlekeep, then our accomplice will be convinced to sacrifice herself to gain our ends."

Her? Raf's ears pricked. Who? Who could it be? But these cagey old men would keep their secrets to themselves. Never mind, Raf would find the answer on his own. It must be a servant or a lady-in-waiting, suborned by his father with promises of wealth or a marriage contract, perhaps even to Kyl, who would be a **king**. Across the room, his elder brother dug something from his ear, observed it with interest, then flicked it away and put the same finger in a nostril. Raf grinned. Oh, what a lovely husband Kyl would make—what a grand lord and monarch.

\* \* \* \* \*

Outside the council chambers, Eowin D'Ar steeled himself for the ordeal to come. Exhaustion threatened to overtake him, but he'd swallowed a cautious dose of Girkin's wonderful potion. It had eased the pain in his joints considerably and made him both lightheaded and clear-minded. An odd contradiction in terms. Somehow the Grand Envoy must not only conduct this meeting, but also control it as well, not an easy task for so elderly a man after weeks of travel.

The great houses of Xenara had assembled on a moment's

notice. None dared miss tonight's gathering, and while most resided here in the rebuilt portions of Zankos, some had left their homes in Katay and even Birne on the southern coast of the Inland Sea to wait impatiently for the envoy's return. Now they sat within the council chamber, no doubt even more impatient.

"I want water—cold water—brought to the dais," Eowin ordered, and a young male slave with the mark of the royal house tattooed on one smooth cheek rushed off to obey. D'Ar, robes perfect, face serene, stepped across the threshold.

The rumble of private conversation died abruptly, replaced by an expectant silence. Mounted high on the walls, oil lamps in glass chimneys cast a steady light, and chandeliers filled with hundreds of candles blazed overhead. Heat mixed with the strong scents of expensive perfume and sweat offended the nose. Eowin strode to the dais with its low ceremonial fence and allowed a servant to open the gate for him. Three short steps brought him to the lectern.

Along the wall, the aristocratic houses were similarly sectioned off by fences. The D'Gulars had taken a station closest to the entrance, attended by the houses in sympathy with them. Harren affected boredom, while Kyl sat placidly. They'd dressed their hopeful bastard halfling king in fine clothes, but that did nothing to hide the man's empty blue eyes and dull expression. Behind them, Raf leaned forward in his chair, thoroughly engrossed, his fingers idly twisting one side of his long, narrow mustache. Now, there was the bright one in the family. Unfortunately it was a sick, cruel intelligence.

Cold water arrived and was placed before the envoy. He took a sip and let his gaze sweep over the lines of seated men. Olanden and Sandz were there among a dozen others that sided with them and supported their bids for the throne. But there were empty areas, and that brought a deep satisfaction to the old man.

"Well," he said finally, voice clear and strong despite his weariness. "I see our numbers have thinned somewhat. Only three contenders left. If I'd waited a while longer to return, perhaps there'd be none."

"Perhaps," Harren rumbled, "you shouldn't have returned at all, D'Ar."

That brought a murmur of displeasure from the few houses that favored the envoy.

"Where is she?" called Kij, head of the Makalan house. "Why isn't she here, this daughter of Roffo?"

"The queen and her children sleep this night—while we try to settle our differences," Eowin answered.

"And her butcher husband?" demanded Stef D'Layne. "Where's he?"

Rage tightened the envoy's jaw, but he forcibly relaxed. "Don't speak to me of butchers, D'Layne. You left three infant daughters on the plain to die, so you might claim a firstborn son."

Stef leaped to his feet. "My right!" he shouted. "By Xenaran law!"

"An ancient law, a barbarian one. Sit down! The palace guard stands outside the door. One word from me and you'll be expelled from this meeting." Under the force of Eowin's gaze, D'Layne backed into his chair and sat.

"Listen to me," the envoy said carefully after another sip of water. "You cannot deny your own guilt in the destruction of Zankos . . . any of you, of us. We brought war to Wynnamyr, and Gaylon Reysson defended his land. Accept that judgment or not, but be forewarned . . . the man is truly a sorcerer. Antagonize him at your own risk."

That didn't set well with any of them. D'Ar let the crowd settle, then spoke again. "Jessmyn D'Gerric, by right of blood, is your queen, but you have far more to gain than that. I've watched her these past weeks. . . . She'll bring to the throne all the strength and intelligence of her father, tempered by the grace and capacity to love that was her mother's. Under her the country will thrive, and one day it will also thrive under her son. Let's stop bickering amongst ourselves and be grateful something of Roffo lives on."

Harren broke the silence that followed.

"We don't want your queen, old man," D'Gular said with vehemence. "She may be Roffo's blood, but she was raised in

Wynnamyr. She knows nothing of us, of our government, of our economy." Harren glared around him. "We won't be ruled by the queen of Wynnamyr, or through her, by her husband. And we reject her son as well."

That brought more angry grumbles from the group of noblemen. Eowin felt what small control he held over them slipping.

"Then, Harren D'Gular," the envoy said coldly, "you're welcome to find another country more to your liking. That goes for the lot of you. The coronation of Jessmyn D'Gerric has been set for two days hence. What you deny, the people of Xenara have taken to their hearts. All your half-blooded claims mean nothing against a true daughter of Roffo."

D'Gular stood slowly. "You conniving old fool. Do you honestly think you've won? And don't count overmuch on Gaylon Reysson. He may be a sorcerer, but a sorcerer is also a man, and men have weaknesses. Put the lady on our throne and see what happens. This is far from over." He stepped out onto the floor and strode to the exit, his family and his allies close on his heels.

The chamber emptied steadily then, and D'Ar could feel the overwhelming hatred in the air. The house of Ar and its sympathizers lingered behind, but the envoy, too tired to offer comfort or encouragement, waved them out. In the emptiness, he finally allowed himself to sag against the lectern, a frail ancient man. Of course Harren would fight back. Eowin had expected no less.

The aristocracy had a choice now—to continue to fight among themselves or join forces against the queen. Unfortunately, of the bunch, it would be D'Gular and his idiot stepson who would win out. The Grand Envoy gathered what strength was left in him and started for the door. He would see the queen safely installed on the throne, but beyond that, his powers would be limited. This body, crippled with old age, could not be driven so hard for much longer, even with Girkin's potion.

\* \* \* \* \*

Nials stood a moment longer, watching the queen. She had gone to sleep almost instantly, even with a stranger in the room. Such a small frail body for so strong a heart, but then Queen Jarath had been delicate, too. At supper, the royal family had eaten little, though the food had been plentiful. Perhaps it was the exotic dishes, so different to their tongues, that stayed their appetites.

The physician smiled to himself. Robyn, the little prince, had had his share of sweet sesame cakes, though, until the children's new nanny, Bessi, stopped him. What a charming creature the tiny boy was—unlike his older brother, who remained quiet and aloof, suspicious of his surroundings and the people in them. The king of Wynnamyr had behaved in much the same manner as his heir. The duke of Gosney hadn't appeared at all.

It was Nials's duty to taste the food brought to the queen and her family, for he had an extensive knowledge of poisons, their tastes and odors. Tonight he'd rejected two meat dishes because their flavors were slightly off. Not poisoned, the man felt certain, but improperly prepared or stored, which made them just as dangerous. The kitchen staff would have to be chastised.

Jessmyn D'Gerric sighed in her sleep and turned, brow furrowed. Her hip still pained her despite the physician's careful manipulations. It frustrated him to be unable to heal the injury immediately, but the damage was a fortnight old. Finally Nials signaled to Sandaal D'Lelan, who sat in the shadows near the foot of the queen's bed. The young woman followed him to the exit.

Guards stood in the hall to either side of the door, silent and unmoving. The physician bade Lady Sandaal good night, then went his own way through the palace. He'd heard the sound of distant voices, which meant the council meeting had ended already. Now he must tend the Grand Envoy.

The old man's chambers lay within the royal sector, and Haldrick knocked on the door lightly. Some time passed before D'Ar responded. Then his gravel voice called, "Enter."

"What's this?" Nials asked, sniffing carefully at the cup

beside the bed, where the envoy sat on the edge of an elevated mattress.

"Something you no doubt would disapprove of," the elderly man answered testily. "How is the queen?"

The palace physician smiled at the memory. "Nearly as feisty as you, milord. I checked the children as well. They're all suffering from exhaustion and dehydration from the journey over the plain, but will recover quickly enough." Nials stuck a fingertip into the cup, then touched it to his tongue. His nose wrinkled in distaste. "They'll recover more quickly than you if you continue to use these medicinal draughts. Jimson uses the body hard."

"I'm well aware of that."

"Then why?"

"I do what I must." Eowin D'Ar waved that subject off. "What do you think of her, Nials? Give me your fair judgment."

"The queen?"

"Is she fit to rule?"

The physician frowned. To judge someone at the first meeting went against his grain. "I find her young, but very bright. Well educated, considering, and extremely sensitive. If she lives long enough, she'll make a fine monarch."

"I need your help, Nials."

Nials didn't like the desperation in the old man's voice. "You have only to ask, milord."

"You must keep her safe . . . and the children. I can't go on much longer. . . ." His voice faded away.

"Rest, milord." The physician pulled the sheets back on the bed, then turned the envoy and pressed him into the mattress, worried. With gentle fingers, he found the pressure points on head, hands, and feet that would ease D'Ar's pain—at least for a little while.

# Ten

Davi had not come to supper the evening before, nor did he appear this morning for the sumptuous meal laid out for the royal family in one of the many inner courtyards. Gaylon felt a touch of annoyance at his duke's absence, but the palace physician had tended to the young man in the late afternoon yesterday and proclaimed him well, though extremely tired. They were all tired, for that matter.

Sandaal served the queen, whose eyes remained red and dark-circled, while Katina and Rose served the irritable young princes their breakfasts. The king, his eyes no less puffy than his wife's, filled his own plate with strange unknown dishes despite the three servants who hovered over him, uncertain what to do.

Her duties done for the moment, Sandaal took a seat near the queen and served herself small portions of food. Across the table from her, Nials Haldrick watched the children with a faint amusement on his face. The Grand Envoy had also failed to appear for the meal, but that was certainly understandable at his age. It would be several days before Eowin had recovered from the long journey south and his night in the council chambers. Even so, according to the physician, the old man was determined to direct Jessmyn's ascension to the throne from his bed.

Robyn stared at his plate, a frown on his full lips. "What's this?"

"Rice with curried fish, milord," Kat said from beside him.

"But where're the eggs? Where's my porridge?" the boy demanded.

"In Xenara, people break their fast with other foods." Rose leaned to fill the youngster's cup with a dark, thick concoction of cinnamon and cocoa. This was much more to the child's liking, since the drink was heavily sweetened with honey.

Gaylon glanced at Thayne. The heir to the throne of Wynnamyr carefully separated the rice from the fish on his plate, but tasted neither. The anonymous piles on the king's plate looked no more appetizing.

Finally Nials took note. "Our new royal family ate little last night, and it seems they eat little this morning. I think perhaps I'll arrange for the kitchen to try to prepare more familiar foods for you—until your palates grow accustomed to Xenaran fare."

"Thank you," Jessmyn said with obvious gratitude, though she had stoutly forced down her own breakfast. "That would be very kind."

She caught her husband's gaze and smiled, tired, swollen eyes lit from within. Since the king's chambers were unfinished, the two had shared a bed last night for the first time in many weeks. Gaylon smiled back, feeling a small rush of heat to his cheeks. She still affected him that way after so many years of marriage—made him feel young and awkward and eager.

A clatter of boot heels in one of the antechambers drew the king's attention. Fitzwal and Toad arrived with three of the palace guard, and from the look on the face of Davi's old retainer something must be wrong.

"Sire." The sergeant bowed deeply.

"Come, Fitzwal. What is it?"

Fitzwal led Toad to the table. "It's milord duke, Sire. He won't answer our knocks, and his apartment door is locked. The chamberlain's master key can't seem to open it neither."

"Was he given a sleeping draught?" Gaylon looked at the physician.

"No, Your Highness," Nials answered. "As I said last night,

he was tired but well when I left him."

A sudden anxiety gripped the king, and outrage followed. "This godsforsaken land! He was well last night, but who knows what's found him since? Davi should never have been put in military quarters."

"We . . . we didn't expect either of you to accompany the queen," the physician stammered. His face had drained of color even as Gaylon's Stone flared an angry blue. "The palace is far from rebuilt. There's so much yet to do."

"I don't want excuses, Haldrick. I want help." The king caught Fitzwal's shoulder. "Take me to him."

Thayne clambered out of his chair. "I want to come, too."

"No," his father snarled. "You're safest here."

Even Rose D'Jal had half risen, pretty eyes filled with worry, but Sandaal reacted not at all, her expression cool and disinterested. Gaylon had no time to contemplate either young woman's behavior. Hurriedly he pushed Nials Haldrick toward the exit after the sergeant and Toad. Fear nagged at the king as they followed wide corridors.

This part of the palace housed only servants and guards. Though clean and spacious and newly refurbished, it was somehow a little darker, a little less fine. Morning found the halls and chambers teeming with those intent upon their early chores. Slippers whispered on the tiles and long robes rustled. Somewhere incense burned. Fitzwal paused finally before a thick wooden door, but no one answered his knock or Nials's.

The chamberlain's key was tried again to no avail. Toad, once an accomplished thief, took a thin bladed dirk to the lock. Nothing worked. At last the king took hold of the latch and felt an icy tingle in his hand. The Stone in the ring on his finger flickered rhythmically. The lock had been magically reinforced somehow. No wonder the key wouldn't open the door.

"Stand away," he murmured and drew on his Sorcerer's Stone gently.

The door could always be destroyed, but it would be easier to counter the subtle spell on the mechanism. A twisting spiral thread of blue spun off the Stone and into the keyhole.

Behind him, Nials Haldrick drew a heavy breath, though Gaylon hardly noticed. The lock snicked, and the door creaked open.

Fitzwal pushed it wide. Morning sunlight did not reach these chambers, and the king searched the gloom. Davyn Darynson lay on a thick mattress in the bedchamber, silent and unmoving, as Gaylon came near. The young man's right hand clutched something on a golden chain against his chest. That fact failed to register at first.

The physician crowded close to lay two fingers on Davi's throat, searching for the beat of a heart.

"Is he . . . ?" The question wouldn't form on Gaylon's lips, the thought too unbearable, but this was a dead man's face, he knew. An internal grief numbed the king.

"He lives," Haldrick muttered. Gently he raised one of Davi's eyelids and peered into the wide, dark pupil, then inspected the duke's fingernails. His nose close to Davi's, he inhaled the unconscious man's breath in search of some faint odor, anything that might tell them what had happened.

"Is it poison?" Fitzwal demanded.

The physician shook his head, perplexed. "I can find no true symptoms of poison or drugs. It's as if he sleeps, only so deeply that he can't hear us." He looked at Gaylon. "Such a sleep must have a cause, though—a blow to the head, a severe illness, or a potion."

Sleep. The king touched the golden chain on Davi's chest, then tugged at it. The duke's grip was iron. Whatever he held in his hand, he wouldn't readily let go of it. Magic. In the dim chamber, Gaylon turned. A chest sat open near one wall, the contents spilled across the floor. The king's Stone began a steady shine as he approached the chest. Within the trunk, a copy of the *Book of Stones* lay under tangled clothing. Blue light glinted off the gilded edges of the pages, off the beaten gold that decorated the heavy wooden cover.

"What is it, milord?" Nials asked.

"The source of our troubles," Gaylon answered bitterly. "The duke sleeps, all right. And he Dreams. Davi has a Sorcerer's Stone."

Fitzwal's brow wrinkled. "No, Sire! I would know if that were so."

"How? It's obvious he's kept it secret. Even from me." Anger welled in Gaylon's chest. "This *Book of Stones* looks far older than mine. It and the Stone must have been the gift that King Zorek brought to Castle Gosney. Only how and why?"

"At least there's no need to worry," Nials said, "if this is a magical sleep he's induced himself."

"Only if he has the power to find his way home. If he even remembers to return." The king had come to the bed once more. Carefully he reached out through his Stone to the other clutched in the young man's right hand. It rejected him with an almost savage jolt of energy, and Gaylon winced at the fiery pain that shot through his own hand. He gazed at Davi's slack features. "Fool! Why didn't you tell me? How can I help you now?"

This must have been how Daryn had felt when Gaylon, just a boy, had wandered away in Dreaming—frustrated and helpless. A thousand thousand worlds awaited the Dreamer, and time meant nothing in that place. The king remembered his own joy of freedom and discovery. Everything else forgotten, he'd laughed and played and shouted among the stars. And might have died there, too.

"We'll take him to his own chambers," Gaylon said.

"Milord," Nials objected. "The plastering isn't done and the apartment is unfurnished yet."

"Then order a bed immediately. Go! All of you."

Fitzwal hesitated on the threshold. "Sire . . ."

"Do as I ask. The duke's rooms are across from mine. I'll meet you there. Send someone back to carry the trunk there."

Alone, Gaylon contemplated his unknowing companion, the slow rise and fall of his chest. Davi had survived the Xenaran war, and for these past years, the king had rightfully considered him a man. At a closer look, though, the duke's face had still not thinned with maturity; the skin remained smooth and unlined. How old? Twenty now. Gods, a boy yet in so many ways.

Davi had inherited this magical bent from his father, and all

this time, the king knew, he'd longed for a Sorcerer's Stone of
his own. And all this time Gaylon had hoped that his duke
would never find one. Such power was fraught with dangers,
to the soul as well as the body. Better if the duke had never
tasted that power, but it was far too late now.

The king slipped one arm under Davi's shoulders, the other
under his knees, and lifted him nearly as easily as one of his
own sons. Lost in Dreaming, the young man might never
return. His body would waste away in time and ultimately fail,
and then the duke of Gosney must be buried in Zankos, far
from family and home.

* * * * *

The first ecstatic rush of flight had faded, and Davi found
himself alone in darkness, floating without direction. Distant
pinpoints of colored light shone with a steady gleam before
him. Stars, he thought. Behind him lay only empty depths.

"Orym!" the duke shouted soundlessly into the void, knowing there would be no answer.

The Dark King had shown him how to let the Stone pull
him into Dreaming, but in his eagerness, Davi had forgotten
to ask Orym how to return. There were other worlds, the
ancient spirit had promised, worlds beyond number, that
awaited a young sorcerer's exploration. The thought had
proven irresistible after being denied the Stone's power for so
long.

That first step had been difficult, though. To Dream, one
must release his hold on the body that ties him so firmly to
this world—a small death of sorts. Davi had overcome the
fear, determined to gain this new and fascinating skill. Over
the long weeks of the journey, he'd begun to believe himself
already an accomplished sorcerer. Now it seemed those memories might have been a little gilded by overconfidence.

The emptiness hemmed him in, and a small touch of panic
seized him. No. The Stone's powers were his. Davi brought
the pendant up before his eyes and stared into the blue glow,
willing himself home. The Stone obeyed, but not as he

expected. Swirling darkness faded in the warmth of an oil lamp.

His mother sat on the edge of her narrow cot, sewing. Her thimble twinkled in the light, and she held the cloth close to her face, green eyes squinting. Age and failing sight had slowed her.

"Mum?" Davi said gently, afraid to startle her, but she didn't stir, only continued her careful stitches.

Such a cold, stern woman. His childhood had been barren of affection, yet he'd never doubted her harsh love. It struck him then that Sandaal D'Lelan was much like his mother, every emotion held tightly in check. Why? Why were they afraid of love? Davi watched his mother with new eyes and understood finally. She had never feared love, but only the loss of it. The pain had proven too much, and so it was with Sandaal.

The duke closed his eyes, saddened, and opened them in another chamber. Unknowing, he'd willed himself elsewhere, and the Stone had obeyed his innermost wish. The sweet, rich voice reached him first, blended with the voice of a mandolin. The duke looked across a wide room bathed in late morning light to where Sandaal D'Lelan sat cross-legged on the end of Robyn's bed. Copper hair mussed, the little prince struggled against sleep, but was already hopelessly lost in the song.

Davi found himself hopelessly lost in the woman's dark beauty. The sight and sound of her brought such terrible longing. Somehow, someday, he must convince Lady D'Lelan that love was worth any risk. Her voice faded, and she turned slowly, eyes searching the shadows of the room.

"Milady," the young man said gently, but she seemed to look beyond him and didn't react to his voice.

Dream . . . He wished himself away again, only this time to somewhere beyond these sorrows. The Stone answered with dizzying swiftness, and the void closed in once more. Darkness flowed around him endlessly, bringing a wild sense of speed. Among those distant pinpoints of light, one grew brighter, a golden glow that turned eternal night to everlasting day.

It occurred to Davi that he should be afraid. The yellow sun rushed toward him, a great roiling ball of flame, then he'd plunged into it, arms flung up over his face. Slowly the young man opened his eyes again. Fire raged around and through him without pain, and yet he felt the incredible sensations of heat and grinding weight, of the continuous explosions of searing energy. Density brought resistance, and he paused at the core of the star.

Power . . . He'd never dreamt of such power, and now something more was happening. His sense of self began to meld with the internal forces around him until he'd joined this magnificent radiant orb, become one with the star. Content, Davi swirled and spiraled and sent tongues of flame dancing into the void. Then, with a last, voiceless shout, he flashed outward in every direction as a wave of light.

* * * * *

Jessmyn gathered her plum skirts and left the women protesting in her chambers. Several times each day she made this journey, and her own coronation wouldn't stop her now. The palace staff rushed along the corridors, offering quick obeisances as they passed. The queen hardly noticed, her mind on other things. Outside, the palace grounds were crowded with merchants and lords and their families, all come to see Jessmyn D'Gerric take her throne. And some, no doubt, hoping she'd trip and break her neck on the way.

Bare wall frames were still visible in the apartment across from her husband's, and the only bit of furniture was a long, low mattress. Davi lay on the bed, his hands on his chest, eyes closed. Rose sat on a cushion beside him.

"How is he?" Jessmyn asked.

The young lady-in-waiting looked up, face haggard and nearly as pale as Davi's. "No change, milady."

"It's kind of you to stay with him," the queen said gently and laid a hand on Rose's shoulder.

For the first time in ages, Gaylon had used his Stone to Dream, but it was a useless gesture. The universe had called the duke of Gosney, and without some idea of the direction taken, her husband might wander forever and never find this one lost Dreamer. It all seemed so hopeless, and Jessmyn felt a sudden urge for tears.

"You need to rest, Rose," she said finally. "I'll send someone to sit with Lord Gosney."

"It's no trouble, Highness," the girl protested. "Honestly. I doze off here. He should see a friendly face when he wakes."

A loving face, Jess thought with some frustration. Rose was sweet, but shallow, and hardly a suitable wife for Davi, yet Sandaal showed no interest in the duke at all. A breathless slave girl appeared in the open doorway.

"Your Majesty, Lord Eowin says to please come to the throne room. The ceremony must begin."

The queen lifted her chin. "Tell the Grand Envoy that he and all of Xenara may wait until my hair is done. Go!"

The young girl dropped a curtsey and fled away with her answer. Rose smiled bleakly up at Jessmyn.

"Lord Eowin will be upset."

"He's been nothing else these last four days," the queen replied. "It's a wonder he's lived so long." She paused on the threshold. "Don't worry, Rose. Our duke will return to us."

All the way back to her apartments, Jess forced herself to believe that. Madness reigned within the dressing chamber. No fewer than ten young noblewomen milled about in confusion, dressed in their own finest clothing. The queen spied Sandaal near the door to the bedroom, watching the chaos with her usual amusement. As always, she wore somber colors and little, if any, makeup, though her glossy black hair had been woven in intricate braids.

A half-dozen ladies pounced on the queen, brushes brandished in their hands. Jess shook them off irritably and pulled Sandaal into the bedroom, then closed the door.

"Milady?"

"Do you truly wish to sit through my whole boring coronation?"

"Of course," the young woman said stoutly, but her expression said otherwise.

Jessmyn turned away. "It's obvious to everyone that you have no feelings for the duke of Gosney, but it's equally obvious how the duke feels about you."

"Your Highness—"

"Wait until I'm done, please." The queen found the edge of the bed and sat. "Sorcery is a dangerous avocation, not to be dealt with lightly. Davi hasn't had his Stone for very long, and no one to train him. For some unknown reason, he thought to train himself, and now he's lost in Dreaming. There's a good chance he'll die. Those of us who love him have all tried to call him home, but I think you might be the one person he'll respond to." Near the door, Sandaal had paled. "Will you go to him for my sake . . . if not for his?"

Lady D'Lelan bowed her head. "I'll do anything you ask of me, Majesty."

"I suppose," Jess sighed, "that that's as much as I can hope for."

In the room beyond, Katina shooed away the overzealous ladies and tended to the queen's hair herself. A wet nurse carried Lilith into the bathing chamber, no doubt to change her diaper. This insanity could not be over too soon to suit Jessmyn. Finally they were ready, the queen's silken train gathered in a dozen gentle hands. She led them down the corridors, all but Sandaal, who had dutifully gone the other way.

The throne room was larger than Castlekeep's great hall and held three tiers of galleries, and though the sun had barely dawned outside, all three were packed. Already the air held the scents of sweat and strong perfume. Low voices rumbled like waves on a distant sea. Jessmyn stood frozen on the brink. A thick purple carpet marked a path over the tiles for her to follow. At the end were gleaming white marble steps and a throne of the same hard, cold stone.

Between her and the throne, she must face the crowd and the many priests and priestesses who spoke for the varied gods of Xenara—all but Mezon, the warrior god, who'd been destroyed by a mere man, a king named Gaylon Reysson. Jessmyn searched the faces around her in hope of seeing her husband, but he had wisely kept away.

At a signal from the Grand Envoy, the musicians began a slow, stately march. The voices of the people faded. Every eye was on her as the queen made her way along the carpet, but not every eye was friendly. The palace guard lined her way, tall and handsome and glittering with gold. Casual wealth lay in all directions, male and female equally decked out in gaudy jewelry and fashionable garb.

The first clutch of priests met her, and Jessmyn knelt to accept their blessings. Incense smoked in golden censers while she was anointed with oil on her forehead and hands. So it was with each of the other four major gods. The queen murmured her thanks to the holy men, though the names of their gods had already been forgotten. Since the destruction of Mezon, Xenara's priests had lost much of their power and influence within the court.

At last Jessmyn reached the dais and once more knelt, this time before the Grand Envoy. Silence had fallen in the huge chamber.

"To you is entrusted the fate of this land," the old man intoned in his gravelly voice. Heavy embroidered robes gave him an illusion of substance, though he seemed to tremble slightly under their weight. In gnarled fingers, Eowin clutched a petite crown of white gold, encrusted with rubies, emeralds, and diamonds. "To you are entrusted the lives of its people." He placed the crown upon her head. "Rule in peace, Jessmyn, daughter of the house of Gerric, daughter of Roffo and Jarath. Rule long and rule well."

The envoy helped the queen of Xenara to her feet, then led her up the stairs to the throne. Lord and merchant watched her closely as she took her father's broad seat, diminished by its size. They would think her small and weak, and Jessmyn must prove them wrong. Now Lord D'Ar brought a scepter of knobbed, polished ebony, unadorned. While the crown reflected her wealth, the scepter reflected her power of life and death over her people. Many a ruler before her had killed with a single blow.

"Come forward, my lords," Eowin called into the crowd of witnesses. "Come forward and swear fealty to your queen."

Only the leaders of the many houses had been placed near-est the throne so they might speak for their families. And after them would come the merchants who, lesser in status, still rivaled the aristocrats in power by virtue of their fortunes. The fact that merchant vied with merchant and noble family with noble family kept the power structure in constant flux. Alliances formed and failed and formed again. Court life here would be anything but sedate.

Jessmyn watched the first group brought to the foot of the dais. Each man in turn went to one knee and mouthed the words that bound him by honor to the queen of Xenara. They bore gifts as well—books, fine silks, perhaps the ownership papers of a well-bred horse. Many were toys for the royal chil-dren. The queen took note of the gifts and oaths honestly given, but also recognized the halfhearted gestures and those offered with disdain. Their faces and names would be remem-bered.

"Your Majesty, may I present Harren of the House of Gular and baron of Gulcrest," the envoy said.

His tone made Jessmyn look at the man below carefully. D'Gular, his dark hair streaked with silver, was tall, nearly Gaylon's height, but double her husband's size. Lord Harren put one knee on the bottom step and bowed his head only slightly. His deep voice boomed in the chamber.

"I accept Jessmyn, daughter of Roffo, as the queen of Xenara. So long as she lives."

Behind him, the onlookers raised brows and began a trou-bled murmur. Jessmyn, her heart thudding in her chest, man-aged a cold smile for the baron.

"Such a man deserves to speak his mind," she said. "Come, milord, and offer your honest counsel."

Harren sneered, then took the stair, almost causing the Grand Envoy a fit of apoplexy. The queen ignored his outrage and waved away the two guards who started toward the throne. D'Gular arrived, the sneer replaced by a conspiratorial grin. He laid his right hand on the great marble arm of the throne and leaned close to whisper.

"You're a lovely wench, more's the pity. This is my counsel—take your children and flee, if you would have them live." Harren glanced around. "Where's the king? But then, he need only rule you and Xenara from the bed."

The queen's reaction caught everyone by surprise, including herself. With a strength far beyond what she normally possessed, Jessmyn slammed a crushing blow against the baron's hand with the dense wooden knob of the scepter. He screamed, toppled backward, and fell down the stairs.

Now his wails turned to a muffled agony, and Jessmyn's stomach churned. The crunch of bone still echoed in her head. But none of her regret was allowed to show. Instead, she stood up, chin held high, and looked out on her subjects.

"Hear me! I alone rule Xenara. Honest counsel will always be considered, deception and disrespect will be dealt with harshly." Jessmyn watched the silent faces. "The next time, I will strike to kill." She sat again on hard, cold marble, the scepter across her lap. "Who is next?"

Someone had come to help Harren D'Gular away, and the rest of the lords approached one by one. There were subtle changes in their attitudes, though, a new deference in their stances. The queen accepted the honors and gifts offered, while the faint trembling in her limbs persisted. Only let this day be done, only let her return to her chambers and gather her family around.

\* \* \* \* \*

Rose had left reluctantly, and Sandaal found herself alone in the room with the duke of Gosney, her mandolin in hand. This was a useless gesture on the queen's part. Davi lay as dead, his body an empty shell, and nothing Sandaal could do would change that. She wandered across the bare tiles. The chamber held nothing but the mattress, a battered trunk, and a box of tools left behind by a plasterer.

One wall opened up on a wrought-iron balcony, and the view of the Inland Sea caught her attention for a time. Gulls swooped over the glittering waters, feeding on schools of tiny fish. Beyond them, tall-masted ships slid eastward toward the docks, their sails furled, their slave crews hard at the oars.

"Can you smell the salt air?" Sandaal asked Davi without hope of an answer. The silence angered her somehow. "What in all the universe can possibly compare with this? Adventure lies on every hand, Davyn Darynson. Only a fool would leave this life willingly—not with music to play and songs to sing. Not with love to win or lose." She moved back to the bed. "Sorcery is an illusion of power, nothing more. It's mostly pretty tricks and nonsense. What has magic ever done for Gaylon Reysson but bring him sorrow? And I promise you, it will only bring him more."

"True enough," someone said.

The duke lay unmoving, face lifeless and empty. Sandaal turned toward the entrance where the king of Wynnamyr stood. His sandy hair was ruffled, his clothing in disorder, and he gripped a squat green bottle of brandy in one hand. More than anything, she noticed the pain behind his hazel eyes.

"Majesty," Lady D'Lelan murmured and curtsied. For once the old hatred wouldn't surface. She had never seen him drunk and vulnerable—a troubled man and not a monster. "Would you prefer to be alone with him?"

Gaylon rocked unsteadily. "No. My wife is being crowned a second time, my duke is lost in Dreaming, and I most definitely don't want to be alone." He found the bed and collapsed on the end of it, just missing Davi's feet. "You seem to understand the price of sorcery better than most."

"Not really," Sandaal dared to answer. "I only hoped to convince Davi that this world is worth living in."

"Is it?"

That gave her pause. "Sometimes . . ."

"Arlin enjoyed living." The king took a swig from his bottle. "So I killed him twice."

"You're being cruel," Lady D'Lelan accused, hating the pain his words brought.

"I am. Tomorrow I'll regret it . . . but now I don't care. You should hate me. I want you to."

"Would that make you feel better? Ease your guilt?"

"It might."

"What if I told you I loved you instead?" Sandaal gazed back across the balcony.

"I would say that you were being cruel."

"Then we've hurt each other enough for one day. I'll leave you here, milord." She reached for her mandolin.

Groaning, Gaylon heaved himself to his feet. "No. There's nothing I can do for him." He found his way to the door, then paused to look back. "Love me?"

Sandaal saw the confusion in his eyes and felt cold satisfaction. Let him wonder. The king used the door frame to push himself out into the corridor, and she listened to his uneven steps fade.

# Eleven

A huge reception and banquet had been planned for after the coronation, but Gaylon knew Jessmyn hoped to have time for a respite before the festivities. The king of Wynnamyr retired to his wife's empty chambers and waited. While he waited, he drank—something he hadn't done in excess since before the Xenaran war. The anger and self-loathing had returned, though, seemingly a thousandfold. Fate had once more taken control of his life, leading him in unknown and terrifying directions . . . where even a sorcerer went blind.

His inability to help Davi only pulled Gaylon deeper into the morass. Daryn's loss had nearly destroyed the king. To lose Davi now would be unbearable. This was Zorek of Lasony's fault—the meddling old fool. Gods curse him. Angry and frustrated, the king stretched out on Jessmyn's bed, boots and all, and watched the afternoon light from the overhead grating move slowly across the tiles.

Sandaal's statement had only confused him more. Her love was the last thing he expected or wanted. Such a strange, unfathomable young woman, as mysterious as Arlin had been open. Davi was the one who needed her love, that much had become obvious on the journey to Zankos. The lad had managed to keep his Stone a secret, but not his feelings for Lady D'Lelan.

The bottle drained, Gaylon set it aside. He'd never really doubted Jessmyn's abilities to rule, even a nation as huge and complex as Xenara. What he'd never taken into consideration was the fact that she'd want to. Here Gaylon Reysson was nothing more than a consort to a queen, a bitter draught to swallow, but the only alternative was leave his family at risk for a lonely reign in Wynnamyr. The king considered with irritation just how much effort it would take to find another bottle of brandy.

"Milady has surpassed every expectation. . . ."

The outer door had opened, and Eowin D'Ar's voice floated in from the main chamber. Jessmyn answered.

"I maimed a man," she said with low fury and distress. "For life."

"Yes," the envoy agreed. "But if you hadn't struck D'Gular down for his insults, he and his followers would have gained much greater support among the houses. You met his challenge and proved yourself a force to be reckoned with."

"Enough. Go away, Eowin."

"I'll send for your ladies-in-waiting, Majesty."

"No. Just let them wait. I'll call for them when I'm ready."

"Milady, don't dwell overmuch on this incident. You have performed magnificently."

"Please, Lord D'Ar. Get out."

"Yes, milady. Of course, milady." The envoy's tone held amusement.

Gaylon heard the apartment door close, then a rustling of silky material. The queen entered the bedchamber, her long train folded over an arm, her face stormy—until she saw her husband.

"My lord . . ."

"My love," Gaylon said. "What's this I hear? My wife resorts to violence?" He eyed the black scepter she carried.

"I'm not in the mood for teasing." Jessmyn flung the scepter onto the bed beside the king.

"I wouldn't tease about that. I remember once you killed a man to save my life. You're much stronger than you realize."

The queen sank to the edge of the mattress. "I crushed Harren D'Gular's hand—without a thought. It was as if something came over me, something cold and pitiless."

"Self-preservation is a very powerful instinct, my lady. Your father was a hard but honest ruler. In some ways, you're very like him." Gaylon struggled to sit up, then wrapped clumsy arms around his wife.

She pushed him away abruptly. "You stink of brandy."

"With excellent reason."

The queen eyed the empty bottle on the floor. "Gaylon Reysson, what are you doing? Don't desert us now."

"I hadn't planned on going anywhere."

"That's not what I mean, and you know it." Now Jessmyn reached out to gather him in her arms. "I know you're worried, but don't give up on Davi. He's much like Daryn, but very different, too. He's not afraid of magic. He will return to us."

Her certainty brought comfort somehow. Or perhaps it was her embrace. Gaylon pulled her face close to his and found comfort in her kiss. He longed for something more, but the queen once again pushed him firmly away.

"We need to get ready for the banquet."

"We?"

Jessmyn smiled. "It's time the court grew accustomed to your presence, my lord."

"The envoy won't agree."

"The envoy needn't. I'm the queen." Jess turned her shoulder, offering the tiny row of buttons that fastened the back of her gown. "Help me, please. Then go clean up. I need you beside me more than ever tonight."

\* \* \* \* \*

Feelings ran high among the houses that still followed Harren D'Gular. Outrage bound some of them all the tighter to D'Gular's purpose, but some had expediently found other alliances after Harren had suffered the new queen's wrath. From his place near the manse's upstairs railing, Raf watched the comings and goings with high interest. Below, a small crowd of grumbling men spilled out from the library and into the entry hall. His father was not among them. The physician tended him alone in his bedchamber, and the muffled shrieks of pain as the bones were set had finally ceased a short while ago.

Raf felt a delicious joy at his father's agony . . . and a strange sorrow. Harren was—had been—one of the finest swordsmen in Xenara, one of the finest bowmen, and with one blow, the queen had crippled him forever. She had badly miscalculated in that. A vengeful man, Harren would never quit until Jessmyn D'Gerric was dead and his own stepson on the throne.

"What're we gonna do?"

Kyl had arrived unnoticed, and Raf glanced up at the big man with faint disgust. Dressed in rumpled black satin, his brother's face still appeared smooth and childlike, though he was well into middle age. His round cheeks at the moment were sticky with what might be peach juice.

"We go to the banquet," Raf told him.

"Is Papa coming?"

"I doubt it."

"But we shouldn't—"

Raf took Kyl's elbow. "Don't worry, Brother. Let's clean you up. Then we'll go to meet the queen. You'll like that."

"She's very pretty," Kyl agreed, then frowned. "But she hurt Papa. Will she hurt me?"

"I won't let her," Raf said and led him into his bedroom.

Kyl took the dampened cloth offered and scrubbed at his face while Raf tried to tuck the satin shirt back into place. As a young child, Raf had loved this slow, gentle brother who had spent hours playing with him, but the years had pried them apart—that and Raf's resentment of Kyl's royal blood and his importance to their scheming father. Now Kyl represented a rare opportunity for Raf to meddle in Harren's affairs. That thought brought a deep pleasure.

"What do you think you're doing?" Stef D'Layne demanded of them at the foot of the stairs. The group of men milling around him in the hall grew silent.

"We're going to meet the queen," Kyl said happily. "And eat lots of food."

"No. Absolutely not." D'Layne's fingers closed on Kyl's arm. "We've decided in the absence of your father to forego the coronation banquet—as a protest." The others rumbled their agreement. "Let Jessmyn D'Gerric feel the anger of the most important houses in the realm."

Raf laughed outright. "She won't even miss the lot of you. Come, Kyl. We mustn't be late."

His brother only looked confused, but Stef's craggy face reddened.

"I forbid it!"

"*You* forbid it? In *my* house?" Raf laid a hand on the dagger at his belt.

"Your father—" D'Layne began to bluster.

"Is asleep in his chambers. Go wake him if you dare." Raf took Kyl's other arm. "Meanwhile, we're going to a banquet."

Stef snarled in frustration. "You blasted young pup! You'd put our heir to the throne in jeopardy for these foolish power games of yours?"

"What jeopardy?" Raf snarled back. "We're simply going to dinner."

"Then, by the gods, we'll all go!" D'Layne signaled to the others.

"Suit yourselves." Raf turned away to hide his grin.

He'd taken the reins from his unknowing father, and now the rest fell in line to follow him. It was all too easy. Outside, stableboys rushed to bring them saddled mounts. The palace grounds would be too packed for easy access with a carriage, and they were already late. Raf waited impatiently while Kyl was helped onto his horse, then they rode away down the narrow city street together, leaving his father's allies to scramble for their own mounts.

Zankos had only just been rebuilt over the past few years, yet the salt air had already aged the buildings. Rampant poverty had added its own patina of squalor, until this new city looked as old as the last. Kyl grinned at the children who played on the cobbles, bobbing his overlarge head in amusement. The front of his shirt was wet with sweat and drool.

Evening softened the heat somewhat, and shadows filled the canyonlike streets. Raf endured the stench of the raw sewage in the gutters. Twice he tossed coins to beggars along the way. Not very much money, but it would outrage his father should he ever find out. Petty rebellions behind the old man's back were all that his youngest son had been able to muster for most of his life. That was about to change.

The Milliners Street led the brothers in a winding route through the upper city, then down toward the Inland Sea at last. Below them, both sets of tall gates to the palace grounds were open. Raf observed the activity—the clutches of guards stationed throughout the area, the brightly clothed merchants and fashionable noblemen moving in separate groups toward the white marble palace.

"Good food?" Kyl asked, shifting in his saddle, doubt once more on his old-young face.

"Certainly." Raf turned his gelding onto the wide royal boulevard. "But I want you to behave, Kyl. Use your spoon and your napkin. And don't pick your nose."

"All right." The man's brow furrowed. "Will I be king, Raf? Like Papa says?"

The question startled Raf. "I don't know. Being king isn't nearly so nice as Papa wants you to believe. A baron's life is much better, I think."

"Then I want to be a baron."

"You should tell Papa that."

A sudden fear flashed in Kyl's eyes and faded again with whatever thought had brought it. He grinned and shook the reins, clucking to his horse. "I can smell sesame cakes!"

Raf sighed and let his brother lead the way. It had been easy to be jealous of the attention Kyl got from Harren, but now the resentment began to dissipate. To hate such a simple-minded man seemed foolish now. Kyl had been no better treated by his stepfather, and for that and other outrages, Raf would exact his own revenge.

Exuberant, Kyl pushed his way past lord and merchant and guard, and Raf followed. The fabulous scents of roasting meat reached them on the warm, dusty breeze. In time, their horses were taken away, and Kyl, apprehensive in the crush of the crowd, began to fidget.

"This way," Raf said gently and took his arm once more.

The flood of banqueters carried them across the grounds, through the courtyards, and into the main dining hall of the palace. A dozen tables, the entire length of the room, had been laid out with linens and golden dinnerware. Each place had been meticulously assigned by station and status. Raf led Kyl to the head of the table where his family's colors decorated the chairs and boldly took his father's seat. Kyl took the seat beside him, reaching immediately with both hands for the plates of appetizers.

"Sit back and behave," Raf growled.

His brother dropped the food, face crumpling. "I'm hungry."

"You're always hungry." But Kyl's tangible hurt made Raf take the man's plate and fill it carefully. "One at a time," he said and patted his brother's hand. "Eat slowly. Savor the tastes." Harren had never tried to groom Kyl for his royal role, nor teach him manners, long ago convinced this idiot son was incapable of learning. Kyl would, after all, be only a figurehead.

The last of the diners filed in and found their places. Conversation seemed friendly enough here on neutral ground, though merchant and nobleman had little to say to one another. Silence fell with the call of trumpets, and the queen of Xenara entered, attended by her ladies. Gaylon Reysson strode beside her in bright scarlet garb that clashed with his wife's beautiful violet gown. He eyed the crowd defiantly, one arm entwined in the queen's. The ring on his royal finger flashed a brilliant blue for an instant, and Kyl gasped.

"I want a ring," he said petulantly. "I want a pretty stone like that."

"Hush," Raf snapped. There were troubled murmurs up and down the line of tables.

Jessmyn carried the heavy ebony scepter that had crushed Harren's hand. This, too, caused a stir, but with it she signaled the servants, and great platters of food began to arrive. The lavish sights and smells distracted everyone, especially Kyl.

The guests were served first, something never done before. Whole beef carcasses were carried in, each stuffed with lamb, which were in turn stuffed with fowl. Raf had never seen anything quite so elaborate in the old king's court, but then he'd never seen a coronation feast. Roffo had ruled nearly fifty years.

The very best wines were poured—Wynnamyran vintages, aged to perfection, and behind it all came the strains of sweet music. At last the royal table was served and everyone began to eat. Raf filled Kyl's plate again and again, wondering how the man could possibly ingest so much food without getting ill. On his own plate, he took only small amounts of several dishes and ate slowly. The wine, however, proved his weakness, and he drank enough to lighten his head and his mood.

Raf ignored the pointed angry looks from Stef and his people at the next table. Finally the desserts arrived, incredibly rich yet somehow light. Kyl positively crowed with delight over them and soon had his face and the napkin tucked in his collar smeared with goo. The wine helped Raf let go of the embarrassment. They were half brothers, bound by blood, and Kyl could no more help what he was than Raf could.

Now the queen began to receive visitors at her table, a small but steady stream of petitioners seeking largess and small favors or offering gifts. Most were merchants with hopes of lower import taxes and higher status in the eyes of the new ruling family. Largo Mensen waddled up to the royal board, an immense man in height and weight. Mensen Trade Company was the biggest mercantile firm in the country. Wealth among the merchants was displayed in how well fed they and their families were. The wives were often as enormous as their husbands, the children round-faced.

The noblemen, on the other hand, showed their wealth in jewelry, fine clothing, and education, taking pride in slender, muscular bodies and quick minds—all except Kyl, of course, who could barely ride, let alone use sword and bow. "My little merchant," his mother had been fond of saying. Raf twisted the ends of his long mustache and watched Largo Mensen bow and fawn.

"Come," he said to Kyl and hastily pulled his brother's bib free, then cleaned his face as best he could. "Let's meet the queen."

The fear returned to Kyl's dull blue eyes. "I don't want to."

"I told you I'd keep you safe. Now come along." Raf pulled the man upright.

Mensen lumbered away just as Raf arrived. He took Kyl past the merchants already queued up, aware of their angry indignant looks. Flustered, the head chamberlain failed to introduce them.

"Your Majesties," young D'Gular said and bowed deeply to the queen. A sharp elbow in Kyl's side reminded him to bow.

Jessmyn D'Gerric widened her pale green eyes only slightly. "Are you always so rude, milord?"

"Always," Raf answered. "It's one of the many traits I inherited from my father."

"Who is . . . ?"

"Harren D'Gular."

Next to the queen, the king scowled, but Jessmyn's expression softened. "I'm very sor—"

"No, milady," Raf interrupted. "You must never apologize for your actions. King Roffo would have opened my father's head like a melon . . . but then Harren would never have dared to speak to him in such a manner."

The queen glanced down at her plate. "Thank you, Lord D'Gular. Is there something I might do for you?"

"You've already done more than you know." Raf grinned, then sobered abruptly. "No. There's something I wish to do for you. Beware of Largo Mensen, Highness. The man, I'm told, is set to take a competitor's trade company and has used illicit means to this end. He's a liar and a cheat and not to be trusted in the least."

"Oh?" Jessmyn said, amused. "But of course I can trust you. . . ."

Raf shook his head. "No, milady. I'm as untrustworthy as the rest of my countrymen. Perhaps it's something in the air we breathe." He leaned toward her, voice hushed. "Please, madam. This land isn't worth your life. Let the houses bring themselves to ruin, not you."

The king of Wynnamyr brought his right hand up in warning, and at the flash of blue from his ring, Kyl blundered forward, eyes huge.

"He means no harm," Raf said quickly, fearing the sorcerer's unpredictable nature. "Kyl, no . . ."

"It's pretty," his brother muttered, his gaze on the Stone. Then it shifted to Jessmyn. "You're pretty, too." His cheeks reddened suddenly, and he looked away.

"Thank you," the queen said, reaching out to touch the cloth of the big man's sleeve. "What are your names?"

"I'm Rafel," Raf answered for him. "This is Kyl, my half brother, milady . . . and yours. The one my father would put on the throne in your stead."

His answer disturbed her, but Jessmyn D'Gerric hid it well. "How good to meet you at last," she told Kyl with genuine warmth.

"I don't want to be a king," Kyl said, round eyes on the scepter beside the queen's plate. "I want to be a baron." Then he confided, "I'm not very smart."

"Some think I'm not very smart either," Jessmyn added.

Raf felt a pang at his brother's words. Slow-witted he might be, but his awareness of the fact stunned Raf. Tonight Kyl had shown a wide range of emotions—fear, anxiety, happiness. There was far more to Kyl than Raf would have believed. The brothers had been close once, until Raf had grown up and Kyl hadn't.

The queen's eyes had settled on Raf once more. "Thank you for your warnings, milord. Now, is there something I might do for you?"

"I had hoped to get your permission to dance with Lady D'Lelan tonight," Raf said, unable to think of anything else. "But she doesn't seem to be here."

Gaylon Reysson's expression grew even more grim, and young D'Gular wondered why. Before him, the queen smiled faintly.

"Sandaal was unable to attend tonight, but I'll tell her you asked after her. I'm sure she'll be pleased."

Raf doubted that, but he bowed again and took Kyl back to their seats at the table. The food and music lasted well into the night. Sometime near dawn, the king of Wynnamyr murmured in his tired queen's ear and left her alone at their table. Raf, more than a little drunk, watched him disappear into a corridor beyond a pair of palace guards.

Kyl had fallen asleep, head nestled on an elbow, his snores barely audible over the voices around them, and Raf envied him that unself-conscious peace. The Layne and Makalan clans still sat at their tables, unwilling to leave until the D'Gular brothers did—which was the only reason Raf, bored to death, had stayed so long. His father would hear of this, of his youngest son's audacity, of his quiet conversation with the queen. Harren would be outraged, but Raf no longer cared.

* * * * *

Thayne woke in the dark chamber, and for a brief moment, he imagined gray stone walls around him. But the night air was far too warm, the scents all wrong. Zankos. That brought a momentary ache of homesickness. Everyone was kind here, the servants and slaves, and many spoke Wynnamyran, though Katina had schooled Thayne in Xenaran on the journey here. Even little Robyn got his wants and needs across with a happy mixture of the two tongues.

The princes got everything they could want—except freedom. Since their arrival over a week ago, Thayne had not once been allowed to visit his Lasony pony. Davi hadn't come to see them either, though a steady stream of children their own ages came to play. Only the prince and heir didn't see himself as a child any longer, and their games annoyed him.

A distant strain of music drifted into the room on a night breeze. Somewhere in the palace, the adults still celebrated his mother's coronation. Thayne and Robyn had watched the earlier ceremony from a high wrought-iron balcony in the council chambers. Rose had told him the chambers were also used as a theater where plays were staged. Aside from an occasional troupe of jugglers traveling through Keeptown, entertainment had always been rare in Wynnamyr. Plays were something only read about in books.

Thayne pushed aside his thin sheet and sat up. Faint moonlight created eerie shadows in the corners, transformed the toys across the room into strange immobile creatures. Robyn stirred in his bed, and their nanny on a mattress near Lilith's crib made a low moaning sound that raised bumps on Thayne's arms. Sleep seemed impossible now, but to lie and stare into the darkness held little appeal.

Barefooted, he made his way to the door. Oil lamps flickered in the corridor beyond, and the music was louder now. The red tiles beneath his feet felt cool. Thayne followed the sounds first, then realized the risk of discovery would be far greater near the banquet hall. He turned and headed in the opposite direction. The choices of paths were numerous, the palace a great mysterious world all its own. Three floors rose above the ground, each smaller than the last under the high domed roof.

Thayne unhooked an oil lamp from its wall bracket and took the first broad staircase upward. The rooms above were as yet unfinished, filled with stacks of lumber and buckets to mix plaster. In some hidden corners, the walls remained blackened and scorched—a testament to his father's powerful sorcery. Like the ants in a damaged hill, however, the Xenarans had swarmed back to rebuild and begin again.

Along another corridor, the prince paused, listening. Some tiny sound had stopped him, the scurrying of a mouse perhaps. Now the quiet lay heavy, and instead of the banquet music, there came the muffled sounds of Zankos outside the palace grounds, the lonely clang of ships' bells. The city never slept, or so the Grand Envoy said.

Another smaller staircase led Thayne to the highest level, an open-sided cupola. The view dazzled him. Zankos seemed close enough to touch. Behind lighted windows, he saw women in bright garb, and the streets below were crowded with celebrants. The Inland Sea lay dark and empty to the south. Somewhere horses nickered, sleepy night sounds. Sojii would be among them, and suddenly Thayne longed more than ever to be home at Castlekeep with his old playmates and Davi. There his mother was also a queen, but happy.

The prince and heir of Wynnamyr and Xenara leaned against the iron railing and drew a deep breath of moist salt air rich with the scent of night-blooming jasmine. This would be his kingdom one day, or so the Grand Envoy told him. Behind him came the quick patter of slippered feet upon the tiles. Thayne never had a chance to turn and face his attacker.

*  *  *  *  *

Gaylon found Davi alone in his chambers. Nothing had changed. The young man on the bed still clutched the pendant to his chest, his face slack and empty. In a week's time, the flesh had melted from his cheeks, and day by day his pallor grew worse. He dreamt his life away, and nothing the king of Wynnamyr could do would wake him. Why had Sandaal left him unattended?

Davi's *Book of Stones* still lay in the open trunk. The gold trim on the cover was hand-beaten, the runes carved into the wood with careful, ornate skill. An ancient volume, this one— far older than the king's. Such a wondrous, dangerous gift to a youth who desired sorcery above all else. If only Davi had come to Gaylon first . . . but wondering did little good now.

On his hand, the king's Stone flared a sudden blue, but not from his own emotions. He turned to look at the unconscious man on the bed and saw cobalt light stream through Davi's clutched fingers.

"Davi?" Gaylon knelt beside the mattress, afraid to hope. "Davi . . ."

The duke's eyes flickered open, sightless at first. Then horror filled them. He reached up to take a weak grip on Gaylon's shirt.

"Thayne," the youth gasped. "He's fallen from some high

place. . . . I felt it. He's still alive. Find him quickly, before it's too late. Bring him to me." His hand fell back. "I can help." Exhaustion made the words fade.

In turmoil, Gaylon stood. Thayne hurt? The chamber door opened on Sandaal, laden with a tea tray, but the king dodged past her into the corridor, already calling for the palace guard.

# Twelve

For lack of a better plan, the king raced first to the nursery. This might be some dream vision of Davi's, but if it wasn't . . . A half-dozen guardsmen thundered into the chamber with him, and the clamor woke Lilith. Her cries of distress in turn woke the nanny who, terrorized, caught the baby up and tried to flee. Gaylon caught her.

"Where's Thayne?"

"Sleeping, milord!" The woman trembled in his grip, and Lilith continued to wail.

"He's not in his bed. Where would he go?"

Bessi began to sob. "I don't know, milord. I don't know."

In anguish, Gaylon freed her and fled from the room. Some high place, Davi had said. The guard came after him, uncertain of the king's alarm but willing enough to follow. They found one of the many courtyards, and Gaylon paused.

"There may be an injured child . . . Prince Thayne . . . a fall from a balcony, perhaps," he told the soldiers, and he began to take lamps from the walls to pass around. "Spread out and search the palace grounds. You!" The king motioned to one man. "Get the physician. He may still be at the banquet. Say nothing to the queen as yet. Hurry!"

Each guard took an oil lamp and disappeared into the night. Gaylon went his own way, his heart beating wildly, his stomach sick with fear. Let it be a dream, dear gods. But he knew. The paths were all of the same monotonous red tiles that wound around the huge marble structure. Each small shadowed bush brought a rush of panic.

"Milord!"

The king turned at the shout. A pair of guards waved their lanterns, and he followed them back the way they'd come and beyond—to the stable yard. A crowd of soldiers clustered in the dirt near a young olive tree, only a few paces from the palace wall. They parted as Gaylon approached. Nials Haldrick knelt beside a small, still form, and he looked up at the king, face contorted.

"Majesty . . ."

Gaylon dropped to his knees beside his son. By lamplight, he saw the twisted limbs, the blood soaking into the barren soil.

"Is he . . . ?"

"He lives, milord, but only just," the physician said. "I'm sorry—death is inevitable. The skull is cracked, and he bleeds from within."

"No!" Gaylon moaned, then hardened his heart. "Will the pain be worse if I move him?"

"He feels nothing, milord."

The king gathered the limp broken body to his chest as gently as possible. Thayne's chest rose and fell in quick short breaths, and his eyelids fluttered, though only the whites of his eyes showed. Blood leaked from his nose and mouth, and his head seemed flattened behind the left ear. A prince and heir lay dying in his arms. Unaware of the others and blinded by tears, Gaylon carried the boy into the palace.

Warm blood had soaked the red satin shirt by the time he reached Davi's chambers. Sandaal met them at the door, blanching at the sight of Thayne. On the mattress, the duke turned his head slowly, his expression bleak.

"Go," Gaylon told Sandaal, sobs tight in his throat. "Bring the queen." He brought the child to the bed. "The damage is too great, Davi. His life is nearly gone."

Davi's face twisted with hurt and anger. "Put him here beside me. Quickly." When that was done, the young duke reached out two weak and shaking hands to the boy's blood-matted hair, then closed his eyes. The Stone in the pendant on his chest took fire—not a bright glow, but steady.

The king turned away, unable to watch. This was a hopeless gesture on Davi's part. He'd proven his healing powers a number of times on small wounds, minor injuries. It was a rare magic that tended to drain the healer physically and emotionally. Thayne's injuries were far too great, beyond any sorcerous help, and Gaylon had long ago learned the horrible price of refusing a loved one the peace of death.

The door opened, and Jessmyn rushed in, confusion and horror on her pretty, tired face. Gaylon caught her shoulders with blood-sticky hands. Rose and Katina followed more slowly, afraid.

"Nials says Thayne's fallen."

"Yes."

"Let me see him." The queen tried to pull free of his grip.

"My love . . ."

"No!" At the pain in his voice, Jessmyn tore loose and rushed to the bed.

Unwillingly the king went after her. His wife made no sound, only stared at her son's broken body, one hand clamped hard over her mouth. But something had changed, some small thing. Gaylon looked hard and realized Thayne's breathing had slowed and deepened ever so slightly. Davi's breathing moved in time to the boy's now.

"What is he doing?" a voice asked beside him. Nials Haldrick had come into the chamber unnoticed.

"What little he can," the king answered bitterly.

Nials didn't press him further but found a station near the bed from which to watch. Watch and wait. It was all any of them could do. Jessmyn finally came to Gaylon, and they sat on a large cushion, arms entwined, finding comfort in each other.

The sky beyond the wrought-iron grilles began to glow with dawn. Food was brought, but no one ate, no one spoke. Thayne's eyes had ceased to flutter, and the blood no longer flowed from his nose and mouth. Still Gaylon refused the small seed of hope that tried to form. On the bed, Davi was no more conscious than the prince. Neither had moved in all this time.

The king dozed finally until a faint mewling woke him. Everyone gathered near the mattress. It was Thayne who cried, his eyes still closed. Davi, though, had opened his.

"Haldrick . . ." he whispered.

"Here, Lord Gosney," the physician said.

"The skull is nearly healed, but he feels the broken bones now. Bring a draught for the pain."

"I will, milord." Nials leaned close, wonder on his face, while his fingers traced the back of Thayne's head. "Incredible, milord," he murmured in awe, then hurried from the chamber.

"Davi," the queen said gently, but the duke's eyes had closed once more.

Jess looked at Gaylon, worried. Already weak from Dreaming, Davi was using energy he didn't have to spare. The king longed to help him, but this wasn't a gift he shared. His own angry, seething magic wrought only death and destruction. The Stone on his finger glimmered in answer to those faint wild impulses, and Gaylon willed it dark again.

Shadow patterns moved across the floor. The draught was brought and administered. Davi's hands covered the prince's chest and then his stomach. At dusk he moved them once more to cover Thayne's right forearm, where the bone had splintered and broken through the skin. Servants came and went, though Gaylon paid them no mind. His attention remained fixed on the duke's hands, but no matter how hard he stared, the changes came too slowly to see.

Near midnight, Davi finally worked on the last break, the one in the boy's thigh. Thick scar tissue stretched over the worst of the injuries. Rose dared to bring a basin of water to the bed and bathed the dried blood from Thayne's face and hair, cooing to him gently.

"Majesties," she said, voice sharp.

Eyes open, the prince gazed around him, and it took every bit of restraint Gaylon could muster to keep from grabbing him up. The queen wept openly.

"I don't feel very good, Mummy," Thayne muttered.

His father laughed, joy and exhaustion making him giddy. "Got a headache, do you? No wonder. Why were you wandering around in the cupola at night?"

"Was I?" The prince frowned.

"You fell," Jessmyn told him.

"Did I?"

Nials saw the fear on the queen's face. "This is not uncommon with such trauma, milady. The mind wishes to forget."

Thayne had discovered Davi on the mattress beside him. He struggled to turn over, and the duke's left hand fell away from his leg. His right one cupped the pendant.

"Did Davi fix me again?"

"Yes, he did," the queen said.

"Davi?" Thayne caught the duke's chin in small fingers, then glanced up. "Is he asleep?"

His mother nodded. "He's very tired now."

A sick dread began to build suddenly in Gaylon's chest again.

"Can you move Thayne to his own chambers now?" he asked Nials.

"I don't see why not."

Gaylon straightened. "Best do it." He turned to the others. "All of you, go and rest."

"I'll stay with Davi," Sandaal said from beside the physician.

"No, I'll stay with him." The king sent them away as quickly as possible, then returned to the bed. "Davi!" he snapped.

The young man's face had lost all expression once more.

"Davi! Let go of the Stone!" Gaylon cried in his ear. "Don't go back into Dreaming. You won't have the strength to return."

Silence was his only answer. Frustrated, the king paced the tiles a moment before halting beside the bed again. He tried to pry apart the duke's fingers, but they remained iron tight.

"What does it take to make you understand, Davi? No matter how appealing, there's death in Dreaming. Everlasting death. Let me teach you as your father taught me. I can teach you so much." Gaylon shook the man hard. "Davi! You came back to save Thayne. Now save yourself!"

In unison, both Stones flared, nearly blinding Gaylon, and the duke of Gosney slowly opened his eyes.

"Let go of the Stone," the king ordered.

He could see the anguish on Davi's face and remembered how hard it was to give up that feeling of power and comfort—even temporarily.

"Please," Gaylon said and watched the duke release his Stone. "Good. Now you may sleep as long as you like. I won't leave you. I promise."

*     *     *     *     *

Next morning Davi sat propped up with pillows, a bowl of thin gruel on a tray in his lap. The weakness was most pronounced in his hands, and their shaking embarrassed him as he painstakingly guided spoonfuls of food to his mouth. Rose was there to watch him, ready to take the spoon and feed him if necessary. The duke was determined that it wouldn't be necessary.

Nials Haldrick was the first to come calling, long before the bland meal was through. He stood in the entry, his dark eyes aglitter, thoughtful.

"Milord," Rose said and curtsied.

"Could you give us a moment alone, dear?" the physician asked. At Rose's pretty puckered lips, he smiled. "I won't stay long."

The young woman took herself from the chamber, and Haldrick approached the bed. "How's the food?"

"Terrible," Davi grunted.

"But it's all your stomach will tolerate at the moment." Nials began to fidget nervously. "Milord Gosney, I've practiced the healing arts all my life—apprenticed to an elderly physician in Cadjia when I was only five. He saw my potential even then." Now the man stared at his long-fingered hands, and his expression indicated that he found them somehow lacking. "What I witnessed last night in this room goes beyond any form of medicine I've ever known. You're a duke, with money and property and a high station in life . . . but this gift, this power of yours, transcends any worldly endeavors." Finally Haldrick gazed into Davi's eyes. "Join me in helping others. We could learn so much from each other."

The duke of Gosney shook his head slowly. "I can't."

"But why?"

"It hurts too much to . . . to open myself to another's pain."

"Ah." That one word held disappointment. "You're afraid of the pain. But I feel it, too. All good healers suffer for their gift."

"Imagine," Davi said, "what you suffer multiplied a thousandfold."

Nials nodded sadly. "The greater the gift, the greater the pain. I understand, milord. Forgive my intrusion."

There were other things Davi wanted to say, to explain, but exhaustion still tugged at him, leaving him empty of coherent thought. The physician had already gone out the door, and Davi sat alone on his bed, unhappy. Several times throughout that long night, he had felt himself being pulled into death with Thayne. It would have been so easy to let go, to give in to the emptiness, but the Stone had proved the anchor that held them both to life.

Rose returned a good while later, and the duke found the strength to put another spoonful of cold gruel into his mouth before she could rush to help him. Her hopeful eagerness irritated him, but he managed an awkward smile for her. It was Sandaal he wanted most to see.

The younger D'Jal sister came to tuck the sheets around him. "Thayne is resting well, milord. He's tired and sore, but happy. He's already demanding to see you . . . and his pony."

"Where is the Red King?"

"He said he'd be by at supper."

Good. The duke stroked his pendant, thoughtful and a little apprehensive. Gaylon had promised to teach him sorcery, but the king didn't know the whole truth. Orym had wisely kept silent since Davi's waking. Cagey old spirit. Alone, Davi might call the Dark King forth. Instead, he set the bowl aside and settled back in the pillows to sleep.

Dreams came. Vivid, senseless, uncontrolled dreams that harried Davi's rest. They drove him through light and darkness, through fire and ice, until a shake of his shoulder late in the day brought him awake, sweaty and wide-eyed.

"Easy," Gaylon said gently. "It's all right. I suffered the same at first." He pressed a damp cloth to the young duke's forehead. "In time, common dreams will return. Stone-provoked Dreaming has filled your mind with experiences far beyond what it can deal with at the moment. Here." The king helped Davi sit, then placed a frosted chalice in his hands. "A sweet sherbet like nothing you've tasted before, made with a combination of imported fruits. The physician says it will give you much needed strength."

Carefully the duke tilted the cup to his lips, letting the exotic icy flavors flood his tongue. Slushy pinks and oranges had been swirled together in the concoction. Nials Haldrick was right. Not only did the fluid slake Davi's thirst, but the coldness also turned immediately to warmth in his belly. He finished the drink and looked up.

"Is there more?"

That made Gaylon smile. From the table beside him, he brought a ceramic pitcher and filled the chalice once more. This time Davi sipped slowly, aware of the king's speculative gaze. They were alone in the chamber, and the silence drew on.

"You'd think in all this opulence, a man could find a piece of decent furniture," Gaylon said finally, settling himself on a huge satin pillow. "These are made for broader behinds than we have in Wynnamyr. I've commissioned some chairs and a dining table in Zankos. If they get those right, I'll have some real couches made—none of these half-sized curvy things that break your back when you sit on them."

Davi held out his cup for more sherbet before it melted into fruit juice. "Redecorating the palace, are you?"

"Keep a civil tongue," the king said amiably, then switched to the subject that had been on his mind all along. "So tell me about this." He let his right hand slide casually near the duke's pendant and watched both Stones ignite with internal blue fire. "It's not a Gosney heirloom. There's never been a magician in the lot. That leaves your grandmother and a long line of powerful men and women on the Dark King's side. Whose was it?"

Davi gazed at the sheet that covered him, afraid. "In the trunk . . . beside the Book . . . there's a metal box with a letter in it."

"From Edonna?" At the duke's nod, Gaylon went to retrieve it. "My gods, the thing's heavy."

He found the brittle page hidden under the inner lid and carried it back to the bed, eyes already traveling over the tiny scripted lines. Whatever reaction Davi had expected, it didn't come. Absolutely nothing showed on the red-bearded man's face as he sank onto the pillow again. Another silence reigned, far heavier than the last. This time the duke broke it.

"Edonna was wrong about the Stone. There's no evil in it. Look at me. . . . I've worn it this long, and I haven't changed."

"But you have." The sorrow in Gaylon's eyes made Davi's heartbeat quicken. "Minor changes, but they were there all along if I'd known what to look for—you've been short-tempered, secretive, keeping to yourself."

"That's not the Stone's fault. How could I tell anyone? How could I risk its destruction?"

"I'm your king. You should have come to me."

There were equal amounts of accusation and hurt in those words, and the duke felt a sudden shame. "I was afraid."

Gaylon nodded. "And I'll answer you as your father answered me . . . you had every right to be afraid. But you've never been any danger to others, only to yourself. You might have been lost forever in Dreaming."

"No. I had someone teaching me. . . ." Davi caught himself too late, but the king already knew this as well.

"You had Orym, a creature who doesn't serve anyone but himself." The king held up a hand when Davi started to protest. "I don't blame you. I know what it means to want magic badly enough to take such risks. Whatever the Dark King promised you, though, was a lie."

"He's weak, milord. He wants only to meet his end having

done one decent act."

Gaylon laughed bitterly. "What he wanted was for you to be lost in Dreams, leaving him a strong young body to control."

"No . . ."

"Think, Davi. Has there been no hint of Orym's influence over you? That pendant is his last refuge. Kingslayer is destroyed, his bones in the cairns were long ago broken to prevent his return. He's waited a thousand years for a descendant that his Stone might accept. And he found you—all too willing."

"Then Edonna was right," the duke said, pain threading its way through his chest. "The Dark King's Stone must be destroyed." The pain worsened as he pulled the golden chain from around his neck and held the pendant out to Gaylon.

Triumph touched the Red King's eyes, but he made no move to take the Stone. "Do you feel him? Is Orym present now?"

Davi shook his head. "I haven't felt him since we began the Dream spell. He tends to vanish when he senses danger."

"Good," Gaylon muttered. "You'll lure him out later, then together we'll destroy Orym . . . and make the Stone completely yours."

"That can be done?" the duke asked, almost afraid to hope.

"It's been done before, but not easily. We can do nothing less than try. Put the pendant back on and clear your mind. Do nothing to alert him." Gaylon patted Davi's shoulder. "Rest and eat. Gather your strength. Meanwhile, I'll study the spell in my own *Book of Stones.*"

\* \* \* \* \*

Raf D'Gular never rose before noon. The clear, cool morning air of the city had no particular attraction for him, but today he had made an exception—all because of a bit of gossip. One of the palace stableboys had mentioned to one of the D'Gular stableboys that Sandaal D'Lelan, without fail, came to a certain Benjiri confectionery on Sweet Street on the first day of each week. So this day Raf went alone in the early golden light to wait for the lady.

Zankos, it was often said, never slept, but morning found the city quieter at least. The avenues, though, were still crowded with vendors and laborers and lords in rumpled evening finery, many of whom had not yet been to bed.

Young D'Gular heard a phlegmy cough overhead and dodged just in time as the contents of a chamber pot hit the cobbles. He turned the next corner and made his way now among the tall buildings that lined the avenue of the milliners. Here men worked over steaming vats of dye on the sidewalk, stirring in bolts of cloth or skeins of yarn with long wooden paddles. The stones of the road and walkway were blotched with rich indelible colors.

The scents of fresh-baked pastries drew Raf down yet another narrow cobbled roadway. He'd left home without breakfast, before even his father had risen this morning. The old man and his cohorts would be busy later today in a privy council with the queen. Of course, Eowin D'Ar would be there to guide Roffo's daughter through any rough waters, but Raf had a strong feeling that Jessmyn could well take care of herself in such matters.

The thought pleased Raf. He'd dearly love to be there, in hope of seeing his father humbled by Her Majesty once again. This was forbidden, though. Only the house leaders were allowed at privy council. But a private meeting with Sandaal might prove enlightening, might even provide Raf with more and better information regarding his father's most secret schemes.

Raf had come alone—without his brother. Harren, having noticed the sudden interest Raf had taken in Kyl, was for some reason determined now to keep the two apart. Poor Kyl had been locked in his chambers the past two days, and Raf felt a small fury over the animal-like treatment his half brother received at Harren's hand. It had always been thus, though Raf, constantly filled with resentment for Kyl, had never cared before.

The candy shop sat at the far end of the street. A few customers wandered in through the wide front doors, while some, accompanied by eager, happy children, exited with heavy packages in their arms. The morning sun, rising slowly in the southeast, already held a promise of the day's heat to come. Raf passed into the aisles of the cool, breezy store, where little slave boys sat in woven chairs along the walls and pulled ropes to keep huge overhead fans waving.

Rock candy and dried, sugared fruits had been packaged and set in attractive rows on the shelves. The more perishable sweets—chocolates, burnt sugar caramels, and butter candies—were kept in glass cases at the rear of the shop. Kyl loved them all, and Raf found a shopkeeper to wait on him. Sandaal was forgotten for the moment. In the midst of these wonderful sights and smells, Raf chose his half brother's favorites—but not too many. Candy had always been used as a reward for this slow-witted son, and Kyl's teeth and health had suffered for it.

The shopkeeper, an elderly Benjiri man with hair the color of the powered sugar in his candy, patiently and good-naturedly filled his order. Warriors, poets, and the finest of sweets were Benjir's enigmatic gifts to the world.

Young D'Gular had just paid for his goods when Sandaal D'Lelan finally entered, a basket hung over one arm and, as always, that faint mysterious smile on her lips. Her thick black hair had been set in half a dozen braids, then woven over her head, uncovering her long slender neck and smooth shoulders. Raf stared unashamedly until she noticed him.

"Good morning," he said and bowed.

Sandaal eyed him. "Is it? How would you know, Lord D'Gular, when you so seldom see one?"

"With such a caustic wit, my lady, how will you ever find a husband?" the young man countered.

Her only answer was to walk away from him.

"Wait, milady," he said gently and followed her down an aisle.

She continued on. "I haven't any time for you, Raf."

Her blunt tone didn't dissuade him in the least.

"These are nice," he said and dropped a small box of hard orange candies in her basket.

Sandaal removed them. "Go away, milord."

"You wound me, Sandaal. Remember how we played as children in Katay? Remember how Arlin took us riding along the beach?"

Now he had wounded her. The pain flickered briefly across her face and disappeared, and Raf wondered if this driving need to hinder his father was worth the loss of a long friendship. For most of his life, he'd loved Sandaal D'Lelan, offering it up to her jokingly for fear of rejection.

"I don't want you here, Raf," she said. "It'll only cause problems."

That brought hurt and anger. "Ah, that's right. It wouldn't be good to be seen in the company of a D'Gular."

That got him a sidelong look of exasperation. The young woman chose a package of imported dried bananas and went on. Raf trailed her, lips pursed, more determined than ever. Sandaal D'Lelan was the most likely person to be Harren's spy—bright, learned, and with even better reason than most to hate the king of Wynnamyr. Look at the dowdy solemn clothing she wore, the dark grays and blacks of mourning. How to get her to confess her duplicity, though . . .

"He's told me, you know."

"Who?" Sandaal asked, her gaze on the shelves, her mind elsewhere.

"My father. He sent me to help you."

Annoyed, the woman turned dark eyes on him. "Harren D'Gular is concerned with my shopping and sent you to help me? Kind, but unnecessary."

Raf caught her arm in frustration, lowering his voice. "Harren is paying you to spy on the royal household. I want to know what you know about my father's plans."

Sandaal's reaction caught him totally off guard. She jerked her one arm free and struck him with the other hand—not a woman's open-handed slap, but with her fist. Fiery pain shot through Raf's eye and cheekbone and sent him reeling back against the shelves behind him. The fury on the lady's face gave him pause.

"I care nothing for your father's plans," Sandaal snarled,

outrage in every word. "Or yours, you little beast. Now, go home to your nasty little family where you belong."

Raf fingered the small dagger at his belt, feeling his own outrage, but it was an impulse impossible to follow. Such a violent reaction only proved him right. Lady D'Lelan had much to hide, much to be ashamed of. They would meet again soon, Raf vowed silently—alone this time, where he would take the information he wanted by force. And maybe other favors he'd wanted for a very long time. . . .

# Thirteen

Jessmyn took Lilith with her that afternoon and left the princes surrounded by her ladies-in-waiting, their nanny, and two of the palace guards. Thayne's accident had shaken the queen deeply. Never before had she felt so vulnerable and helpless. And yet determined. If they must live in Xenara for now, then the daughter of Roffo must take complete control over this inhospitable country.

The Grand Envoy followed her along the corridors toward the main council chambers, his anxiety all too apparent. An infant at privy council was unheard of, would distract everyone from the work at hand. This would also lessen her in the eyes of the others, reduce her to the role of female and mother rather than queen. Jess continued to ignore the old man's quiet ranting, much to his frustration.

Dead silence fell as they passed through the double doors and into the chamber. This room was small and intimate and held only the voting members, the heads of the noble and merchant houses—around thirty men. The entire council rose immediately to bow, and now the queen bade them sit again. Lilith burbled happily in her arms, revealing two tiny bottom teeth—her first. At five months old, the little princess had grown far more aware of her surroundings. She looked with great interest at the world, head bobbing, arms and legs waving.

Jessmyn noted the disapproving glances among her council

members and also noted Harren D'Gular, seated at the far end
of the long mahogany table, his hand carefully bound and
resting in a sling. The man's complexion was slate gray, his
eyes slightly glazed, but the hatred in them remained obvious.

The court clerk helped Her Majesty settle in her own heavy,
ornate chair, then placed a thick stack of papers at her right
hand, beside the ebony scepter. Eowin D'Ar took his seat at
her left, stooped and worried.

"Gentlemen," Jessmyn D'Gerric said, gazing about the
room. She was unwanted here, even by those who supported
Roffo's heir. Politics in Xenara was a man's territory by long
tradition, and feminine leadership would be anything but welcome.

The top page in the stack bore the signature and seal of
Largo Mensen. The big man straightened in his chair when
Jessmyn took the paper in hand. Lilith still cradled in her left
arm, the queen scanned the text quickly before passing the
document to her clerk.

"No, Master Mensen. Your bid to purchase Caldwil Shipping
is denied."

Largo stiffened in surprise. "Your Majesty, please . . . I've
offered them an honest price. If you will only read the contract. . . ."

"I have, sir. And I find the price anything but honest.
You've bullied your competitors into making no bids at all,
and offer a tenth of the value of the property." The queen
lifted her chin as Mensen made to protest. Across the table,
Sirus Caldwil frowned, uncertain. "It would seem the Caldwil
Company is facing grave financial difficulties due to the loss
of several of their ships off the Leaman Islands—a sudden
plague of pirates, I'm told."

"Milady," Largo dared to interrupt, "by law, I am allowed to
make this purchase. All parties are in agreement. Your
approval is a mere formality."

"I know the law, Mensen. But as of this moment, Caldwil
Shipping is no longer for sale." That statement confused even
the Grand Envoy. "I find that the company's western trade
routes are some of the richest and most profitable in the

realm, and that would tip far too much money, and therefore power, in your direction, sir. The crown, then, will loan Master Caldwil the funds to rebuild his fleet—for a fair interest from his profits, of course." Jess looked directly at Largo. "We will also have the queen's navy escort his ships against further incidence of piracy." It wasn't an outright accusation, but close enough to redden Mensen's face.

The reactions of the council members around her were mixed, but Jess had no time to decipher them. Lily, hungry, made her unhappiness known loud and clear. Embarrassed, Eowin D'Ar waved a servant to the table, no doubt to send for the wet nurse. The queen, however, brought the baby's blanket chastely over her shoulder, then opened her blouse beneath it. The little princess quieted immediately.

Most of the council members merely continued to murmur among themselves, eyeing an angry Largo Mensen. So far, Jessmyn D'Gerric had shocked them at every turn, and to nurse a baby at council was the very least of her outrageous actions. Tea arrived while the queen reviewed the next few petitions. It saddened her as she read them each with care. In Wynnamyr, Gaylon had dealt with nobleman and commoner alike, and while arriving at judgments wasn't always easy, the people still showed one another honesty and courtesy in all matters.

Here in Xenara, every phrase of every document was written in a convoluted language meant to confuse and cloud the issues. Heated arguments broke out constantly among the council members, who sought to cheat one another at every chance. Jessmyn soon had a throbbing headache, and Lilith, sensitive to the moods of those around her, grew cranky.

Far more experienced in Xenaran politics, Eowin D'Ar proved invaluable. The queen took his advice on many matters, though it only meant compromise among thieves for the most part. She had few friends at the beginning of this meeting, and by its end had far more enemies, which only made her headache worse.

The afternoon passed into evening, and the last document in the stack was finally dealt with. Lords and merchants began to gather their things, but the queen of Wynnamyr and all Xenara had one last piece of business to attend to. Rocking the baby gently, she stood.

"Milords . . . as your new queen, I have many duties, none of which I take lightly."

A worried silence fell, and Jess could see the same question on all their well-bred faces. What now?

"I wish to address a millennia-old practice in Xenara that I find cruel and inhumane. And intolerable." The alarm in the Grand Envoy's aging brown eyes only made Jessmyn all the more determined. "I intend to abolish slavery in Xenara."

Harren D'Gular had had nothing to say throughout the entire meeting. Now he pushed back his chair at the far end of the table.

"Her Majesty is insane!" the man said with sharp insolence. He was well out of reach of the queen's ire and her scepter, and surrounded by those who plainly agreed with him. "You would destroy our economy and our country. Tell her, Eowin. Explain to her just what a silly, sentimental woman might accomplish with such an act."

The Grand Envoy looked away. "He's right, milady. Slave labor is the backbone of Xenaran industry."

"Slavery is the shame of any civilized land." Jessmyn held her anger tightly in check. In order for so immense a change to occur, she must not antagonize these men any further. "Milord Envoy, you've told me often enough that you're pleased with my abilities. Don't make the mistake of thinking me a fool now. Any of you!" The queen paused to whisper comfort to her troubled infant daughter, then looked up. "I don't propose to end slavery tomorrow, or even next year . . . but it will end. And that end begins here in my own palace.

"From now on, the slaves in the royal household will receive a small wage as well as their housing and food—until every man, woman, and child may buy his or her freedom. So it will eventually be for all the households in Xenara. With freedom will come citizenship and all the rights thereof."

Jessmyn had expected outrage and anger, and D'Layne and D'Gular did not disappoint her. Some of the other houses, though, were quiet and circumspect. This didn't mean they approved, the queen realized, but it might mean that they would think about her proposal. A victory of sorts, then. Lily had gone to sleep in her arms, and Jess, with the barest of nods to the Grand Envoy, took her leave, her nervous exhaustion well hidden.

\* \* \* \* \*

"Call him," the king said quietly.

Davi, seated on a new chair in Gaylon's chambers, stroked the Stone in his pendant. "He won't come, Sire. Orym senses danger and hides himself deep within the matrix."

"Call him," Gaylon repeated. "He'll come. We're old adversaries, and he won't be able to resist a chance to gloat."

"Gloat?"

"Do it!" the king snapped in irritation. "Or are you protecting him?"

Troubled by the accusation, Davi closed his hand about the Stone, and Gaylon saw it brighten, cobalt light streaming through the young man's fingers. The duke closed his eyes, and, immediately unconscious, his head fell back against the cushioned top of the chair. The king of Wynnamyr smiled grimly. He'd expected as much. Orym had been using the boy all along.

In the center of the room, a faint glow wavered, then steadied, taking form—an immense ancient man with great black curls around a heavily bearded face. He held gnarled hands with twisted yellow fingernails folded before him on his black velvet robes. To bring himself thus, in so clear an image, the Dark King drew heavily on Davi's life-force.

"Gaylon Reysson, Red King and sorcerer," Orym said, his voice slightly hollow. "You wished to see me, and here I am."

"I wish to see you gone forever."

The Dark King's laughter echoed in the chamber. "Then there must be one final battle between us." He glanced at Davi. "But realize . . . win or lose, this young one will surely die. His strength is mine to use, and his powers may prove even greater than yours. The blood of the Dark Kings is unsurpassed in sorcery. Will you risk him for a chance to destroy me?"

"You won't let him die," Gaylon said, his fear held carefully in check. "Davi's the very last of the Dark King's line and your only real hope to live again."

Orym frowned, but a knock at the door distracted them both.

"Who is it?" Gaylon called.

"Sire, it's Katina," came the young woman's voice. "Her Majesty has returned from privy council and wishes to see you immediately."

"Beg her forgiveness, Kat, but tell her I cannot come. Tell everyone I'm not to be disturbed for any reason."

"Milord, the queen is very despondent. . . ."

"I'm sorry, but no. Tell her I'll come as soon as I am able. Now go!"

In the silence that followed, he heard the sound of her soft slippers fade in the hall. Gaylon turned back to Orym's image.

"One of us will die tonight, lost forever. But not here. Zankos has seen enough of my destructive powers, and I won't risk the lives of my family and staff. Since I challenge you, you may choose the battleground."

"It matters not where I kill you, Gaylon Reysson," the Dark King rumbled. "Lead and I'll follow."

Now the king of Wynnamyr closed his eyes, letting the warm blue glow of his own Stone sweep through him. It was not conscious thought that brought him to a huge knoll of land overlooking the Western Sea on Wynnamyr's coast. A heavy gray cloud cover rolled away into the distance, and there the setting sun, fat and golden-red, lay suspended in the narrow space between sea and sky. Cold gray-green water surged restlessly below.

Some mighty upheaval had torn a gigantic hole in the rich earth at the center of the grassy sward. Large gray stones lay scattered in every direction—all that remained of Castle Seward, where Daryn's teacher, Sezran, had once worked and lived. In the fading light, the king gazed at the emptiness.

Only the cries of gulls came to him. This lonely place would suit his purpose well.

Blue light flickered briefly at the edge of the wide maw in the ground. An image formed—not Orym's, however, but Davi's. His green cat's eyes turned on Gaylon.

"Milord, where are we? What is this place?"

But Gaylon had seen the sly glint of blue behind the green eyes. This wasn't Davyn Darynson, duke of Gosney.

"Games," he said with supreme disgust.

Orym, ever cruel, let sudden flames engulf Davi's form, let the body writhe and scream in seeming agony. Despite himself, the vision brought a twisting pain to Gaylon's gut. The resultant anger nearly cost him his life.

A faint blue orb had bobbed away from the flames. Enraged, the king lashed out at it, a heavy wave of cobalt fire that hit nothing but air. The force went on to strike the hillside above the knoll, destroying some of the wind-stunted trees that grew around a pond there.

At the same instant, Orym had struck from high overhead. Searing hot agony created a moment's confusion before Gaylon could call up his Stone's defenses. Enclosed in its protective bubble, he gathered his strength. His clothing still smoldered, and blisters formed quickly on his hands and face.

The *Book of Stones* had offered up no spells for exorcising such creatures as Orym, so deeply entrenched within its stone. In all ways, the murderous Dark King defied logic. For that cunning madness to survive a millennium was beyond reason, but it had. Alone, Gaylon must save the lives of himself and Davi.

He reached deep into his Sorcerer's Stone, drawing on it. Outside his bubble of protection, Orym's forces stormed. The Red King pushed back, gently at first, feeding his own power into Orym's. The old king failed to notice the swelling energies at first, but at the last moment, as the power field erupted outward, Gaylon felt the creature's instant of terror, felt him fling himself away toward the setting sun and beyond.

The billowing blue firestorm roiled into nothingness, and the king sank to his knees on the heat-blasted ground. Pain made him lightheaded, but not so lightheaded as to believe he'd won the battle. In this short respite, he must come up with some plan to drive Orym so far into Dreaming that he might never return—or preferably destroy him.

Wind blew in from the sea now, a sharp, cold wind with demon voices. Words swirled in the Red King's head, faint but growing stronger. On the withered grasses at the sea cliff's edge, sparkling blue fireflies gathered, and then there was Arlin, wounded and pain-wracked. Dark eyes regarded Gaylon with longing.

"I can be yours again," Sandaal's brother said softly. "Let Orym live, and I will, too. He has that power."

"No . . ." Gaylon moaned, fingers against his pliant shield. "No one should have that power. No one must ever have that power again."

Arlin reached out to him. "Look at me. I'm real! I've died for you twice. Let me live. I want to exist—anywhere but in the horrible nadir world you sent me to."

"Lies!" The Red King's voice caught, and tears burned the blisters on his cheeks. "Arlin is long dead, forever gone. Bastard, Orym!" He climbed to his feet, his Stone flaring brightly on one finger. "This only proves your desperation, old man. You're afraid!"

Arlin's image wavered and changed. Now Davi stood on the brink of the cliff, a malicious smile on his lips, Orym's madness in his eyes.

"Afraid?" He sneered. "Not I. But I'll give you one more chance to survive. It would be a shame to waste a talent such as yours." The young duke stepped toward Gaylon. "Once I asked you to join me. Together, no one could stand against us. Together, we could have this world at our feet. Think of it, Gaylon Reysson. I know the rage and longing in your heart— your joy at destruction and death. Give in to it—give in to me—and discover your true powers."

The Red King shook his head. "Give in to your madness? Both in life and death, you've used insanity as an excuse to follow your every whim and desire. But power alone is not enough for me."

"What then?" Davi-Orym demanded. "Is it love you hope to gain? A worthless emotion, and something you'll never have. Sorcerers are hated and feared, never loved. Even their families fear them; the love they profess is tainted with dread."

"I don't believe you," Gaylon said, but doubts had already formed. Was Jessmyn's gentle touch one of love, or merely respect born of fear? He'd given her plenty of reason to be frightened of him. No . . . Orym only wished to confuse him.

Before him, Davi waved his hands hypnotically. "Remember, Sire."

Visions came—those vivid bloody dreams that had haunted him all his life. Gaylon saw himself again, ten years old, a tiny dirk in his gore-smeared hand, two soldiers lying dead at his feet. The elation filled him once more, heady and strong, then suddenly increased a thousandfold. He stood above the Xenara Plain now, with Kingslayer spewing horrible golden death over Roffo's army.

"Stop!" he cried, blistered face buried in blistered hands. The dreams faded, and so did the joy they had brought.

Somewhere near his ear, Davi whispered against the sea wind. "Monster, king, sorcerer . . . you must be what you are. Anything else is a lie. You are more a child of mine than even the duke of Gosney."

"No . . ."

"Give me the boy to use as I please. Join me, and I promise you pleasures beyond anything you've ever imagined."

That soothing, oh-so-logical voice had numbed the Red King. He'd felt the hatred of those around him, known their fear and scorn. Orym's offer of succor, of release from the constant internal war Gaylon waged every moment of his life, was hard to resist. Gods, how he longed to give in to those base urges!

The cost was too high, though. Davi, who had served his king as faithfully as his father, Daryn, had, didn't deserve to lose his life in order for Orym to live again. The Dark King was wrong, too. Gaylon had love. Robyn and Thayne, born to a sorcerer and too young yet to understand others' fears, loved their father unconditionally. And Jessmyn, in a thousand

thousand ways, had proved her love and devotion. Even in
the midst of his misery and pain, he felt a touch of pride. Jessmyn had proven herself a true queen in Xenara, a monarch of
far greater ability than her troubled husband.

Gaylon looked up finally. Davi-Orym stood close to the
protective bubble, held back, but waiting with anticipation.
Something about the duke, though, made the Red King look
more closely in the fading daylight. The young man's skin was
pale, and a fine sheen of sweat covered his face. There was
something more than Orym's madness in the green eyes—
pain, hidden deep, but it was there. So. The backwash of their
combined energies earlier had done more than send Orym
fleeing. The old sorcerer was somehow injured.

Now he tried gentle persuasion in hope of avoiding another
confrontation. Gaylon shivered. The ploy had very nearly
worked. The old king had perceived his adversary's strongest,
darkest desires.

"I can't bear it any longer," the king of Wynnamyr murmured, his sorrow genuine. He'd fought those desires too
long, and one day would surely lose. The knowledge struck
him hard. Orym, then, must be destroyed at any cost, and
Gaylon knew now that he would pay any price. "Love has
brought me only misery. . . ."

"Yes, yes!" the Dark King agreed. "So it will always be.
Accept my offer. You'll never regret it."

"Then give me your hand in pledge." Gaylon reached out
through the faint blue bubble to the duke.

After the slightest hesitation, Orym took the hand with
Davi's. The king of Wynnamyr clasped it hard and jerked the
man forward into the bubble with him. The touch of the
shield brought agony to Davi's face as he passed through it,
but Gaylon didn't wait for him to recover. He wrapped his
ringed hand in the pendant chain that hung from the duke's
neck. Stone met Stone, and the shriek of their meeting soared
to deafening heights.

"No!" The Dark King screamed. His mouth formed the
word, but his voice was lost.

The sudden surge of energy within burst the bubble around

them, and Gaylon, his body engulfed in blue fire, felt himself hurled away. Davi/Orym came with him, still caught by the chain. The Red King's fingers loosened slightly, and the Stones parted, their fire dying. But the world had already vanished. Starless black night had taken its place. They tumbled together through the darkness, their mutual agony silent. Then the links that held the pendant parted, and Orym was swept away, shouting soundlessly.

Another bubble formed around Gaylon, golden this time. With it came the loss of pain, the loss of all sensation. He understood now where he was . . . in that space where the newly dead floated before going on to whatever fate awaited them, never to return. It was here he'd come in search of Arlin to bring him home again, back to life, only to kill him again later.

Relief washed through the king of Wynnamyr. At last, the peace of death. He had destroyed Orym and given up the pain of life himself. Those he'd left behind would be far better off for his loss, and never again would he have to struggle against the internal rage and hatred and shame that had always ruled him.

The walls of the bubble thickened slowly, though they stretched at his touch. In the blackness beyond, he could see a few other globes bobbing, moving in random patterns, distorted and blurred by the curve of his own bubble's wall. Orym would be among them now. Had he, too, found peace? That seemed hardly punishment enough for the horrors he'd inflicted on his world and his people. Gaylon, though, had perpetrated his own brand of evil and deserved no less punishment. The only difference between them was that the Red King had welcomed death, while the Dark King had fought it desperately for a thousand years. This golden bubble would seem a trap to him, not freedom.

"Gaylon!"

The word filled his head, not his ears, but he recognized Davi's voice, muted over a great distance of time and space. The Red King stared at the pendant, its chain still wrapped in his fingers. Both Stones remained dark. These were illusions.

Neither he nor the Stones existed here. Somewhere in the universe, in the city of Zankos, perhaps, Davyn Daryson stood over his dead king's body.

"Gaylon!" This time the soundless word brought a curious pain with it—Davi's.

"I'm all right, my duke," Gaylon murmured. "Raise Thayne well, with all the love I can never give him. Help him to be the wise and gentle ruler I could never be."

Davi, so far away, so filled with anger and heartache, refused to listen. The Red King could feel an almost physical tug on his being.

"Don't!" he begged. "It's too late. Let me be at peace finally."

In answer, Orym's Stone began to glow a faint blue glow. The young duke's equally faint voice came again.

"Come back, milord. Don't leave us, I beg you! Use the power of my Stone to lead you home from Dreaming. Jessmyn needs you now more than ever. The children need their father. I need you."

This wasn't Dreaming, this was death. Despite himself, Gaylon felt the walls of the bubble again. It had suddenly become a prison. No! There could be no going back. Death must be final if there could be any balance to life. He'd learned that painful lesson from Arlin. The king's own Stone remained dark, its powers lost to him.

"Leave me be!" he raged at Davi, but it was already too late. The desire for life had filled him again. He clutched the pendant tightly, and as Orym's Stone neared his own, the blue glow passed from one to the other. What might happen if they touched once more? Perhaps another eruption that would end his existence now and forever.

Determined, Gaylon brought the Stones together, but instead of another burst of firestorm, his Stone drew steadily from the other, growing brighter and brighter. With the glow came a surge of energy, a feeling of great strength. The king reached out and tore the globe open as easily as if it had been made of cobwebs, then dove through into the darkness beyond.

There he made himself another bubble with his Stone, blue this time and protective against the death that floated all around him. Home. He wanted to be *home*. All his misery and rage seemed as nothing now compared to what he had nearly left behind. Eyes closed, Gaylon willed himself back to Zankos.

# Fourteen

Davi saw the Stone in Gaylon's ring take life and knew that he had somehow won. The tears he'd so tightly held in check finally flowed. They were alone in the chamber, and the duke had awakened with the certain knowledge that Orym was gone from his Stone. It was then Davi found his king lying prone on the tiles, his face and hands and clothing blistered and burned.

Gaylon had fought the Dark King, and both, it seemed, had lost the battle. The man's heart was still, his burned face slack. Davi had witnessed something of this sort before, after the final confrontation between the Red King and the warrior god Mezon. Then Gaylon had lain like dead for well over a month, lost in Dreaming, until the love of his wife and the reluctant help of Sezran had brought him back.

Only Sezran was gone now, and Davi, less than half trained in the ways of the sorcerer, would be lost in Dreaming himself should he attempt to find his lord. Worse, a cold dread had begun to fill the duke's chest. There was something different this time, something the duke couldn't figure. After the Xenaran war, Davi had been certain his king lived. Now he felt no such certainty.

So he crouched beside Gaylon, calling his name, frantically demanding his return. A Gosney defended the Red Kings; it was his purpose in life. When nothing else seemed to get through to Gaylon, Davi used his Stone to reach into his lord's. It, too, seemed empty of life. Gently he poured his own energy into the other Stone, until at last it began to draw hungrily. Light flickered deep within Gaylon's ring, then finally brightened. Sobbing, Davi buried his face in the king's chest.

The injured man drew a ragged breath and stirred weakly. "Ow," he murmured.

"Milord." The duke lifted his head and saw Gaylon's eyes open, filled with agony.

"Do you . . ." the king whispered. "Do you think you can heal these burns? I . . . I don't want to alarm Jessmyn."

Davi nodded through his tears. "Yes."

The wounds were bad, but not nearly as bad as Thayne's had been. The power of the Stone helped greatly, and now its power was his completely. Davi drew the energy to him, filling his mind with a warm orange light, a healing light. With it, he bathed Gaylon, then watched without seeing as the blisters and burns shrank and the red inflamed skin cooled. The king's pain eased.

"Better," he said. "Much better." Gaylon got carefully to his feet, staring down at his ruined clothing. "Jessmyn made this shirt for me. It took her nearly a month. How am I going to explain away its disappearance?"

Davi helped him go through a closet in search of fresh apparel, his thoughts in turmoil.

"What happened, Sire?" he asked finally, when Gaylon only continued to ramble on about what to wear. "I know Orym is gone. I feel it—a strange emptiness in the Stone. How did you manage to defeat the Dark King?"

"By a desperate, foolish act—one I hope you never find the need to use." Gaylon refused to say more on the subject. Instead he busied himself dressing, his movements as stiff as an old man's. "I owe you my life once again, Davi."

"No, Sire. I'm a Gosney." Davi glanced down at the toes of his boots. "I had an ulterior motive, though. I need your help to master my Stone—now that it's truly mine. You're the only one who can train me."

"As a teacher, you may find me sadly lacking, but I'll do the best I can by you, my duke." Gaylon pulled on his last boot.

"The queen needs me, but I'd best go alone. By the look of the shadows, not much time has passed. Or has it?"

"No, I don't think so. The queen would have grown worried." Again the duke gazed at the floor. "I'm grateful, milord——for your breaking Orym's hold on me. He's truly dead."

"Dead and Stoneless. He'll never haunt this world again. And both of us are finally free of his influence . . . forever." The king gathered the burned, scorched clothing and stuffed it in the bottom of a trunk. The smell of smoke still hung faintly on the air. "If you wish to wait here, you're welcome," he told Davi. "I don't know how long I'll be."

The duke sighed. "I'm tired. I think I'll go to my apartments and rest."

"Of course," Gaylon agreed with sympathy. "I'd forgotten how much your healing powers drain you."

"You need rest as well."

"I will soon, I promise."

Davi watched him move away down the corridor. If anything, the king seemed to have more energy than usual, not less. He was pale still, but had recovered from his misadventures. For a brief moment, the duke let himself wonder just what had really happened between the two sorcerers in that final battle. Then he turned and headed toward his own rooms. The Stone on his chest warmed him, filled him with ecstasy. His! All his, now and forever.

*　*　*　*　*

The king's limbs shook a little, and bright moments of remembered pain caught him unaware as he walked. Gaylon ignored it all, intent on one thing—seeing his wife and beautiful children. The hurt and shame of the past were still with him, but buried for the moment under the joy of the life that had been restored to him.

Katina met him at the door to the queen's apartments. Face troubled, she bade him enter. Somewhere in another room, Sandaal played the mandolin, her sweet voice in accompaniment, but behind the music, Gaylon heard a sound that made his heart ache suddenly. Jessmyn sobbed brokenly, her tears nearly hidden behind Lady D'Lelan's song.

Gaylon paused there in the antechamber. "The queen cries. . . ."

"She's been this way since privy council ended," Kat said. "Nothing we do seems to help. Lilith is with the wet nurse, and Rose has taken the princes to the nursery to play."

"What happened in the council?" the king asked.

"Her Majesty won't say, but the Grand Envoy seemed most upset. The meeting went on for more than half the day. She returned tired and depressed."

"Take me to her, please."

Kat nodded. "Yes, milord. This way."

The apartment was huge, even larger than Gaylon's and far more richly accoutred. Beautiful silk hangings draped windows and walls. Tall bookshelves held myriad tomes, though all appeared to be in Xenaran. Nothing of Wynnamyr, the king noted, existed here. Those things the queen had brought with her must have remained unpacked in the chests, considered too crude by comparison to Zankos's stylish trappings.

Sandaal glanced up as they entered the queen's bedchamber, and her voice faded away. The mattress shook gently under Jessmyn's sobs, and every few moments she hiccuped into a pillow.

The king sat beside her, laying a hand softly on her shoulder. "My lady?"

She drew her knees up and curled into a ball until Gaylon pulled her over.

"Jessmyn, please. What can I do to ease your sorrow?"

She tried to tell him, her mouth working uselessly, but the sobs continued to rack her, making speech impossible. The king gathered her up in his arms.

"Ssshhh," he murmured, rocking her gently, then noticed Sandaal and Katina still in the room. "You may go," Gaylon told them. "I'll take care of her now."

The two women hesitated, uncertain.

"Go," the king said firmly, and when they had left, he turned his gaze back on Jessmyn. "Who hurt you, my love?

Only give me a name, and he'll share your sorrow a thousand-fold, I promise."

The queen only shook her head wordlessly. Her eyes were swollen and red with tears, her throat constricted. Gaylon found a cup of water beside the bed and helped her sip from it. Her body still shuddered, but at last she found her voice.

"I . . . I don't know . . . what's happening to me. I felt so . . . so sad, I began to cry . . . and then I couldn't . . . stop."

"Sad about what, dearest?"

"Everything," the queen answered in misery. "I felt their hatred at privy council. Everything I did was wrong, no matter what. Nothing pleased them. I wanted to prove myself strong, but I'm not. I want to go home, Gaylon. Now, tonight. I want to see cool evergreen forests and the Great River. I need to see Lady Keth and hear her children fighting with mine. I want my cold stone walls around me again." Her voice faded into sobs, and the hiccups grew worse.

Gaylon drew her tighter against his chest. "I have always been proud of you, but never so much as since our arrival here. If I hadn't been such a fool all these years, I would have recognized the incredible wisdom and strength in you long ago. We might have sat side by side in council at Castlekeep. How much more quickly the land might have recovered from war with you to help guide the people."

"No," the queen muttered.

"Yes! Let these idiot councilmen howl and gnash their teeth. It's not what you say or do, but what you are that angers them. They want a man on the throne, and so they shall have one day, when Thayne finally rules both countries. Until then, I know you'll prove to be the finest monarch, male or female, that Xenara has ever had."

The king leaned over to kiss her lips. "What's more, you make my life worth living, beloved."

At the threshold of the chamber, someone cleared his throat, and Gaylon glanced up. The Grand Envoy stood just outside the door, obviously embarrassed.

"I knocked, Your Majesties, but no one answered, so I let myself in. Please forgive my intrusion."

"Is it important?" Gaylon demanded with a touch of irritation. This old man had caused his wife enough grief.

"I believe it is, milord," Eowin replied.

"Then enter."

In his arms, Jessmyn tried to stanch her tears, and the king helped her sit up, back snugged to a stack of thick pillows.

Eowin approached, eyes glittering. "Oh, milady. I'm so sorry to have put you through this, but I'm even more ashamed that I doubted you when you needed me most." He smiled faintly. "But you must know what my people in the city have reported. After privy council, many of the members dispersed to taverns. With time to think and rest, most of them have come to agree that their new queen is both canny and just. Many that were outright enemies are now, while hardly friends, at least respectful of the daughter of Roffo." The Grand Envoy leaned nearer. "They'll fight you still on the issue of slavery, but you've won a great victory, Your Highness. Instead of tears of sorrow, these should be tears of joy."

Doubt in her swollen eyes, Jessmyn watched the elderly man, but the king began to laugh.

"Perhaps your councilmen are not all the idiots I took them for," he said. "See, my lady? You're a far greater stateswoman than you'd believe."

"It's true," added Eowin. "I shall never doubt you again, Highness. Can you forgive me?"

The queen managed a smile. "Lord D'Ar, it was your knowledge that brought me this far."

"I merely supplied you with the information, but you decided how best to use it." The Grand Envoy dared to pat the young queen's arm. "Now, madam, tell me you'll rest easy tonight. If you like, I'll have your dinner served here."

"Yes, please," Jessmyn said, her words still nasal from a stuffed nose.

Eowin D'Ar bowed stiffly and turned away. When they were alone again, the queen left the bed to find a cloth and wet it in a basin.

"He's not well." She pressed the damp rag to her swollen eyes.

"The Grand Envoy?" Gaylon asked. "He's never been very well."

"It's grown worse since we arrived. So long a journey taxed him badly enough. Here, his duties are far too much for a man his age . . . yet there's no one who could possibly replace him."

"Have you mentioned this to Lord Haldrick?"

Jessmyn nodded, her eyes still covered. "Nials does what he can, but he's worried, too."

"Well, my love, you are the queen of Xenara. Order your Grand Envoy to take better care of himself."

That made the queen peek out from under the cloth, smiling. "A royal order might be just what he needs."

"What I need," Gaylon said, grinning back at her, "is dinner, and afterward a visit with my children. Then a night alone with the queen of Wynnamyr and all Xenara."

Jessmyn cocked her head. "You're certainly more cheerful than usual, my lord."

"I certainly am," the king agreed.

*   *   *   *   *

Davi spent his night in the *Book of Stones,* far too restless and excited to sleep. So many mysteries, so many tales of other sorcerers in other ages. Fascination held him tight under the glow of a hanging oil lamp in his bedchamber, the huge volume spread open on a wide, low table before him.

There'd been a time when magic had reigned in all the lands along the Western Sea. Every court had had its magician, and sorcerous battles were commonplace occurrences. What a strange and wondrous age to have lived in. It was sad to think of magic's slow decline, to think of a world in which magic would eventually disappear altogether.

While this particular Book followed the rise of the Dark Kings in Wyndland—later called Wynnamyr—it ended before the destruction of Orym's empire. This left a great task for the young duke of Gosney. With Gaylon's help, he must add all the history that followed the Dark Kings, along with any new spells devised and included in His Majesty's *Book of Stones*. This particular task would take many long years of arduous labor. Likewise, Gaylon would search this Book for any lost information to add to his own copy. Few now sought the mysteries of sorcery, since common folk still feared and despised it. Little information was exchanged between magicians because few would admit to the practice.

Davi ran his thumbnail idly across the rough edges of the closed pages until it snagged in one spot. Many times the *Book of Stones* offered answers to difficult questions or needed wisdom in this manner. The binding creaked as he opened the tome to the indicated page. Tiny endless runes marched over the paper without the relief of punctuation, headings, or breaks of any kind.

The duke held his Stone up to the page and watched as the runes changed by the soft blue light, forming text he could understand. He had learned in time to see the words individually—though they ran into one another—so that now the reading went quickly. The spell that caught his eye, however, slowed him.

*If a sorcerer seeks a hidden truth, let him heed this casting.*

It was a simple formula, yet different from any Davi had ever seen or practiced. This spell involved the use of the Book itself, a tome that a magician protected with his life and let no other touch.

His eyes blurred, as they always did when he spent long periods of time peering at the tiny runes. A knock at the door made him jump. The door was locked.

"Who?" the duke called.

"It's Sandaal, milord. May I enter?"

The pull of the Book and his Stone were strong, but so was the pull of his memories of the lady on warm starlit nights. Davi rose to let her in. Sandaal stood a moment on the threshold, her long black hair loose and flowing over her shoulders. In her hand, she held her ebony mandolin.

Her gaze drifted over his face, then turned downward. "I thought you might like to play some music. It's been a while." The young woman looked beyond him into the chamber. "But if you're busy . . ."

Davi wavered. Since her vigilance over him when he was lost in Dreaming, she'd had nothing to say to him. Her behavior never ceased to confuse and enchant him, yet her warmth could turn to ice quickly. The Sorcerer's Stone held diverse mysteries, and some were dangerous, but not so dangerous as Sandaal D'Lelan with her beauty and mercurial moods. Still, he found himself stepping aside.

"Please . . . come in."

She wore jasmine perfume, or it had followed her in from the gardens. The sweet scent brought a moment of longing for Castlekeep and a quick stab of desire, then Davi's attention wandered to the *Book of Stones* laid out on the table.

"Perhaps you have some wine?" Lady D'Lelan asked, reminding him of his lapse in manners.

"Yes, of course."

It was Xenaran wine from the southern provinces beyond the Inland Sea and not much to his liking, but the duke poured them each a glass. Sandaal chose cushions beside a low table, and he brought her the drink. The king's new upholstered chairs and sofas were apparently not to her liking. Davi settled beside her, as he had so many nights on their journey here, willing to accept whatever she would offer— music, song, conversation.

Her gray silk gown shimmered in the lamplight, spread over her lap where she sat cross-legged on the pillows. Davi kept his eyes from the curve of her breasts by concentrating on his wine.

"What's it like," the young woman said finally, after a long sip of her drink, "to be a sorcerer? To have control over unseen powers?"

"Frightening," Davi answered with sincerity, "and exhilarating. Beyond that, it defies explanation."

"The Stone on your chest is much larger than the one in the king's ring. Does this make you a more powerful wizard?"

"Hardly. The power is in the wielder, to whom the Stone only reacts." The duke's brow furrowed. "Why do you ask these questions?"

"Curiosity," Sandaal said. "I want to know if it's possible for a woman to wield a Stone."

Davi nodded. "It's more than possible. Before and during the reign of the Dark Kings, female sorcerers were some of the greatest in the land. After the people rose up against magic, though . . . well, I know of no living sorceress today, but there might be some in other lands."

"And how would I find a Sorcerer's Stone?"

"You won't. I know. I searched for a very long time. If magic is in you, a Stone may find you one day."

Sandaal's face revealed nothing, and Davi wondered at this sudden interest in sorcery.

"Will you do something for me?" she asked suddenly.

"Anything," he answered without thought, his own aching love for her obvious.

"I've never witnessed magic. The king of Wynnamyr seems to despise the use of it."

The request troubled Davi. On the lute, he could perform, but sorcery? What's more, his skills were poor yet, and anything done for Sandaal's sake must be fabulous. He wanted her love, too. The duke stood slowly.

"Come onto the terrace with me. . . ."

A summer night breeze brought a mixture of fragrances, sweet and tangy. City lights twinkled on the hillsides. Lady D'Lelan went to the railing, drawing a deep breath of warm air. The duke stood back from her, his hand on his Stone, eyes half closed. The pendant began a soft blue glow that brightened and brightened again. In his mind, he imagined a bird with brilliant iridescent feathers. The creature came to life on the palm of his left hand, and Davi held it out to Sandaal.

For one brief instant, he saw a rare look of fear in her dark eyes, but she reached out to touch the bird gently. It cocked its head to peer with one eye at her. Then, with a fluting voice, it opened its wings and took flight. Showers of red and gold and blue sparks followed the little animal into the starry sky until it disappeared high above them.

"Was it real?" Sandaal asked, gaze still turned upturned.

"No."

"So beautiful . . ." The words were whispered. She pulled her attention back to earth. "It seems there's a gentle side to magic. Or is that all you're capable of, Davyn Darynson? Could you fight if you had to? Could you destroy an enemy?"

"What enemy? Yours or mine?"

"I can take care of my own enemies," Sandaal answered, a touch of scorn in her voice.

Davi had hoped to impress her, but once again things had somehow gone awry. "You wanted to play music," he said in hopes of diverting her. "I'll get my lute."

"No. Never mind. I've other things to do tonight."

The young woman found her mandolin among the pillows and headed toward the door. Davi caught up with her there.

"Please come again tomorrow night," he begged and hated himself for it.

"Perhaps . . ." She offered him that dry half smile of hers, then closed the door on him.

Sighing, the duke returned to the table and his *Book of Stones*.

\* \* \* \* \*

Someone woke Robyn deep in the night with a hand pressed gently over his mouth.

"Shhhh," whispered the tall, slender form that bent over him. "Come with me, little prince."

The child recognized the exotic perfume of one of his mother's ladies-in-waiting, if not the quiet voice. He curled one hand in the woman's soft silken skirts, then rubbed his right eye with the other.

"Katina? Sandaal? Where we going?"

"Shhhh," came the answer, and he was gathered up in strong arms. Long hair brushed his face.

They didn't go into the lighted corridor, but out through another door that led to a terrace. In faint starlight, Robyn was set down barefoot on the warm tiles.

"Am I going to see my mama?" he asked, not quite fully awake yet.

"Yes," the woman answered, still in a whisper. She took his hand tightly in hers and led him across the terrace to the stairs.

The steps were difficult for so small a boy, especially in shadowy darkness, and only her grip on his hand kept him from stumbling. On a terrace below, they paused at the sound of sandal steps. Robyn was dragged back against the wall, mouth covered again, as two palace guards passed by.

This was a game, the little prince decided. He loved games, even in the middle of the night. His mother would explain the reasons, and he wanted very much to talk to her anyway. Just before he'd fallen asleep, Thayne had said he would take Robyn for a walk on Sojii if Mama and Papa let him. Usually Thayne was very selfish with his things, especially his Lasony pony.

"Come," the lady murmured and pulled him forward along the terrace and then out into the gardens beyond.

They were near the sea wall now. Ships' bells clanged in the distance, rocked by the slow roll of the tide. Behind them, Zankos's clamor was muted, blown inland by the sea wind.

"My mama's out here?" Robyn asked, curious now but not afraid.

This time the woman didn't answer. Her sweet fragrance mixed with the scent of citrus blooms as she crouched down beside the boy, long hair hiding her face. Robyn saw starlight glint off of something long and shiny, felt an instant of sharp pain in his chest, then nothing more.

\* \* \* \* \*

Davi had fallen asleep with the *Book of Stones* for his pillow. This brought bizarre and incomprehensible dreams, but nothing more, though it was a practice Gaylon might have cautioned against. The young duke's Stone could easily answer the subconscious wish as well as the conscious.

The hurried pounding on his door dragged him back to wakefulness that morning, and, his mind a little fuzzy with sleep yet, he answered it. Rose, her hair mussed and eyes puffy, stood on his threshold, a single palace guard behind her.

"Milord, Prince Robyn has disappeared."

Davi blinked. "What?"

"He's gone from the nursery."

"Have the king and queen been told?"

"No." Now there was stark fear on Rose D'Jal's face. "I hoped he might be found first. If he's only wandered off, it would be senseless to alarm Their Majesties."

"They must be told, Rose. Who was watching the children last night?" A strange foreboding had settled in the pit of the duke's stomach.

"Their nanny, Bessi. She's with Thayne and Lilith now, but she remembers hearing nothing." The young woman looked up. "She's so afraid, milord."

"So am I," Davi muttered, then, "Go quickly and inform the king and queen. I'll join the search."

He didn't bother to change his clothes, only donned slippers and ran his fingers through his hair. Robyn, where are you? But the duke had always been more closely bonded to Thayne, and now he couldn't sense anything of the youngest prince. A four-year-old boy would go exploring at any opportunity. He'd simply awakened before everyone else and gone off to play. That rationale did nothing to ease Davi's dread.

Palace guards and servants hurried along the corridors. The duke passed them all without a word, headed for one of the many staircases that led to the palace's second tier. Guards had searched there already, no doubt, but Davi kept on until he reached the huge third floor cupola. From here the view in all directions was magnificent. The red glow of the rising sun spread across the city's tall buildings beyond the wall and through the palace gardens below. Plants and trees threw long shadows westward.

With his Stone-enhanced vision, the duke carefully studied the grounds until at last, in the thin shadow of the southern wall, he saw a tiny mound of light cloth. The dread multiplied a thousandfold. Now the stairs tripped and hindered him as he rushed down them. In the hall, he barked orders in Wynnamyran at a palace guard, then noticed the confusion on the man's face.

"Follow me," Davi snarled in the Xenaran tongue.

The ground sloped downhill to the seawall, not steeply but steadily. It seemed forever before they reached the spot he'd noted from the cupola above. There, already in tears, Davi fell to his knees beside the tiny body of the prince. Glazed eyes, the color of the sky, stared into infinity, and the duke touched the cold, bluish skin of the child's baby face.

On the front of the little nightshirt was a small red stain around a slit from a sharp blade. It had been neatly done. Robyn had not suffered, but the thought brought no comfort. Davi gathered the boy up, noting the stiffened limbs. Death had found him a while before.

"Oh, gods!" he moaned through his tears. "Why? Why?"

The climb back to the palace offered no answers, only serving to drag the duke deeper into a morass of stunned grief. Gaylon and Jessmyn waited at the top of the gentle slope, the queen in nightdress and robe, the king in breeks, shirtless and barefoot.

Jess said nothing, only came forward to take the child from Davi's arms, but her eyes were huge with disbelief. The king spoke, making demands. His duke failed to hear him, his attention on Jessmyn and her burden. No tears had fallen yet. Her mouth worked soundlessly for a moment, then her gaze fixed on Davi.

"Heal him," she said faintly. "Please, Davi."

Her plea tore his heart. "I can't, milady. He's already dead."

Angered at his reply, the queen turned to her husband. "Use your Stone, Gaylon. Bring him back."

The king's face crumpled. "Jess, I can't do that. You know I can't do that."

"You brought Arlin back from the dead," she said, eyes still dry. "Isn't a son more important than a friend?"

"My love, the consequences of necromancy are too great. I brought Arlin back only to destroy him again."

"I don't care about the consequences. We'll protect him, keep him safe. Gaylon, I beg you. Bring Robyn back!" Now the queen's voice rose with hysteria.

Forcibly the king pulled his younger son from his wife's arms. "Death cannot be denied . . . only accepted."

Jess backed away from him, horror on her pale face. "No!" she shrieked, and turned and fled.

# Fifteen

Thayne rode Sojii along the beach, aware of the splash her hooves made in the tiny wavelets that slid onto the shore. Behind him rode half a dozen palace guards—constant companions now, even at night. The water, sparked gold by the morning sunlight, had trapped the young prince's gaze. Far to the southwest, ships under full sail scudded over the Inland Sea, some headed toward the ports of Zankos and Katay, while others veered right, on their way to the Inland Isles and the far southern ports.

The water here along the shore was brackish and foul with waste from the city. Thayne wrinkled his nose at the smell, but pushed Sojii on, unwilling to return to the stables. Within the palace grounds, they made ready for Robyn's funeral procession, and the crown prince couldn't bear the weight of his mother's sorrow and anger any longer. His father, too, had lost all sense of reality. The king had begun to terrorize Zankos in his outrage and grief.

Determined to find the murderer, he'd systematically gone through the servants and guards first, then sought out the opposing aristocratic houses. Anyone, male or female, without proof of whereabouts two nights before was unceremoniously thrown into the underground dungeons just outside the palace walls. There they awaited the judgment of an outraged sorcerer-king who had already destroyed the city of Zankos once.

Thayne shivered despite the warm day. His own guilt lay heavy in his chest. He'd slept while Robyn died. If only he'd awakened when they'd come for his brother, but both he and their governess had heard absolutely nothing. The shiver ran deeper. What if they had come for the eldest prince that night? Now shame was added to the guilt. The son and heir of a king should be more than willing to die in his little brother's stead.

Sojii danced a step under him, and Thayne nudged her into a lope. His guards followed, their half-armor and weapons clanking. The white pony's thick mane slapped his face in the wind, and she fought him for more rein. Finally Thayne gave her her head and felt her stride lengthen under him until they were racing headlong through the shallow surf. If only they could run faster, perhaps they could somehow outdistance the pain and the misery, but it followed close on their heels.

Robyn had never gotten to ride Sojii, though he'd begged many times. When his older brother had finally given in, it had been too late. It seemed they'd fought all the time over every little thing, as siblings often did, shouting hateful words at one another, even coming to blows. Thayne had actually hit his little brother. The thought horrified him now, and wind and tears stung his eyes.

The most frightening thing, though, was his parents' behavior. While the king raged at the world, the prince's mother walked about in a daze, sometimes crying, mostly silent. They seemed to have lost all reason, both in deep mourning, but worse yet, a great rift had grown between them. Husband and wife refused to speak to one another or suffer each other's company, all because the king refused to use his powers of necromancy to bring Robyn back to life.

"Thayne!"

The shout came from behind him, barely audible above the drum of hooves and the wind. Thayne twisted in the saddle to look back. The duke of Gosney followed on a sweated and foam-flecked Crystal. Unhappily the prince reined his mount in.

Davi halted beside him. "It's time to return. Your mother is frantic with worry. It's cruel to leave her alone so long at a time like this."

"I can't return, Davi," the boy said with a shake of his head. "I'm no help to anyone, and it hurts too much to see my mother suffering."

The duke scooped him from Sojii and onto his own animal. "Nevertheless, you have to come back. A prince and heir will face many difficult tasks in his lifetime. This is only one of them."

Guard in tow, they returned to the palace stables, leading Sojii at a calm walk so the horses had cooled by the time they arrived. The grounds were strangely quiet, and the few stable-boys about behaved in a subdued manner. Thayne wanted to groom his little mare first—anything to avoid the inevitable—but the duke hustled him along a path through the gardens. Everything remained still. Even the always bustling city seemed hushed on the morning air.

They found the queen in the main courtyard, surrounded by her ladies-in-waiting and Nials Haldrick. Rose held Lilith, cooing to the baby, while Sandaal played soothing music on her mandolin. At sight of Thayne, his mother left her couch to rush to him. He stared up into her swollen face and endured her almost painful embrace, and then her fingers gripped his right hand tightly.

"Where have you been? I've been so frightened."

"I told you I was going riding, Mama."

"Did you?" Jessmyn's frown turned immediately to a sad smile. "Come eat. There're sesame cakes and stuffed dates and almond candies. They were Robyn's favorites."

"I know, Mama."

There'd be tears next. Her lightning-quick mood changes hurt Thayne and scared him, too, though Master Haldrick had said they were normal for a mother struck with sudden grief. The duke had gone to talk with the physician. They spoke in low tones, and Haldrick shook his head a couple of times.

"Why?" the queen asked the air around her. "Why?"

This was a question she had voiced hundreds of times over the last two days, and as always, they were followed by tears. Katina came to wrap strong arms around the woman while she sobbed brokenly, but Thayne, without any comfort to offer, turned and rushed away across the courtyard toward the nearest palace entrance. The duke and physician hurried after him.

Their company and sympathy unwanted, the prince dodged into another corridor and ran in hopes of losing them. Random turns brought him finally to the last place in the world he wanted to be—the palace's main chamber, the equivalent to Castlekeep's great hall, only many times larger. Here was where his mother's coronation had been held. Now the huge chamber was filled with flowers, and in the midst of all those blooms lay a tiny coffin.

Thayne stood panting, coppery hair plastered with sweat to his forehead. Something pulled him across the hall against his wishes, pulled him toward the little casket that sat on a wide pedestal at the center of the floor. They had dressed the small prince in a red satin outfit, the one he had worn to watch his mother crowned queen of all Xenara. His face had been powdered to hide the bluish cast of his skin, and his eyes were closed. Sleeping . . .

"Wake up, Robyn," his big brother ordered gently. "Wake up so Mama won't cry anymore, and Papa can rest." The little body, once so animated, failed to respond. "Does it hurt?" Thayne asked. "Does death hurt?"

"No," the king answered from behind him, and the child's heart nearly stopped.

"Death brings true peace, Thayne. I promise you, Robyn isn't suffering. Not . . . as we are." His father's arm encircled the boy's shoulders.

"Let's go home, Papa," the prince said, voice quavering. "They hate us here. No one wants us. Let's take Mama and Lilith and go home to Wynnamyr. I don't ever want to be king of this place—not where they kill little children. I want to go back to Castlekeep." Despite a sudden aching homesickness, no tears fell.

The king pulled him close. "I wish we could, but not now. Not after what's happened. There's got to be an accounting for Robyn. But people change and so do countries. This sort of thing will stop happening if your mother remains on the

hrone, Thayne—if you someday take her place as a wise and
ust king."

"No," the prince muttered, his attention on Robyn's pale,
empty face. "Have you found the ones who did this, Papa?"

"Not yet," his father growled. "And the dungeons are full."

Thayne looked up, the rage and pain finally too much.
"You should kill them all and destroy the city again. These are
horrible people. They don't deserve to live." He'd stunned the
king with that statement, but the next question hurt him. "If
you really have the power with your Stone to bring Robyn
back to us, Papa, you've got to do it. For Mama's sake."

"By now your little brother has passed far beyond my
reach." The heaviness in the king's voice was not lost on
Thayne. "Necromancy carries too high a price, Thayne. Your
mother's in such pain, she's forgotten the consequences of
such magic. It's best for all of us if you never speak of this
again." He caught the boy's shoulders in his hands. "That goes
for speaking of Zankos's destruction as well—but at least
you've made me think. In my own pain, I've overstepped myself and abused my powers. I can't arrest an entire city for a
single crime, however hideous. These aren't all horrible people, Son, and they shouldn't be made to suffer for what a few
bad ones have done."

Now his father stared at the tiny body in the casket. "Go
back to your mother. The funeral begins soon, and you're all
she has at the moment. I'll have the guards release those I
unjustly imprisoned." He turned away, then paused. "Please,
Thayne . . . learn from my mistakes."

The prince watched the tall slender man cross to the nearest
exit and thought that he would never be the king his father
was. To rule both Wynnamyr and Xenara one day seemed
impossible, even terrifying. His throat grew tight, and the first
sobs nearly strangled him. The world was falling apart around
him. Nothing would ever be right again, not without Robyn.
The cloying odor of the flowers forced the boy to finally
move, sent him at a run toward the corridors to find his way
back to the main courtyard and his mother.

*  *  *  *  *

Jessmyn lay on the low couch in her apartments while Nials Haldrick gently massaged her hands. His touch soothed her mental turmoil, if only for a brief time. She'd drunk the valerian tea they'd brought her, but could face none of the meal. Tears welled behind her eyes as they had the last two days, ever ready to fall. The queen hated tears, hated crying. To her, they indicated a basic weakness, something a monarch must never show, yet she had lost all control over her emotions.

In this age, a mother worried about her children for many reasons. Illness and accident claimed many young lives every year. The peasants of Wynnamyr had large families, not only to provide help with their farms, but also because inevitably some of their young ones would be lost. This was a sad reality, given the lack of medicines and qualified physicians.

To have a child murdered, though, made the loss all the more devastating. Murdered. Did the killer have children of his own? If so, how could he love and defend them and still be able to stab another child—a toddler—in the heart? It made no sense. Nothing made sense anymore to Jessmyn.

The physician's fingertips traveled to her shoulders and neck, digging deep into muscle as hard as rock, then followed her jawline. All the while, Jessmyn found herself listening for a small familiar voice to call her name, some part of her convinced that Gaylon had relented and used his powers.

The funeral procession would begin soon. In so warm a climate, the dead were dealt with in all haste, and the queen had already held off as long as she could. The Grand Envoy, old and unwell to begin with, was confined to bed, but Rose and Kat and Sandaal stood waiting in somber gowns. Thayne, his face frozen in some unreadable mask, paced out on the private terrace. The last two of their party, Gaylon and Davi, had gone to release the new prisoners from the dungeon. The queen failed to understand this sudden change of heart in her husband. Among those he turned loose might well be the man or men who had assassinated his own little son.

The thought angered Jessmyn, and that anger was compounded by Gaylon's refusal to save Robyn. Deep inside her, she knew the king had made the only choice he could, and that that choice had caused him far worse pain than even she suffered. Her own hurt, however, made it impossible to accept, and the anger helped her survive the loss of a child.

Out on the grounds a trumpet sounded, an achingly sorrowful series of notes. The duke of Gosney had returned, and now he assisted Nials in helping Jessmyn rise from the couch. Her head spun a little, and Davi steadied her, a hand on her elbow.

"Milady?" he asked. "Are you all right?"

She nodded wordlessly, afraid the tears would betray her again.

"She'll need your support out to the coach," the physician murmured.

"Mama?" Thayne stoutly took her other elbow, though he had to reach up to do so.

After that, almost everything was a blur. The queen vaguely remembered the coach, where she sat with the sleeping Lilith clutched in her arms and her ladies and her son seated around her. The sun hung dreamlike in a cloudless sky overhead. Robyn's flower-shrouded coffin rode near the head of the procession, and Jessmyn searched the faces of the people who lined Zankos's streets, wondering. Was it you who killed my son? Or you?

What touched her most, though, were the tears in so many eyes. It seemed odd that anyone in this land would care for a child they'd perhaps seen once if at all, the son of a woman so many of them didn't truly want for their queen. Some of the women openly sobbed, and the cool breeze that touched Jessmyn's cheeks reminded her that her own tears still flowed.

At some point, she realized that Gaylon and Davi rode behind them, both dressed in black with black ribbons tied about their heads in the Xenaran fashion of mourning. Those who recognized the sorcerer-king stared openly, some curious, some appalled, most without expression. This was a time of sorrow, not animosity.

Much of the populace followed the funeral procession up

out of the city and onto the plain. There, a pyre had been
built, a small one, and on it they lay Robyn's small casket. The
king lit the fire with a torch, not his Stone, and stood back to
watch the flames devour the body of his young son. Sandaal
stood close to Jessmyn, a hand tight about her arm—for support and to stop any impulse of the queen's to fling herself
forward.

Jessmyn, stunned, stood fast, however. Now she must
accept absolutely the loss of a little red-haired toddler who
had so often clung to her skirts with grubby hands—a tiny
boy whose hugs and wet kisses had brought her such joy.

"No . . ." the queen said softly and collapsed bonelessly into
Lady D'Lelan's arms.

*　*　*　*　*

The duke of Gosney held Thayne tight against his chest. He
crouched with the boy on the tiles of the main courtyard,
where the funeral buffet had been set out. Lords and ladies of
Zankos drifted by, all with dour expressions, whether feigned
or not. For a very long time, the crown prince clung to Davi,
his face buried in the young man's shoulder. There were no
tears, only this desperate need for an anchor. The duke felt
Thayne's moods as always, felt the struggle for strength mixed
with grief and guilt.

Nothing he could say would help the prince. Time alone
would heal the pain of loss, but his helplessness dragged at
Davi. Jessmyn paused beside them, a small plate of cold food
in her hands. After collapsing at the funeral, she had somehow taken control of herself again. The finality of the funeral
pyre seemed to have brought her to her senses, at least for the
moment. Now she served the Xenaran nobility with her own
hands, regal and graceful as she moved about the courtyard,
truly a queen.

"Would you eat something, milord?" Jessmyn asked, voice
gentle but clear.

"Thank you," the duke replied. Thayne's grip around his
neck had loosened slightly, and Davi reached for the plate.

The queen touched her son's head. "Are you hungry, Thayne?"

"No, Mama," the child said, pulling away from Davi finally.

"You must eat, darling."

"I will. Later, Mama, I promise."

His mother nodded, eyes unfocused, vision again turned inward and distant. She moved on to speak with another group of finely dressed ladies, none of whom Davi recognized.

"I want to ride Sojii," Thayne said suddenly. "I want to saddle her and ride away and never come back."

The duke set his plate on a nearby low table. "Where would you go?"

"Anywhere away from here."

"No matter where you go, Thayne, nothing will change," Davi told him in a soft voice. "Robyn will still be dead. But your parents will have lost their other son. I don't think you really want to hurt them like that. . . ."

"No," the boy sighed, exhausted from grief.

"Why don't you lie down for a while on one of the couches. No one will mind."

Thayne nodded dully and crossed the wide yard to an empty couch. The duke followed the child with his eyes, then caught sight of Gaylon seated in a far corner, Sandaal in the chair beside him. They leaned close in quiet conversation, and Lady D'Lelan touched the king's hand with light fingers. Despite himself, Davi felt a twinge of jealousy. The lady-in-waiting, after all, merely soothed the troubled husband of her queen. Jealousy had no purpose except to cause distrust and pain. Consciously the duke forced the feeling aside. There'd been really very little between the two of them, duke and lady, since their arrival at Zankos.

Davi noticed Master Mensen at a buffet table, heaping his plate with everything he could reach. The big merchant enjoyed the food, if not the company. On impulse, the duke retrieved his own dish and went to meet the man.

Largo looked up, then grunted, "Ah, the duke of Gosney. How do you fare, sir?"

"Well enough. And you, Master Mensen?"

"Quite good, thank you. Quite good." Largo glanced around. "Though, of course, 'tis a sad time for everyone."

"It is," Davi agreed, picking idly at the food on his plate with his fingers. "Could I ask you a few questions, sir?"

This didn't please the merchant. "What kind of questions? I've already gone round and round with Her Majesty's husband. I was asleep in my bed, my dear wife beside me, when the poor child was murdered. I'm not responsible for what happened."

"Of course you aren't," the duke soothed. "I've no doubt of your innocence, but you might help me find whoever hired the assassin."

"How? I'm a simple merchant with little or no dealings with the aristocracy."

The aristocracy? Davi pushed on. "You've heard rumors then. What are the people saying among themselves that they wouldn't say to the king of Wynnamyr?"

"Not much." The big man shrugged. "They have suspicions, but that's all."

"Let me hear those suspicions."

"So that your sorcerer-king can take his revenge? Hardly. Whoever it was did a despicable thing, but these are my countrymen, and I won't set them up to be butchered."

Davi's jaw tightened. "Gaylon Reysson isn't looking for revenge, only justice. No one but the guilty will be punished."

"So you say, Lord Gosney. But I have no reason to love or trust your Red King."

"I'll be sure to tell the queen of your reluctance then, Master Mensen," the duke said coolly. "I'm sure she'll take it into account the next time the privy council meets."

Largo's face reddened. "There's no need of that." He glanced around him at the small groups of people, then murmured, "Look to someone within your own household for the answers to your questions."

"Who?"

"That I don't know. Now if you'll excuse me . . ." The merchant took his overloaded plate to another table, but his appetite seemed poor all of a sudden.

"Look to someone within your own household." Davi considered that with ice in his belly. Who? And could the big man be trusted? Probably not, but the duke would nevertheless begin his search here within the palace walls.

He gazed across the courtyard once more and found the king and Sandaal still sequestered in a corner, speaking earnestly. A moment later Gaylon rose and strode away to one of the many corridors that radiated out from the yard. Lady D'Lelan sat awhile longer, then she, too, stood and followed the king into the palace.

\* \* \* \* \*

Sandaal's sympathy had been bad enough, Gaylon decided, but her quiet, gentle devotion had completely unnerved him. She was a complicated woman, highly intelligent, talented, and beautiful, but her behavior mystified him. Jessmyn was all these things, too, and her behavior mystified him no less. For so many years, the king had relied on her deep strengths for his own survival. Her love and support had buoyed him during the constant upheaval of his life.

That support had been withdrawn, though, since Robyn's death. The queen, standing in the same room with her husband, seemed a thousand leagues away. No amount of reasoning would change the fact that Jessmyn's tiny son was forever gone, or that Gaylon Reysson had had the power to save him.

He headed without direction down the halls of the palace, intent on leaving the pain behind. No matter the horrible consequences if the king had called up the spirit of the Stone to bring Robyn back from death—this loss was his fault, and he would carry the guilt with him always. The corridors, light and airy, twisted their way through the great structure, but Gaylon paid no heed.

Slippered footsteps behind him made the king turn. Lady D'Lelan had followed. Annoyed, he halted on the red tiles.

"Milord, forgive me," the young woman said, contrite.

Gaylon sighed. "There's no need, but I'd rather be left to myself for the while."

"Highness, please." Sandaal looked down at her black silk slippers. "Your hurt and sorrow are so strong that you mustn't be alone. Let me help you. . . ."

"No one can help me, milady. Go away. Go back to the funeral celebration and comfort Davi, if you will. He's the one who loves you."

Lady D'Lelan's serene face altered, anger flashing in her dark eyes. "He loves his Sorcerer's Stone above all else, just as you do, Gaylon Reysson. I pity your poor queen with a sorcerer for a husband instead of a man. But I could make you one, if you'd let me."

The tone of voice, the impudence, enraged the king. He caught her upper arms in his hands and jerked her toward him, but somehow his intentions changed as she neared. Fingers digging deep into her soft flesh, Gaylon trapped her mouth with his. He had never kissed a woman other than Jessmyn, and the danger, the guilt, only excited him all the more.

Sandaal didn't fight the kiss, though it was rough, even cruel. Instead, her arms wound tightly around his neck. Her lips, sweet as honey, pressed eagerly against his, and the king felt himself slipping deeper into her trap. The woman was a sorceress in her own right, capable of bewitching the men around her. Gaylon gave in to her spell willingly, taking comfort where it was freely offered.

The sudden sharp tread of boots on the tile floor made the king abruptly disengage from the kiss. Davi stood in the corridor, his face impassive.

"Excuse me, milord," he said carefully and turned away.

"Davi, wait!" Gaylon called, but the young man had already passed around a corner and disappeared.

The king cursed bitterly and pulled Sandaal's hand from his neck. She wore a faint smile now, as if somehow pleased with herself. Irritated, Gaylon pushed her from him.

"Go away, Lady D'Lelan . . . and stay away from me. I've a wife I love and a dear friend who loves you. We've sorrows

enough to deal with at the moment. I don't want to hurt my
family any more than I already have."

"Certainly, Majesty." Sandaal curtsied, the smile still on her
lips. "But you can't deny my love. There are some things
beyond even your powers." Her tone carried the same infuriating insolence as before, and she reached for him again.

This time Gaylon called on his Stone. A bright shimmering
blue curtain formed between them, and Lady D'Lelan backed
against the wall with a frightened gasp.

"Whatever it is you feel for me, it isn't love, milady," the
king said. "I've wronged you, taken everything and everyone
you've ever cared for from you. What I can't make you understand is the suffering that's caused me—each moment of each
and every day. I loved Arlin as a brother, too. I've never had a
friend so close or caring, and never will again." He let his blue
barrier waver between them. "If you can't forgive me, Sandaal,
I understand. I'll never forgive myself. But don't play these
hurtful games. Don't say you love me—"

"But I do! I swear by all the gods, I do."

A sad hopelessness filled Gaylon. "Then I'm doomed to hurt
you again. I can't return your love, now or ever. And the sad-
dest thing of all is the pain this will cause Davi. Or do you
even care?"

The look in the young woman's eyes proved she did, but as
quickly as that look came, it disappeared. To the king of Wynnamyr, Xenaran motives seemed unfathomable, but Sandaal's
confused him utterly. Enough to know she cared about the
duke of Gosney.

"Go away," Gaylon said again, gruff and angry. "Leave me
be."

Her lips pursed, and the lady opened her mouth, but the
king cut her off.

"Go!"

Sandaal D'Lelan turned slowly and walked down the corridor, toward the council chambers where the others mourned
Robyn. The Stone's blue light faded into empty air, and the
king stood awhile longer, his attention on the city beyond the
palace walls. Lamps flickered there in the dusk, but the

citizens were subdued this evening. The usual shouts, the clatter of hooves, and rumble of wagon wheels had ceased. The common folk of Zankos grieved with their queen.

Davi must somehow be found, Gaylon realized. Some explanation of what the duke had witnessed must be made, otherwise a rift would develop between them, to grow steadily wider. Sandaal's timing had been perfect. What worse moment to complicate already complicated matters? Or perhaps she'd merely seen an opportunity and seized it. Whatever the king told his duke, it would have to keep Lady D'Lelan's image pure in the young man's sight. With a troubled sigh, Gaylon headed back to the council chambers.

*　*　*　*　*

Raf D'Gular found he didn't enjoy the queen's sorrow nearly as much as he'd hoped. Perhaps the fact that he'd lost three young brothers to illness and accident had something to do with it. His own mother's grief had remained vivid despite the years.

The funeral buffet had not disappointed him, though. Despite his slender shape, Raf had an enormous appetite that rivaled even Kyl's. His father, also in attendance, disdained the tables loaded with food, however, possibly because he could no longer eat with any grace. The sling had been discarded, but his right hand remained tightly bound and nearly useless.

His youngest son stayed well clear of the old man, unwilling to be the brunt of his anger in front of a crowd. Kyl had been left at home, much to his unhappiness, but Raf had promised to bring him a sack of goodies from the buffet. All around, the huge chamber was filled to overflowing, and among the aristocrats and merchants were a number of commoners—something King Roffo would never have allowed. This queen ruled like no other before her, and only time could measure her worth. So far, young D'Gular enjoyed her unorthodox methods, but having nothing, he had nothing to lose under her rule. Unlike his father.

Rose and Katina D'Jal appeared near the buffet table not far from Raf. In dark clothes, their fair skin looked almost bloodless, and Rose's eyes were swollen and red. D'Gular contemplated them. Kat had not been crying. Her strength had always been the greater of the two sisters. Perhaps it was the elder D'Jal sister who spied for Raf's father. But, no, neither woman had the intelligence for such business.

He searched the crowd for Sandaal but found the queen first. Prince Thayne clung to her hand tightly, his eyes glazed. Devastation marked Jessmyn's lovely face, and she had aged a dozen years over the past few days. The Grand Envoy, stooped and crippled, stood beside her, offering comfort, but the king of Wynnamyr was nowhere near.

Gaylon Reysson, a head taller than most of those around him, stood at the far end of the chamber . . . with Sandaal D'Lelan, the woman leaning close, a hand on the king's arm. Raf saw her briefly through a break in the crowd. For a moment only, they were lost from view; then, as the intervening group of people moved again, the man and woman were gone. His interest pricked, young D'Gular shoved his way impolitely through the mourners to the exit nearest where the king had stood.

This corridor led into the palace, toward the royal apartments or back to the kitchens and the servants' quarters. Raf chose the former direction and moved at a hurried walk. The low murmurs of the crowded council chambers dimmed until he heard the distant rap of boot heels on the tiles. Much closer came the quiet sound of slippers. D'Gular followed at a careful pace, intent on the pursuit and what it might reveal.

Sandaal hurried to catch up with the king, and Raf hurried, too—so much so that he nearly revealed himself. Around the next curve in the corridor, where it opened up on one of the palace's many terraces, the king of Wynnamyr had paused in the dusky air. There Lady D'Lelan caught him. Raf backed two quick steps down the hall and waited, trying to silence his ragged breathing.

They argued, king and lady, over strange things. A long silence fell, and Raf dared to venture a look. Gaylon Reysson stood locked in Sandaal's embrace, their kiss urgent and hard. Boot steps behind him made D'Gular dive into the thick evening shadows of a recessed doorway. The duke of Gosney walked past, unaware, then stopped dead in the passage, his pale face gone even paler.

"Excuse me, milord," he said, voice empty of emotion, then turned and rushed back the way he'd come.

"Davi, wait!" the king cried, but the young man had already disappeared.

Deep in his shadows, Raf grinned. Whatever the duke's relationship to Lady D'Lelan, he had just had a shattering revelation—and Gaylon Reysson, Davi's sworn lord and king, had been the cause. What a wonderfully complicated predicament.

The voices on the terrace had lowered. Raf once more dared to leave his hiding place to better hear their words. The two argued again briefly, then Sandaal made a sudden proclamation of love for the king of Wynnamyr. That news stunned D'Gular. Elation followed swiftly, though. With that one act, the woman had finally convinced Raf of her duplicity.

In all the years Raf D'Gular had known her, Sandaal had shown love for no one. So painful a childhood, filled with loss and mistreatment, had left her deeply scarred within, left her a cold and distant woman. Raf had always been attracted to her, had at one time shamelessly pursued her, but the lady allowed herself no real friends, let alone lovers—her defenses were that strong. Sandaal was D'Gular's only romantic failure, something that still frustrated him.

On the terrace, the king of Wynnamyr made his choice. His wife and family were far more important to him, and this he made utterly plain to the young woman. Raf wished he could see the lady's face, now that she had felt rejection, too, but Gaylon's steps sent him into hiding again.

The king swept by, headed back to the council chambers. After a momentary quiet, Sandaal followed—well behind Gaylon Reysson. Raf let her pass, then trailed after her at a distance, his mind churning over this turn of events. Within the chamber, the subdued crowd still managed to create an undercurrent of sound, the murmur of hundreds of voices.

Servants moved through the room, collecting empty plates and cups.

Young D'Gular found a fresh cup filled with a golden Xenaran wine and drank as he searched the area for Jessmyn D'Gerric. She stood with a small group of merchants at the foot of the dais. Raf refilled his drink and wound his way through the crowd to the stairs of the queen's throne.

"Forgive me, sirs," she was saying, "but I cannot discuss policy now. Another privy council is scheduled three days hence. Bring your questions to me then. I'll be glad to answer them."

The merchants bowed and turned away, frustration on their faces. How rude to approach Her Majesty at a time like this, Raf thought. He slipped quickly to the queen's side, the wine cup held out to her. She looked up in surprise, but took the offering anyway.

"I was instructed by the Grand Envoy to eat or drink nothing before it was tasted." Jessmyn eyed her visitor thoughtfully. "Would you poison me, Lord D'Gular?"

"There's only one way to know for certain," he answered, and taking the cup from her, he sipped the wine. A moment later, he grinned. "Still alive. But then how could I harm such a beautiful queen?"

That brought a faint smile to Jessmyn's lips, though her eyes remained bleak. She retrieved the wine and drank. Raf straightened his shoulders.

"My honest condolences, lady. Our houses may be enemies, but we needn't be. Have they discovered the person responsible for your son's murder?"

Jessmyn's smile faded. "No, and it's something I prefer not to think about. . . ."

"I know, milady," Raf said, his voice low, his attention on the small groups around them, "and I'm so sorry to bring the subject up, but I would like to help if I might. Being a member of one of your opposing houses, I have the chance to gather information. In Xenara, information is our most important weapon."

"Your lack of loyalty makes me leery, sir." The queen

continued to sip from her wine. "What of your father and brother?"

Young D'Gular looked away. "I've no love for my father for many reasons, and my brother is merely his pawn. I would deal honestly with you, madam."

"Really? And what would you ask in return?"

"Your friendship, Highness. Nothing more."

The queen's smile returned. "Nothing more? You sound less and less like a Xenaran."

"You're in agreement with Harren in that," Raf muttered.

"What will the others do, should they learn you're spying for Jessmyn D'Gerric?"

"Kill me." Again the young man looked away. "I already have information to pass to you as a show of my good faith. Are you strong enough to bear it?"

"This news is that weighty?"

"Indeed, milady. It will test our new relationship like nothing else could."

The queen's fingers tightened on the cup. "Tell me."

"A short while ago," D'Gular told her, "while I walked in the corridors, I came across the king, your husband, on the northern terrace in the embrace of Sandaal D'Lelan. They were kissing, milady."

Jessmyn's eyes clouded, filled with confusion and hurt, then a touch of anger. "Are you being cruel, milord?"

"No, Majesty. To add so much to your sorrow would seem cruel, but this is something you need to know. I only wish it were not so."

"If it is so," Her Majesty said, her voice tight, "I will expect you to keep this information, any information concerning the royal family, to yourself. Is that clearly understood?"

Raf bowed. "Certainly, madam. Merely send for me if you wish my services." He turned and walked away as quickly as was seemly. A queen's wrath could be dangerous.

There were other dangers, though. From the midst of a small crowd, a hand caught Raf's upper arm in a grip so tight it brought shooting pain. His father, a huge glowering bear of a man, dragged him to the side, away from the others.

"You seem to have the queen's ear, boy. What lies have you been telling her of me?"

Raf tried to wrench his arm free and failed. "We spoke," he said, teeth gritted against the pain, "only of simple things—of funerals and sorrow. Your name never came up."

"Well, see that it doesn't," Harren grunted. "For if I find the faintest hint that my dealings are known to the queen, you'll suffer for it, Raf. I swear to you."

"I know nothing of your dealings," his son dared to say. "I'm never allowed at your secret meetings with the others."

"Because I don't trust you, boy. Your allegiance is to yourself alone. Now, stay clear of Her Majesty and of Kyl or suffer my wrath. That's a promise, boy."

"Yes, Father," Raf answered quietly, eyes downcast to hide his outrage. "I'll obey milord's orders."

Somewhat appeased, Harren let go of his son's arm. He returned to his covey of friends, Raf forgotten. The young man pushed his way through the crowd, furious, toward the outer doors, then paused by one of the loaded buffet tables. The first thing he'd do once at home would be to see Kyl, bringing him the promised cakes and candies. Only defiance of his father could ease his anger.

# Sixteen

Davi had returned to his chambers, unable to face the queen and the crowd that attended Robyn's funeral again. After his initial fury, a strange calm had descended upon him. Already he found excuses for the two people he loved most in this world. Was it so terrible for Sandaal to be attracted to the king of Wynnamyr? And Gaylon, sorcerer though he be, was also a man, and not immune to the charms of so beautiful a woman. A kiss was only a kiss, after all.

The pain of betrayal remained, however, a sick hurt that threatened to choke the duke. So blinded by love and so tired by his endless hours of work in the *Book of Stones*, he'd never once imagined that something might be happening between Gaylon and Lady Sandaal. Fool! And what of Jessmyn? This could break her heart. At all cost, the queen must never learn of her husband's lapse.

A knock at his waiting-room door startled him. Davi considered ignoring it, but the knock came again, louder, more urgent.

"Davi! Please let me in."

The sound of Sandaal's voice made the hurt throb all the deeper in his chest, but the young duke of Gosney rose slowly to his feet. The woman had reached to knock again when Davi pulled the door open. Wavy black hair fell to her waist, and kohl darkened her black eyes. Her gown, also black, was made of layer upon layer of sheer silk. The sight of her brought Davi even worse pain.

"Davi, you must let me explain . . ." she began as she stepped over the threshold.

"There's no need," the young man answered tonelessly. "I can accept what's happened . . . but what of the queen? Have you thought of the pain she already suffers?"

"I never meant to hurt anyone, milord." She found a seat near his and settled into it. "It was impulse, Davi . . . nothing more. I felt his grief, his confusion and loss, and the need to bring him comfort overpowered me." Sandaal stared into Davi's eyes. "He simply responded to my need out of his own devastation. You mustn't blame him, Davi, not after Robyn's loss."

The duke wanted desperately to believe her. Why hadn't he thought of this one simple explanation himself? On the surface, her logic seemed flawless. Davi felt the heartache ease, but only a little.

Lady D'Lelan went on. "You must have faith in me, milord. Did you think that there'd been other secret meetings between the king and I? There hasn't, and never will be. You are the dearest person in the world to me, Davi."

Hope soared, along with confusion. "Truth?" the duke asked.

"Truth . . ."

"Then why, in all this time, have you never let me know? You've hidden your feelings too well."

"Because," Sandaal answered uneasily, "you have other, more important, things in your life—your king and your magic. And there are things about me that I can never tell you. Sadly, Davi, our love was impossible from the start."

"Why? Your love has been all I ever wanted from that first night we met. I know more than enough of your suffering as a child. Do you think I care about your past, so long as you share your future with me? Magic hasn't kept Gaylon Reysson from being a husband and father."

"Nor has it made him happy. No," Lady D'Lelan murmured, "I never meant to love you . . . and should never have let you love me." Davi detected remorse in her voice and wondered why. Sandaal stared into infinity. "It matters little now, for I'll be gone soon."

"Gone?" the duke echoed. "Where? Why? You can't leave. I won't let you."

She smiled sadly as she stood. "There's no way you can stop me—not even with your Sorcerer's Stone—and you can't follow, milord." Sandaal's hand had found the door latch. "Good-bye, Davyn, son of Daryn." The young woman slipped out, closing the door behind her.

Davi stood frozen, unable to follow. The finality of her words weighted him down, and the only emotion he could muster was anger.

She loves me, she loves me not. . . . The childhood rhyme circled in his head until he thought it might burst. None of what the woman had said made any sense. What cruelty to admit her love finally, then just as quickly take it back. The memory of her lips pressed to Gaylon's only deepened the hurt. The duke had never felt the touch of those soft lips. Next came self-loathing. This was his own fault, so clumsy and awkward in the matters of courtship, he'd failed to win her heart.

In the midst of all the palace upheaval, there was no one even to ask advice. Somehow, despite everything Lady D'Lelan had said, Davi would win her back, prove himself worthy of her love. Finally he turned to the one thing that could bring him comfort still—the *Book of Stones*.

\* \* \* \* \*

The main chamber had emptied somewhat in the late afternoon. Exhausted, the queen remained on her throne, accepting the occasional condolences offered by lords and merchants. The wine had been flowing freely, and not a few were slightly unsteady on their feet. Gaylon had returned to the council chambers earlier, but spent his time on the floor among the mourners. Once or twice he glanced Jessmyn's way; then his eyes shifted aside, and he would find another full cup of wine to empty.

Rose and Katina stayed close by, tending to Her Majesty's needs as best they could while keeping watch on baby Lilith. Thayne, no doubt sick of the whole business, remained seated at the foot of the dais where his mother could see him. At last, when Lilith grew restless and cranky, the queen called four of the guards to her and directed them to return the prince and princess to their rooms. Rose would go as well. The young lady-in-waiting took the cooing baby in her arms.

First, though, Thayne ascended the steps two at a time to the throne to hug Jessmyn, throwing his arms tightly around her neck.

"Don't worry, Mama. We'll be all right."

"Of course you will," she agreed, still unreasonably afraid. She watched him leave in his fine dark quilted breeks and coat, the tall guards close on either side. The tousled red hair and freckles were so like Robyn's—other than that the two boys had been as different as day from night. From the very beginning, Thayne had disdained childhood, even babyhood. He carried himself always with an inherent dignity—undoubtedly a future king. Robyn, though, had let Jessmyn cherish his infancy, let her dote on him. . . .

Her eyes blurred, and she fought the sob that had started in her chest. Katina arrived immediately with a handkerchief.

The queen blinked her tears away. "Kat, please find my husband. There's something I must discuss with him."

"Yes, milady," the young woman said dutifully and headed down the stairs and into the crowd.

Perhaps these were things better left said in the privacy of their shared bedchamber. Jessmyn drew a ragged breath. Perhaps they were things best never said. Raf was the son of her greatest enemy, though it was well known that father and son shared little love. Young D'Gular's impish smile could mean many things. Only there had always been honesty and openness between husband and wife—even in the worst of times. Raf might have somehow misinterpreted what he'd seen and heard, and only Gaylon could put things in true perspective.

Kat found the king at the far end of the hall—an easy enough task, for the man stood nearly half a head taller than most of the guests. His steps slightly unsteady, Gaylon wove his way through the mourners toward the dais. Katina came with him, stopped now and then by relatives along the way. The king arrived, his climb to the throne slow and trudging, while Kat remained below.

"My lord," Jessmyn said gently, but though he faced her, Gaylon's hazel eyes gazed beyond her shoulder. "I was about to leave the chamber. I've mourned in public long enough. Would you retire with me?"

He nodded. "Certainly, my lady."

His voice, his stance, every move seemed wrong. Raf had neither lied nor been mistaken, and Gaylon, gifted sorcerer that he was, had no knack for deception.

"It's true, then," the queen said, fighting to keep the sorrow from her voice.

"What?" Gaylon asked.

"It's true what I've heard about you and Lady D'Lelan."

The king paled. "Since when do you listen to gossip, Jess?"

"Only when you prove it true by your actions."

"And what tale were you brought so quickly?" Gaylon demanded, on the defensive.

"A tale of stolen kisses in empty corridors."

"Not so empty after all. It was Davi that told you." The king made a fist of his right hand, and his Stone glittered blue with his anger. "In all our years of marriage, I have never once been unfaithful. Why should you doubt me now, my lady?"

"Because perhaps your love for me has waned, Gaylon Reysson," Jessmyn flared, then heard herself say the unforgivable. "You didn't love me enough to bring Robyn back to me."

Gaylon's face contorted, not with rage but with remorse and agony.

"My lord, wait!" Jess called, though he was already down the long steps and headed across the chamber, roughly shoving others out of his way as he went.

The cruelty of what she'd done struck the queen hard. To blame her husband for the nature of magic was impossible. She had already come to that conclusion, yet somehow, deep inside her, the resentment still dwelled. A freshet of tears began to flow, and her pent-up emotions spilled forth. Her heartbroken wails brought Nials Haldrick at a run. Kat and the Grand Envoy arrived moments later, but Jessmyn was barely aware of any of them, barely aware of the physician as he scooped her into his arms and took her from the hall.

*　*　*　*　*

Davi had told her. So there was betrayal in all directions. The king paced among the young orange trees clustered near the north wall. Bats, dark silhouettes against a darker sky, flashed by overhead in the evening air. The city beyond the palace grounds had begun to come back to life. Official mourning by Xenaran customs would last a fortnight, but Zankos was a city of commerce, a shipping port filled with foreign sailors who sought recreation.

Nothing remained of Robyn now but memories and the black headbands worn by the men of the immediate family and their retainers. Gaylon had gone to the nursery to bid Thayne good night, his anger and frustration at Jessmyn carefully hidden. That one empty mattress near the others had stabbed him in the heart.

Worse were the doubts now. Perhaps he should have sought Robyn's soul and brought it back. Perhaps the sorcerer-king might have found a way to forgo payment this one time. But how? Death and life were a delicate balance. The price for one life was the loss of another—another as dear as the first. Not a choice Gaylon would willingly make again.

So he paced among the trees with their tangled branches and waxy green leaves. Jasmine perfumed the warm air. His love for Jessmyn had never been stronger, yet how could he convince her of this? Especially after a tryst with Sandaal D'Lelan, however brief and unwanted. Gods, he hated this land! There was nothing here he wanted, nothing to hold him but his family—what was left of it.

The children could be sent away, back to Wynnamyr, but even there their safety could not be assured, not against the plots of powerful and wealthy Xenarans. These men—these creatures—wanted Jessmyn off the throne and one of their own placed there. Surely she would see now the futility of try-ing to rule Xenara. Let them put another on the throne, and Thayne might be free of the obligations set on him by his grandparents.

But, no. The blood of Roffo would always have a claim to this kingdom, and thereby be a threat. Gaylon struck futilely at a nearby branch, and the sharp ends of the twigs tore the flesh on his hand. The pain felt good, a small punishment for failing his dear wife when she'd needed him most. Only time would heal their true wounds, if they were given the time. Divided as they were, in emotional turmoil, the royal family was at its weakest and most vulnerable. Now, of all times, Gaylon must be vigilant.

Tired, he paused to lean against the high palace wall that caged them in, trapped them here. Tonight the king would sleep in his own apartments. Best to leave Jessmyn alone until she'd had time to think, to remember the love they had shared from early childhood. Then he might explain what had really happened on the terrace with Lady D'Lelan.

First, though, Gaylon must find Davi. His world must be falling to ruin as well. While nothing had truly happened, San-daal had meant it to. The young duke's love had been mis-placed all along, and for that cruelty, Gaylon couldn't forgive the lady. Still, in Davi's eyes, the king would be the villain here. Oh, gods, what a tangled, hopeless mess!

Guards challenged him at the palace's northern entrance, then snapped salutes and let him through. The great council hall held only servants and slaves, clearing away the food and dishes, mopping the soiled tiles. Guards walking their watches passed him in the corridors. Within the royal quarters, Katina met him at the door to the queen's apartments.

"How is my lady?" Gaylon demanded gruffly.

Kat's eyes were puffy and red. "Her Majesty is resting. Mas-ter Haldrick has given her a sleeping draught . . . strong enough to make her sleep through both night and day. What . . ." the young woman began, then fell silent.

"Go on," the king said.

"Milady grew hysterical after speaking with you, Sire. May I know what was said?"

"No!" Gaylon snapped and strode away, the anger reasserting itself.

His knocks on Davi's door went unanswered. The king let himself into the apartment and found it empty. The *Book of Stones* lay open on the wide desk with a fat candle flickering beside it. The wax dripped down the sides of the taper, tearlike. Gaylon's Stone began to glow as his hand neared the tome. Davi had been here recently, seeking solace in the Book.

Too tired to await the young man's return, the king left the room for his own chambers. He paused at the door, touched by a tiny apprehension, but only darkness greeted him within and a breath of cool, scented air. The Stone in his ring brightened, creating a soft blue glow about him. His own *Book of Stones* lay near. Exhaustion sent him to the armoire to disrobe.

In breeks and stockings, the king searched for his nightshirt. The madness in the palace the last few days had left the servants busy and disorganized. A gentle stir of the air brought that faint scent again—jasmine. Gaylon froze.

"Who's there?" he asked, already certain.

"Milord." Sandaal's voice, husky and low, came to him from the direction of the bedchamber.

The king held his ring high, brightening the Stone, and blue light fled into the corners of the room. Sandaal D'Lelan stood on the bedchamber threshold, covered in the Stone's light and nothing more. Gaylon's gaze remained fixed on the smooth glowing skin, the swell of her breasts, the slender curve of her hips and narrow waist. Her beauty trapped him, held him transfixed and speechless. Long blue-black hair glistened, drifting over her nakedness, caressing her body.

Gaylon felt a sudden ache in his loins that made him grit his teeth and broke the spell momentarily.

"Get out of here. Now."

"No, milord." A single tear slid down a perfect cheek. "I cannot live without your love. If you will not have me, then use your Sorcerer's Stone to destroy me now and end my suffering."

Her words held the power of truth, or so it seemed. The king felt her longing and hope, her desire, and despite himself, it tugged at him, pulled him toward her. Sandaal caught his ringed hand in hers and kissed his fingertips. A jolt of passion slammed through him, unlike anything he'd ever felt. The world disappeared around him, wife and children and recent sorrows all forgotten.

Nothing existed but the gentle pull of her hands as she led him into the bedchamber, and there by the bed, her lips found his. Sandaal guided his own hand to cup one firm breast. Deep inside, a tiny voice cried an alarm, but the scent of her, the feel of her made him deaf.

Gently the lady pushed him back on the mattress. He watched distantly as she took his right arm and placed it on the small table beside the bed, the wrist turned up.

"No!" someone screamed and broke the spell.

Out of reflex, Gaylon snatched his arm back just as a sword blade drove into the hardwood with enough force to divide the table. The crash of furniture woke him further. Sandaal raised the sword again, aimed at the king's head this time, and he struck at her with his Stone, a brilliant flash of cobalt that somehow met another of equal strength.

The explosion of that meeting of such magical powers flung Sandaal across the chamber. Gaylon was sent rolling off the mattress and onto the floor. The bright light faded as he got to his knees, and there was Davi, duke of Gosney, standing on the threshold, his Sorcerer's Stone glowing a dangerous blue.

"Murderous bitch!" the king said through his teeth. "Why?"

Sandaal stood, naked still, defiant yet afraid. She refused to answer.

"What better way to kill a sorcerer?" Davi said for her. "She planned to separate your hand and Stone from your body. Then, rendered powerless, you'd be easy to destroy. Right, my love?"

The woman remained stubbornly silent.

"It was you who killed Cally, you who pushed Thayne from

the cupola." Davi's voice grew heavier as he spoke. "It was you who killed Robyn."

"No," Sandaal said suddenly, adamant.

"Yes," the king snarled. His rage had built again, his Stone brightening dangerously. "For all these cruel things, you'll die."

"Wait, milord!" the duke said desperately when Gaylon raised his hand. "You must leave her to Xenaran justice."

"It's my family she's harmed. It's my son's blood on her hands."

Lady D'Lelan had finally realized her fate lay in these two men's hands. She wrapped a sheet about her body, gaze darting between Gaylon and Davi.

The duke shook his head. "Milord, Lady D'Lelan is only an agent of whoever it is that means to destroy Roffo's bloodline. Hold her in the dungeons, let her own people use Xenaran torture to get what answers she might refuse us. Think, Sire. Hold your powers."

Gaylon was torn. His own thoughtless lust had nearly cost him his life, and that shame brought an anger all its own, but it would also have left his family undefended. The moment of unthinking rage had passed, however. The thought of killing a women, even a callous assassin, didn't set well.

"So be it," he said wearily. "Let this brutal, pitiless country deal with its own. And for Robyn's death, may your suffering be endless, Lady D'Lelan."

"I didn't kill him," Sandaal almost whispered. She looked up. "Your life was all I ever wanted, Gaylon Reysson—for Arlin, for my mother, for all my sisters and brothers. I would never harm a child. Never!"

"Tell your lies to the master of the dungeons, woman. Davi, bring the guard. We'll soon get to the bottom of this, and one or more of the great houses of Xenara will die with Sandaal D'Lelan."

Lady D'Lelan's anger returned. "May I dress first?" she asked without a hint of fear, then gathered her dress from a chair without waiting an answer.

As she dressed, the king finally realized what trauma Davi

was going through. His deep green eyes watched her every move, gazed sadly on the dark silken gown that covered her beautiful skin. Love was not something easily given up. Love often went on after betrayal after betrayal. And that was love Gaylon saw in his young duke's face.

Davi's grip on Sandaal's arm was tight, though, rough even. "We'll find you new quarters tonight, milady," he said coldly. "Something suitable."

"Davi . . . I swear I didn't—"

"Be quiet. Your words have no power over me now . . . or ever again."

After they were gone, Gaylon sat heavily on the mattress, confused and worried. Sandaal's sword still lay on the tiles near the shattered table. She had very nearly accomplished her aim tonight. That thought made him shiver.

# Seventeen

A dozen palace guards escorted them through the high gates under fluttering torchlight. One, an over-captain, had caught Sandaal's other arm in an iron grip, fingers digging deep. Near the end of her emotional limits, the young woman still fought to keep her head up, her face clear of expression. The duke of Gosney held her opposite arm, and while his grasp was not so rough, neither was it gentle.

She had failed completely, after long years of work and planning and taking advantage of every situation. Lady D'Lelan's steps grew heavy with remorse. The promise of revenge to a dead brother had been such an awful burden for a twelve-year-old girl . . . but it had helped her survive, given her purpose when all else was gone.

They approached the dungeons, a series of dank catacombs dug into the hillsides near where the temple of Mezon had stood. The simple outer portals had been cut from granite and told nothing of the horrors that awaited within. Sandaal had heard stories, though. On the edge of the dark stairs, she pulled back sharply and earned herself a sudden blow to the face from the over-captain.

When the soldier tried to strike her again, however, Davi caught the man's wrist with his free hand. The pendant on the duke's chest began to glow, and the captain's mouth contorted with agony.

"You will not take liberties with her ladyship," the duke told him in a quiet, eminently cold, voice. He loosed the man, and his Sorcerer's Stone's frightening glow faded.

Sandaal saw the anger on the soldier's face, but also saw the fear and a new respect. The palace guard would be more careful in the treatment of their prisoner now, and for that much, the lady was profoundly grateful. In Xenara's deadly games of politics, losers never dared hope for justice—only a swift end.

They led her beneath the stone arch of the entrance. The stairs spiraled down into darkness, and the stench that rose up from the depths made Lady D'Lelan feel ill. The duke had released her arm.

"I'll return later with the Grand Envoy," he was informing the over-captain.

Comprehension brought a sudden tightening in Sandaal's chest. "No, milord! Please! Don't leave me in this place."

"I've no choice," Davi answered, and the deep green eyes regarding her seemed made of ice.

Lady D'Lelan grabbed his arm in panic. "I beg you, Davi. Let me go. I'll disappear and never return. No one will ever know what happened to me. It'll be as if I died."

"You'll die soon enough," the captain growled with some amusement.

"Shut up," Gosney said sharply, his gaze still on Sandaal. "Your faithlessness means nothing to me, milady. I might even forgive your spying and plotting against Their Majesties. . . . Only you've murdered two children—one an unborn babe— and tried to murder another. No doubt Lilith would have been next."

"No, Davi, listen to me! Why would I do such a thing? I loved Robyn. I've loved the children always. My quarrel was with the king alone." Lady D'Lelan drew a ragged breath. "I'm guilty of attempting to assassinate the king of Wynnamyr, nothing more. By Xenaran law, I can be executed for that alone, only I don't want to die with you thinking I would do such monstrous things as murder babes! I didn't . . . I couldn't."

Davyn Darynson shook his head. "Words . . . you've always been so good with them. What better revenge on the man

who killed your family than to kill his?" When she broke into
tears of frustration, he only laughed bitterly. "You're wasting
your time, milady. That cold heart of yours has finally betrayed
you."

He called the leader of the soldiers aside and spoke briefly
with him, then left her there with a small troop of unsympa-
thetic guards. Their captain pushed her toward the curving
stone steps. The torchlight wavered in a draught, and her tears
blinded her enough to make her stumble continually on the
stairs. The thought of dying terrified and angered her. With
her death, Gaylon Reysson would have completed his destruction of the house of Lelan. All her careful plans had come to
naught.

The stench of burning flesh wafted up the stairwell followed
immediately by a series of hysterical screams. Wide-eyed, Sandaal looked around her and saw smiles on the lips of the
guards. They herded her down endless steps and finally into a
dark chamber with an enormous brazier at its center. Against
the mountain of coals that glowed there, shadowed figures
moved. The screams had died back to muffled whimpers.

"What's this?" someone asked in a husky, gravelly voice.

"She tried to kill the king of Wynnamyr," the captain
answered, chuckling.

"Well, well." The fellow moved into the torchlight, and Lady
D'Lelan saw a man of massive build, shirtless and sweating
from the heat. "We ain't had none so pretty in many a year,
nor so well dressed. Welcome, milady, to Jake's dungeon.
We're the finest equipped in all the land." He bowed grace-
fully despite his size. "The law must be satisfied, of course,
but I won't execute you for trying to assassinate Gaylon Reysson . . . oh, no. Only for failing to accomplish it." The man
threw back his head and bellowed with laughter. The palace
guards joined him.

"Bring her here," Jake ordered, and Sandaal was caught
again in a rough hand and pulled to the wall after the dungeon
master.

Chains rattled on their racks as he made his choice. "These
should be small enough."

Sandaal watched him fasten the cuffs around her wrists. The links of chain were huge and heavy and fell nearly to her feet.

"Put her in number three for now." Jake threw a big ring of keys to a soldier. Someone moaned from a table in the shadows beyond the brazier, and the big man turned. "Don't worry, lad. I ain't forgot you."

The guard led Sandaal down a narrow passageway. The stink of urine and feces was nearly overpowered by the stench of rotting flesh. They stopped by an oaken door, solid but for a tiny slot near the top. The young soldier pushed the door inward, then turned to her. Alone in the hall with only a rush light flickering in a bracket, he jerked her close, a rough gloved hand caressing her through the dark silk.

The lady pulled back suddenly, spinning away as she did. The heavy chain gathered enough momentum and height to catch the guard along the side of his head and send him staggering into the wall. His shout of pain and outrage brought the others at a run. Any chance for retribution was lost with their presence, and her captor merely glared at Sandaal, a hand to his jaw. Jake only roared with amusement at the sight of blood.

"Oh, this's gonna be better than we've had in a long while." The master shoved Lady D'Lelan into her cell. "Breaking you, my dear, is going to be a pleasure."

*   *   *   *   *

The quiet of the palace in mourning had been shattered by shouts and running booted feet along the corridors. Jessmyn, deep in a drugged sleep, struggled toward consciousness and failed. Then later someone sobbed brokenly near the head of the bed. Katina, the queen realized. By the light of a single oil lamp, Jess reached out an arm almost too heavy to lift.

"What is it, my dear?" she mumbled, still fighting the sleeping draught Nials had given her.

"It's Sandaal," Kat answered, and the sobs grew worse. "They've arrested her for trying to assassinate the king . . . and for Robyn's murder."

A long moment passed while Lady D'Jal continued to weep and the queen tried to make sense of what she'd heard. Master Haldrick's strong potion had distanced her from her own emotions. Exhausted, she felt no desire for tears, nor any tolerance of another's.

"Stop that!" Her Majesty commanded. "Tell me what's happened."

Kat blew her nose wetly into a silk hanky, then dabbed at her eyes. "I only know a little. It was Rose who found out. . . ."

"What?" Jessmyn couldn't hide her exasperation. "Found out what?"

"That Sandaal went to the king's apartments tonight. . . ." Here Katina grew very uneasy. "That she went there to seduce and kill your husband. She failed only because the duke arrived in time to shout a warning. The king tried to destroy Lady D'Lelan then, but Davi saved her with his own magic. The bedchamber is wrecked, milady—furniture and clothing burned."

The queen groaned. What madness was this? Sandaal had long ago made her peace with Gaylon, and no one could be so foolish as to attack a sorcerer. In their months together, Jess had grown close to the young woman, as close as Sandaal allowed anyone to come. The queen had learned in that time that Lady D'Lelan was both intelligent and sane. None of this made any sense.

Katina D'Jal continued to cry quietly. "Sandaal was sent to spy on you, Your Highness, to gather information for the opposing houses. It was she who killed Robyn and pushed Thayne from the cupola."

"No . . ." Jessmyn's confusion deepened. "Lady D'Lelan loves the children. She'd never do anything to harm them." The anger and irritation grew stronger. "What kind of proof do they have to condemn Sandaal of Robyn's murder?"

"Rose . . ." Katina began to sob so uncontrollably that her words grew difficult to understand. "Rose found a letter, a contract, in Sandaal's rooms . . . and a small box of gold coins. Payment for her services, though we have yet to learn who the employer is." The young woman buried her face in her hands. "She's always behaved strangely, but we had to take into account her sad childhood. Now look what she's done. You gave her your trust, and she betrayed you, Majesty." Kat's grief caught in her throat. "Oh, Robyn, that dear sweet little boy . . ."

"Be quiet!" Jess snapped, afraid of falling into that deep well of sorrow again. "Where is Lady D'Lelan?"

"They took her to the dungeons, milady."

"The dungeons? Dear gods." The queen dragged herself upright on the bed. "Stop sniveling, Kat. I need some paper, a stylus, and an ink pot from the desk. Hurry."

"But why?" The D'Jal woman's hands shook, and now she had the hiccups.

"Never mind," the queen muttered.

Dressed only in her nightgown, Jessmyn made her way into the private library. Haldrick's sleeping draught had her still dizzy, caused her limbs to refuse to obey, but Jess found the desk and the things she needed. Only her fingers refused to hold the pen right, and her confused words, half in Wynnamyran, half in Xenaran, slanted across the page, barely legible. Still, it would have to do. The queen reached for a stick of wax and her royal seal.

An attempt on the king's life was a serious crime, but Jessmyn couldn't condemn Lady D'Lelan, not when she had lost Arlin and her entire family to Gaylon. Even the king, given time to think, would understand and forgive. Unfortunately time was something they had little of. With a piece of paper and a box of coins for proof, the Xenaran people would also lay Robyn's death at Sandaal's feet and demand her immediate public execution. The queen had known Lady D'Lelan long enough to know she could not possibly be responsible for Robyn's death.

Katina had followed her into the library, and now she peered over Jessmyn's shoulder at the page on the desk. "The dungeon master won't honor this, milady. The king intends to execute Lady D'Lelan in the morning and has ordered her held in the catacombs until then."

"Oh, has he?" Jess said with a sudden peevishness. "Gaylon may be king of Wynnamyr, but I am queen of Xenara, and I will make the judgments here. I wish to be dressed . . . immediately." The queen stood, swaying, then sat down hard on the chair.

Lady D'Jal caught her elbow to steady her. "Your Highness, you must rest. Master Haldrick wants you to sleep the night and day through. He's very much worried about your health. I should never have awakened you."

"And when I did wake, everything would be over, and Sandaal dead." Jessmyn's anger heightened. "How dare he do this to me—take control of my country while I slept!"

"Majesty, I don't think the king meant to do any such thing—"

"I want to be dressed. Now. And send for some strong, hot cocoa from the kitchens. I need something to fight off Nials's potion. We'll bring Sandaal from the dungeons ourselves." That startled Kat, but before she could interrupt, the queen went on. "Someone plans to make Sandaal D'Lelan—guilty or not—a scapegoat for all that's happened. I intend to prevent that."

Katina looked deeply troubled. "Milady, please . . . the evidence is undeniable. Sandaal is guilty. Let others take care of this foul business. You've endured too much as it is."

"Not another word," the queen said firmly. "If you wish to remain my lady-in-waiting, you'll do as I ask. Immediately."

Unhappily Katina led her lady to her dressing chamber and began to choose a gown from the closet. Jessmyn wondered at her reluctance. The woman had loved Robyn deeply, but she had also spent months with Lady D'Lelan—certainly long enough to have formed some sort of loyalty.

And what of Davi? Had he, too, been turned so easily against Sandaal? Whatever the evidence, whatever had happened, the queen wanted to hear the young lady's explanation from her own lips. Jessmyn slipped her feet into her sandals just as the hot cocoa arrived.

"Thank you," she said gratefully, then realized it was Nials Haldrick who had handed her the cup, not Katina.

"You hadn't planned on leaving your bed tonight?" the physician asked, his tone severe.

The queen glared at her lady-in-waiting. "Tattletale." She turned back to Nials. "I *am* leaving my bed tonight, sir. As I would on any night one of my ladies is thrown in the dungeons."

"And what can you possibly accomplish, Highness, by a midnight visit to the catacombs—other than catching some dire illness?"

"What do you suggest, then?" Jessmyn demanded.

"Where have you laid your scepter, my queen? This is your country. Speak with your husband first. Inform him there'll be a trial under Xenaran law, over which you will sit in judgment."

Jess gnawed her lip. Gaylon would have usurped her power, given the chance—just as some of the noble houses had feared. It had taken weeks of grueling labor to prove to the Xenarans that she was their queen; now it was time to prove it to her husband.

"Master Haldrick," the queen said, "an excellent suggestion. But first I must speak with the Grand Envoy."

"Lord D'Ar was put to bed long ago, milady. Because of his age, he's at even greater risk to illness than you."

"Then let him stay abed." Jessmyn stood. "I'll speak with him there." Ignoring the physician's frown, she left the chamber. Katina followed close on her heels.

*　*　*　*　*

Davi returned to the king's chambers. The halls swarmed with palace guards now, searching for the enemy, while the enemy—a beautiful young noblewoman—had already been secured in the catacombs of Zankos. The duke ground his teeth and refused to think of what he'd done. The stench of the dungeons clung to his skin and hair and clothing. A bath, though, would do little to wash away the guilt.

Rose stopped him at the entrance to the children's quarters. Tearful, she buried her face against his chest, her fingers clutching his shoulders convulsively. Davi hesitated, then took the D'Jal sister in his arms. The sweet scent of rose oil filled his nostrils.

"What's wrong?" he asked and touched one soft, wet cheek.

"It just can't be, milord. It just can't!"

"What? What can't be?"

Rose continued as if she hadn't heard. "I had to get my shawl. The one she borrowed . . . This . . . this box fell from a shelf, and coins spilled out. More than a hundred Xenaran decos. All gold." The young woman sniffed loudly. "There was a paper inside. I gave it all to the king."

"Whose gold? Whose paper?" the duke said in frustration. "I can't understand anything you're saying, Rose."

"Sandaal's," Rose answered dully. "It's Sandaal's gold and her paper. A contract to kill little Robyn. But I just can't believe it."

The dark rage began to build in Davi's gut again. "Who wrote the contract?"

"It was torn off the page . . . that part."

"And you found these things in Sandaal's room?"

"Yes, milord . . . though I wish I hadn't. Gods, but I wish I hadn't." The D'Jal sister pressed against him even tighter. "I'm so sorry, Davi. I know how much you cared for her."

The duke untangled himself from her grip. "The king and queen have suffered far more than I. Save your sorrow for them. How are Thayne and Lilith?"

"They sleep. . . ." The quick change of subjects confused Rose, but she continued in her original direction. "Perhaps, milord, you might let me ease your pain a little. Only give me the chance, and I know I could make you very happy."

"You might . . . someday" Davi said, hiding his anger.

He walked quickly down the corridors to the king's apartments and found the door wide open. Five over-captains shared the main chamber with the king. Gaylon, eyes fever bright, gave his orders and sent them away, then turned to refill his crystal cup with a viscous amber brandy.

"Where do they go?" Davi asked and filled himself a cup.

"Some go into town to question the heads of the opposing houses. Some return to Lady D'Lelan's chambers to continue the search."

"Xenaran gold and a letter of contract isn't enough for you?"

"You learned of that already?"

Davi nodded. "From Rose." A touch of bitterness flavored his words. "How convenient that she find this evidence now."

"Does it really matter? Lady D'Lelan has been building her tower of deceit ever higher and higher. Now it's crumbled and left her to her fate." Then Gaylon took pity on his duke. "No one can escape his fate, Davi. Not even a sorcerer-king."

"I know. . . ."

"The evidence Rose found has only made things all the clearer for me. I've made the right decision—the only decision, considering. But I need the name of Sandaal's employer if possible." The king eyed Davi thoughtfully. "You told the over-captain what I wanted done?"

The duke gritted his teeth again. "I told him."

"Good. Hold on, Davi, please. I need you now more than ever. I need your strength and wisdom. Your love for the lady makes everything so much more difficult for you, but you understand why I've done what I've done." Gaylon searched his duke's face. "You do understand?"

"Too well, milord. Given a chance, I might have once died for Sandaal D'Lelan. But she forced me to choose between her and my Red King." The anger flowered once more deep inside him. "I only want it all to be over with as quickly as possible, for her sake as well as ours."

"Milords . . ."

The scratchy, aged voice made them turn toward the threshold. There stood Eowin D'Ar, in a yellow satin robe, beside the queen. Nials Haldrick, on the old man's other side, held a bony arm to keep him steady.

Gaylon frowned deeply. "What are the two of you doing out of bed at this time of night?"

"Her Majesty has come to speak with you," the Grand Envoy answered. "About Sandaal D'Lelan."

"She needn't have troubled," the king said. His face softened, though, when he glanced at Jessmyn. "Everything has been taken care of."

"That's the problem, Highness." Eowin stopped to clear his throat. "The queen of Xenara feels these are matters best left to her judgment."

"Absolutely not," Gaylon growled. He turned to his wife. "This is the one thing you should never have to face, my lady. You've had enough sorrow already."

Jessmyn's lip quivered. "It will cause me worse sorrow to know my husband has usurped my powers as queen of Xenara."

"That isn't so," the king flared, and the Stone on his finger came to life. "How could you think such a thing, Jess?"

"How can I not?"

Gaylon crossed the thick carpet to her. "This is not a Xenaran concern. I was attacked by an assassin and am within my rights to demand retribution."

"And only I can pass judgment," Jessmyn said coldly. "After I've heard the testimony and reviewed the evidence."

"But what good will that do?" the king demanded. "Except waste time and cause all our misery to go on that much longer."

The queen's jaw tightened. "I'm not convinced of Lady D'Lelan's guilt."

"Not convinced! Ask Davi, then. He was there. She would have killed me, woman."

"Why?" Jessmyn asked, tone gentle. "What have you ever done to her that she might seek revenge?"

Gaylon's mouth clamped shut, and Davi saw defeat in his tired hazel eyes.

His wife cocked her head. "I don't believe Sandaal would murder a child. I believe her only crime is the attempted assassination of a king—a grievous offense in any land. But since we are Wynnamyran, considered weak for our humanity and foolish for our love of simpler lives, we may also show mercy without causing outrage."

"I doubt that very much." Nials Haldrick spoke for the first time. "Majesty, think. If you show leniency, you'll lose respect. What's more, these are a callous people. Here in Xenara, executions are considered high entertainment. They won't thank you for saving Lady D'Lelan . . . not at all."

"I won't have her die," the queen said, jaw tight. "She has served us faithfully these many months—"

"Because it suited her plans," Gaylon cut in. He frowned at his wife. "No matter what, we can never trust Sandaal again. I won't have her around me waiting for another chance."

"Then we'll exile her," Jessmyn said in a rush. "Send her away."

The king looked to Nials for support, and Davi saw a sudden doubt in the queen's eyes. Even royalty must observe the laws of the land. The hard, cruel facts were finally coming clear to Jess.

"An attempt on a king's life," the physician said, "is the gravest of crimes." He dared to cross to the queen and take her small hands in his. "Milady, you've worked hard to win the houses over. Don't jeopardize the ground you've gained and prove yourself a silly sentimental woman after all. The last queen to rule Xenara did just that and brought herself a disastrous reign."

The stricken expression on Jessmyn's face made Davi's heart ache, though the reality of Sandaal's impending execution had failed to reach him yet. Very little of this made sense to him anymore. He imagined it now, Lady D'Lelan's body as lifeless as tiny Robyn's had been.

The image shattered him suddenly, the sight of her dark eyes closed forever. In all the time Davi had known her, the woman had kept him confused and wondering—one moment thoughtful and kind, the next cold and even cruel, but the thought of losing her brought a pain too deep to tolerate.

The Grand Envoy spoke, his voice weak but clear. "The council will sit in judgment with the queen first thing in the morning. We cannot waste a moment, since the entire city knows by now what's transpired here. They'll watch us most carefully to see how we react."

"We . . ." muttered Jessmyn bitterly, pale and drawn. It would be her judgment alone, and the guilt on her shoulders. "At least keep Lady D'Lelan imprisoned here in the palace."

"It cannot be, milady," Eowin answered. "There are . . . things we must learn."

The queen understood that reference all too well. If possible, she grew even paler, and dread washed through Davi. He felt the lady's eyes on him and glanced up. Jessmyn said nothing, but her gaze put a great weight on the duke of Gosney.

"Fair night, milords," she said, tone thick with irony, and turned to leave. Katina followed quickly on her heels.

\* \* \* \* \*

The absence of light made Sandaal's other senses all the more acute. Sounds and smells assailed her. Soft moans of despair filtered through the oaken door to her cell, and occasionally, from the main chamber, came shrieks of agony. Despite the cold air, Lady D'Lelan's skin prickled with sweat. The stink filled her nostrils, gagging her periodically.

She lay sprawled on a foul bed of damp straw, which had become the home of other creatures. Something tiny and many-legged crawled over Sandaal's bare leg, and she squealed, scrabbling away as quickly as possible, the chains at her wrists rattling. There was nowhere to go, though. A slick stone wall stopped her, and she squatted there in the filth, sobs caught in her throat.

Tears couldn't help her now. A surge of anger replaced the self-pity. She had made her choices, all along aware of the consequences. If Gaylon Reysson had been destroyed, her chances of escape had been few. Death was the ultimate goal of all living things, but a quick, clean death at the hand of a soldier was far preferable to this. Sandaal kept a vial of poison in her chamber, an honorable retreat after the assassination of a king, but one she could not reach at the moment.

Wavering light appeared beyond the tiny barred window slot of her chamber door. A key turned, and the door swung wide. Torchlight caused bizarre shadows to flutter against the dark walls. The man who held the torch wobbled across the straw toward her. His right leg seemed considerably shorter than the left, and he walked with the right foot twisted sideways. He wore no shirt, and whatever the cause of his deformed limb, his arms and chest were well muscled, huge.

"Come, dearie." He closed fingers hard around one of San-daal's shackled wrists. "The master summons ye."

The young woman started to fight, panic rising, then gave in to the hopelessness. Though she went willingly, her captor took pleasure in jerking her about. When she fell, he dragged her partway down the corridor before letting her rise.

"Here, Robet, be nice," the master of the dungeon growled from his place near the center of the main chamber.

Robet pulled her along, no more gently than before, and the two men shared knowing chuckles. They'd called him Jake, Sandaal remembered. Shirtless, like his assistant, the man must weigh twice as much, and his bare arms and chest were slick with fresh blood. Lady D'Lelan looked down at the table despite herself. The master's last victim still lay on the hard stone surface, dead.

They'd cut off his hands and feet and left them in a pile on the floor, along with his tongue and eyes. Blood dripped steadily from the table edge into two nearly full buckets set beneath it. Sandaal's stomach churned and bile rose in her throat.

"I'll . . . I'll tell you anything you wish to know," she said, her eyes on the gore.

"Certainly, milady," the master returned. "Most certainly."

That brought another round of chuckles. Jake pushed the body from the table, then dragged it away into the shadows. Robet caught the young woman's chains and jerked her for-ward. Sandaal broke, filled with such terror and horror that her strength doubled, even tripled. She jerked back on the chains hard enough to tear them free. They were her only weapon, and she whipped them into Robet's face.

The man screamed and fell back, but her victory was short-lived. Jake caught a handful of the lady's long hair from behind and swung her into the table. Before she could recover, he slammed a fist into the side of her head, knocking her to the floor.

Red-hot pain flared behind her eyes, and then a dark cur-tain slipped over her vision. Distantly Sandaal felt hands grip her, lift her. When the darkness faded, she found herself on the table, wrists and ankles fastened to the corners with iron bands. Robet leaned over her, a bloody track across his face, a wide grin revealing yellowed teeth.

"What'll we take first?" he asked. "An eye?"

The master appeared, a small knife in his hand. "First the bitch's tongue, I think."

# Eighteen

Unable to sleep, Davi wandered the corridors. The search of the palace had ended long since with nothing more of the assassination plot revealed—only those first bits of damning evidence to show for the effort. Guards stood by strategic doors in half-armor and helms, armed with lances and swords, proof that more would happen this night. The duke crossed the soldiers' paths wordlessly, too tired and sick at heart to respond to quiet greetings.

He caressed the Stone on his chest, finding comfort in the rough surface, the faint tingle of power through his fingertips. No hint of Orym had come to Davi since Gaylon Reysson had confronted the Dark King. Perhaps that ancient monster had finally been destroyed, though now the joy in that was gone. In the silence of a long deserted hall, the duke heard a sound—the scuff of a shoe or a boot. He paused momentarily, then went on. The sound came again, a furtive little scrape of leather against stone.

Davi ducked around a corner and pressed himself back to the wall, one hand on the hilt of the dagger at his belt. While the corridors still teemed with soldiers at their stations, there was no one here who could be truly trusted. A short time passed before the quiet, careful footsteps resumed, but when the assailant rounded the corner, the duke at first grabbed only empty air.

A mild and confused scuffle followed, and Davi, a hand tangled in red hair, felt the prick of a knife point just above his knee.

"How dare you!" his captive snarled, then looked up. "Davi?"

The duke released the boy. "Milord Prince, hasn't your mother suffered enough? This is not the time or place for games."

"This is not a game! I . . ." Thayne slowed, eyeing him warily. "I'm going to rescue Lady D'Lelan from the dungeons."

"What?"

"I can't believe you'd let her die," the boy accused. "She trusted you. She loves you."

"She tried to kill your father, Thayne. There's nothing either one of us can do to help her."

"But I will," Thayne snapped imperiously.

Davi shook his head. "No. You're going right back to bed. We've enough troubles as it is."

He reached to take the boy's arm, but Thayne caught him with a vicious kick to the kneecap and fled away down the hall. Limping and cursing bitterly, the duke followed. On a broad, dark terrace, he lost the prince. The wind brought tavern music and the clatter of hooves on cobblestones over the palace wall, which hid the sounds of the small boy. No matter. Thayne was headed to the dungeons.

It struck Davi as strange that Lady D'Lelan, murderer and assassin, would inspire such devotion in the very ones she'd been sent to destroy. Frustrated and angry with himself as much as the situation, the duke headed for the dungeons. The price of loyalty had gotten suddenly very high, and being forced to take sides brought unbelievable pain.

A guard at the palace gates had stopped Thayne. Davi could hear the boy's high, indignant voice arguing.

"What's the problem here?" the duke demanded.

The soldier bowed hastily. "Milord, I cannot let the prince pass, nor can I escort him back to the nursery because I'm here alone tonight."

"Why can't I pass?" Thayne growled in indignation.

"Majesty," the young guard said, "there are assassins about, and Zankos is never safe at night." He looked to Davi imploringly. "Perhaps you would take His Majesty back to bed, milord?"

"No!"

Davi caught the boy's elbow. "I'll take responsibility for the prince. Let us pass."

"Yes, milord," the guard replied slowly, obviously troubled. He opened the small pedestrian gate to the right of the huge double-doored one. Oil lamps on posts lit the steep roadway into Zankos.

"Come," Davi said to Thayne and led him down a narrower road.

"We're going to the dungeons?" the prince asked.

"Yes."

"We're going to save Sandaal?"

The duke sighed. "I suppose so, though no good'll come of it." Thayne pulled his dirk, and Davi shook his head. "There'll be no violence. We'll simply ask that the lady be released in our custody."

"But I want to rescue her," the prince said with some disappointment.

"And so we shall . . . but without trouble."

Another guard met them at the stone portal to the dungeons. This was not a soldier of the palace. His uniform, while designed in the same colors of the royal house of Roffo, was slightly different and far shabbier. The man himself had failed to bathe or shave lately, and wine stained the bottom of his tunic where it showed under the tarnished cuirass.

"We've come to see the master of the dungeon," Davi informed the guard, who grunted and stood aside to let them pass.

"Not a very pleasant fellow," the prince observed as they started down the long stairs. "It really smells bad in here."

Davi didn't answer. The torches in sconces along the wall threw fluttering shadows on the steps, making them all the more difficult to traverse.

"Watch your footing," he told the boy.

A high sharp scream, immediately cut off, made them freeze

on the stairway.

"Dear gods," Thayne cried and rushed downward, taking three steps at a leap.

"Wait!" The duke followed, the sound of the shriek echoing in his ear, his fear for Thayne goading him.

At the foot of the stairs, Davi collided with the prince, and they both very nearly fell. Thayne shuddered in the duke's grip, and Davi finally understood the fear the boy wrestled with.

Barely audible, Thayne whispered, "We must get Sandaal out of here."

The duke of Gosney agreed. Somehow the dungeons seemed worse since his last visit, the stench stronger, the air more chill.

The prince eyed the choice of corridors before them. "Which way?"

"This one," Davi answered and started into the tunnel on the left.

Now laughter filtered to them, a coarse, cruel laughter that made the hair on the duke's neck prickle. Thayne grabbed one of Davi's hands and dragged him hurriedly forward. His urgency pushed the duke into a clumsy run. Brighter lights appeared, and they slid to a stop in a wide smoky chamber.

Two burly shirtless men, bent over a stone slab, straightened at the sight of them.

"What do you want?" the larger one demanded, then noticed this guests' apparel. "Milords."

Davi recognized the master of the dungeon and noticed the bloody knife in his hands. The small shadowy form on the table lay still. "We've come for Lady D'Lelan."

The lesser man looked annoyed. "We ain't got the information yet that His Majesty wants."

"It's Sandaal," Thayne gasped suddenly, and ran to the table.

"Stay back," the master snarled. "We won't have children down here—not even princes."

Thayne ignored him. "Give me the keys." His small hands plucked at the bands on the prisoner's wrist. When Jake refused, the boy turned to Davi. "They've hurt her. She's bleeding."

"Give the keys to the prince," the duke said carefully, a sick feeling in the pit of his stomach.

The master glared back. "I already have my orders. I'll need to hear otherwise from the queen before I'll loose this woman."

"You'll take the orders of a duke and be glad." Davi's fingers closed over his Sorcerer's Stone, and bright blue light flooded the cavern. No violence, he had promised himself, but that was not to be. "Release the lady now!"

A wind gathered, rushing along the walls, turning the flames of the torches into fiery streamers. The master's assistant let out a low howl of terror and backed away from the table, but the master stood fast, defiant.

"Thayne!" the duke shouted above the gale. "Get down!"

The prince ducked under the table just as Davi's sorcerous wind blasted into Jake. The man staggered and fell, his knife flying free. Thayne had escaped to the far side of the table, then ducked behind the duke for protection against the wind. With effort, Davi gathered his powers again and stilled the gale. Fire burned in his gut, though, seeking release. The urge to destroy the master of the dungeon built in him, all his anger and fear turned to a sudden vile elation. Even so, he fought them down and stepped to the stone slab.

Sandaal's eyes were closed in the blue glow of the duke's Stone, and her face was bloodied. Long cuts scored her cheeks and forehead, her bare shoulders. Among the cuts were deep burns that had blackened the skin, and the nails on the fingers of her left hand had been torn out. Sight of the wounds brought another surge of overpowering rage. Davi's Stone flared even brighter.

"Davi, no!"

Thayne's voice, barely heard, came as if from a great distance. Fury washed through the duke, and under him the ground heaved. So there was some of Orym left, if not in the Stone, then in Davi—an ancestral connection that might never be destroyed so long as the duke lived. Frozen in astonished horror, the master of the dungeon at last recognized his danger. He fled shrieking toward the tunnels, his assistant close behind. A clamor of terrified voices filled the air from prisoners trapped in their cells, in the dark, alone.

Davi struck at the two fleeing men, then somehow managed to divert the energy at the last possible moment. Blue fire slammed into the lintel of the tunnel entrance, and chunks of rock exploded into the chamber. A piece of debris glanced off the master's hairless skull, knocking him to the floor, unconscious. The other man never faltered but kept on running. Thayne rushed to the table and fumbled with the key at Sandaal's cuffed wrists. The iron bands fell away.

"I need your help, milord," the boy said through chattering teeth.

Rage still seethed in Davi, and mindlessly he gathered power for another strike at the helpless master. Then Thayne's hands gripped his wrist in desperation.

"No! Sandaal's hurt, and we have to get her away. Now!"

Her pale, bloody, and burned face glowed eerily in the light of the Stone. Davi let his rage go, felt it leeched away by a rush of sorrow. The Stone flickered and died on his breast. Thayne had unlocked the cuffs from the young woman's ankles, and the duke gathered her up in his arms. Blood smeared the sleeve of his shirt. She felt impossibly light.

"Sandaal," he murmured to her, clutching her tight to his chest. "Sandaal."

She didn't respond. The pain had put her deep into a merciful unconsciousness.

"Come on. . . ."

The prince led Davi through an obstacle course of rocks and rubble and back to the stairs. They stepped around the dungeon master, leaving him there on the floor alive or dead, blood leaking from his scalp. The duke hardly cared. With Sandaal in his arms, the climb took longer and required far more energy. He was sweating profusely by the time they made the top.

"She needs doctoring," Thayne said. "We must get Nials Haldrick."

"No," Davi snapped. "I'll try to heal her . . . or we can find someone in the city, someone who doesn't know who she is or what's happened. Then we'll put her on a ship to somewhere far away and safe."

The prince nodded, and Davi noticed tears on his cheeks, glinting in the torchlight. Such a traumatic night, and far from done. The past week had been horrible for the boy . . . for all of them. Legs leaden, the duke started out. Another long climb took them into Zankos. Much of the night had passed, and with dawn so close, the streets were as empty as they ever were. Tired lords and ladies huddled or leaned against lampposts, awaiting carriages, while slaves swept the sidewalks and cobbles.

Groups of sailors passed them, drunk and noisy, but no one even glanced at Davi and his burden or the well-dressed child with him. The stink of the dungeons faded finally in the salt breeze that blew up from the sea. Thayne stopped to talk with one of the slaves, then hurried back to Davi.

"There's an inn at the end of this street. We can get a room there."

"Good." The duke let the boy lead. The sky to the east, above the buildings, had begun to lighten, and in his arms, Sandaal stirred. A faint moan escaped her battered lips. "Shhhh," Davi whispered.

"Here," Thayne called and pushed open the huge door of the Cricket Inn.

The duke brushed past him. "Find the landlord."

There was no need. A bell attached to the door jangled and brought the owner, a fat little man in a satin robe, down a broad staircase. This was not one of the better inns, but shabby and dirty and run-down. The landlord's gown was frayed at the hems and stained with wine. He fought back a yawn, then rubbed his eyes.

"I charge a gold deco a day, in advance. It's more for clean linens and . . ." The fellow paused, his gaze on Sandaal. "No, no. This won't do. You'll have to go elsewhere, milord. I don't allow no trouble here."

"She's hurt," Thayne said, outrage in his tone.

"Yes, and whoever done that will likely come looking for

her. Good night, milords." The man bowed and backed away.

"We're staying," Davi growled, then pushed past their protesting host to the staircase. "Which room?"

"Milord—"

"Which room?"

"I'll call the guard," the landlord blustered.

"Then there will be trouble," Davi promised him, "and lots of it. Which room?"

"Blast you, sir. At the end of the hall on the right . . . Number Four."

Sandaal moaned again, and Davi heard the pain in her voice. Legs wobbly and weak, he made it to the landing and down the hall. Thayne beat him to the room, opening the door for him. By the time Davi found the bed and laid his burden gently on it, the prince had found and lit the lamp. He went back to close the door in the landlord's red face.

"Can you help her?" Thayne asked, unable to hide his worry. "Like you helped me when I fell?"

The duke drew a long breath of air, doubly aware of his exhaustion. "I'm not sure."

"Should I go look for a physician, then?"

"Let me try first." Davi leaned over Sandaal and brushed away the hair that had gotten caught in the blood on her face. By the lamplight, the wounds looked even worse than they first had. Such cruelty made the duke grind his teeth.

"Let your Stone help you."

The duke glanced at Thayne and saw hope in his tired blue eyes. Perhaps the Stone could help. They were separate magics, the Stone and the healing powers, but the one might aid the other. It had seemed so the night Davi had healed Thayne after his fall from the palace cupola. Already a blue light flickered deep in the pendant on its chain, answering his subconscious desire. Davi put both hands out, one hovering over Sandaal's bloodied face, the other over her left hand. An internal warmth began, spreading quickly through his body, and the duke closed his eyes. They were gritty with exhaustion.

The warmth soothed him—too much—and he felt as if he were drifting on water, farther and farther away from all the misery. His attention scattered abruptly, and he woke with a start.

"Davi?"

On the bed, Lady D'Lelan had awakened, too. She stared, eyes open, at Davi. Her flesh was still burned and bleeding, and while agony informed her face, she remained silent.

"I'm sorry," the duke said quietly and closed his eyes once more.

This time he drew on the power, refusing to let the warmth distract him. He envisioned Sandaal's face and hand as they had been—smooth, soft skin, unblemished and whole. The process fatigued him even further, until at last he slipped bonelessly to the floor beside the bed.

Thayne squatted beside him. "Are you all right?"

"Yes," the duke answered, his voice no more than a croak. "What of Sandaal?"

"Better," the lady answered from her bed.

Davi dragged himself upright. Indeed, Sandaal had much improved. The cuts on her face had closed, the burns had partially healed. Even the fingertips had sealed over, though the nails were still gone. The lady was definitely better, but better wasn't good enough. Unfortunately, Davi's resources were exhausted.

"How do you feel?" the duke asked, gazing down on her.

Sandaal looked away. "The pain is less—much less, thank you."

"Then sleep for a while, milady," Davi told her. "We'll find passage for you on the ship that leaves soonest."

"To where?"

"Does it matter?" The duke pulled a purse from his belt. "If you're careful, this should keep you well enough for a time wherever you go. If you write me, I'll send more."

Thayne came to lean across the worn bedclothes. "I should go with you, milady. You'll need a man to defend you."

"Thank you, Majesty," Sandaal replied and managed a smile. "But you will need to rule Xenara one day."

"I don't want to rule Xenara. It's a nasty place, filled with mean, nasty people." The prince shook his head. "No. I've decided what to do. We'll go away together, milady, and when I'm old enough, you'll be my wife."

"I'm afraid I won't be suitable as wife to any man now." Sandaal touched her face gingerly.

"The scars will hardly show," Thayne said, peering close. "But I'd love you no matter what." His gaze faltered. "You tried to kill my father, which was a very foolish thing, and I think I know why you tried. It doesn't matter to me. I've loved you since the first time we met. Only Davi has, too, and I couldn't hurt him by taking you away."

Lady D'Lelan smiled again. "You're a dear, sweet child, and wise beyond your years."

"If you'll wait for me to grow up, I know I'll make a good husband."

"I'm certain of it," the young woman said, then turned her eyes to Davi. "But . . ."

Thayne sighed heavily. "But you love another. I understand."

"No," Sandaal said. "That's not it. Since my brother died, since my whole family died, I haven't been able to love anyone. I doubt I ever will. Thank you both for saving my life, but it's time for you to go. I won't take your money, Lord Gosney." When Davi opened his mouth to protest, she continued. "Please take a message for me to Raf D'Gular. He runs his father's import business and has contacts in all the countries south and east of here. I have my own money put aside."

"Do you?" The old feelings of betrayal and anger washed through the duke once more. "Don't count on the gold that was found in your chambers."

Lady D'Lelan frowned. "What are you saying?"

"Harren D'Gular is the queen's greatest enemy. That you would turn to Raf, a member of the House of Gular, in a time of trouble makes me wonder, milady."

"Raf and I have known each other since childhood," Sandaal said. "He's opposed his father for as long as I can remember." She gazed at the duke. "You confuse me, Davi. You risked the king's ire to save me, yet you seem as willing to judge me guilty as all the rest. Why?"

"I'll send your message to Raf D'Gular," Davi answered and strode to the door. "Come, my prince."

Thayne balked. "Sandaal shouldn't be left here alone."

"Majesty," Lady D'Lelan said, "I appreciate your concern and thank you for bravely coming to my rescue, but your father already believes me a murderer and traitor. If you fail to return to the palace, the king will think the worst, and nothing will stop him from finding me."

The prince nodded unhappily, then took her unhurt hand and kissed the fingers. "If you ever need me again . . ." Eyes filled with loss and sorrow, he went out into the hall through the door that Davi held open for him.

The duke of Gosney walked away from the room without a backward glance, aware that Thayne followed. Outside on the street, the morning sun glared in his tired eyes, and it took a moment to orient himself. Citizens already gathered on the walkways to start their daily shopping. Davi motioned to Thayne to keep up. The misery the duke felt over Sandaal had been replaced by another thought: Gaylon Reysson, sorcerer-king, would be incensed by this betrayal. The worst was yet to come.

\*   \*   \*   \*   \*

Raf returned from a night of revels blurry-eyed and still somewhat drunk. In the early morning, the house was still, and the thump of his fashionably thick-heeled shoes on the stairs seemed overloud. Sunlight had found the eastern windows of the upper story, a promise of the summer heat to come later in the day, but now the air remained cool, and D'Gular wanted nothing more than to find his bed and sleep.

But behind his bedroom door he heard a gentle sobbing. Perplexed, Raf let himself into the chamber and discovered Kyl hunched in a chair beside the bed, head down, his broad shoulders shaking.

"Kyl?" Raf asked.

The would-be king of Xenara looked up, and his sobs intensified at sight of his younger brother. That soft round face, uncreased by time, had one swollen, purpled cheek. Raf gritted his teeth. This was Harren's doing, punishment for some minor infraction, not that the pain meant anything to Kyl. He sobbed over the verbal abuse that inevitably came with his father's blows.

"Here," Raf said and offered Kyl a silk handkerchief from his pocket. "Don't cry. Was Father drinking again?"

The older sibling shook his head. "I told him what you said. I told him I didn't want to be king. Everyone was there, and when they left, he got very angry."

So there had been another meeting this past night. Kyl's anguish forgotten, Raf sat down beside him on the bed, intent.

"Do you remember what they talked about?"

"Who?"

"Father. Stef and Kij and the others."

Kyl's tears slowed, his sorrow momentarily forgotten. He wiped his running nose on an already damp sleeve. "They talked like they always do."

That talk would have made little sense to Kyl. Raf took his brother's hand and squeezed gently.

"Try to remember. Please. Were they angry . . . or happy, perhaps?"

The bigger man furrowed his brow. "Angry at first. Then happy."

"About what?"

"About . . ." murmured Kyl, eyes focused on the far wall, then his face lighted. "I know. Lord Aikim had been at the palace. He said someone tried to kill King Gaylon, and they put her in the dungeon."

"Her?" For some reason, Raf felt a sick jolt. "Who?"

"Lady Sandaal." Kyl frowned again. "Why would she hurt the king?"

Raf didn't answer. His mind raced, trying to understand. Kyl could be wrong, could have misremembered, but young D'Gular's heart told him differently. After a moment, he realized his brother was speaking again.

"Father hit me. I said I didn't want to go . . . I didn't want to kill the queen because she's so pretty and kind. Father hit me and said I was diso . . . disobedient. Is that bad, Raf? Am I bad?"

"No," the younger brother told him. "You're not bad, Kyl. But how do the fools plan to kill the queen?"

"With soldiers . . . lots of soldiers to raid the palace. More of the noble houses have joined us. They think the queen is weak now since her little boy died."

"My gods . . ." Raf muttered in awe. "No matter the queen's weakness. I can't believe their audacity to think they'll overcome a sorcerer-king."

"The king will be taken care of," Kyl pronounced.

"How?"

Kyl only stared at Raf, eyes puffy from so many tears, his young-old face empty.

"You don't know, do you?" Nor would he know what had become of Sandaal D'Lelan. The situation had somehow turned insane over a single night.

Raf laughed suddenly, startling his brother. This was madness, all of it. The noble houses of Xenara would lay siege to the royal palace, something not done in centuries, and Gaylon Reysson would retaliate as he had seven years previously. No matter that the sword of the Dark King, Orym, had been destroyed. Death and distruction would rain on Zankos once more.

A soft knock at the bedroom door diverted young D'Gular's attention. "Come," he said, and Kef, an ancient manservant, entered.

"A message, Milord Raf." The old man held out a bit of brown paper.

"From whom?"

Kef shook his grizzled head. " 'Twas left at the front door by a boy."

The note told of Sandaal's desire to see Lord Raf at the Cricket Inn on the Masons' Avenue. It was signed by Davyn Darynson, Duke of Gosney. Then she was safe. . . . An unrecognized tension drained from him, and Raf felt suffused with relief and the desire to see the beautiful woman.

"I have to go out," he told his brother.

Kyl looked troubled. "I want to come with you."

"No. For now, rest here. Sleep on my bed until I return." Raf turned to the servant. "See to him, Kef. I'll be back as soon as possible."

"Aye, milord."

The man's reply went unnoted. Raf was already closing the door, his thoughts filled with questions for Lady D'Lelan.

\* \* \* \* \*

Gaylon refused to let his guard go into the city that morning to search for the escaped Lady D' Lelan. His wife's reign had proven disastrous from the very start, and now a young sorcerer—in the company of a young prince—had defied his sovereign and stolen away an assassin from the dungeons.

In the king's outrage, though, was mixed a good portion of relief, and that only served to make him more angry at himself. How could he rule a kingdom when he couldn't handle the duke of Gosney or his very own son?

His broad terrace opened up on a view of the Inland Sea, and there he stood now, shirtless, the taste of the salt breeze on his tongue and the cool, damp feel of it against his cheek. In Zankos, the heat would already be approaching unbearable limits. Jessmyn stirred on the bed in the chamber behind him.

She had gathered her strength once more, as she had each time tragedy struck in her life, but she had slept nearly an entire night and day. Gaylon didn't blame her. In dreams, even unmagical dreams, a certain peace and control could be maintained. If anything, he envied her the peace that sleep had brought her. Somehow the madness had left her, once again leaving him the strong determined woman that he so dearly loved.

"My lord," he heard her murmur and turned to go to the side of the bed.

"My love."

His smile was reflected by hers briefly. Then the queen yawned and rubbed her eyes. "Have they returned yet?"

"Our enemies of the state?"

"Who else?"

"No. If Thayne weren't with the duke, I'd be worried." Gaylon leaned down to kiss her. "Are you certain they weren't on a mission for their queen?"

Jess nodded. "I'm certain. But only because they didn't give me a chance to ask them first. Are you terribly angry?"

"Furious." The king kissed her again. "With luck, Lady D'Lelan will take the next ship to some distant foreign land, and that will be the end of it."

"What if Davi goes with her?" his wife asked gently, gazing into his eyes.

The thought gave Gaylon pause. "Do you think he might?"

"He loves her very much, and she him."

"And their love has been no easier than ever ours was," the king added. "No. Davi is my duke. He'll never leave me."

Jessmyn reached out to stroke his cheek. "Davi's more than just your duke, my love. He's a sorcerer now, with untold powers. In many ways, he's already left you."

The truth hurt. Gaylon tried to hide his pain without success. He gathered the queen in his arms and hugged her close, then changed the subject. "You don't believe Sandaal killed Robyn . . . ?"

"She's a strange young woman," Jess agreed, "capable of many things, and while I wanted very much to condemn her, I knew all along that she wasn't responsible for Robyn's death."

"Someone is," the king said grimly. "And by the gods, that someone will pay. I swear it." In his arms, his wife trembled.

# Nineteen

Alone in the tavern bedchamber, Sandaal dozed, slipping in and out of a light sleep. There were things she must do, things she must remember, but in easing her pain, the duke of Gosney had allowed her respite from her cares. The day grew hot and sultry outside, and through the shuttered windows, the rumble of carriages and arguing voices invaded the lady's dreams.

"Dearest," someone whispered near her ear, then soft, warm lips touched hers.

"Raf?"

He sat on the edge of the bed and brushed loose hair from her face. "What have they done to you, my darling?" His pity and concern only angered her.

"No more than any assassin deserves." Bitterness colored her words.

"Assassin?" Young D'Gular touched the half-healed slashes on her cheeks. "Milady, I spend an evening dancing and dining and return home to receive a strange note from the Wynnamyran duke of Gosney. He asks that I spirit you onto the first sailing vessel that leaves Zankos. What am I to think?"

Sandaal closed her eyes momentarily. "Last night, Raf . . . Last night I tried to kill Gaylon Reysson."

A strange muffled sound made her look up. Raf's face was contorted with stifled laughter.

"You," he managed, "tried to kill a sorcerer?" Her expression caused his amusement to fade. "Sandaal, I know you too well. I can't believe you'd ever try anything so foolish."

"I had . . . magical help." Sandaal ignored the question in his eyes. "It hardly matters. I failed and was imprisoned. The duke and Prince Thayne freed me."

"And so you must flee the country," Raf added. He pursed full, sensuous lips. "We'll flee together, then. I've nothing to hold me here."

"Except Kyl."

Young D'Gular grimaced. Sandaal had known him always to be callous, self-serving, and cruel, but his one saving grace—the one thing that attracted Lady D'Lelan to him—was his devotion to his retarded brother, even though Raf had tried to hide it in seeming hatred.

"He'll come with us."

Sandaal shook her head. "No, Raf. Someday you must take Kyl away from here, but not with me. I'll be a fugitive for the rest of my life."

"Which may not be long without my help," Raf said. "You can't survive alone, milady." His expression turned thoughtful. "But then . . . you may not have to leave at all."

"What do you mean?"

"There just might be a change of regimes in the near future." The young man smiled. "It seems the royal family's recent misfortune has finally provided a common cause for the Xenaran nobility. An attack on the palace has been planned."

Sandaal felt an odd twinge of panic. "When?"

"That I don't know, but soon, I imagine."

"Surely they don't think they can overcome an entire garrison."

"Apparently they, too, have some sort of magical help or knowledge." Raf stood up and began to pace. "Perhaps the wisest thing for us, after all, is to run."

"Your father needs Kyl."

"Yes," Raf agreed. "Harren would be absolutely distraught if the Xenaran throne is taken, and he can find no son to place on it."

"That would please you, though." Sandaal noted the sparkle in the young lord's dark eyes. "Make whatever plans you wish, Raf. They matter little to me. I have decided to return to the palace."

"For all the gods' sakes, why?" Raf demanded, and Lady D'Lelan wondered at her own intentions.

"Someone must warn them."

"You're mad!" Young D'Gular paused by the bed again. "You must take the first ship away. I'll warn the palace."

Sandaal gazed at him hard. "No, you won't. It involves too much risk and not enough profit."

"I swear I will—"

"Don't bother." Lady D'Lelan found the strength somehow to struggle upright on the mattress.

"Then let me help," Raf insisted. "I'm the one with the information, and I'm the one most likely to get more. Let me go with you to Her Highness."

"You would destroy your own family?"

The young man shrugged. "I'd destroy my father . . . happily." He helped her to stand. "Come, we'll pay a visit to the queen."

\* \* \* \* \*

Davi returned the prince to his chambers. By the sidelong looks from the palace guard, the duke knew that their recent escapades had not gone unnoted. Still, no one tried to halt them. Thayne, overly tired, had little to say when they finally arrived at his door.

"Don't worry," the duke told him. "Just rest and let me take care of everything."

Rose appeared suddenly in the antechamber to cluck over the boy and glare at Davi. She closed the door in the man's face before he had a chance to utter a word. Well . . . His own exhaustion blurred his thinking, and the duke wandered away down the corridors, deeper into the palace. His directionless travels brought him to the queen's apartments some unknown time later. Hand raised to knock, the duke paused, uncertain, but then the door opened and Gaylon stood before him.

A wry smile touched the king's lips. "Come in . . . if you dare."

Davi groaned inwardly, but took that brave step over the threshold.

"Where is she?" Gaylon asked calmly, following his duke into the main sitting room.

"Gone . . ."

"Gone where?"

"Leave the boy be," Jessmyn said from the entrance to the bedchamber. "He's tired and hungry."

"And disobedient and wicked." The king threw up his hands in irritation. "He's got to be punished . . . or else no one will obey me."

"No," said Davi, much to his own surprise. The Stone on his breast took fire and life. "I won't be punished."

Gaylon's Stone brightened in answer.

"Stop it! Both of you!" The queen stepped between them. "As ruler of Xenara, I will mete out punishment if it's due. All that matters now is that Sandaal is safely away from the city."

Gaylon's irritation seemed to grow, but the light faded from the Stone in his ring. The duke willed his own Stone dark, then felt Jessmyn's hand touch his arm.

"What of Thayne?" she asked.

"He's fine. I left him with Rose at the nursery. I didn't want him to come with me to the dungeons, but he insisted. I couldn't stop him."

The queen smiled. "I know. He's a brave boy and fool-hardy, and quite taken with Lady D'Lelan. Where will she go, do you think?"

"I don't know," Davi answered. "I told her to write when she needs more money. I doubt she will, though."

"Too proud," the king grunted with obvious contempt.

Jessmyn's face expressed sympathy. "I thought you might go with her, Davi."

"And leave my Red King?" The duke turned away lest his own expression betray him.

Another knock at the outer door brought silence. Irritated, the king of Wynnamyr went to answer it.

"What are you doing here?" Davi heard him ask.

Raf D'Gular answered. "I'm looking for Her Majesty. She's not in her chambers." The young man pushed by Gaylon and walked into the room.

The king's Stone flared a deadly blue, but Jessmyn stopped him. "No, my lord. Let him speak."

"Highness," Raf said gently and bowed. "Lady D'Lelan wishes to see you in the cupola."

The queen's eyes widened. "But how . . . ?"

"It was all too easy to gain entrance. The palace guard is still in upheaval. After all that's happened, they're no longer certain who is enemy and who is not." Young D'Gular smiled impudently at the king. "This must be remedied soon if any of you are to survive."

"Survive what?" Davi demanded.

"Come to the cupola and find out."

Once more the queen calmed her angry husband. "He hasn't come to harm us, Gaylon. Only to taunt us, as he does everyone."

"Then let's proceed," Raf said and headed to the exit.

The duke followed the others reluctantly. He disliked D'Gular, and the thought of seeing Sandaal only brought more pain, but he still sensed the anger in Gaylon. The lady might yet be in danger.

The open airy cupola remained cool in the early afternoon sun. Sandaal stood at the far railing, her back to Raf and his group, her eyes on the Inland Sea. Dirt smudged the long skirts of her gown, and the bodice was torn in several places. Jessmyn gasped when the young woman finally turned. The cuts on her face were still angry and red, and the bruises only emphasized her pallor.

Lady D'Lelan bowed. "Don't fret, Your Highness. What you see is nothing more than I deserved."

"And what do you deserve," Gaylon snapped, "for the murder of a prince?"

"I didn't kill Robyn." Sandaal gazed at the king steadily.

"Though if I'd been under your dungeon master's knife much longer, I might have confessed to it . . . and to anything else you like."

"Gaylon . . ." The queen eyed her husband angrily.

The king looked away. "Assassins, male or female, receive the same treatment."

"In my kingdom, no one receives such treatment—not even assassins. I'll see to it." Jessmyn took Sandaal's elbow gently and guided her to a lounge chair. "I want Nials to see you immediately, my dear."

"No." Lady D'Lelan shook her head. "Raf has learned something that may save a lot of lives—yours included, milady." She gestured at D'Gular. "Tell them."

Raf smiled again. "You should know . . . I only come here at Sandaal's behest. I have little interest in politics."

"Raf, tell them!"

"All right." The young man flinched at Sandaal's harsh tone. "My father, with the help of his allies, plans to invade the palace."

"Impossible!" Gaylon snarled. "The House of D'Gular has alienated far too many of the highborn families."

"No," Raf told him. "Since the little prince's death, the queen has been . . ." He glanced at Jessmyn, brows furrowed. "Her Majesty has not been behaving rationally. The Xenaran people have taken this as a sign of weakness, and my father has managed to convince many more houses to stand with him."

"When?" the queen asked. "When do they plan this attack?"

"I don't know, milady. I only know it must come soon. They can't risk your winning the people back to you. And they know the king's secret now."

Davi stared at Gaylon, apprehension twisting in his gut. "His secret?"

"They know he won't use his powers to harm others."

"How do they know?" the king demanded.

"I told them." That infuriating smile touched Raf's full lips once more.

Jessmyn drew a deep breath. "And how did you come to know?"

"I spoke to him about it," Sandaal admitted with a touch of hostility. "I saw the king withhold his powers over and over again, in certain situations." She stared hard at Gaylon. "Do you think that makes you noble? Well, it doesn't." The lady turned to Jessmyn. "He's had others do the hurting and the harm for him ever since I joined the royal family. Eventually I realized that he no longer had the heart to use his most powerful magic. That's why I tried to cut off his hand, to separate him completely from his magic forever. Before I killed him, I wanted him to suffer as my brother suffered."

The duke of Gosney felt something stir deep within the Stone pendant, drawn to the overpowering hatred that emanated from Sandaal.

"Enough!" said the queen. "What's past is past. We have the immediate future to deal with now. How shall we go about defending ourselves?"

Gaylon paced to the cupola railing. "We need more information. Can you get it for us, Raf?"

"No," the young man answered simply. "I've risked enough in telling you what I have. I'm in no one's employ."

"And if I order you?" Jessmyn asked.

Raf smiled sweetly. "The answer is still no, milady."

"Then perhaps," the king said just as sweetly, "you might like a nice long stay in our dungeons?"

D'Gular's lips tightened, but it was the queen who replied. "I forbid any retaliation against Lord Raf. He's done more than his duty to a new and troublesome monarch. You may go, boy."

Being called a boy didn't please Raf. He stiffened. "I'd rather stay."

"Oh, no," Jess told him. "A man without allegiance to anyone but himself can be trusted to serve only himself. There's no need for you to know any more about us than you already do. Farewell, Lord D'Gular." She gestured to Davi. "See him out, please . . . and well away from our doors and windows."

The duke bowed and led Raf to the stairs and down. Young D'Gular no longer smiled, and Davi took a small pleasure in that. At the bottom of the final staircase, Raf slowed.

"Sandaal tells me you healed her."

Davi said nothing, refusing to be drawn into idle conversation with the man. Finally Raf spoke again.

"I thought all along there might be something fey about you, Gosney. How is it that Wynnamyr breeds so many magicians? Is it something in the air or the water?" D'Gular hurried to keep up with his silent escort. "You've bewitched Sandaal somehow. I've never seen her so confused or hurt, or so much in love. All my life, I've tried to win her heart. I've tried to claim her beauty, her voice, and her sharp, clear mind for my own, but I was always merely a friend—no more, no less." A bitterness crept into Raf's voice. "She was waiting for you."

The duke would have closed his ears if he could have. A familiar dull pain ached in his chest. The fact of Sandaal's love altered nothing. She had tried to kill a king, and other than accomplishing that deed, there was no higher crime in any land. A pair of soldiers appeared in the corridor ahead of the two men, and Davi called out to them.

"Take this man to the outer gates. He's forbidden to return to the palace."

Raf's smile suddenly returned, more radiant than ever. "Ah, well, it's good-bye, then. At least I have the satisfaction of knowing your love is as doomed as mine."

Teeth gritted, the duke of Gosney turned and strode away.

\* \* \* \* \*

Nials Haldrick pinched the candle flame out, and a thicker darkness slipped over the chamber. For a time, he listened to Lady D'Lelan's breathing. It had finally evened after the administration of a strong draught of valerian. Now only rest and time could heal the young woman's wounds. Davi had brought the process well along, though.

A brief envy washed over the physician. Such miraculous powers in one young duke. If only . . . Thoughts like these were unworthy of a healer, he chided mentally. Best to be grateful for his own talents, however minor in comparison.

Uneasy, Nials directed his attention to the night beyond the open chamber windows.

Earlier in the day, while Gaylon Reysson attempted to secure the palace, the physician had become aware of something odd. It seemed that the constant noise of the city beyond the walls had grown muted. The rhythm of life in Zankos had altered, however minutely. No one else had noticed, but Nials felt an unreasonable fear. Over all else, he detected a growing tension, a raw malignancy that threatened every living soul within the palace grounds.

Sandaal moaned faintly in her sleep, and the sound raised gooseflesh on the physician's arms. There was nothing more he could do here, though he was reluctant to leave. The thick, close darkness somehow brought comfort. A rattle of armored men moving along the corridor outside finally roused Nials. On impulse, he bent to kiss the lady's cheek, then found his way blindly to the door.

The palace bustled despite it being so late at night. All gates had been closed and barred that afternoon. Supplies were always kept stored against possible siege, but the palace guard had dwindled in numbers over the years since Roffo's death. The king of Wynnamyr found himself with fewer than two hundred men, so he'd quickly drafted all male members of the household staff, slave and freeman alike, who could wield a weapon.

The long winding route to his own chambers took Nials through the servants' quarters and the kitchens. One of the soups in a huge kettle on the stove smelled wonderful, but he was too tired to eat. His own soft bed awaited him. At the last curve in the corridor, a young slave caught up with him.

"Master Haldrick," the boy panted. He wore strapped across his chest a scaled leather cuirass several sizes too large. A heavy short sword hung from a wide belt at his waist, though he looked to be no more than eleven or twelve years of age. "Sir, come quick. You're needed at the cupola."

"Why?" the physician asked irritably. The cupola lay at the top and on the far side of the palace from his chambers.

The young soldier's face was still red and sweaty from

exertion, and Nials saw fear in the boy's eyes.

"The queen . . ." the youngster began and then faltered. "The queen is very upset and . . . acting strangely. We don't know what to do, milord."

"What of the king?"

"He sent me, milord. He doesn't know what to do, either."

Dear gods, what now? Nials gave up his hopes of bed and rest and quickly followed the boy back along the corridor.

\*   \*   \*   \*   \*

Late in the night, Jessmyn finally dozed, sprawled on a long couch in the king's apartment. Davi had not paid her much attention of late. His duties were endless, and now he stood with Gaylon while the king consulted his captains and an ornate map of the palace and grounds. They had doubled the guard on the wall and set a second barrier inside the main gates.

A story had been devised for the good citizens of Zankos who traded daily with the palace. It seemed that Nials Haldrick had discovered a virulent and deadly illness in one of the new servants from Benjir. While the sickness had so far remained isolated, the good physician felt it best to quarantine the palace for the while and thereby avoid an epidemic. Once the gates were closed and locked, the frantic preparations within were hidden from Zankos.

Davi studied the faces of the six captains who listened with rapt attention to the king of Wynnamyr. They were young men, though older than the duke, and untried. Nearly a decade had passed since Xenara's fatal confrontation with Wynnamyr. The land had hardly recovered from such destruction, and the children who had survived had finally come of age. With so few of them, though, Xenara dared no aggressions against its enemies—only trained their young to defend what was left of their own nation.

"What of our weapons?" Gaylon asked. He ran fingers through his hair in agitation, then stroked his red-gold beard. No one answered. "Well?"

Nav Deskin, a tall, lean man with sharp features, found his tongue. "We've a few hauberks and catch poles left—only because they're ancient and wieldy and no one wants to use them. The swords and pikes and bows have all been handed out, but more than a few of our men will fight bare-handed, milord."

"It hardly matters," Gaylon growled. "They wouldn't know what to do with a sword if they had one."

Nav's elder brother, Lyn, spoke up. "Milord, surely D'Gular and his lot will turn back when they see that we're ready for them. And if you merely lit your Sorcerer's Stone, they'd run. Lord Gosney has his, as well . . ."

"Don't count overmuch on magic," the king warned, and Davi agreed.

Behind them, in the shadows of the room, a mewling wail arose. The unearthly sound brought ice to Davi's heart and made him spin around. The queen writhed on the couch, caught in the grip of some terrible dream. Again she wailed, then woke suddenly, shuddering and in tears. Gaylon rushed to take her in his arms.

"No!" She shoved him away. "Where are Thayne and Lily?"

"In the nursery, my love."

"Bring them here. Now! Hurry."

Gaylon gestured to one of his captains, and the man left quickly to do the queen's bidding. Jessmyn wasn't satisfied, though. She began to pace back and forth across the wide floor.

"Jess . . . please," her husband pleaded.

The queen stopped before Lyn. "Captain, find a dozen of the servants and bring them to me. I want all the furnishings on the second floor taken to the staircase that leads up to the cupola.

"Highness?" The man gazed at her in confusion.

"Do it . . . now."

Her voice sounded perfectly rational, despite words that made little sense. Lyn Deskin hurried out into the corridor and disappeared. An uneasy quiet settled over the chamber until Davi broke it.

"Majesty," he said gently, "perhaps you should rest awhile longer. I could take you to your chambers. . . ."

The queen's face went blank momentarily, then she frowned, uncertain, and Gaylon gave Davi a tiny nod of approval.

Jessmyn drew herself up. "You don't really understand, do you?" She eyed the others. "Any of you."

"My love—" Gaylon said.

"My reign will be the shortest in Xenaran history . . . less than a hundred days." The queen began to weep again, silent tears that dripped from her chin. "How will I save my children?"

"Mum? Da?" Thayne stood in the antechamber with Rose beside him, tiny Lilith in her arms. The child, a sleeping gown still over his breeches, had heavy dark circles under his eyes. He gave Davi only the barest glance before going to his mother.

Jess scrubbed the tears from her cheeks and managed a smile for the boy. "My darling! Come give me a hug. Then we must hurry."

"Hurry where?" The prince accepted her embrace and returned it.

"To the cupola." At Thayne's sudden look of apprehension, the queen hugged him tighter. "It's all right, darling." She took the baby from Rose's arms. "Please, Rose, go to the kitchen and tell the cooks I want food and water brought to the cupola, enough for a dozen people for several days. Go quickly."

Rose, doubtful, looked to the king for reassurance.

"I'll go with you," Thayne offered stoutly, then fought down a yawn.

At His Majesty's nod, the D'Jal sister left the apartment with the prince, followed by the remaining officers, who would return to their commands. Gaylon returned to his map and his thoughts. Soon the wavering light within the main chamber began to dim as the candles burned down to puddles of wax.

Davi took it upon himself to replace them. He needed that simple mindless chore to calm his nerves. Life with the Wynnamyran court had never been boring, but here in Xenara, he'd found nothing but turmoil. Worse, the duke feared that Jessmyn was losing her mind. All the sorrow and loss had finally brought her to the breaking point.

"Send for Haldrick," Gaylon whispered when Davi leaned to put another taper in the holder on the map table.

In the queen's arms, Lilith burbled happily, wide awake now. Jessmyn rocked her and sang in a soft, sweet voice, almost as if she'd forgotten her earlier anxiety. The first set of servants arrived, over a dozen men. They appeared quiet and subdued, possibly exhausted by a long day and night of hard labor.

"We're going to the cupola now," the queen informed her husband.

Gaylon hesitated briefly. "Shall I come with you?"

"If you like." Her answer was cool and indifferent. Without a backward glance, Jess led her entourage out into the hallway.

"Stay with her, Davi," the king ordered. He picked the duke's cuirass from the pile of armor on the floor and handed it to him.

"But aren't you . . ."

"I'll come later. I've things to see to first."

The queen's insanity soon grew all the more clear. Helpless, Davi watched as the palace servants carried basket after basket of breads and fruits up the long stairs to the upper story of the building. Water jugs were brought as well, and then Jessmyn ordered the furnishings from every chamber and apartment stacked at the mid-point of the staircase and down to the foot.

"Milady," the duke said finally, following as Jess took Thayne and Lily up the steps to the cupola. "Do you realize how mad your actions appear to the servants?"

The queen smiled. "And to you, Davi." She put the baby into a crib taken from her chambers. "What do you think I'm doing?"

"You're making it impossible for anyone to gain the upper floor . . . or for you to get down. But why?"

"I'm trying to keep alive the children I have left."

"So are we, Majesty. Look around you. No one will get by these walls."

"Yes, they will," Jessmyn answered simply and continued to pat Lilith, soothing her back into sleep.

Davi's unreasonable fear returned. "How do you know that?"

That made the queen pause. "I saw it in a dream." She took Davi to the southern railing. "There. At the seawall."

The duke peered into the night at the vague outline of the wall against the darker background of the Inland Sea. A sudden burst of light struck him in the eyes, then a brilliant yellow-orange flower of fire blossomed from the far wall high into the air. Next came a thunder that shook the palace to its foundation, and debris began to rain from the sky.

Lilith shrieked in terror, and the queen rushed to take her up. Davi hadn't moved. Jessmyn's insanity had swept him up. None of this could be real. None of it. Below, by the fading glow of the fire, the duke saw movement in the dark. Moments later, a great mass of armed men swarmed over the wreckage and into the palace grounds.

Jessmyn was screaming in the room behind Davi, calling for the servants to bring the furniture to barricade the stairs. From somewhere, he heard his name being shouted over and over. The king's voice. Davi turned to go and found Jess alone with the baby. Both mother and child were wailing. The servants had deserted her all too quickly.

"Thayne . . ." the queen sobbed. "He wouldn't obey me. He's . . . he's gone to fight. Bring him back to me, Davi. Please!"

The duke stood, torn. Jessmyn should not be left here undefended.

"I'll send men to guard the stairs," he called to her and ran past her to the steps.

Gaylon met him below, rigged in half-armor, a bared sword already in his hand. "How did she know this would happen?" he demanded breathlessly.

"A dream, milord. Thayne's disappeared . . . gone to fight, I think. The queen is wild with fear."

Both men headed directly toward the break in the wall and the army that flooded through it. Shouting in outrage, the queen's defenders engaged the enemy beneath the citrus and olive trees. The clang of metal weapons grew heavier, louder, and were joined by the screams of men in mortal pain. Davi felt the Stone at his chest warm, felt the hateful presence of Orym on the edges of his mind. The hated creature still existed within the pendant, then. Angry, Davi refused the old man, pushing him away.

"I'll search for Thayne out here," the king shouted above the clamor, unaware of Davi's plight. "Have the servants search the palace, then return to me."

Such a command did not set well with Davi—to be separated from his lord while the battle raged. The trees closest to the wall had caught fire, lighting the predawn darkness with an orange glow. From this vantage, it looked as if half of the men of Zankos had joined D'Gular's forces.

A familiar figure darted from among the knots of struggling men. Nav Deskin had somehow found his way through all the madness to come stand by the king, sword at the ready. Blood flowed sluggishly from a wound in the captain's upper arm.

"Have you been near the breach?" Gaylon demanded.

Nav grimaced in pain. "Aye, milord."

"Quick, man." The king caught his officer's good arm in a hard grip. "Did you learn the size of the enemy forces? How, in all the gods' names, did they break through?"

"A guard from the southeast tower says the boulevard is packed with men all the way into the city proper. He says the streets were empty one moment, then full the next. They're mercenaries, Highness. The great houses have employed soldiers of fortune from at least a half-dozen countries."

Gaylon remained calm despite such devastating news. "How did they manage the breach?"

"By magic, milord. It must be," the captain answered. "Fire exploded through a mortar-and-stone wall as wide as you are high, milord. That's well beyond the capabilities of mere men." Nav gazed at his king, uncertain. "Isn't it, milord?"

"No," Gaylon said grimly. "Mere men are all too capable of finding new and better ways to wage war."

"If it is magic," Nav insisted, "then you must use your own to fight it. We cannot stand against sorcery, milord."

The king's face reddened, then paled. "I've told you already what the price of my sorcery would be. Are you willing to be the first sacrifice?" He pushed his right hand under the soldier's nose, and the Stone in his ring pulsed blue. Nav shook his head violently.

A sudden uproar drew their attention back to the fray. The palace guard, with servants as their only allies, arrived at the seawall from every part of the grounds. Banded together, the king's small army somehow rallied and began to press the enemy back into the rubble, back through the break in the wall.

Gaylon grabbed the duke by a shoulder. "Go! Tell the women in the palace to search for the prince. We've got to find Thayne before it's too late."

Davi ran, dodging along the flagstone path through wind-driven smoke and the first hazy light of morning. Once, long ago on a similar dawn, he and the king had led their Wynn-namyran army against a foe with more than ten times their numbers. As hopeless as that had seemed, this small battle was somehow far more desperate. The king had thought to keep his people safe within these high thick walls, but they might find themselves trapped here instead with nowhere to run.

A sudden heat warmed the metal at the back of Davi's cuirass. The sky brightened overhead momentarily, then a roll of thunder slammed through the trees, shaking the earth. Behind the duke, another section of the wall exploded inward. Those nearest the blast, friend or enemy, died in a hail of stone. Magic . . .

The madness outside was replaced by a deadly silence within the palace. Davi ran, directionless, through the empty halls and chambers of the bottom floor, then up the stairs to the second. The heavy gold pendant thumped against his cuirass with every step, and he stopped briefly on the first balcony to look out over the battle. Already bodies were strewn through the wreckage of the once stately gardens.

The duke slammed a fist against the carved stone railing, furious with himself. With the help of the Sorcerer's Stone, this madness could be quickly ended. But Davyn could not do it alone. He would have to give himself over to Orym, let him take control of the Stone through the duke. What was his own life, his soul, against the hundreds that fought below? What of the queen . . . and Thayne? Tiny Lilith? What of the Red King, whose life meant more to a Gosney than his own?

Dangerous thinking, and more than a little foolish. Orym would never keep such a bargain. Instead, he would use Davi to gather all his stormy powers again. No one who opposed him would survive, and those who did survive would long for oblivion. No, old man, Davi thought. Never.

"Davi!"

He turned at Thayne's shout and saw the boy take the last few steps to the top of the stairs. The prince's face was flushed and sweating, and his blue eyes glittered with barely contained terror. Davi caught him up in a tight hug.

"Where did you go?" he growled in sudden anger.

"To get Sandaal. And Katina, but I couldn't find them anywhere."

The duke straightened. "Your mother's frantic. Get up to the cupola. Now!"

"But they've broken in, Davi." The glitter in the prince's eyes turned to tears. "Did you see how they destroyed the wall? We won't be safe here. The whole palace will fall, and we'll be crushed. There's too many—"

"Stop!" The duke hugged Thayne again. "You've got to be brave for your mother, for Lily."

The prince pulled away. "Use your Stone, Davi. Please! You saved me once."

"But not with the Stone, Thayne, and this is entirely different."

"I'd use my Stone if I had one. I'd save us all! You want me to be brave, but you're not. Both you and my father have

Sorcerer's Stones, but why won't you use them? We're going to die if you don't!" The tears had stopped, the boy's fear and sorrow turned to fury. With an angry, wordless cry of frustration, Thayne fled down the corridor toward the staircase to the cupola.

# Twenty

Davi watched the prince weave through the partially completed barricade on the staircase. The jumble of furniture would not have stopped a determined assault, but it might have slowed down the inevitable. For the moment, Jessmyn and her children were safe. The duke paused briefly at the balcony railing, one hand on the cool marble. The insanity below had worsened. One breach in the wall might have been defensible; two were proving impossible to keep blocked.

Smoke drifted over the battleground, obscuring much from Davi's view, but he could still see the king well enough. Gaylon's peaked helm had a red silk scarf tied to the tip, and his shield was as bright, painted red and gold and white. He had joined the battle, and while his captains scrambled to defend him, the king continued to cut and slash through the opposing forces. That seemed to keep him always a long pace ahead of his protectors. His sword moved with lightning speed, and dead and dying enemies lay in every direction at his feet.

Davi reach for his own sword hilt. A sense of wrongness had suddenly twisted in his stomach, so intense it nearly doubled him over. Behind him, he heard a noise on the steps.

"They're going after the Red King!" Sandaal cried. "They know he won't defend himself with the Sorcerer's Stone. Help him!"

This was the woman who longed to see Gaylon Reysson dead above all else; this was the woman who would have killed the king herself. Now she fled to the railing and pointed down into the fray. Davi followed the gesture with his eyes. Gaylon's brilliant red scarf floated in the wind and smoke, bobbing as the man swung first his blade and then his shield. A gathering of enemy forces had begun, though.

There were horses with riders on the field for the first time, and the duke saw more of them scrabbling over the shattered stone of the wall. The palace horses hadn't been saddled, due to the suddenness of the attack. D'Gular's riders put their advantage to good use and pushed their animals over the wounded as well as the dead. They were headed for the King of Wynnamyr—every one of them.

"Do something," Sandaal said again, her voice quiet now with a breathless fear.

"You don't know what you ask." The Stone in Davi's pendant flared blue and brilliant, despite every effort to keep it dark.

The young woman grew bitter. "If you can't master the Stone, Davyn Darynson, then give the pendant to me."

"No," Davi snarled and clutched the Stone possessively. "You'll die."

"But at least I'll have tried! Use your Stone, milord!"

He wanted to scream that he didn't know how, but that was a lie. Even now, some part of him reached out to the forces held tight within the tiny gray pebble. Connection brought incredible joy, a wild infusion of energy that surged through him, growing stronger and stronger. From some great distance, the duke of Gosney watched himself. He saw himself fling back his head and scream a challenge to the great houses of Xenara, to those who had dared to threaten the queen and her family.

When the echoes died, absolute silence had fallen over the field. Swords and pikes were stilled, and the men who wielded them stood with their eyes on the palace. Somewhere deep inside his being, Davi's own actions terrified him. Worse, he could not be certain that they *were* his own actions. An ocean of outrage and fury filled him, then burst free, and a glowing blue tendril of light flashed out from the duke's fingertips.

Without knowing, he had chosen a target—the armored man at the front of the enemy line. Harren D'Gular, Davi realized at the last moment. The forest green tabard of the Gular household covered the lord's half-armor, and he sat a fine chestnut stallion. Then the Stone's blue fire engulfed him.

Both man and horse shrieked in terror and agony, and the stallion flung itself backward into the men who clustered near. Several fell beneath trampling hoofs, unnoticed by the others, who clambered to safety. Blue fire still burned star bright, and though the dying horse continued to stagger, Harren D'Gular had ceased his cries. His charred body had welded to the saddle. At last the stallion toppled and lay still.

"Lord Gosney!" The king's frantic shout was brought on the wind. "Take care what you do!"

Davi licked his lips, frightened of the ecstasy that D'Gular's death had brought him. The pendant's blue glow dimmed slowly. Where was Orym? He should be here, gleeful and gloating, ready to take control of the Sorcerer's Stone, and through it, the duke.

Below, the mercenaries and the palace guard, all of whom had watched the fiery destruction of Harren, seemed to remember finally the business of war. Someone halfheartedly struck the shield of an opponent with a sword, but the resultant clang encouraged the others. The battle began again in earnest. Only those who had directly followed Lord D'Gular remained undecided and confused.

"Is that it?" Sandaal asked. "That's all you can do?"

Davi glared at her. "The king is safe."

"For the moment." The young woman shook her head, frustrated. "You have the power to end this fight before too many lives have been taken."

"Leave me be!"

Davi wanted to run, to join the king on the field and fight with something tangible—a sword—but the Stone at his breast took fire again. This time, the duke felt a cold sickness. A darkness had come, bringing the stench of death in Davi's nostrils and a foul taste to his tongue. Sandaal seemed to sense something, too, for she glanced around, her expression troubled.

"He's here," Lady D'Lelan whispered, and there was outright fear in her voice.

"Who?"

"Orym . . ."

Davi felt a mild shock. "What do you know of Orym?"

"Too much," the lady answered. Then her eyes fixed on something behind the duke's right shoulder.

No. This couldn't be. Gaylon had finally destroyed Orym. Slowly Davi turned, already certain what he would find. The Dark King floated in the shadow of the wall, a benign smile on his thick lips. On the duke's chest, the Stone's light intensified, and he willed it dark—to no effect. An unhappy thought occurred to him. His control over the pendant may have always been illusory.

"My children," Orym murmured, his voice hollow and omnidirectional.

"I don't want you here." Davi continued to fight the Stone's glow.

"He's smelled the blood," Sandaal said with disgust. "He's tasted the death. He won't go until he's had his fill of both."

The Dark King's gaze fixed on Lady D'Lelan. "Such a clever young woman . . . and such a great disappointment. I'd thought to let you have the Stone if Davi didn't survive. But you failed me, child. You failed to kill the Red King."

Sandaal said nothing, though she held her head high, as if in challenge. Still, Davi saw the fear in her eyes and wondered.

So they had both been used by Orym, and that explained so much of Sandaal's strange behavior. The thought brought a cold rage to the duke, but along with that fierce emotion, he noticed the Stone in the pendant brightening perceptibly. Now a tiny bit of hope formed. Perhaps the Sorcerer's Stone was not completely beyond his control. Determined, the duke calmed himself.

"Go away, old man. I've no time for a lesson today," Davi

said brusquely and returned his attention to the turmoil. The palace guards had fought their way to the second breach and desperately tried to block the ragged opening. So far, the queen's men had closed it only briefly with their dead bodies.

"Ah, but a lesson is what you'll get, my young friend—the final lesson."

Beside the duke, Orym drew more light from the air, set it swirling and sparkling, until the faint outline of his body had taken on more substance, more definition. Sandaal hissed in revulsion when the Dark King's feet settled to the tile floor. He had become flesh and blood—or very like—and only his eyes remained ethereal . . . insane.

"These are your last moments of life, boy," Orym said with pleasure. "You've done all I wanted, and I no longer need you." He reached for the Stone on Davi's chest—or perhaps for his throat.

"No!" Lady D'Lelan cried, and the duke stepped back out of the old man's immediate reach.

"If . . . if I've done . . ." The duke heard the quaver in his own voice and felt embarrassed. "If I've done all you wanted, then grant me one last boon."

"What?"

"Let me win this battle for Gaylon Reysson." Davi saw doubt in Orym's mad eyes and hurried on. "Unless, of course, you're afraid I'll destroy you once I have the power under my control."

Orym laughed, a deep booming sound that seemed to shake the floor. He regarded Sandaal now, and though she cowered when the Dark King approached, she didn't move. Short, fat fingers played in her hair a moment, then slipped down to find one breast.

"Stop it," Davi snapped. Tears of fear and outrage spilled down Lady D'Lelan's cheeks. "Leave her be!"

"But only for a while," Orym promised the young woman. He ran the same fingers over the marble railing, enthralled with the sensation. "I'd forgotten," he murmured in wonder. "I've forgotten so—"

A brilliant yellow flash against the sky nearly blinded Davi.

Thunder rolled over the palace grounds again. Automatically the duke grabbed for a pillar just as the ground lurched, and another section of the wall fragmented. This time, though, huge chunks of stone were hurled into the palace itself. One piece narrowly missed the Dark King, and he dodged aside with an infuriated shriek.

Made so aware of his vulnerability, Orym would take the Sorcerer's Stone. Davi caught the pendant up in his fist and closed his eyes, opening his mind to the blue energy that pulsed within the Stone. The instant he connected, the Dark King's hand closed over his, and the Stone answered its first master, too.

The world around them disappeared with a sickening jolt that was felt, not seen. Davi opened his eyes on gentle rolling earth that swept away to the west. Here clouds obscured the sun, and a cold wind blew, chilling Davi's sweaty face. Ragged mountains stretched high to the north and east, and behind the duke lay a crumbling castle. Gosney. The Stone had brought them to Castle Gosney.

"Milord Duke, what happened?"

The sound of Gaylon's voice made Davi turn. Orym had vanished, but the tall Red King stood by in knee-high meadow grasses, his bloodied sword in one hand, his helm in the other. A faint sheen of sweat covered his face and matted his sandy blond hair to his skull. But something in the man's stance was all wrong.

"These are the same games you played with Gaylon," the duke spat, grateful that his voice didn't shake.

The king had described his battle with Orym, who had tried the very same tricks. The duke must not fall for any of it. Before him, the Red King melted into nothingness, and Orym laughed, taunting him. Everything Gaylon had taught him about sorcery, everything he had read in the *Book of Stones*, must be put to good use if Davi was to survive.

A blue orb dodged suddenly away from the flames, and without thought, Davi attacked. The fury of his own assault astonished him, though the wave hit nothing. The force went on to strike the northwest tower of the castle, and mortared stones toppled to the ground.

At the same instant, Orym struck back. Searing pain distracted the duke momentarily, but the Stone answered his unconscious need, and Davi drew Gaylon's soft protective bubble around himself. Singed and shuddering, he felt the pain of numerous burns, and the stench of burning cloth filled his nose.

The hopelessness of the situation hit Davi nearly as hard as the Dark King's magical blow. He could never survive Orym's attack, only die here in this lonely place. The pain of the burns gnawed at him while the duke tried to clear his mind, tried to think of some means of escape.

There was no escape, though. Somehow the young man must fight as he had never fought before. Davi reached deep within the matrix of the Stone whose power he shared with the Dark King and drew on it. Blue fire raged about him, held at bay by the bubble. Pain turned quickly to agony and worse, but still he held on.

Outside, Orym's flames began to diminish slightly. Davi gathered his strength and pulled harder at the Stone's forces, trapping them within the matrix. The Dark King roared in outrage as his firestorm faltered, then flickered and winked out.

Davi used the moment to break from the bubble and send the trapped energies back at his enemy. Furious and shrieking, Orym fled, a bright blue star that shot skyward and disappeared. Davi collapsed to his knees in the silence. Then movement caught his eye. Robyn stood on the edge of the meadow in his bloodstained nightgown.

"I want to live again," the little prince said softly. "Orym could show you how to do it."

"No," Davi said in misery. His love for the boy overwhelmed him. This was how Orym had tempted the Red King. This was also how Gaylon had come to ruin for Arlin D'Lelan, and now the duke understood why. "No," he repeated, more to convince himself than anyone else. "You're a ghost. You don't exist. Get away from me!"

Robyn reached out to him with small dimpled hands. "I'm real, Davi. Help me live. I want to live—"

"Lies!" The duke struggled against tears, and his voice quavered. "You aren't Robyn. The prince is dead, forever gone!" He pushed himself to his feet, the stone flaring bright on his chest. "You monster, Orym. Stop this now!"

Robyn's image wavered and enlongated. Now it was Sandaal who stood before Davi, a malicious smile on her lips, Orym's madness in her dark eyes.

"Are you a coward?" she asked, sneering. "I offered your precious Red King a chance to join me, but he was afraid." The young woman stepped toward Davi. "Join me, Davi. Together no one can stand against us. Together we can have this world at our feet. Think of it, Davyn Darynson. I know the longing in your heart. I know the joy you feel at destruction and death. . . ."

"I'm not like Gaylon!" the duke said vehemently.

"No?" Sandaal stepped closer still.

"Keep away."

Against Davi's chest, the pendant grew icy hot—in answer to Orym, not the duke. To defend himself, Davi would have to attack the image of Sandaal. Doubt made him stay his hand.

Lady D'Lelan's fingers entwined at the back of his neck, and the duke found himself frozen by her touch, so like the icy hot sensation of the Stone. Trapped, he watched as she brought her face near his, that perfect smile on her perfect lips, and then his vision seemed to blur. The woman's pale features began to melt away from around those hard dark eyes until only the skull remained, with its sharp, jutting cheekbones. Davi panicked and flailed and found himself still trapped by her iron grip.

At last the Stone answered his desire and loosed an erratic burst of energy that destroyed this version of reality. Castle Gosney dissolved. Gray sky washed away and took the landscape with it. Sandaal's bony fingers vanished from around the duke's neck, and he found himself floating in a vast nothingness. In that formless void, only the Stone continued to glow.

Davi fought to create another reality, imagining his hand tight around the pendant.

Orym's heavy laughter echoed in his ear. "Child! Give up. You have no real powers. Only what I've given you all along."

"No!" Davi shouted back. "You're lying." He'd felt the Stone answer his call, knew the joy of control. This was a trick of Orym's.

"Then show me creation, boy. Build me a universe."

In the long emptiness that followed, the duke tried, but the irrefutable nothingness remained. Davi tried again . . . and again, and each time the Stone's blue energy seemed to evade him. Each attempt exhausted him further and made the Dark King laugh all the harder.

Out there, though, in some unimaginable distance, a tiny darkness began to gather. It sucked the nothingness inward voraciously, until sheer density reversed the process and spewed the darkness outward, as light now. Swirling galaxies formed in uncountable numbers, each fabulous and unique. Davi felt a touch of pride, and then wondered. Was this his creation . . . or Orym's?

The answer came in a wave of directionless blue fire that swept over the duke, bringing incredible agony to already blistered skin. Desperate, Davi willed himself away once more. He had revealed his true power by creating another universe, and now the Dark King feared him. Orym must destroy the duke's life essence in order to exist again, in order to have full use of the Stone.

Dodging blast after blast of blue flames exhausted Davi and made him realize how desperate his situation was. He couldn't possibly survive Orym's assault alone. He needed help, and soon. Eyes clamped shut, the duke imagined a familiar place, willing it so. Light and color erupted together around him, and the sounds of battle filled his ears. The duke found himself sprawled on the tattered lawns of the palace. A hand in a red leather glove reached down to him.

"Where're your weapons?" the king demanded and jerked him upright, then beat an enemy soldier back with three light-ning strokes of his sword.

Davi retrieved the blade of a fallen comrade just in time to parry a low sword thrust. An instant later, he dispatched the man who had tried to deliver the killing blow. King and duke fought side by side for a while, smoke harsh in their throats, sweat stinging their eyes. Orym, in his guise as Sandaal, had apparently not followed Davi here . . . from that one Dream to this one. The thought made the duke wonder. Had the Stone returned him to reality, or created another for him?

They had cleared a small space around them. Gaylon stood panting and let two young guards defend him for the moment. "What happened to you?" he demanded, eyes on the duke's blistered face and hands.

"Orym," Davi told him and watched the king's expression turn bitter. "I need your help, milord."

Gaylon shook his head. "I failed to destroy Orym before. What makes you think I can do it now?"

"All I ask is that you try, Sire."

A cloud of dirty gray smoke drifted over them, and from it rushed a pair of mercenaries. The duke ran one through, then turned to aid his king. Gaylon drove at his opponent, and the man dodged away, only to find Davi's blade there to receive him.

The king left a third opponent dead in the trampled grasses and brought Davi through the groups of fighters to the edge of the newest breach in the wall. There the trees still burned and crackled, and stones continued to tumble from the upper reaches.

"When Orym comes again," Gaylon said, "he'll most likely destroy as much around him as he can." He offered Davi a nasty grin. "Best to take ourselves among the enemy, don't you think?"

The duke grinned back, despite his awareness of the danger they would face.

"Let's go, then."

They pressed through breaks in the fighting, headed toward the latest breach in the palace wall, only engaging the foe when they must. A pike slammed into Davi's steel cuirass from behind, nearly bowling him over. Gaylon dispatched the attacker and then steadied his duke. This close to the wall, the strong stench of sulfur clogged their nostrils.

The king and the duke had arrived so quickly that no one had taken notice of their arrival. Now the enemy began to converge on them in force. There was hardly time for worry, though, for at that moment Orym arrived in a whirl of raging blue fire tthat erupted above them. Instantly both men surrounded themselves with luminous bubble shields and watched as dozens of enemy soldiers and horses were consumed in flames.

The blisters on Davi's arms had burst with the latest onslaught of heat, and the pain was hard to ignore, but ignore it he must. He'd come for Gaylon's help in hope that the two of them together might once and for all destroy the Dark King . . . or be destroyed themselves. How to go about it was the question, though.

Only one thing came to mind. Gaylon had nearly ended Orym's existence by touching the two Stones together. They had been Dream Stones then, powerful images of the true Stones but images all the same. The hot blue flames around them began to dissipate, and Davi saw the Red King press his ringed hand to the bubble's surface. His mouth worked, but the words were lost behind the shield. Perhaps he'd had the same thought. Davi took up Orym's pendant and pressed it to the wall of his own bubble, feeling it stretch at his touch. Gaylon nodded, then motioned to the shield around him.

They would have to give up their protection, in which case they might perish along with the Dark King. Gaylon had survived the first battle, but then so had Orym. The flames had vanished, and so had the old wizard. Davi looked at the devastation around him and felt ill. In only moments, the Dark King had wiped out nearly a quarter of the enemy forces and a significant number of the palace guards. Death and agony seemed to nourish the evil sorcerer, bringing him great strength and joy.

The sounds of battle had died away, and now all that could be heard were the moans of the injured and dying. Stark silence reigned about the king of Wynnamyr and his duke. Nothing lived here. Gaylon's muffled voice broke the quiet.

"The cagey old bastard," the king shouted to Davi. "He's

figured out our plan, and the coward's run off."

The duke shook his head. "Not without his pendant. He'd never leave that behind. It's time to face him." Davi willed the shield gone, and it burst like a soap bubble.

"Are you crazy?" Gaylon demanded.

"Perhaps." The duke took the pendant in his hand, then lifted it high into the air over his head. "Here it is, Orym! Come and take it . . . if you can!"

Beneath the king's feet, the ground began to rumble, but no light or thunder arrived to herald another breach in the wall. Gaylon deserted his own shield and came to stand beside Davi.

"You're right," Gaylon said. "He's here."

"But not close enough. When he comes, it'll be sudden. He'll try to separate us."

The king eyed the sky above them. "Can you feel him? Like you feel Thayne? There's a blood tie between you, after all."

The idea caused a wave of nausea that made Davi forget the pain of his burns. If he opened himself to Orym, he'd know the moment the creature attacked, but he'd also give the Dark King a chance to attack him from within. That risk was too horrible to contemplate, but yet what other opportunity could they hope for?

"Stand close," he told the Red King, then shut his eyes and reached out for Orym.

At first there was only emptiness, which left him with an awareness of every hurt and ache in his body. Then an icy tendril wrapped itself about his being. Hatred came, so intense that Davi felt he might drown in it. Lust and rage filled him, dragging him into an endless succession of corrupt and festering emotions. The duke wallowed in the filth. Orym suddenly recognized the young man's touch and joyfully, blindly rushed in to take complete control.

"Now!" Davi cried, and he felt the Red King grab the hand that held the pendant.

At the same instant, Gaylon wrapped his free arm around the duke, and a whirling disorientation swept over Davi. Orym was still there, his essence twined in the duke's, but with the black ugliness, Davi felt incredible desperation. The Dark King fought to hold on against Gaylon's assault. It was the king of Wynnamyr who controlled the powers of both Stones now. With them, he tore at Orym's grip on the duke.

"Kill us both!" Davi shouted wordlessly and knew Gaylon would do it before letting the Dark King have him.

"No!" someone screamed in his head. "No!"

First panic swept through Davi; then a ripping sensation brought sudden agony. Something wrenched the duke away and sent him spinning into empty darkness.

*  *  *  *  *

"Davi?"

That gently spoken word found him. The young man struggled toward the voice—Sandaal's voice. It seemed ages before he had the strength to open his eyes.

"Milady . . ." His throat felt raw and hot.

"Easy," Sandaal murmured and cradled his head, bringing a cup of water to his lips. The taste was divine.

He lay in his own chambers. Someone had covered his arms with wet cloths, and now the pain of his burns asserted itself.

"What of the battle?"

"It's over. We won . . . though there's not much left of the palace wall. Between you, the king, and our enemy, we're lucky to have anything left."

"The king?"

"In his own chamber, being tended to. He's not as bad off as you, but Nials says you'll both be up soon."

The door to the chamber creaked open, and Thayne poked his head in. "Is he awake?" the boy asked.

"He is," Davi answered, his voice rough from smoke and exhaustion. "Come in."

Thayne rushed to the bed, grinning. "Milord Duke, you missed all the excitement!" The prince leaned on the mattress, his face flushed. "When the Dark King came to fight with my father, all the soldiers who followed the House of Gular ran away." He paused. "So did the palace guards, but that doesn't really matter."

"What of the queen and Lily?"

Sandaal answered. "Her Majesty is also recovering, now that her children are safe. She's—"

"Da says Orym is gone forever," Thayne interrupted. "He almost took you with him, though." The boy eyed Davi's pendant. "Now you're a sorcerer . . . a real sorcerer."

"Not quite. But someday soon, I hope." Davi glanced up at Lady D'Lelan. "What about you, milady? How do you fare?"

"Well enough, sir," the young woman answered, her gaze downcast. "I may yet sail from this place. It all depends. . . ."

"I want you to stay," Thayne said sharply. "I'm a prince and you have to obey me."

The duke reached for her hand and found his arm almost too heavy to lift. "I also want you to stay."

"After all that's happened, it may not be possible."

Her words held a hint of sadness, and Davi longed to hold her close, but he had no strength. Somehow he must convince the king and queen to pardon Sandaal D'Lelan. The thought of her sailing away brought him misery. Thayne began to bounce against the edge of the mattress, and suddenly the duke needed to be alone, to rest and heal. His eyes grew heavy, and though he fought to stay awake, the duke of Gosney drifted into sleep.

# Twenty-One

Jessmyn D'Gerric, queen of all Xenara, allowed her husband to lead her across the long chamber to the raised dais and up the stairs to her throne. A moment later, he took his own seat in the king's great carved marble chair, hazel eyes focused, but unseeing, on the crush of citizens that filled the hall.

Afternoon sun filtered in through the wrought-iron openings in the high domed ceiling, and the air had quickly grown stuffy and warm. Three days before, Harren D'Gular and his followers had all been destroyed. Or rather, all but one young woman—the last living member of the House of Lelan.

The people of Zankos, however, cried out for more blood— they hadn't had near enough—and so Jessmyn had been obliged to put Sandaal D'Lelan on trial. Only by judging the young woman innocent in front of her subjects could the queen finally convince them of that fact. Being certain herself of Sandaal's innocence was not enough. Every bit of evidence collected so far had proven her to be the opposite, and there was no one left alive to tell them who had truly been a part of the conspiracy.

The gentle murmur of voices faded to silence as the Grand Envoy came into the chamber, his silk robes trailing on the tiles. He went to stand at a table placed on the floor before the thrones, facing the audience, then unfolded a piece of thick parchment.

"Hear me, citizens of Xenara. You have asked your queen to sit in judgment today over one of your own. So shall it be."

Eowin D'Ar waved a hand to the guards standing at the back of the chamber. "Bring to us Sandaal D'Lelan, who has been accused of the murder of a royal child and the betrayal of the realm. Come forward, also, those who have truthful knowledge of these allegations to offer to the court. All others remain silent and await the queen's reckoning."

A motley collection of Zankos's citzens separated from the crowd and came to sit in chairs lined up at the front of the gallery on the right. Male and female, lord and servant, they greeted one another as old friends, each determined to tell his story and help condemn the accused. The queen drummed fingertips impatiently on the arms of her throne. These witnesses held far more interest in revenge than in justice.

A pair of guards escorted Sandaal down the aisle, and the crowd began a soft rumble of discontent. They had already judged the woman guilty and preferred to attend her execution. A small wooden docket had been placed before the Grand Envoy, a place for the accused to stand throughout the trial. Jessmyn fretted as she watched Lady D'Lelan placed inside the little fenced area. The injuries inflicted by the dungeon master had not completely healed yet, and Sandaal was still too weak to be asked to stand for so long a period.

The scars remained visible on her face, and her eyes were circled with dark rings. She wore a plain gown of gray silk, with her dark hair knotted at the base of her neck, and stood with her head down, showing no interest in anything that went on around her.

"Who will speak for Lady Sandaal D'Lelan?" the envoy asked loudly.

To no one's surprise, Davi answered, "I will!" from his station to the left of the king's throne. He took the steps to the floor, none too steady himself after combat with the Dark King. Like Sandaal's, his face would possibly be scarred for life. He paused on the tiles to bow to the envoy.

Eowin spared him a tiny smile, then shuffled through a stack of papers on the table and chose another to read aloud.

"Sandaal D'Lelan, last daughter and child of Resha and Mendal of the House of Lelan, these are the charges against you: That you have been in the hire of Harren D'Gular, and for payment and personal revenge did bring him knowledge of the royal family.

"That you, on the third day of the past seventh spring sevennight, pushed Thayne, Crown Prince of Wynnamyr and Xenara, from the cupola of the palace in an attempt to end his life.

"That you, on the fifth morning of the first summer sevennight, did willfully murder Robyn, the Second Prince of Wynnamyr and Xenara. For these crimes are you now judged.

"How plead you?"

Jessmyn listened to the accusations, mind numb to the memories of a tiny red-haired son. In Eowin's voice, though, she'd heard a quaver from something other than his great age. Fury? It had never occurred to the queen that her Grand Envoy might believe Sandaal guilty.

"How plead you?" the old man repeated.

In the stillness that followed, Lady D'Lelan looked up just long enough to say, "I am innocent, milord."

That mild, almost casual, answer angered the good citizens in the galleries, and guards were sent to quiet the ones who shouted loudest. The envoy waited for order, then read once more from his parchment.

"The queen will hear the statement of Rinerd Malwik, employee of the royal house."

Malwik, a tall, extremely thin man in the robes of the household staff, came forward. Orginally from Katay and nearing middle age, he was chamberlain to the royal quarters. His expression grave, he bowed to the envoy, then told his story. He had, on several occasions, seen Lady D'Lelan leave the palace late at night and return the next day. This, plus the visits of Raf D'Gular to her chambers, led the servant to believe Sandaal to be deeply involved in the plot to put Kyl D'Gular on the throne.

The last statement brought Davi to his feet. "Raf D'Gular despised his father, as everyone knows. If his visits to Lady

D'Lelan were political at all, they were spent plotting against
Harren, not the queen." The duke glared at the crowd. "As for
those nights spent outside the palace walls . . . they were
spent with me. And I dare any of you to question my loyalty
to Her Majesty."

Malwik would have liked to be offended by the duke's
response, but scattered laughter from the onlookers stopped
him. Such an open admission of nightly rendezvous had
caught the people by surprise, even delighted them. Annoyed,
Jessmyn glanced across at her husband. His thoughts were on
something else altogether, fingertips stroking the Stone in his
ring. The faint blue glimmer that answered his touch gave the
queen some hope.

Now a parade of witnesses came to stand before the accused. Sandaal had the right to answer each accusation, but
she remained silent. Only Davi continued to try to refute the
mounting evidence. His efforts were noble if not always
entirely logical, and Jessmyn began to despair. Lord D'Ar had
taken his role as prosecutor very much to heart, so much so
that several times guards had been sent to end his shouting
matches with the duke.

The final two witnesses called to testify against Sandaal
were the D'Jal sisters. Katina answered the envoy's questions
honestly, but with obvious distress. The queen's ladies-in-
waiting had become more than friends during their service to
the royal family, and no matter how reclusive Sandaal's
behavior, Kat had grown to love her.

From her elevated position, Jessmyn watched Rose approach, the last to face the accused. Some bitter emotion
crossed the younger D'Jal sister's face and disappeared; then
the same sweet smile she always wore reappeared. Her part
of the tale rambled some, and the envoy repeatedly had to
bring her back to the subject. Even so, Rose's testimony
proved to be the most damaging of all.

A keen lover of gossip, she also had a keen memory and
could relate conversations and incidents with amazingly accu-
rate detail. Even the Grand Envoy appeared astonished by her
accounts of his own dealings with the D'Jal woman. Jessmyn

listened with a growing apprehension, while the duke of Gosney actually ranted and turned red in the face.

"Sandaal is my dearest friend," Rose said loudly, "but I must speak the truth. Is that not so, Milord Envoy?"

"Of course, child."

"Well, she must have been working for the D'Gulars from the very beginning, even while we were in Wynnamyr. Just after we first arrived, we went shopping in Keeptown, and Sandaal met a Xenaran sailor there. They didn't speak for long, and the sailor hurried off. I thought it strange at the time, then forgot all about it . . . even when the duke of Gosney returned and I heard that he and the prince had been attacked by Xenaran sailors in Mill Town."

The queen watched a stunned Davi leap to his feet.

"She lies!" the duke cried and paused before Rose, incredulous. "You call yourself her friend and then say things that can't be true?"

The young woman looked prettily perturbed. "But they are true, milord. Why else would I say them?"

"Why else indeed?" Davi snarled at her.

"Lord Gosney," Eowin D'Ar warned, "this behavior will not help Lady D'Lelan."

The duke backed up several steps, his gaze intent on Rose's sweet face. Troubled, she could not meet his eyes, looking down instead. Sandaal hadn't stirred at the accusation or even at Gosney's outburst. Davi leaned on the railing, head close to hers.

"Why won't you defend yourself against this?" he demanded. "Or is this true about the Xenaran sailor?"

Lady D'Lelan kept her head bowed, silent still, but Davi saw a tear fall and splatter on the gray material of her skirt. His heart gave a ragged thud in his chest. It could not be true, any of it. He'd made the mistake of doubting the lady before, but not now . . . not ever again.

"If you please, Lady D'Jal," the envoy said, "continue with the rest of your observations."

"Well . . ." Rose seemed to ponder a moment. "On our journey here, the queen took a terrible fall from her horse. Everyone thought her saddle straps had worn with age, but I happened upon a strange bottle among Sandaal's belongings soon afterward. You see, I wanted to borrow some kohl. . . ." The woman frowned. "Only this bottle contained a liquid that smelled very sour, even more sour than vinegar. It was some sort of acid. But surely there's another reason for Sandaal to have such a bottle. Can't acid be used for other things besides eating away the leather of a girth?"

The grumble within the crowd grew louder, and Davi could only stand frozen, infuriated by the D'Jal sister's outrageousness. To have such precise knowledge of each crime could mean only one thing. Rose D'Jal was the assassin, enticed by D'Gular wealth to spy on the royal family and murder whenever the opportunity presented itself.

The duke opened his mouth to shout this revelation to the good citizens of Zankos, then halted. No one would believe him, simply because they didn't want to. There must be proof—undeniable proof—that the younger D'Jal sister was the murderess they sought. Rose continued her tale of unlikely coincidence, and not a soul questioned her. Except perhaps the king and queen.

Davi looked up. Jessmyn's attention was fixed on the duke of Gosney, and when she realized she had his attention, the queen made clear her greatest desire. With eyes alone, she conveyed her sorrow and fear . . . and her hope. Determined, Davi spun around. The double doors that led from the chamber seemed leagues away. He paused briefly before the Grand Envoy.

"Milord," the duke said, interrupting Rose. "Let the lady continue to speak her filth for a short time longer. I'll return soon."

Once more he paused, this time to spit on the floor at Lady D'Jal's slippered feet. She gasped and took a step backward.

"Lord Gosney!" Eowin bellowed with far more force than his frail body seemed capable of.

Davi only gave him a wolfish grin and strode down the aisle to the great doors. A guard hastened to open one side and let him through. In the corridor beyond, Nials Haldrick waited, face pale under an unruly mass of black curls.

"Where are you going?" the physician asked. "You can't desert her now."

Davi scowled at the man. "I don't intend to." He started away again, this time with Nials hurrying to keep up.

"You won't let them execute her," the man said breathlessly. "You've got your Stone—"

"You think that's an answer to every problem?" the duke demanded with a touch of fury in his voice.

"No . . . but it may come to that."

"It won't," Davi promised. "You'll have your magic, though. Wait and watch."

They skirted the empty kitchens, rushing along bare hallways. At last Davi found the door to his own quarters and hurried within. The *Book of Stones* lay on the table as he'd left it. No one dared disturb the massive tome, not even to dust the cover. A faint energy emanated from the Book, just enough for even the dullest of servants to sense.

The duke leaned over to gather the heavy volume in his arms, and his pendant glimmered in response.

"What are you doing now?" Nials's tone grew plaintive.

"There's a spell. . . ." Davi had already started back down the passage. "I found it long ago, and it just may do the trick."

"Trick? You don't have time for tricks. And how will you find this spell again after so long? Did you mark its place?"

Davi fought back irritation. "No. Every spell is a gift from the Book, and my need will also guide me."

"Is there anything I can do?"

"Only stay clear, physician. The magic of the Sorcerer's Stone is never safe."

The words came breathlessly under so heavy a load, and Davi struggled on down the corridors, only barely aware of Nials behind him. Another guard, eyes wide, opened one side of the double doors to let him into the great chamber. The Grand Envoy still asked questions of Rose D'Jal, which the young woman answered readily. Davi paid no attention, intent only on the tome hugged to his chest.

The sight of him, Book in arms, glowing Stone caught on

the gold trim of the cover, caused gasps among the onlookers. Soon even the envoy lost his voice. At his startled look, Rose glanced behind her and paled at the sight of the duke and his burden. Davi carried the *Book of Stones* to Eowin's table and laid it open on the surface.

The pages had opened at the spell of truthsayers, confirming the duke's faith in the magic. His Stone held out over the Book, he murmured the words to call up the powers.

"Here," D'Ar said angrily. "What are you doing?"

"I plan to find the truth . . . among all the lies that have been spoken today." Davi caught Sandaal by a wrist and jerked her from the small fenced-in area, then forced her hand onto the open page of the Book. In his other hand, he held the Sorcerer's Stone, its glow brilliant as fire now. "Tell me, Lady D'Lelan, have you ever taken money from Harren D'Gular and his people for the hire of your services?"

The young woman kept her head down, silent, until Davi took her shoulders and shook her hard.

"Tell me! Were you hired by D'Gular?" The duke pushed her hand once more onto the paper of the tome.

"No," Sandaal said softly, but anger edged that one word.

"Louder!"

"No!"

Eowin D'Ar gathered himself up, indignant. "And what does this prove, milord? Certainly she'll deny the charges against her."

"This proves her denial to be true," the duke said, unable to hide his pleasure. "The *Book of Stones* metes out a crueler justice than even the Xenarans, believe me. Had she lied, the Book would have destroyed her."

For the first time, Sandaal raised her head, outrage in her dark eyes. No matter. Davi had done what he must.

"So you say," the Grand Envoy snapped. "Those of us without magic will hardly take your word, milord."

"I don't expect you to." The duke glanced around at the myriad faces in the crowd. "I'll prove my point by finding the real assassin. I need your permission, though, to use the Book on every man and woman in this hall."

"What?"

Davi had not spoken to the throng, but the envoy's astounded reaction brought several to their feet.

"Impossible!" Eowin blustered. He gazed up at the king and queen in helpless agitation.

Jessmyn had heard the duke's request, though, and now she stood and gathered her plum-colored silk skirts, then took the dais stair to the floor. Her smile was radiant as she placed a hand on the Book.

"Ask me, Milord Gosney," she said. "But first, does the Book punish a small untruth as severely as a great lie?"

"I don't know, milady." Davi smiled back at her.

"Then perhaps we best not test the powers that way."

"No, best not," the duke agreed. He asked the same question of Jessmyn that he'd asked of Lady D'Lelan. The queen's answer was the same, and no harm befell her.

This failed to impress D'Ar. "Majesty, if we ask everyone in the hall—and presumably everyone in the entire city, should it come to that—we'll be here a fortnight or longer. Surely you don't expect us—"

"But I do, Milord Envoy. There is undoubtly more than one of my staff involved in this intrigue. I'd be well pleased if all the guilty were brought to justice. There'll always be time enough for truth in my realm, sir, no matter how long it takes." The queen gestured toward the small group seated on chairs beside the aisle. "Katina? Come forward, child, and prove your honesty."

The fear in the eldest D'Jal sister's face made Davi wonder, but it was fear of magic, not of the truth. Katina denied being an accomplice, one slender hand firmly on the page filled with tiny ancient runes. Absolved, she returned to her seat. The envoy, still very much irritated, called the chamberlain next.

Rinerd Malwik's story had changed, however. He was no longer so certain of who and what he had seen, and Davi felt a touch of elation. Whether the chamberlain believed in the magic or not, he had decided to be honest, even though it cost him the ridicule of his friends and employers.

Embarrassed, he also returned to his chair.

Soon after, Davi led the queen back up the stair to her throne. Gaylon watched the proceedings, bright-eyed and interested, but offered his duke no advice or counsel. He seemed content to remain an observer and nothing more. Davi let the envoy choose each witness, and very few were as sure of Sandaal's guilt as they had once been.

When at last Rose was called for the second time, the duke noticed a sheen of perspiration on the young woman's forehead. Her reluctant approach further irritated Eowin D'Ar.

"Come, come," the old man growled. "We've none of us had supper yet." Nor likely would, anytime soon.

"You're teasing us, aren't you, Davi?" Rose murmured, her hands gripped tightly together. "Nothing will happen."

Davi grinned. "Lie and find out." He took her wrist gently and put her hand on the page. "Did you, Rose D'Jal, in any manner perform acts of spying or assassination for the House of Gular?"

To confess to such crimes meant suffering and execution. Perhaps the risk of facing an unknown magic seemed the lesser of the two evils. Whatever her reasonings, Rose D'Jal opened her mouth.

"No," she said clearly, without a trace of fear now.

But when the young woman tried to remove her hand from the Book, she found it stuck fast. Her face twisted with a sudden rage, and she pointed at Sandaal with the forefinger of her free hand.

"She's the assassin! She pushed Thayne from the cupola. She murdered the baby prince!" Still her hand was welded to the ancient paper, and she used her left to try to free the right. Her fury faded suddenly, replaced by a twinge of pain. "No!" Rose looked to someone standing near the seated witnesses, her gazed fixed on Nials Haldrick for the moment.

Eowin tried to rush to help her, but the duke held him back. A faint blue glow had come to outline the edges of the tome, and it traveled slowly over the woman's fingers. The pain turned quickly to agony, and Davi watched the flesh of her hand begin to melt and fall away. All the while, hot blue light crawled farther up her arm, accelerating as it climbed.

Rose held her screams back until the women in the crowds began to shriek in horror, then she could no longer curb the pain. Her wails pierced the ears of the onlookers and set their teeth on edge, and Davi stood frozen, unable to help, unable to turn and look away. Her fine blonde hair caught fire, crackling and spitting, creating a blue aura about the young woman's head.

The screams died away as the blue flame consumed her. Now only bone and sinew kept the body upright, propped against the table, and azure fire danced in the sockets that had once held her beautiful blue eyes. Even the cries of the horrified citizens had stopped, and Davi could hear someone sobbing. Katina collapsed on the tiles and continued to weep.

The duke took her shoulders. "I'm so sorry, Kat."

"But she couldn't have done all those awful things," the elder sister lamented. "Your Book is wrong! You punished the wrong one."

A wave of sick fear washed through Davi. Could she be right?

"Let me tend to her," the physician said, crouching beside them.

"The wrong one," Katina sobbed. "You know, Nials. She could never do that. You've loved her too long, and you know this can't be true."

It struck Davi then, and he gazed at the physician. "How do you know, Nials?"

The man turned gentle black eyes on the duke. "Milord, are you certain you want to ask me that question?"

"I'll ask it with your hand on the Book."

"There's no need." Nials sighed. "Rose and I were lovers. I knew she had been suborned all along."

Davi swallowed back outrage. "But you're a healer, a man who saves lives. How could you allow her—"

"How could I not?" the physician returned, his voice calm. "This land has suffered enough at the hands of the Red King. Xenara needs its own governing body, not a foreign-raised queen on its throne. Kyl D'Gular would have been a figurehead for the first truly autonomous rule in Xenara—and, I had hoped, the beginning of the end for monarchy." Nials eyed the duke. "Harren had to do something to drive Jessmyn D'Gerric from this country. Would you rather he killed the mother than the child?"

Without thought, Davi struck him, a sharp jab to the man's jaw that made him stagger sideways. The duke's attack caused a near riot, bringing shouts from the guards as well as the onlookers. Even the queen and king came to their feet and rushed down the stairs of the dais. Eowin D'Ar explained the situation to Their Highnesses while the guards quieted the crowd. Nials Haldrick was well loved and respected by the people of Zankos.

The physician stood quietly, awaiting his fate, eyes filled with sorrow over his loss. At last Jessmyn turned to him.

"Did you personally participate in any of Harren's plots in any way?" she asked.

"No, milady."

"Neither did he try to stop them," Davi said angrily. "This man is as much a traitor as Rose ever thought to be. He would have let Sandaal die to protect himself from complicity. He deserves an assassin's execution."

The queen ignored him. "Master Haldrick, since my arrival here, you have been as close to my person as any other servant. You had plenty of opportunity to cause harm, yet you never raised a hand against me."

Nials gazed at her steadfastly, neither ashamed nor proud of himself. To absolve him of these crimes seemed ludicrous, though, and Davi gritted his teeth, then felt a hand come to rest lightly on his shoulder. In the king's ring, his Stone glittered softly.

"She has her reasons, Davi." Gaylon's face reflected his duke's unhappiness. "Trust her."

Davi bridled, but held his tongue. The citizens in the gallery kept silent, afraid to miss even the most quietly spoken word.

"It is not my purpose," the queen went on, "to annihilate the loyal opposition. This land needs you, Nials Haldrick, not only as the wonderful healer that you've proven to be, but also as a man intent on caring for all his people's needs. All I ask is that you speak openly of those things that anger you, not harbor them in secret, where they might fester again and bring us close to civil war."

The physician frowned, unable to comprehend the lady's words at first. Jessmyn paused to glance around at the crowds that lined each wall.

"Master Haldrick is right. I am a daughter of Roffo D'Gerric, but I'm also foreign raised. Wynnmar is my realm, and I miss its forests and green glades, its rivers and streams. Forgive me, all of you, but I would return home with my husband to that land."

The audience managed a quiet mumble of awe, and beyond the queen, Gaylon turned, disbelief on his tired face.

"Xenara is a fabulous country, and I want to thank the many who made me welcome here, but it's time for us to go. I'll leave in my stead my eldest son, Thayne, to rule. And as his regent, the duke of Gosney, who has proven his abilities as counselor and lord over the last few months."

The queen crossed to Sandaal, then took her hand. Lady D'Lelan looked nonplussed but allowed herself to be led to Davi. Her hand was placed in the duke's, warm and firm, yet soft. The ache that brought nearly caused him tears.

Jess smiled. "I will not leave, though, until these two young people have been joined in marriage. They've suffered apart long enough. Sandaal D'Lelan has been proven innocent of murder and betrayal. As for her attempt on my husband's life, she was not without honest reasons for her hatred. Better to take the king out of reach than ask the young lady to forgive him."

The queen had gone to Gaylon's side, now, and took his left hand in hers, and the king's hazel eyes sparkled, suddenly filled with life.

"No," Sandaal said loudly. "Don't leave Xenara, Your Majesties. You need fear nothing from me ever again."

Those in the crowd seemed to agree, but Jessmyn only shook her head, then gave her startled husband a lingering kiss on the lips. That brought hoots and whoops from every one, and Davi followed suit, kissing Sandaal's battered lips with his blistered ones.

Through Thayne, the duke of Gosney would hold the power of a king, and through the Stone, he would wield the power of a sorcerer. Both these forces must be used to guide and instruct a young ruler, a task that frightened Davi somewhat. The touch of Sandaal's gentle lips against his own, however, caused the doubts to slip away almost as quickly as they formed. No. There may be troubled times ahead, but with this strong and beautiful lady beside him, he could, and would, be able to face anything.